"One of the wildest and hardest heists in science fiction."
Lotusland Comics

"Timely and compelling, *BREAK OUT* does what science fiction does best; uses a veil of strangeness to explore deeply human issues. A can't miss series!"
David Booher (*Specs, Canto, Killer Queens, Rain*)

"The team behind *BREAK OUT* have their collective finger on the pulse of current societal issues, while deftly weaving it all into an engaging teen action-adventure."
Jeremy Holt (*Made in Korea, Virtually Yours*)

"*BREAK OUT* is a timely and necessary story and I can't wait to see where it goes next."
Stephanie Phillips (*Grim, Harley Quinn, Wonder Woman*)

"*BREAK OUT* rolls all the fun of a Spielberg coming-of-age science fiction film and an episode of *Black Mirror* together to create one heck of a thrill ride."
Kenny Porter (*The Flash, DC· Mech*)

"A mix of genuine ominous terror and hope."
AIPT

"The thrill of a great heist story, infused with genuine pathos and a shocking, timely relevance."
Mat Groom (*Inferno Girl Red, Self-Made, The Rise of Ultraman*)

"A masterful blend of high-concept sci-fi action and all too relevant social issues, *BREAK OUT* is a must read comic."
Rich Douek (*The Ocean Takes Us, Sea of Sorrows, Road of Bones*)

"Kaplan is zeroed in on the existential crises of today, and Santos and Wordie bring the book's complex cast of endangered—but fiercely driven—young people to vivid life."
Steve Foxe (*X-Men '92, Party & Prey, Archer &Armstrong Forever*)

"An interstellar heist with a heartfelt human core, ***BREAK OUT*** **confronts real-world fears with out-of-this-world teenage rebellion."**

David Pepose (*Savage Avengers, Fantastic Four, Scout's Honor*)

"*BREAK OUT* gives us a premise in which we can examine our relationships with one another and the world we're creating for future generations."

Darcy Van Poelgeest (*Little Bird, The Bright Queen*)

"Smart, salient and powerful–*BREAK OUT* is a comic that demands your attention and will leave you hungry for more."

Michael Moreci (*Barbaric, The Plot, Wasted Space*)

"The perfect amalgam of excellent writing and detailed art."

Major Spoilers

"*BREAK OUT* offers a thought-provoking examination of today's youth and the problems they face, through Kaplan's always captivating lens."

Steven Scott (NYT Best Seller *They Called Us Enemy*)

"*BREAK OUT* is a brilliant allegory for our times, where everyone under twenty suffers for the sins of everyone older. The comic series for RIGHT NOW!"

Brian Schirmer (*Quests Aside, Fairlady, Black Jack Ketchum*)

"*BREAK OUT* is about the past haunting the present and the future and the few who refuse to give in. This is a book for our time."

Chris Condon (*That Texas Blood*)

"*BREAK OUT* does what so many good sci-fi stories do, entertain and examine our world."

Graphic Policy

"*BREAK OUT* is a genre mashup like you've never seen, rooted in real stakes and emotions. I can't wait to see where this one goes."

Ibrahim Moustafa (*Count, RetroActive, James Bond*)

BREAK OUT™

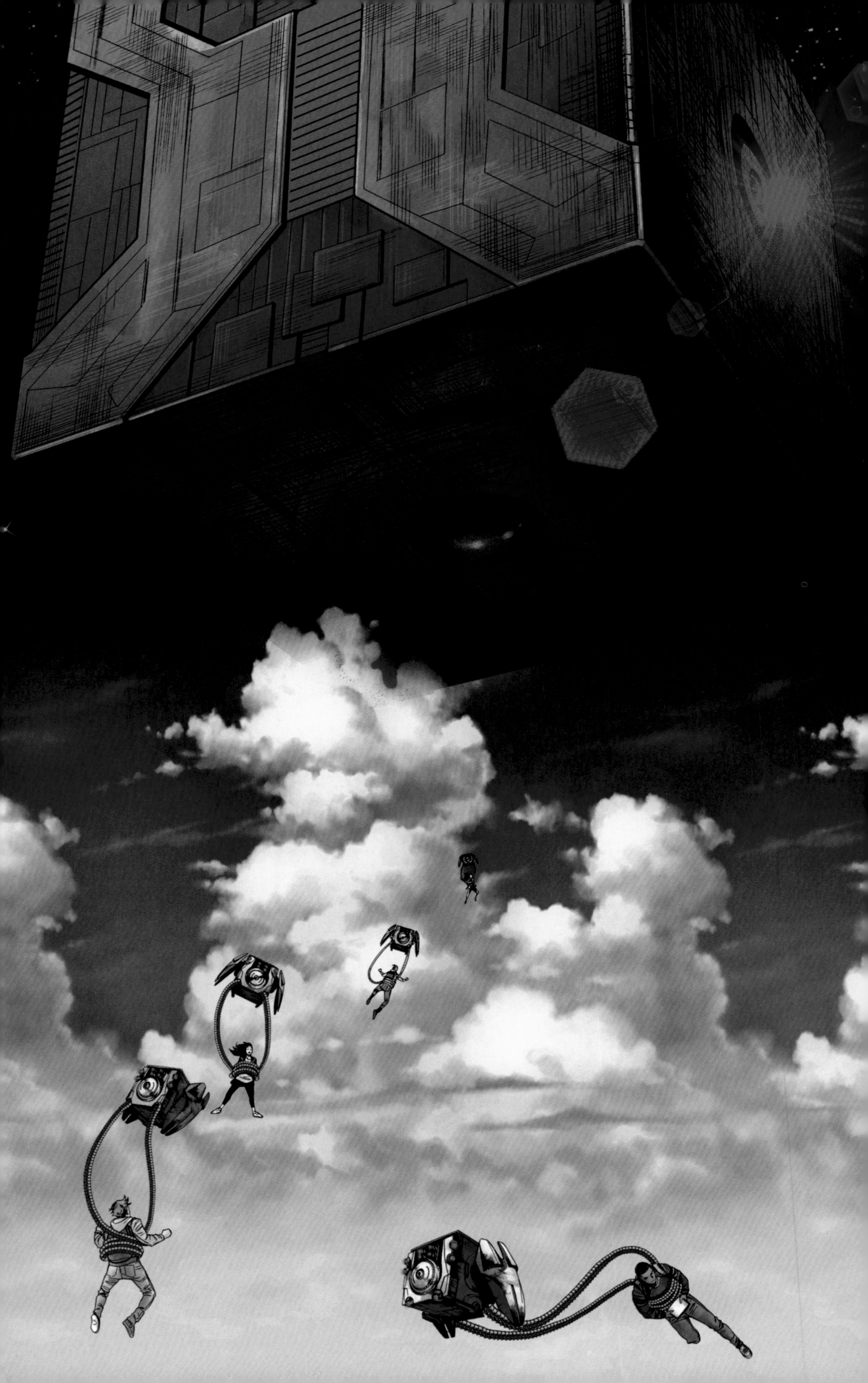

BREAK OUT ™

SCRIPT BY
ZACK KAPLAN

LINE ART
WILTON SANTOS

COLORS
JASON WORDIE

LETTERS
JIM CAMPBELL

FRONT COVER AND
CHAPTER BREAK ART BY
ADAM GORHAM

DARK HORSE BOOKS

PRESIDENT AND PUBLISHER / MIKE RICHARDSON
EDITOR / SPENCER CUSHING
ASSOCIATE EDITOR / KONNER KNUDSEN
COLLECTION DESIGNER / ANITA MAGAÑA
DIGITAL ART TECHNICIAN / JOSIE CHRISTENSEN

Neil Hankerson, Executive Vice President • Tom Weddle, Chief Financial Officer • Dale LaFountain, Chief Information Officer • Tim Wiesch, Vice President of Licensing • Vanessa Todd-Holmes, Vice President of Production and Scheduling • Mark Bernardi, Vice President of Book Trade and Digital Sales • Randy Lahrman, Vice President of Product Development and Sales • Ken Lizzi, General Counsel • Dave Marshall, Editor in Chief • Davey Estrada, Editorial Director • Chris Warner, Senior Books Editor • Cara O'Neil, Senior Director of Marketing • Cary Grazzini, Director of Specialty Projects • Lia Ribacchi, Art Director • Michael Gombos, Senior Director of Licensed Publications • Kari Yadro, Director of Custom Programs • Kari Torson, Director of International Licensing • Christina Niece, Director of Scheduling

ads@darkhorse.com I ComicShopLocator.com

This volume collects issue #1 through #4 of the Dark Horse comic book series *Break Out*

Published by Dark Horse Books
A division of Dark Horse Comics LLC
10956 SE Main Street
Milwaukie, OR 97222
DarkHorse.com
To find a comics shop in your area, visit comicshoplocator.com

Library of Congress Cataloging-in-Publication Data

Names: Kaplan, Zack, author. I Santos, Wilton, artist. I Wordie, Jason (Colorist), colourist. I Campbell, Jim (Letterer), letterer. I Gorham, Adam, artist.
Title: Break out / script, Zack Kaplan ; line art, Wilton Santos ; colors, Jason Wordie ; lettering, Jim Campbell ; front cover and chapter break art by Adam Gorham.
Description: First edition. I Milwaukie, OR : Dark Horse Books, 2022- I v. 1: "This volume collects issue #1 through #4 of the Dark Horse comic book series Break Out" I Summary: "Mysterious and massive cube spaceships from another dimension materialize over our cities around the globe. They routinely abduct teenagers to be held inside their floating prison ships. And the world accepts it as inevitable. But not Liam Watts. His younger brother has been taken. And Liam is tired of "thoughts and prayers". Now, in a "take back our future" anthem, Liam must assemble a skilled team of ordinary high school students and in just a few weeks, they must plan a heist to infiltrate a hi-tech prison ship a mile in the sky. But what they'll find there will throw their plans into turmoil and challenge their resolve. How do you break out of a prison that's not even from this world?"-- Provided by publisher.
Identifiers: LCCN 2022022324 (print) I LCCN 2022022325 (ebook) I ISBN 9781506729893 (trade paperback) I ISBN 9781506729893 (ebook)
Subjects: LCGFT: Science fiction comics. I Graphic novels.
Classification: LCC PN6728.B673 K37 2022 (print) I LCC PN6728.B673 (ebook) I DDC 741.5/973--dc23/eng/20220610
LC record available at https://lccn.loc.gov/2022022324
LC ebook record available at https://lccn.loc.gov/2022022325

First edition: April 2023
EBook ISBN 978-1-50672-990-9
ISBN 978-1-50672-989-3
1 3 5 7 9 10 8 6 4 2
Printed in China

ART BY RAFAEL ALBUQUERQUE

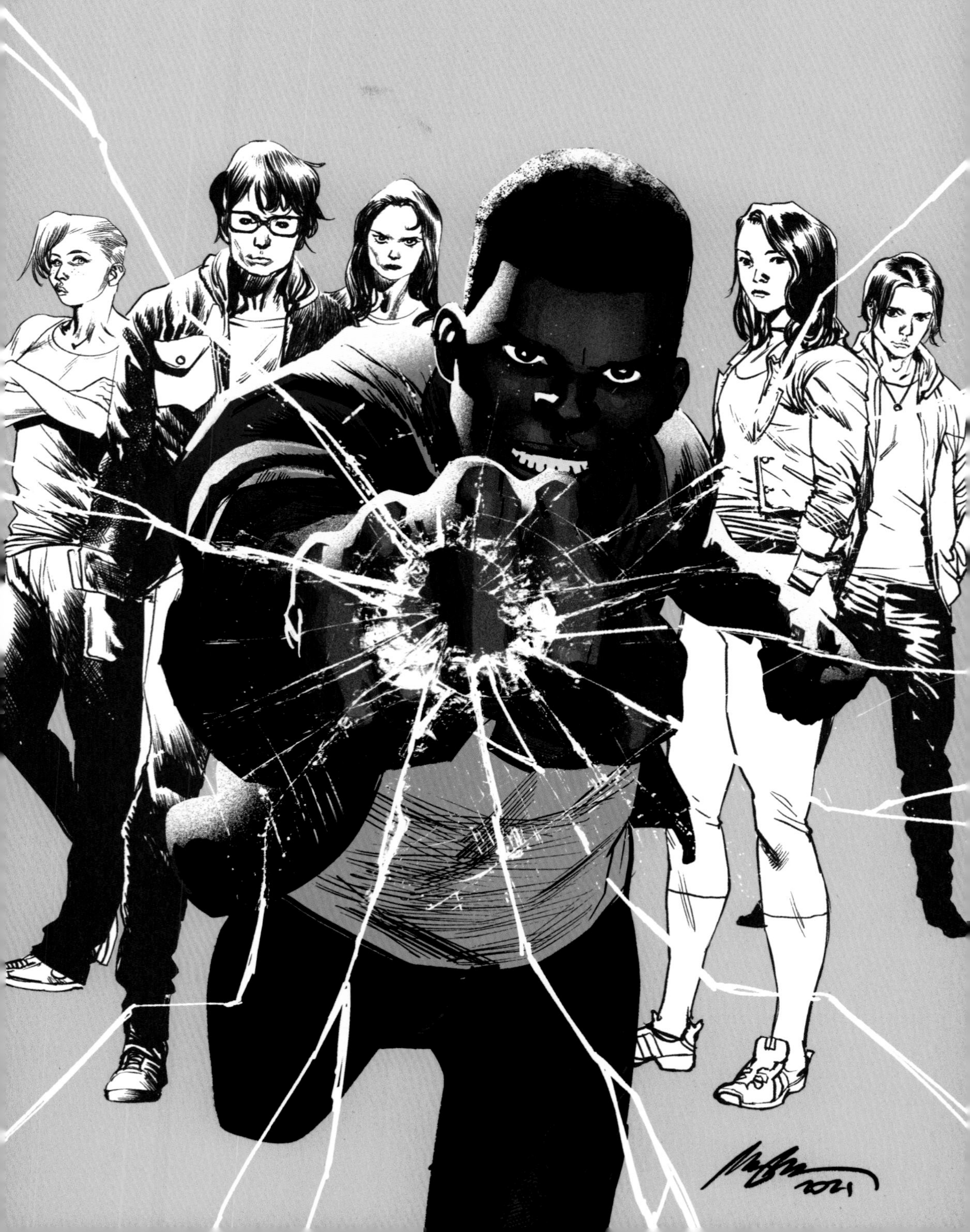

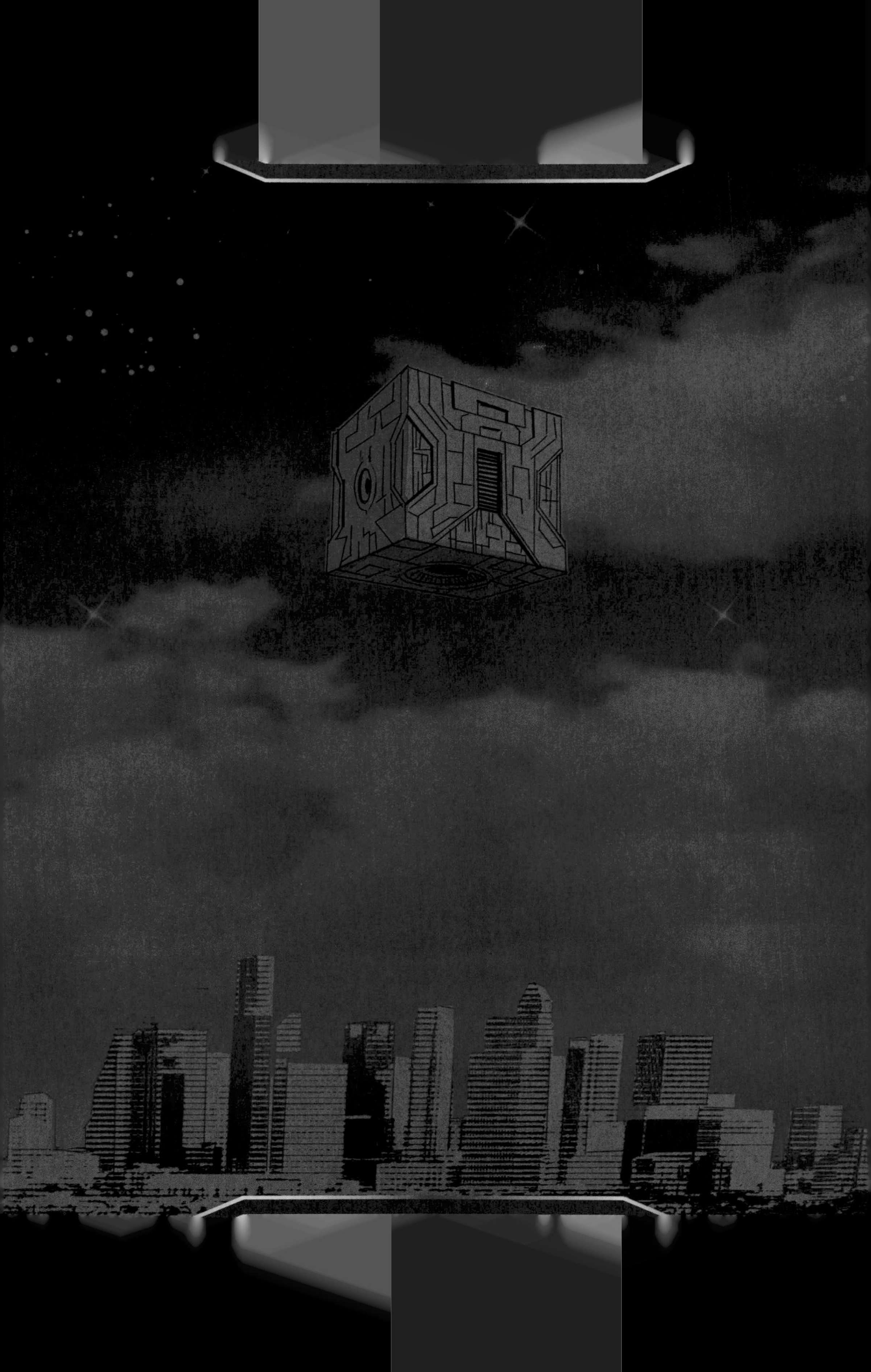

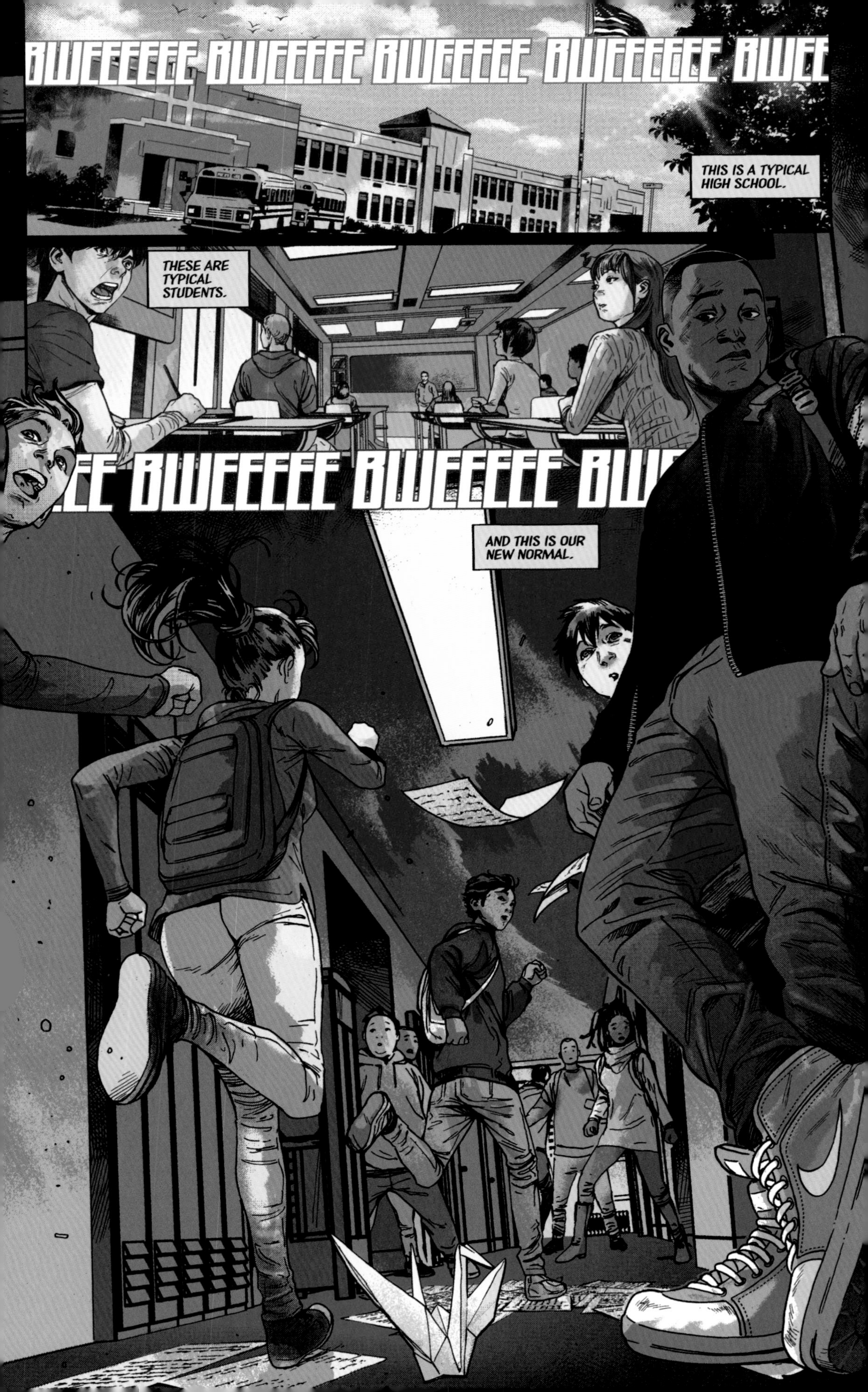
BWEEEEEE BWEEEEEE BWEEEEEE BWEEEEEEE BWEE
THIS IS A TYPICAL HIGH SCHOOL.
THESE ARE TYPICAL STUDENTS.
EEE BWEEEEEE BWEEEEEE BW
AND THIS IS OUR NEW NORMAL.

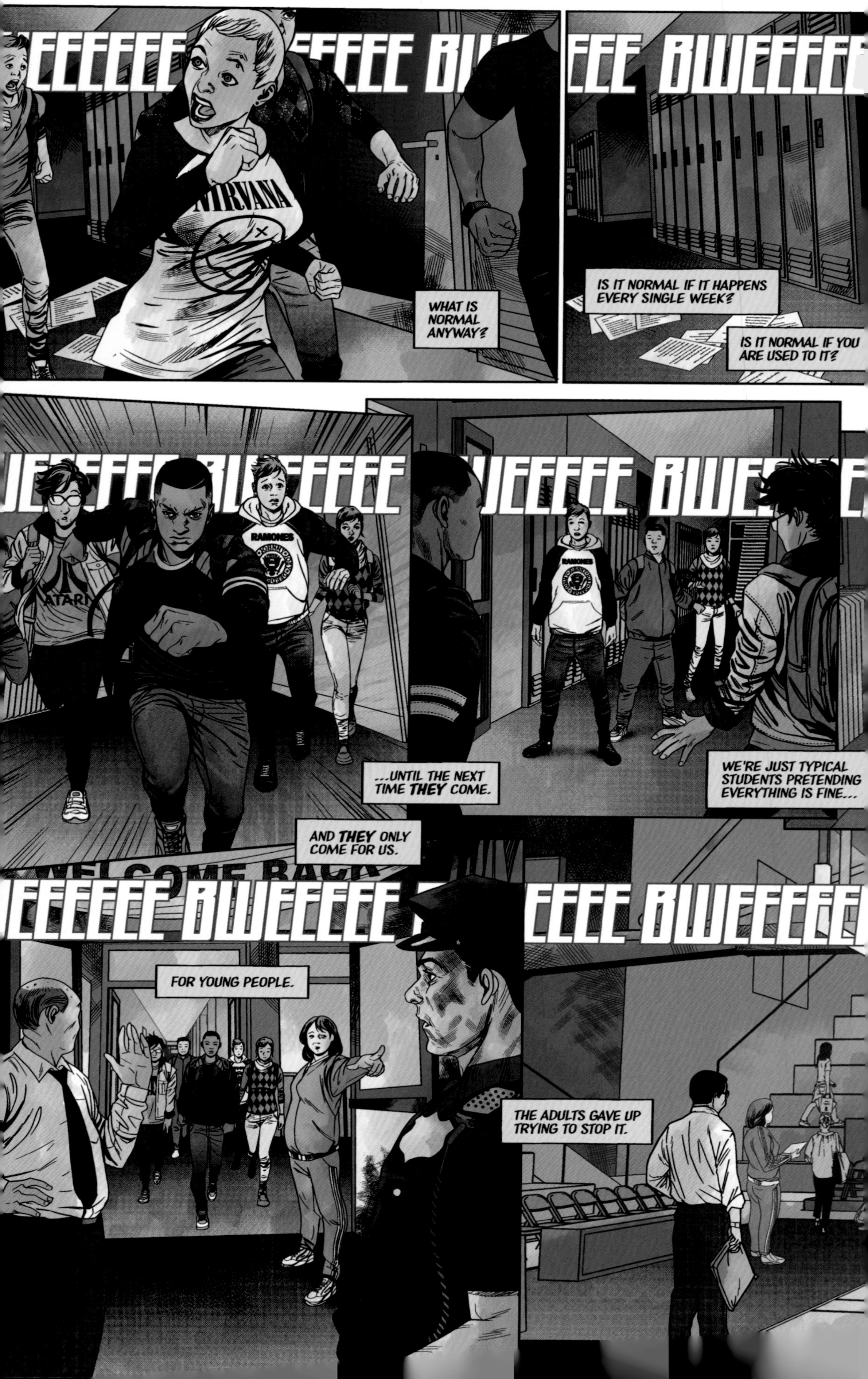
BWEEEEE BWEEEEE BWEEEEE
NIRVANA
WHAT IS NORMAL ANYWAY?
IS IT NORMAL IF IT HAPPENS EVERY SINGLE WEEK?
IS IT NORMAL IF YOU ARE USED TO IT?
BWEEEEE BWEEEEE
ATARI
RAMONES
...UNTIL THE NEXT TIME THEY COME.
AND THEY ONLY COME FOR US.
BWEEEEE BWEEEEE
WE'RE JUST TYPICAL STUDENTS PRETENDING EVERYTHING IS FINE...
BWEEEEE BWEEEEE BWEEEEE
FOR YOUNG PEOPLE.
THE ADULTS GAVE UP TRYING TO STOP IT.

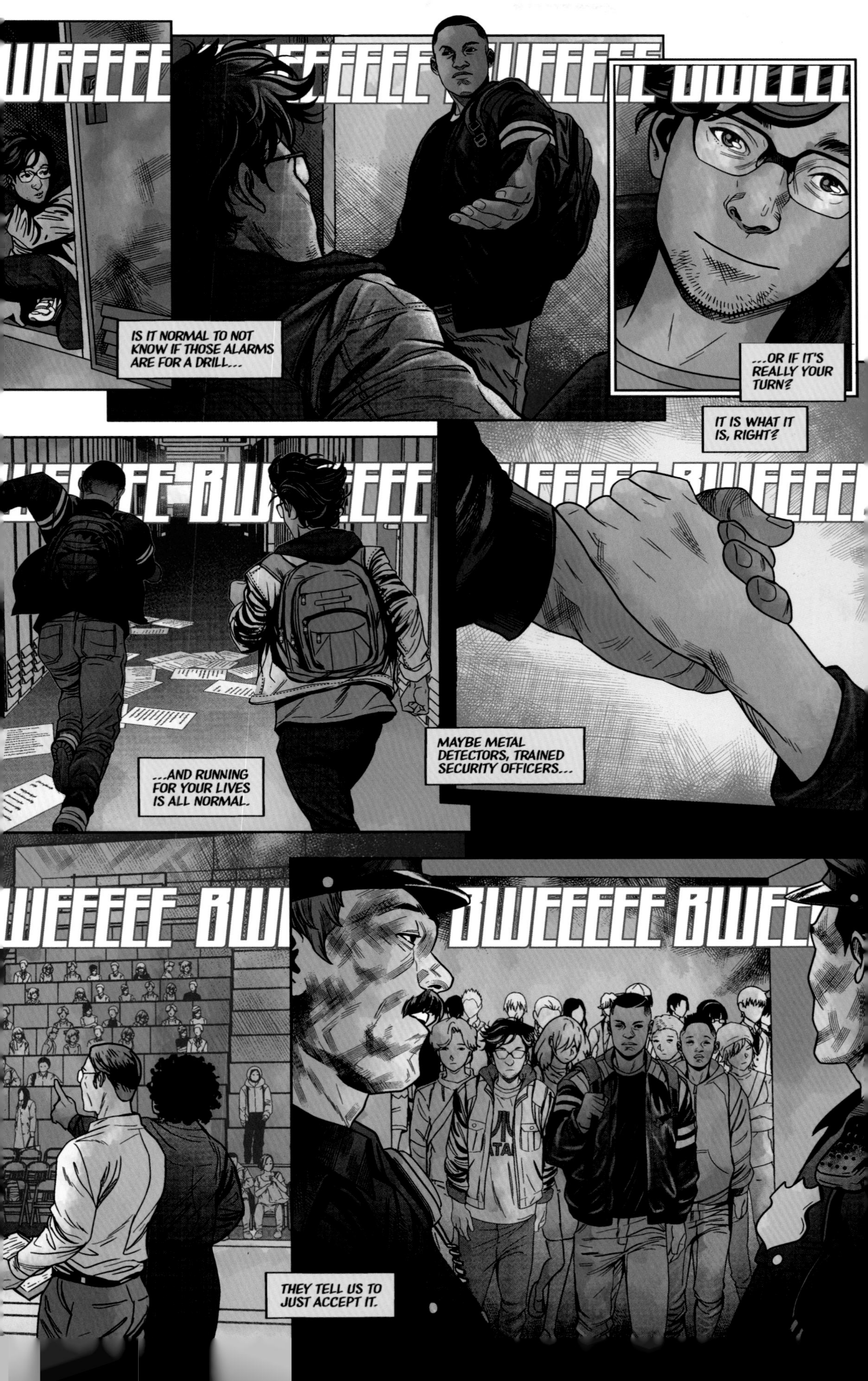
IS IT NORMAL TO NOT KNOW IF THOSE ALARMS ARE FOR A DRILL...
...OR IF IT'S REALLY YOUR TURN?
IT IS WHAT IT IS, RIGHT?
...AND RUNNING FOR YOUR LIVES IS ALL NORMAL.
MAYBE METAL DETECTORS, TRAINED SECURITY OFFICERS...
THEY TELL US TO JUST ACCEPT IT.

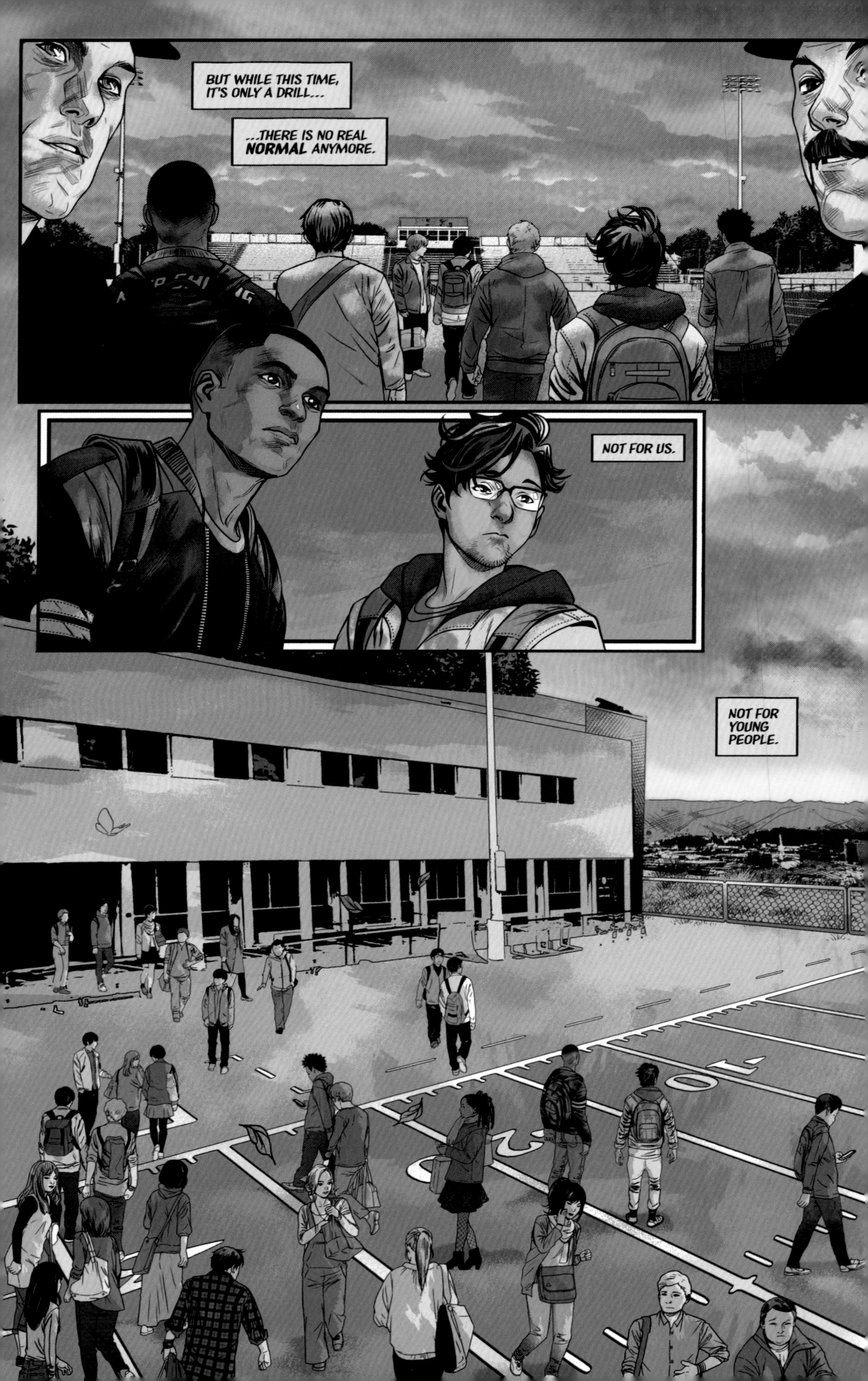
BUT WHILE THIS TIME, IT'S ONLY A DRILL...
...THERE IS NO REAL NORMAL ANYMORE.
NOT FOR US.
NOT FOR YOUNG PEOPLE.

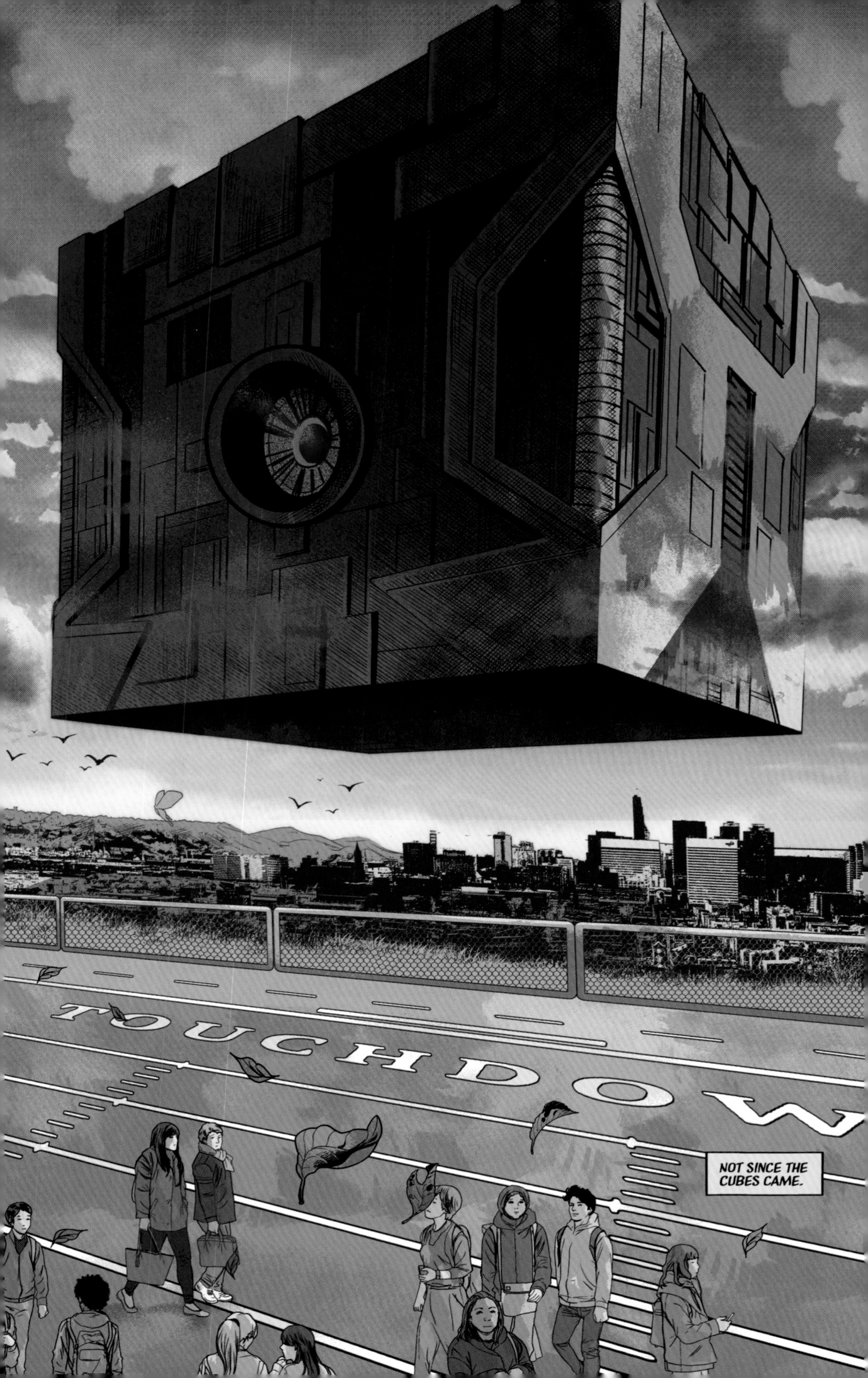
TOUCHDOW
NOT SINCE THE CUBES CAME.

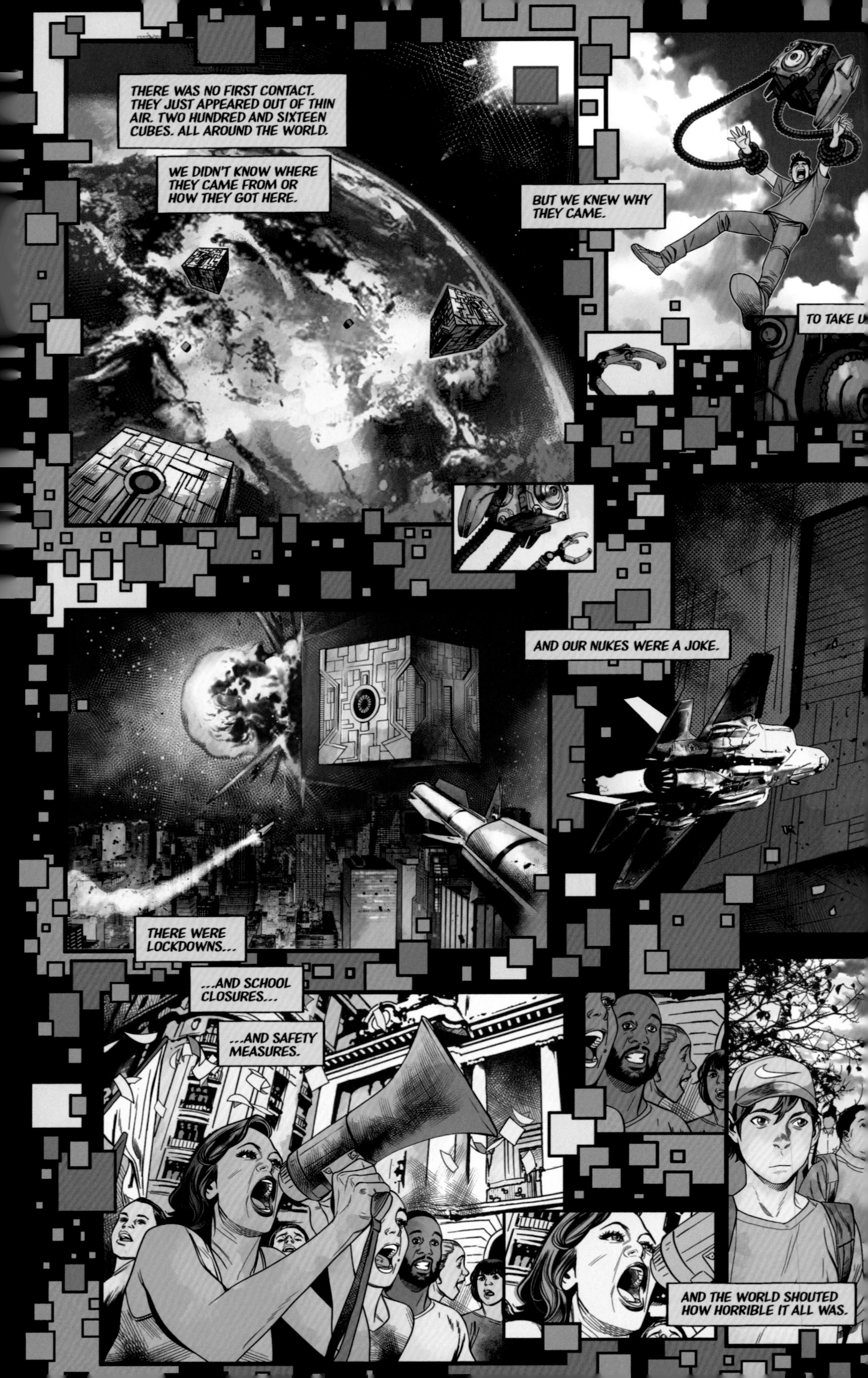
THERE WAS NO FIRST CONTACT. THEY JUST APPEARED OUT OF THIN AIR. TWO HUNDRED AND SIXTEEN CUBES. ALL AROUND THE WORLD.
WE DIDN'T KNOW WHERE THEY CAME FROM OR HOW THEY GOT HERE.
BUT WE KNEW WHY THEY CAME.
TO TAKE U
AND OUR NUKES WERE A JOKE.
THERE WERE LOCKDOWNS...
...AND SCHOOL CLOSURES...
...AND SAFETY MEASURES.
AND THE WORLD SHOUTED HOW HORRIBLE IT ALL WAS.

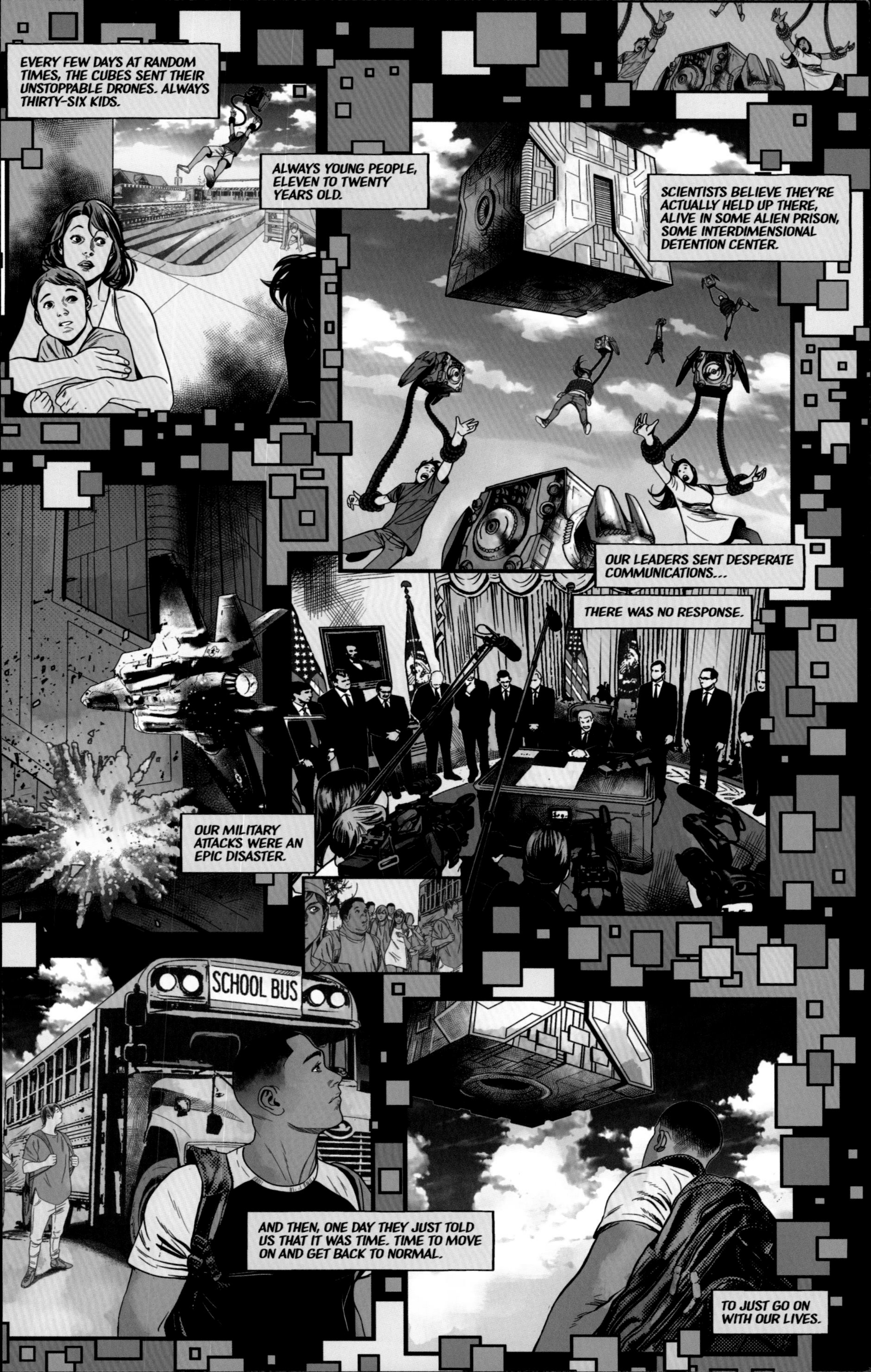
EVERY FEW DAYS AT RANDOM TIMES, THE CUBES SENT THEIR UNSTOPPABLE DRONES. ALWAYS THIRTY-SIX KIDS.
ALWAYS YOUNG PEOPLE, ELEVEN TO TWENTY YEARS OLD.
SCIENTISTS BELIEVE THEY'RE ACTUALLY HELD UP THERE, ALIVE IN SOME ALIEN PRISON, SOME INTERDIMENSIONAL DETENTION CENTER.
OUR LEADERS SENT DESPERATE COMMUNICATIONS...
THERE WAS NO RESPONSE.
OUR MILITARY ATTACKS WERE AN EPIC DISASTER.
SCHOOL BUS
AND THEN, ONE DAY THEY JUST TOLD US THAT IT WAS TIME. TIME TO MOVE ON AND GET BACK TO NORMAL.
TO JUST GO ON WITH OUR LIVES.

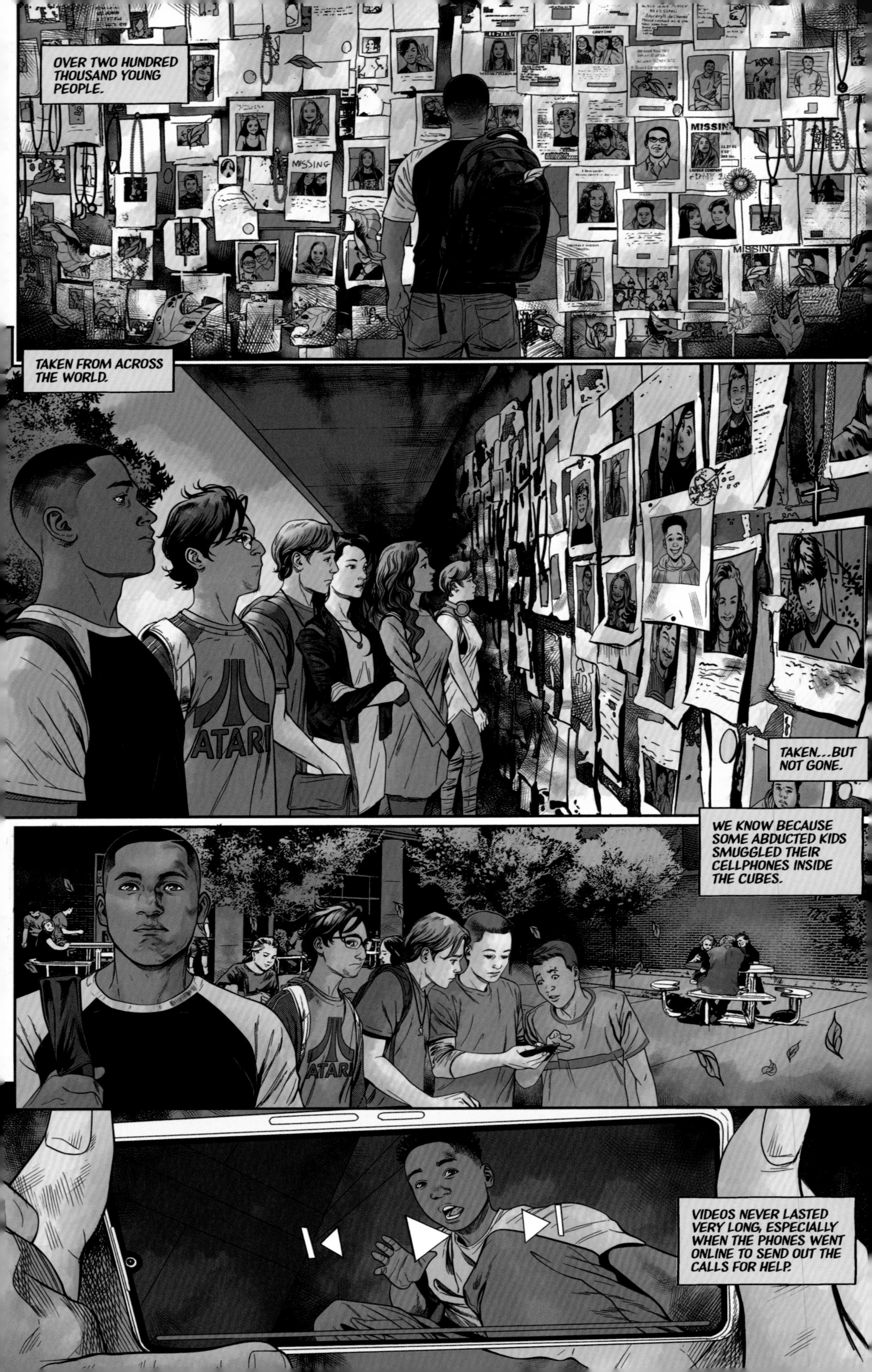

OVER TWO HUNDRED THOUSAND YOUNG PEOPLE.
MISSING
MISSING
TAKEN FROM ACROSS THE WORLD.
ATARI
TAKEN...BUT NOT GONE.
WE KNOW BECAUSE SOME ABDUCTED KIDS SMUGGLED THEIR CELLPHONES INSIDE THE CUBES.
ATARI
VIDEOS NEVER LASTED VERY LONG, ESPECIALLY WHEN THE PHONES WENT ONLINE TO SEND OUT THE CALLS FOR HELP.

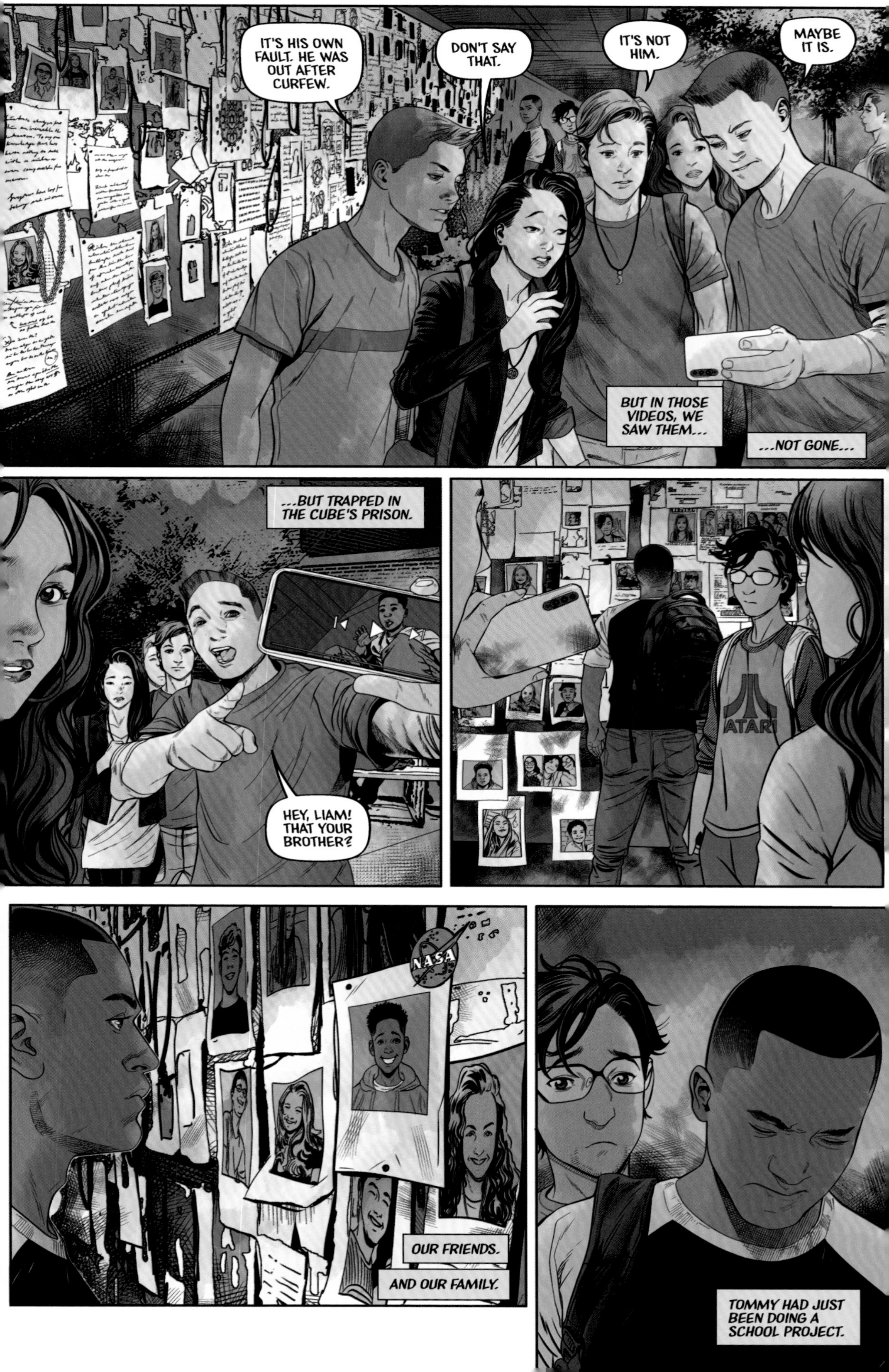
IT'S HIS OWN FAULT. HE WAS OUT AFTER CURFEW.
DON'T SAY THAT.
IT'S NOT HIM.
MAYBE IT IS.
BUT IN THOSE VIDEOS, WE SAW THEM...
...NOT GONE...
...BUT TRAPPED IN THE CUBE'S PRISON.
HEY, LIAM! THAT YOUR BROTHER?
ATARI
NASA
OUR FRIENDS.
AND OUR FAMILY.
TOMMY HAD JUST BEEN DOING A SCHOOL PROJECT.

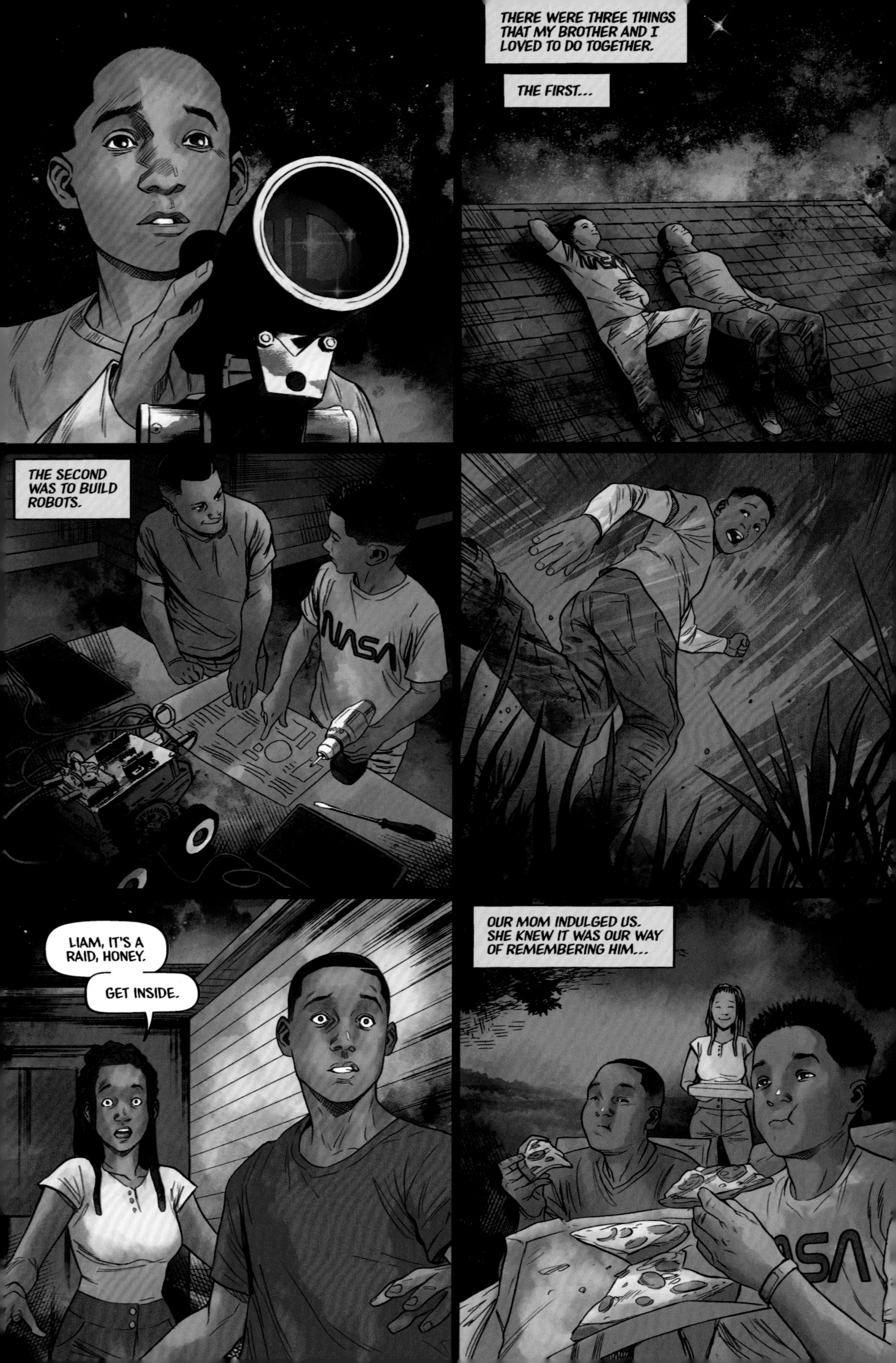

THERE WERE THREE THINGS THAT MY BROTHER AND I LOVED TO DO TOGETHER.
THE FIRST...
NASA
THE SECOND WAS TO BUILD ROBOTS.
NASA
LIAM, IT'S A RAID, HONEY.
GET INSIDE.
OUR MOM INDULGED US. SHE KNEW IT WAS OUR WAY OF REMEMBERING HIM...

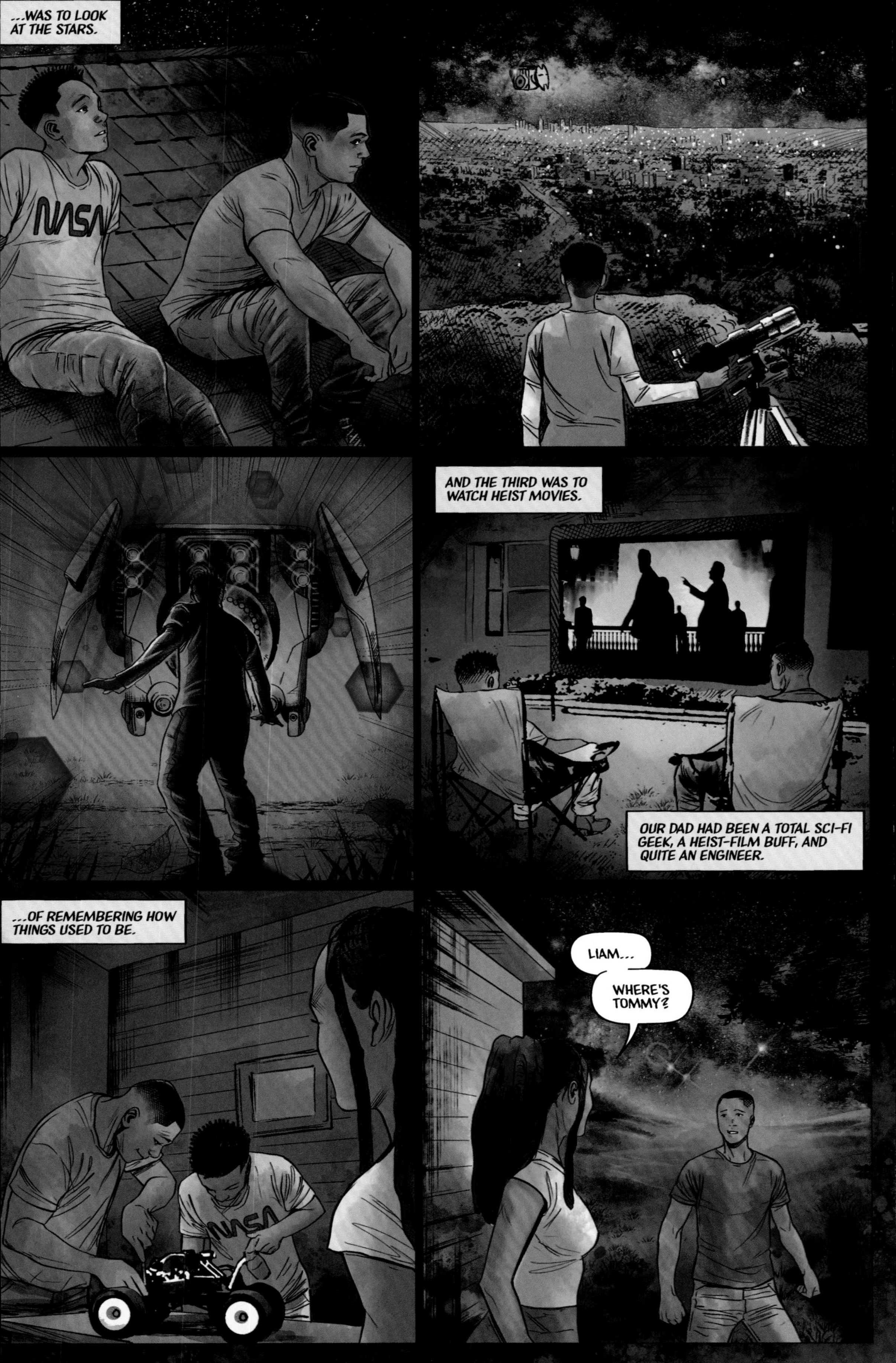
...WAS TO LOOK
AT THE STARS.
AND THE THIRD WAS TO
WATCH HEIST MOVIES.
OUR DAD HAD BEEN A TOTAL SCI-FI
GEEK, A HEIST-FILM BUFF, AND
QUITE AN ENGINEER.
...OF REMEMBERING HOW
THINGS USED TO BE.
LIAM...
WHERE'S
TOMMY?

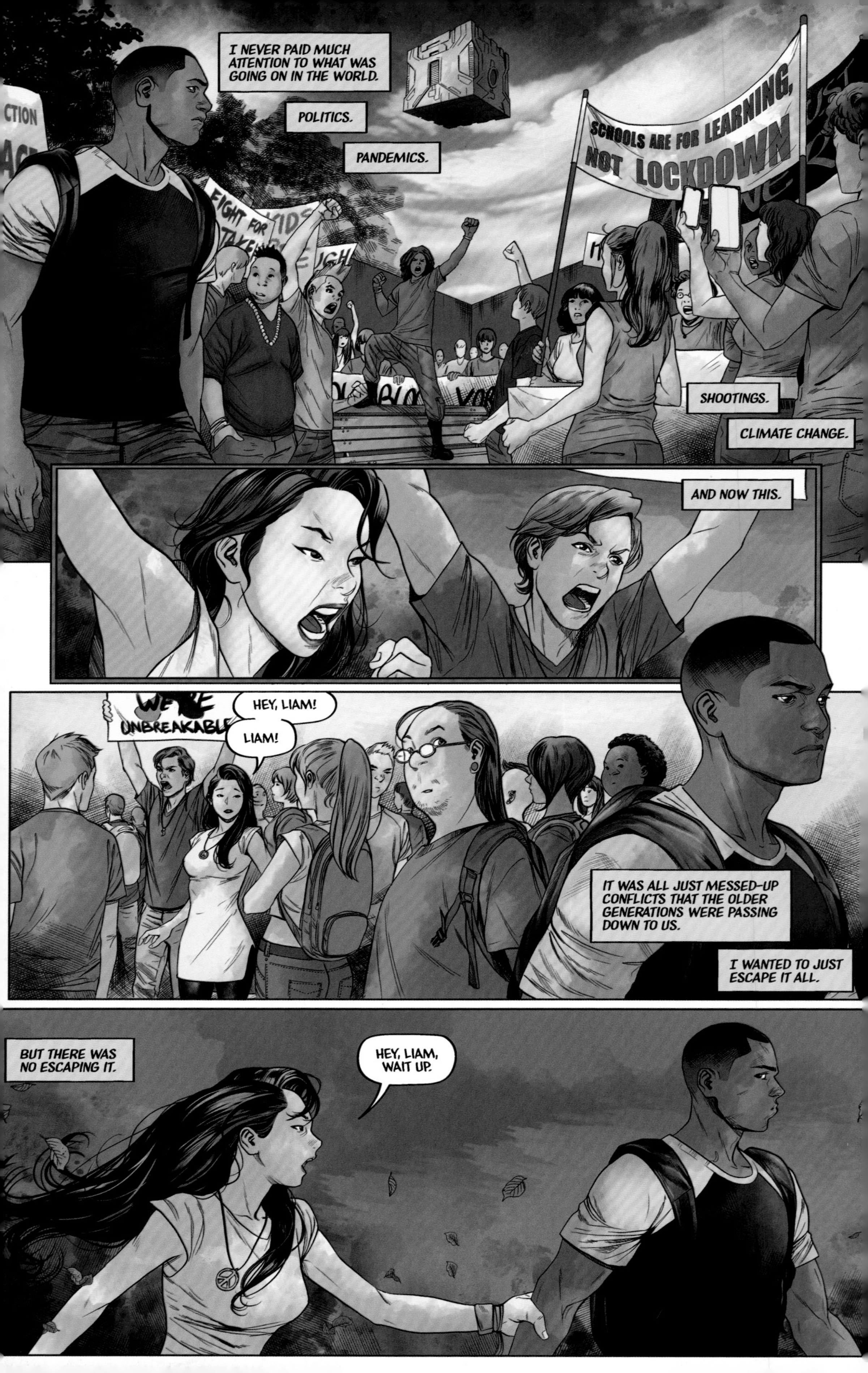
I NEVER PAID MUCH ATTENTION TO WHAT WAS GOING ON IN THE WORLD.
POLITICS.
PANDEMICS.
SCHOOLS ARE FOR LEARNING, NOT LOCKDOWN
FIGHT FOR
SHOOTINGS.
CLIMATE CHANGE.
AND NOW THIS.
UNBREAKABLE
HEY, LIAM!
LIAM!
IT WAS ALL JUST MESSED-UP CONFLICTS THAT THE OLDER GENERATIONS WERE PASSING DOWN TO US.
I WANTED TO JUST ESCAPE IT ALL.
BUT THERE WAS NO ESCAPING IT.
HEY, LIAM, WAIT UP.

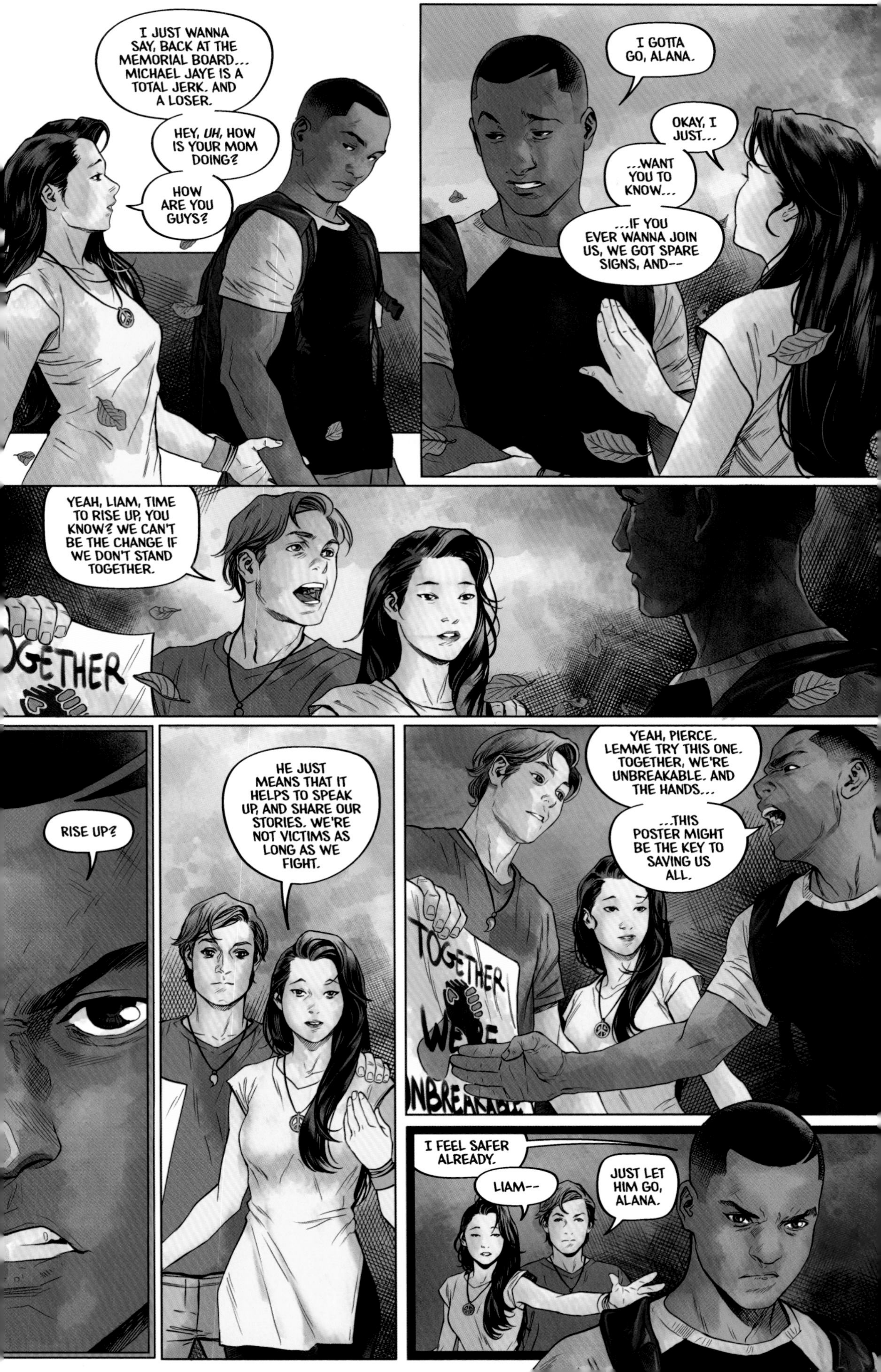

I JUST WANNA SAY, BACK AT THE MEMORIAL BOARD... MICHAEL JAYE IS A TOTAL JERK. AND A LOSER.
HEY, *UH*, HOW IS YOUR MOM DOING?
HOW ARE YOU GUYS?
I GOTTA GO, ALANA.
OKAY, I JUST...
...WANT YOU TO KNOW...
...IF YOU EVER WANNA JOIN US, WE GOT SPARE SIGNS, AND--
YEAH, LIAM, TIME TO RISE UP, YOU KNOW? WE CAN'T BE THE CHANGE IF WE DON'T STAND TOGETHER.
GETHER
RISE UP?
HE JUST MEANS THAT IT HELPS TO SPEAK UP, AND SHARE OUR STORIES. WE'RE NOT VICTIMS AS LONG AS WE FIGHT.
YEAH, PIERCE. LEMME TRY THIS ONE. TOGETHER, WE'RE UNBREAKABLE. AND THE HANDS...
...THIS POSTER MIGHT BE THE KEY TO SAVING US ALL.
TOGETHER
I FEEL SAFER ALREADY.
LIAM--
JUST LET HIM GO, ALANA.

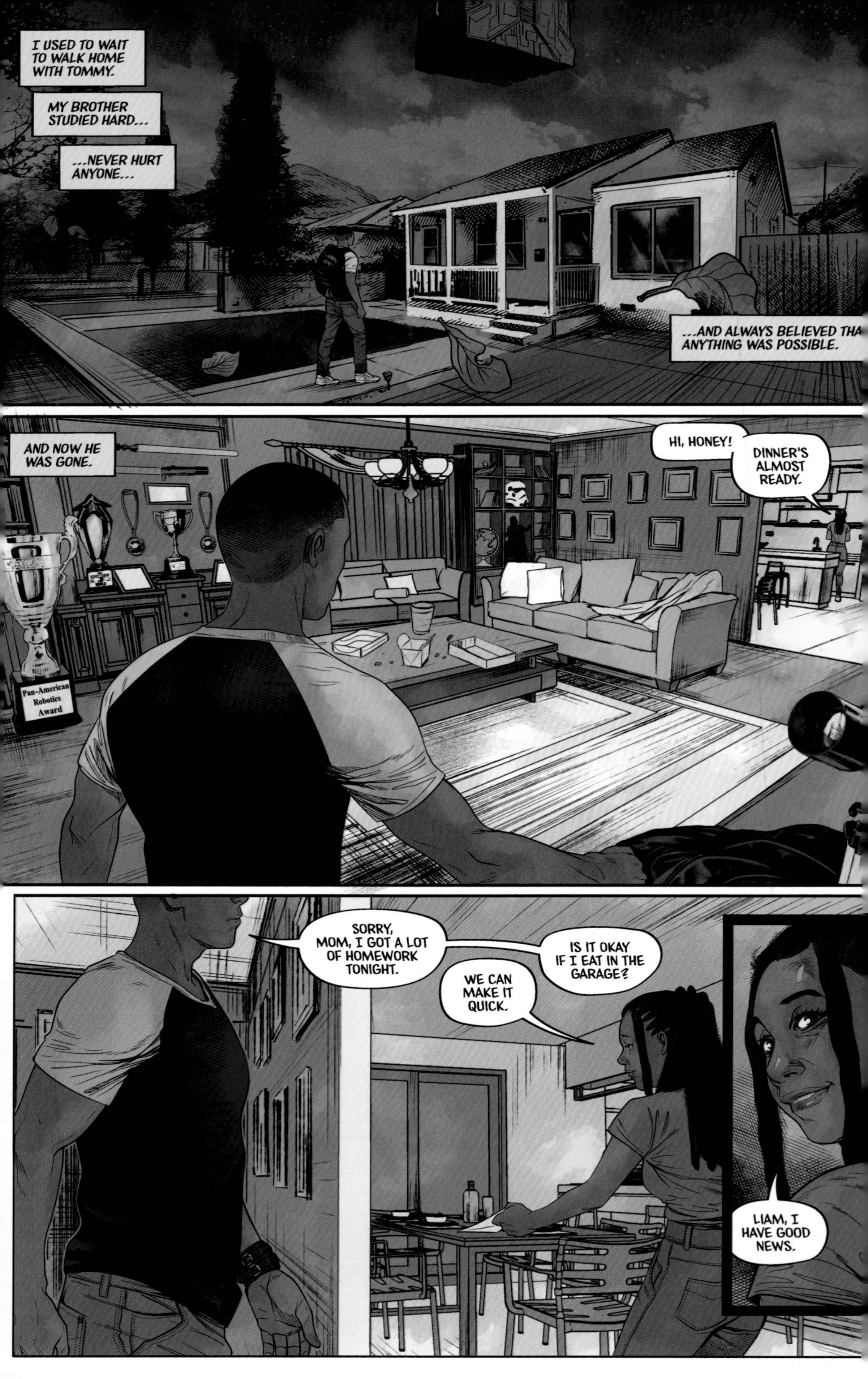
I USED TO WAIT TO WALK HOME WITH TOMMY.
MY BROTHER STUDIED HARD...
...NEVER HURT ANYONE...
...AND ALWAYS BELIEVED THA ANYTHING WAS POSSIBLE.
AND NOW HE WAS GONE.
Pan-American Robotics Award
HI, HONEY!
DINNER'S ALMOST READY.
SORRY, MOM, I GOT A LOT OF HOMEWORK TONIGHT.
IS IT OKAY IF I EAT IN THE GARAGE?
WE CAN MAKE IT QUICK.
LIAM, I HAVE GOOD NEWS.

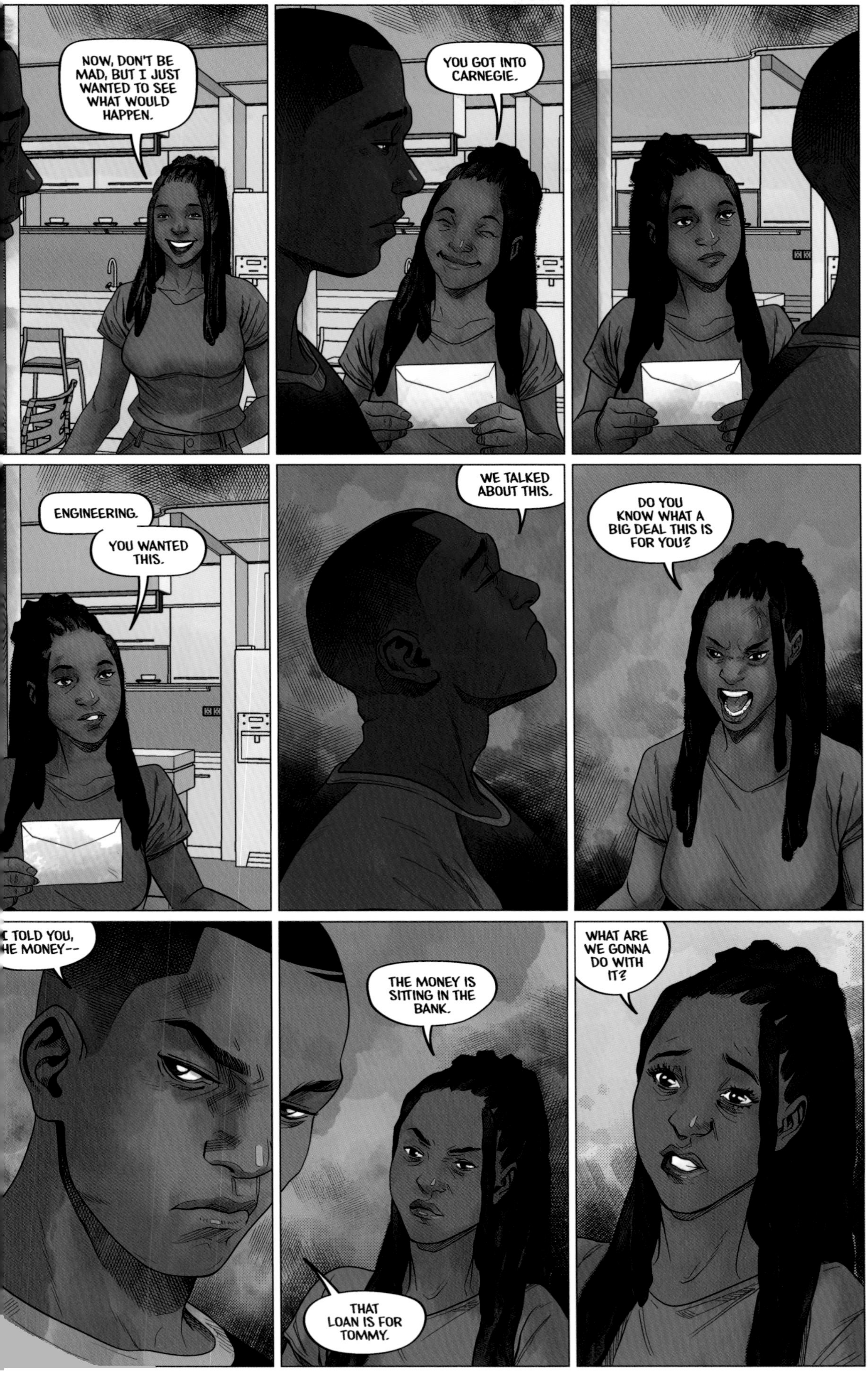
NOW, DON'T BE MAD, BUT I JUST WANTED TO SEE WHAT WOULD HAPPEN.
YOU GOT INTO CARNEGIE.
ENGINEERING.
YOU WANTED THIS.
WE TALKED ABOUT THIS.
DO YOU KNOW WHAT A BIG DEAL THIS IS FOR YOU?
I TOLD YOU, THE MONEY--
THE MONEY IS SITTING IN THE BANK.
THAT LOAN IS FOR TOMMY.
WHAT ARE WE GONNA DO WITH IT?

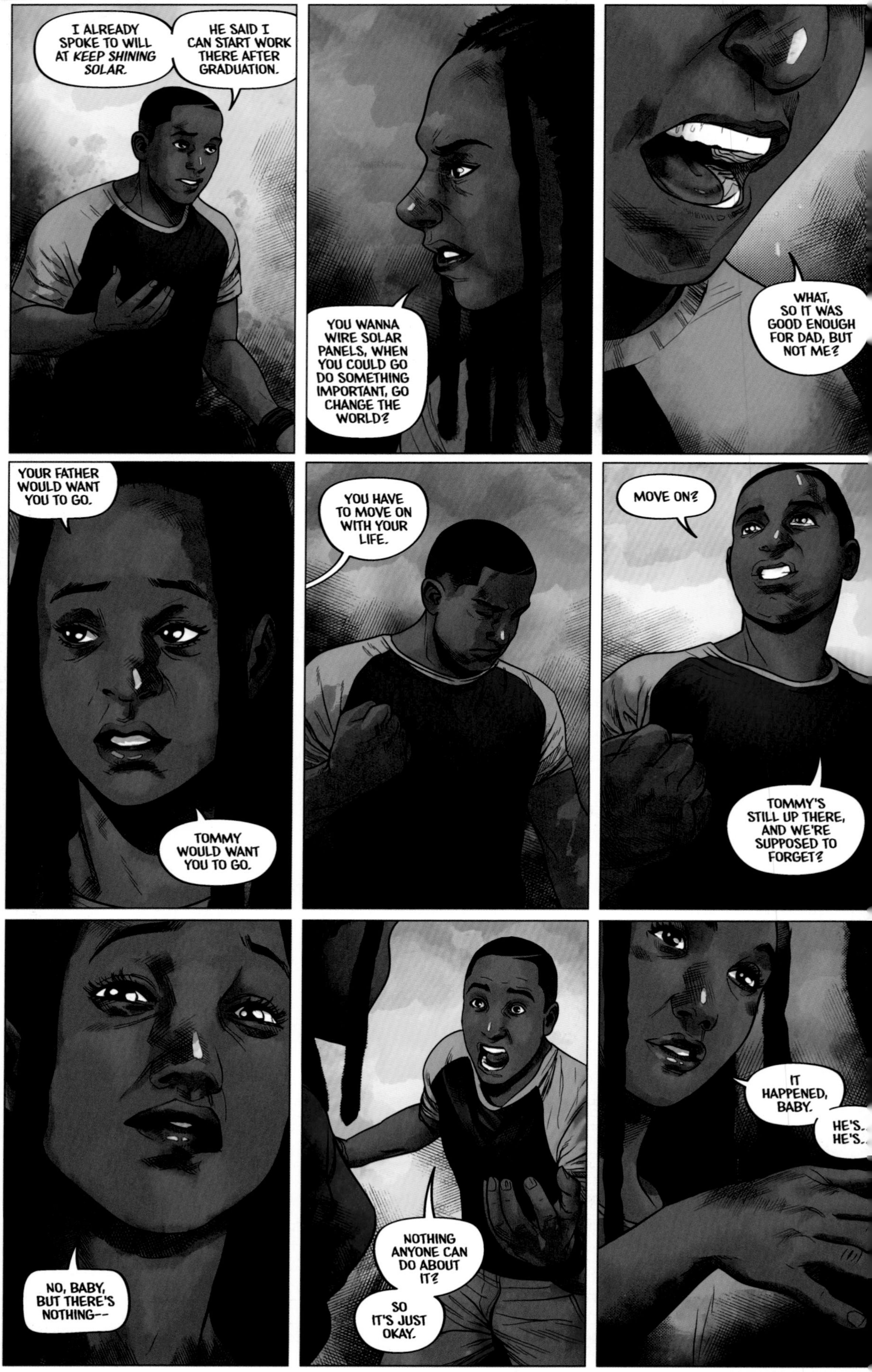
I ALREADY SPOKE TO WILL AT KEEP SHINING SOLAR.
HE SAID I CAN START WORK THERE AFTER GRADUATION.
YOU WANNA WIRE SOLAR PANELS, WHEN YOU COULD GO DO SOMETHING IMPORTANT, GO CHANGE THE WORLD?
WHAT, SO IT WAS GOOD ENOUGH FOR DAD, BUT NOT ME?
YOUR FATHER WOULD WANT YOU TO GO.
TOMMY WOULD WANT YOU TO GO.
YOU HAVE TO MOVE ON WITH YOUR LIFE.
MOVE ON?
TOMMY'S STILL UP THERE, AND WE'RE SUPPOSED TO FORGET?
NO, BABY, BUT THERE'S NOTHING--
NOTHING ANYONE CAN DO ABOUT IT?
SO IT'S JUST OKAY.
IT HAPPENED, BABY.
HE'S... HE'S...

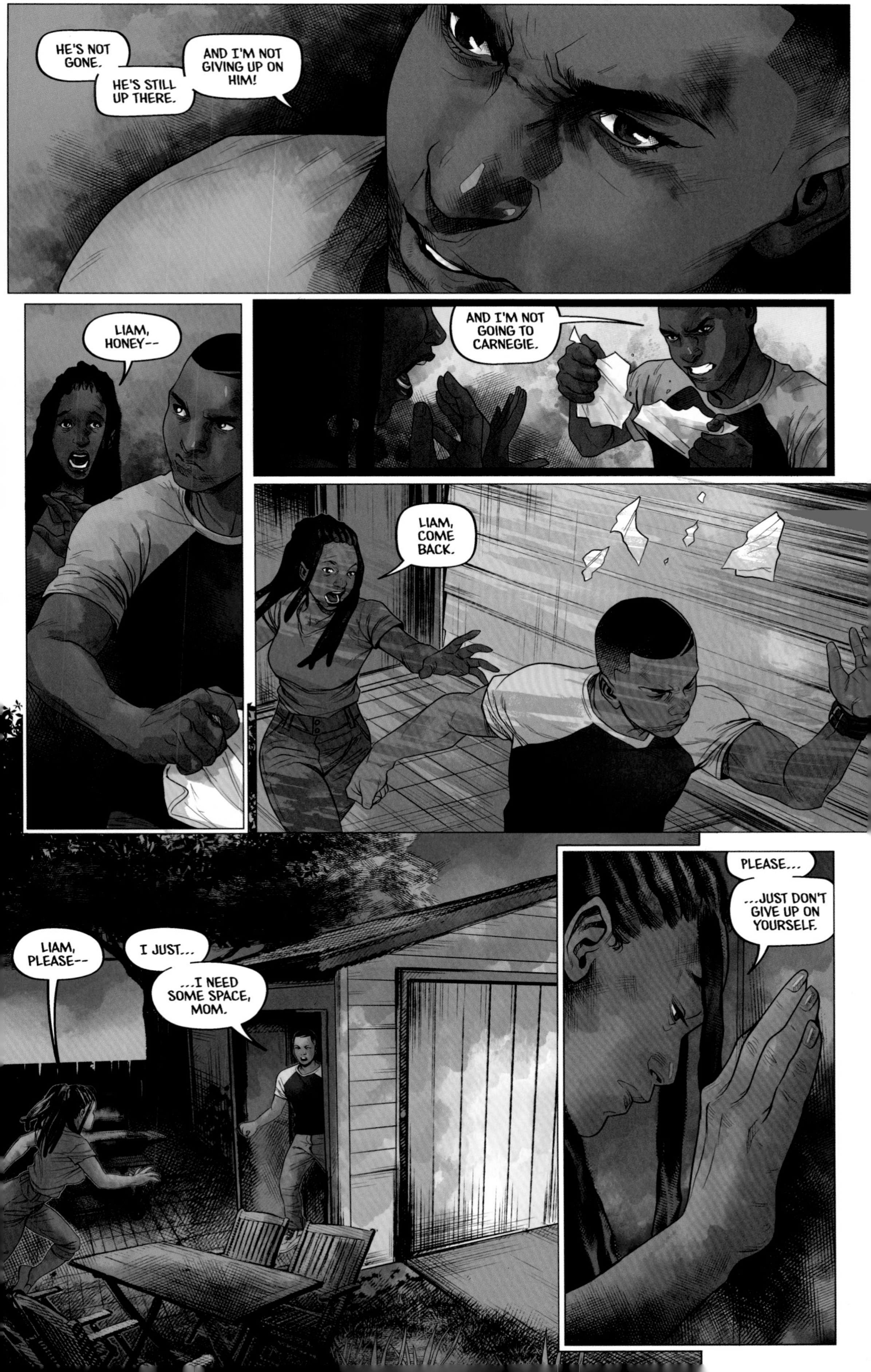
HE'S NOT GONE.
HE'S STILL UP THERE.
AND I'M NOT GIVING UP ON HIM!
LIAM, HONEY--
AND I'M NOT GOING TO CARNEGIE.
LIAM, COME BACK.
LIAM, PLEASE--
I JUST...
...I NEED SOME SPACE, MOM.
PLEASE...
...JUST DON'T GIVE UP ON YOURSELF.

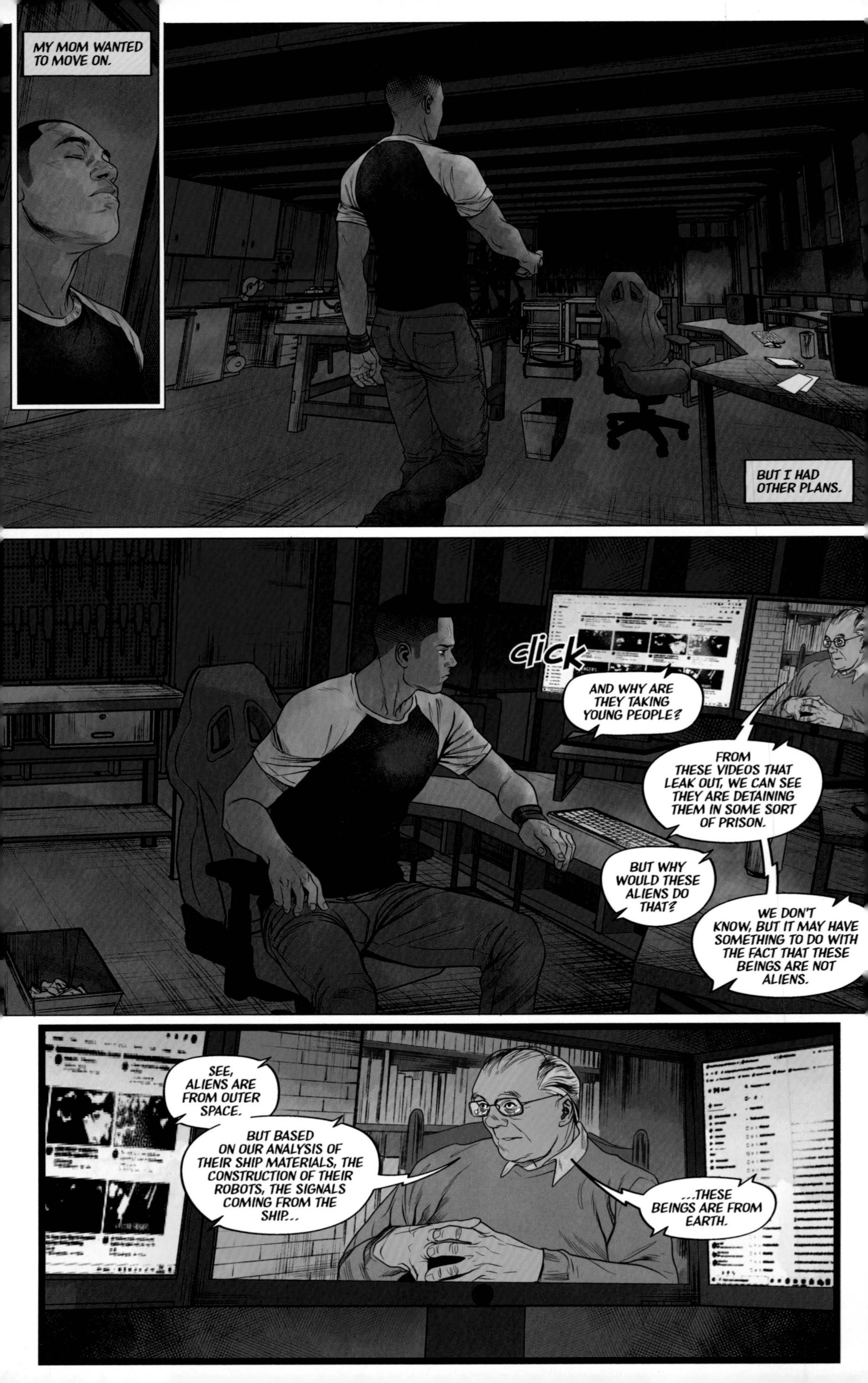
MY MOM WANTED TO MOVE ON.
BUT I HAD OTHER PLANS.
CLICK
AND WHY ARE THEY TAKING YOUNG PEOPLE?
FROM THESE VIDEOS THAT LEAK OUT, WE CAN SEE THEY ARE DETAINING THEM IN SOME SORT OF PRISON.
BUT WHY WOULD THESE ALIENS DO THAT?
WE DON'T KNOW, BUT IT MAY HAVE SOMETHING TO DO WITH THE FACT THAT THESE BEINGS ARE NOT ALIENS.
SEE, ALIENS ARE FROM OUTER SPACE.
BUT BASED ON OUR ANALYSIS OF THEIR SHIP MATERIALS, THE CONSTRUCTION OF THEIR ROBOTS, THE SIGNALS COMING FROM THE SHIP...
...THESE BEINGS ARE FROM EARTH.

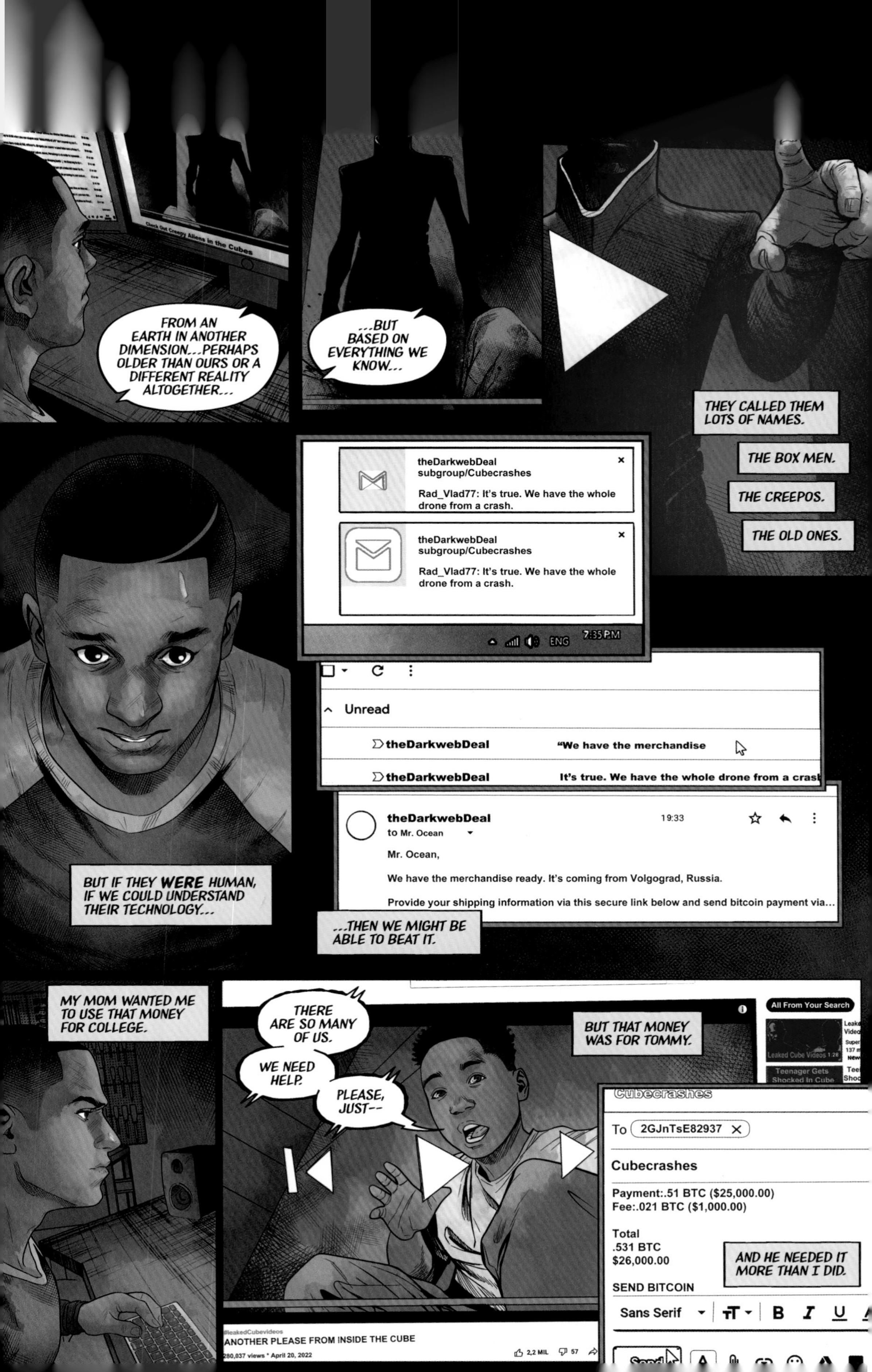
Check Out Creepy Aliens in the Cubes
FROM AN EARTH IN ANOTHER DIMENSION...PERHAPS OLDER THAN OURS OR A DIFFERENT REALITY ALTOGETHER...
...BUT BASED ON EVERYTHING WE KNOW...
THEY CALLED THEM LOTS OF NAMES.
THE BOX MEN.
THE CREEPOS.
THE OLD ONES.
theDarkwebDeal
subgroup/Cubecrashes
Rad_Vlad77: It's true. We have the whole drone from a crash.
theDarkwebDeal
subgroup/Cubecrashes
Rad_Vlad77: It's true. We have the whole drone from a crash.
ENG 7:35 PM
Unread
theDarkwebDeal "We have the merchandise
theDarkwebDeal It's true. We have the whole drone from a crash
theDarkwebDeal 19:33
to Mr. Ocean
Mr. Ocean,
We have the merchandise ready. It's coming from Volgograd, Russia.
Provide your shipping information via this secure link below and send bitcoin payment via...
BUT IF THEY **WERE** HUMAN, IF WE COULD UNDERSTAND THEIR TECHNOLOGY...
...THEN WE MIGHT BE ABLE TO BEAT IT.
MY MOM WANTED ME TO USE THAT MONEY FOR COLLEGE.
THERE ARE SO MANY OF US.
WE NEED HELP.
PLEASE, JUST--
BUT THAT MONEY WAS FOR TOMMY.
All From Your Search
Leaked Cube Videos 1:28
Teenager Gets Shocked In Cube
#leakedCubevideos
ANOTHER PLEASE FROM INSIDE THE CUBE
280,037 views * April 20, 2022
2,2 MIL 57
Cubecrashes
To 2GJnTsE82937
Cubecrashes
Payment:.51 BTC ($25,000.00)
Fee:.021 BTC ($1,000.00)
Total
.531 BTC
$26,000.00
SEND BITCOIN
AND HE NEEDED IT MORE THAN I DID.
Sans Serif
B I U
Send

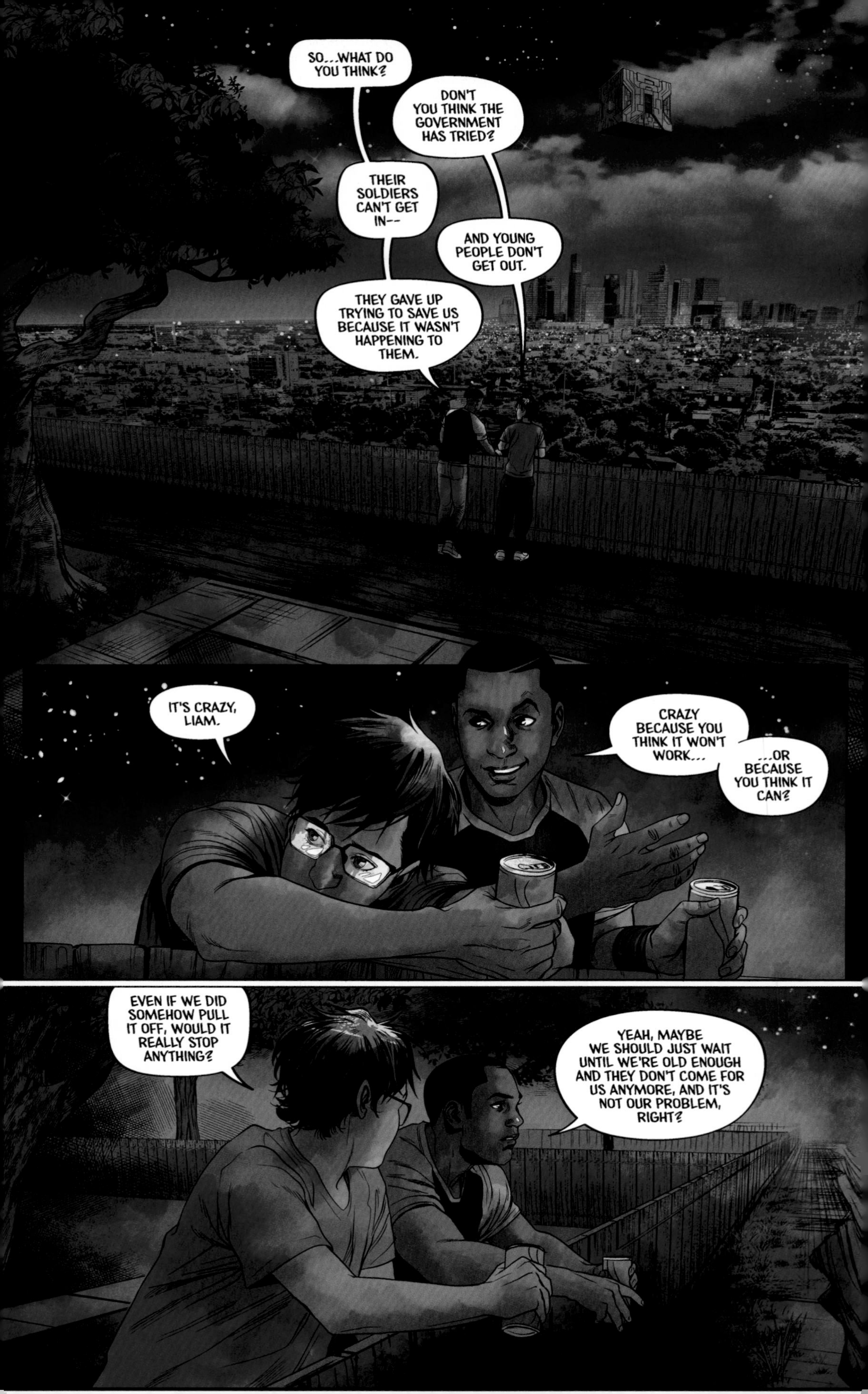
SO...WHAT DO YOU THINK?
DON'T YOU THINK THE GOVERNMENT HAS TRIED?
THEIR SOLDIERS CAN'T GET IN--
AND YOUNG PEOPLE DON'T GET OUT.
THEY GAVE UP TRYING TO SAVE US BECAUSE IT WASN'T HAPPENING TO THEM.
IT'S CRAZY, LIAM.
CRAZY BECAUSE YOU THINK IT WON'T WORK...
...OR BECAUSE YOU THINK IT CAN?
EVEN IF WE DID SOMEHOW PULL IT OFF, WOULD IT REALLY STOP ANYTHING?
YEAH, MAYBE WE SHOULD JUST WAIT UNTIL WE'RE OLD ENOUGH AND THEY DON'T COME FOR US ANYMORE, AND IT'S NOT OUR PROBLEM, RIGHT?

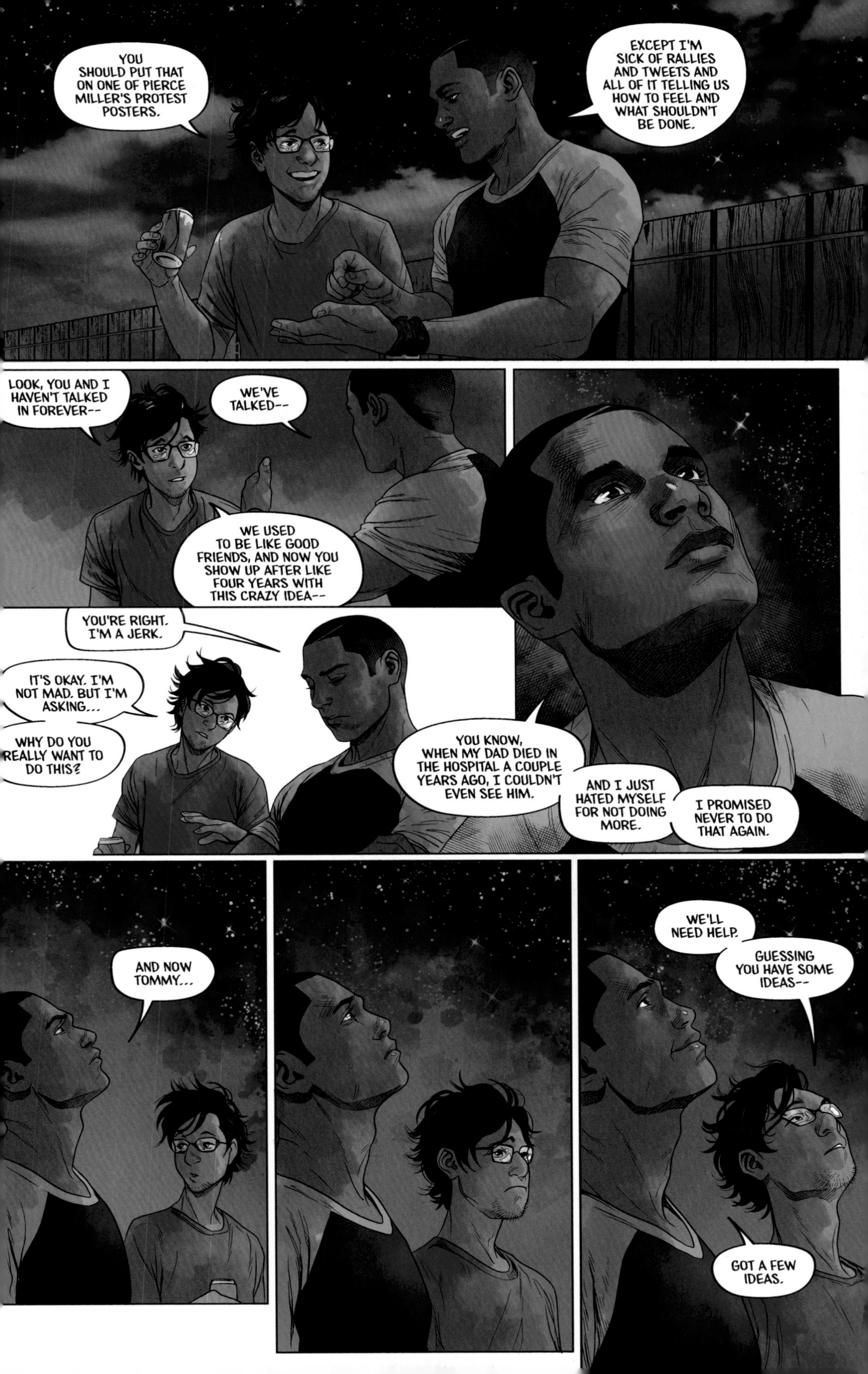
YOU SHOULD PUT THAT ON ONE OF PIERCE MILLER'S PROTEST POSTERS.
EXCEPT I'M SICK OF RALLIES AND TWEETS AND ALL OF IT TELLING US HOW TO FEEL AND WHAT SHOULDN'T BE DONE.
LOOK, YOU AND I HAVEN'T TALKED IN FOREVER--
WE'VE TALKED--
WE USED TO BE LIKE GOOD FRIENDS, AND NOW YOU SHOW UP AFTER LIKE FOUR YEARS WITH THIS CRAZY IDEA--
YOU'RE RIGHT. I'M A JERK.
IT'S OKAY. I'M NOT MAD. BUT I'M ASKING...
WHY DO YOU REALLY WANT TO DO THIS?
YOU KNOW, WHEN MY DAD DIED IN THE HOSPITAL A COUPLE YEARS AGO, I COULDN'T EVEN SEE HIM.
AND I JUST HATED MYSELF FOR NOT DOING MORE.
I PROMISED NEVER TO DO THAT AGAIN.
AND NOW TOMMY...
WE'LL NEED HELP.
GUESSING YOU HAVE SOME IDEAS--
GOT A FEW IDEAS.

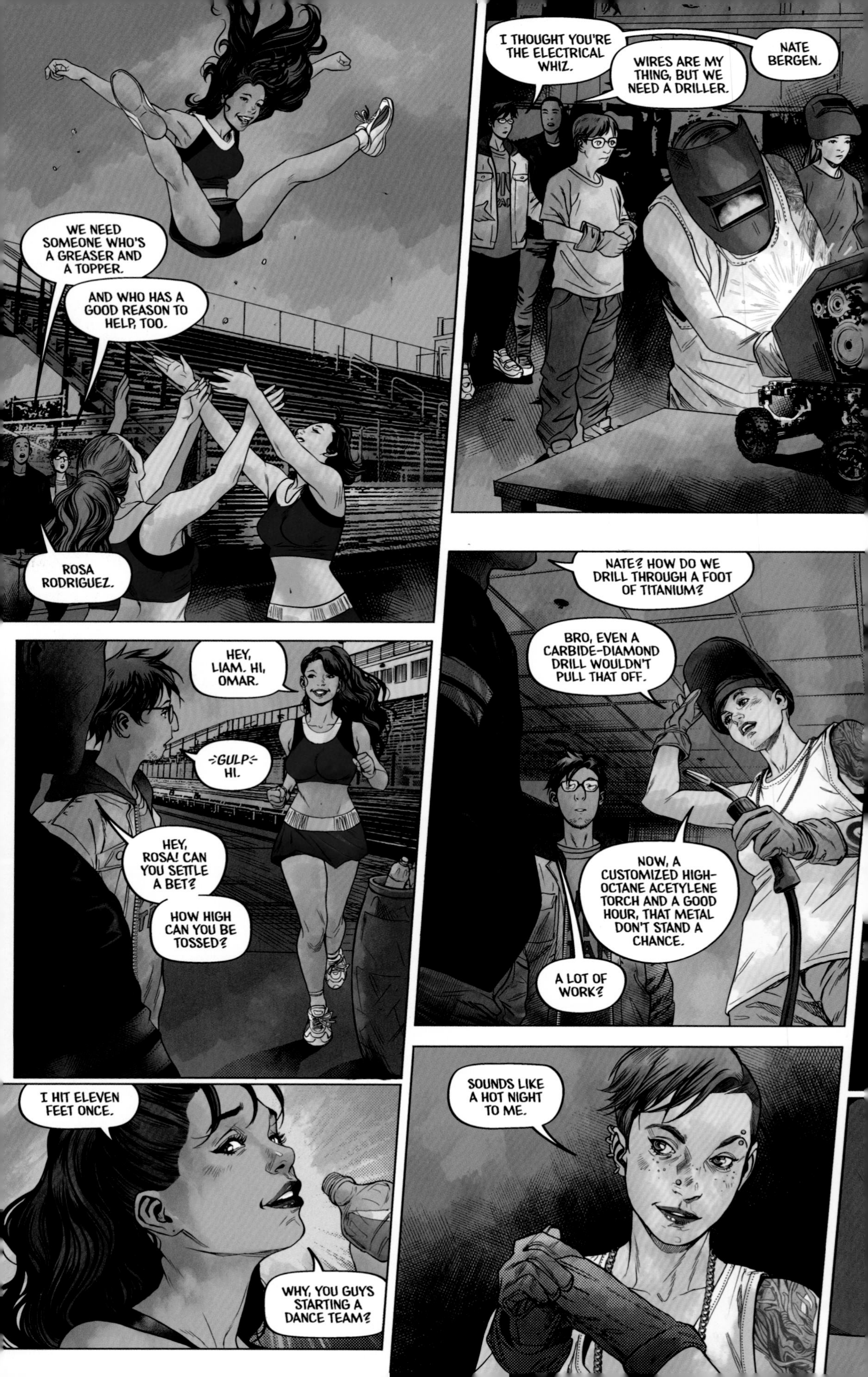
WE NEED SOMEONE WHO'S A GREASER AND A TOPPER.
AND WHO HAS A GOOD REASON TO HELP, TOO.
ROSA RODRIGUEZ.
I THOUGHT YOU'RE THE ELECTRICAL WHIZ.
WIRES ARE MY THING, BUT WE NEED A DRILLER.
NATE BERGEN.
HEY, LIAM. HI, OMAR.
GULP
HI.
HEY, ROSA! CAN YOU SETTLE A BET?
HOW HIGH CAN YOU BE TOSSED?
NATE? HOW DO WE DRILL THROUGH A FOOT OF TITANIUM?
BRO, EVEN A CARBIDE-DIAMOND DRILL WOULDN'T PULL THAT OFF.
NOW, A CUSTOMIZED HIGH-OCTANE ACETYLENE TORCH AND A GOOD HOUR, THAT METAL DON'T STAND A CHANCE.
A LOT OF WORK?
I HIT ELEVEN FEET ONCE.
WHY, YOU GUYS STARTING A DANCE TEAM?
SOUNDS LIKE A HOT NIGHT TO ME.

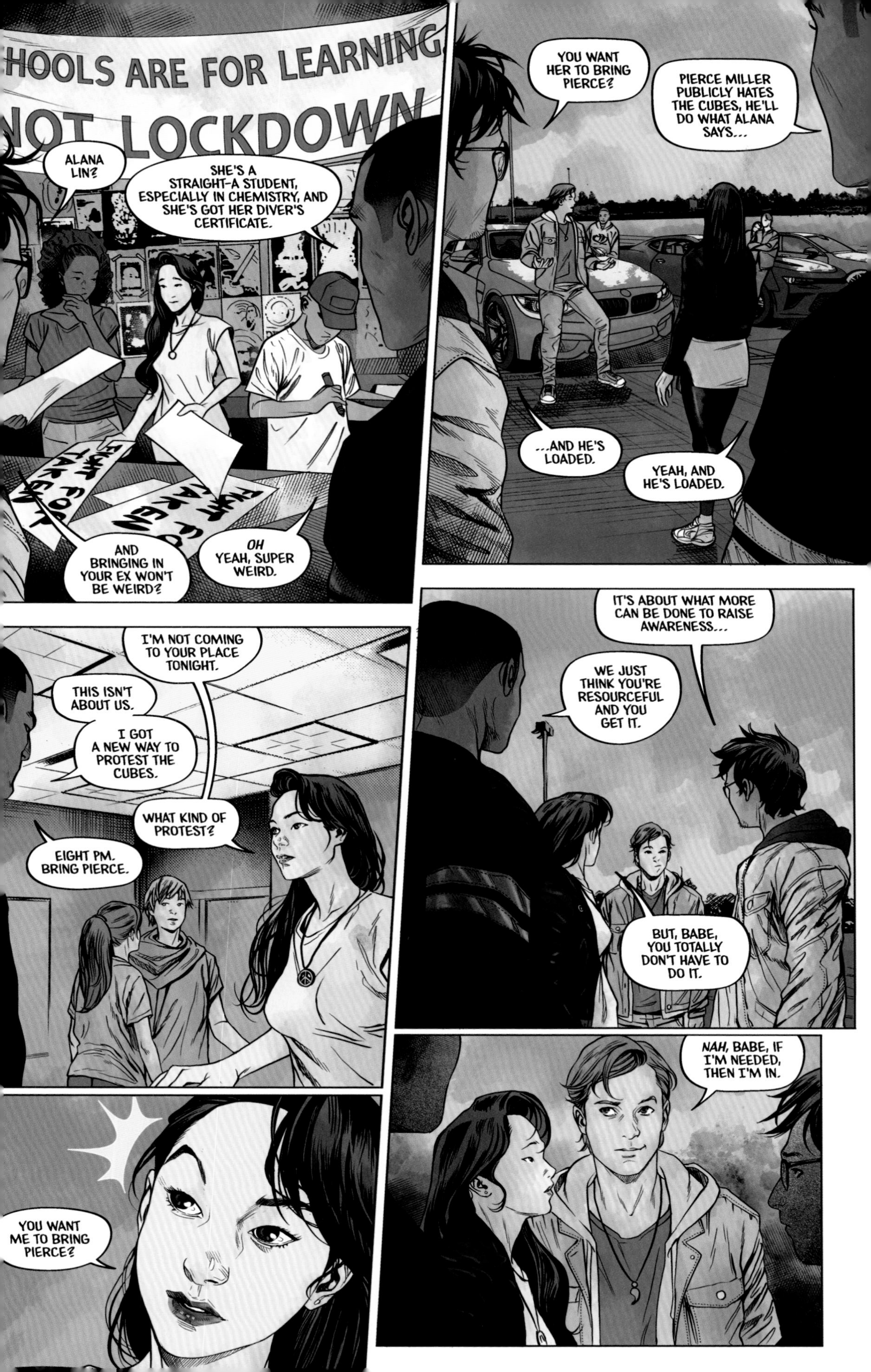

HOOLS ARE FOR LEARNING
NOT LOCKDOWN
ALANA LIN?
SHE'S A STRAIGHT-A STUDENT, ESPECIALLY IN CHEMISTRY, AND SHE'S GOT HER DIVER'S CERTIFICATE.
AND BRINGING IN YOUR EX WON'T BE WEIRD?
OH YEAH, SUPER WEIRD.
YOU WANT HER TO BRING PIERCE?
PIERCE MILLER PUBLICLY HATES THE CUBES, HE'LL DO WHAT ALANA SAYS...
...AND HE'S LOADED.
YEAH, AND HE'S LOADED.
I'M NOT COMING TO YOUR PLACE TONIGHT.
THIS ISN'T ABOUT US.
I GOT A NEW WAY TO PROTEST THE CUBES.
WHAT KIND OF PROTEST?
EIGHT PM. BRING PIERCE.
YOU WANT ME TO BRING PIERCE?
IT'S ABOUT WHAT MORE CAN BE DONE TO RAISE AWARENESS...
WE JUST THINK YOU'RE RESOURCEFUL AND YOU GET IT.
BUT, BABE, YOU TOTALLY DON'T HAVE TO DO IT.
NAH, BABE, IF I'M NEEDED, THEN I'M IN.

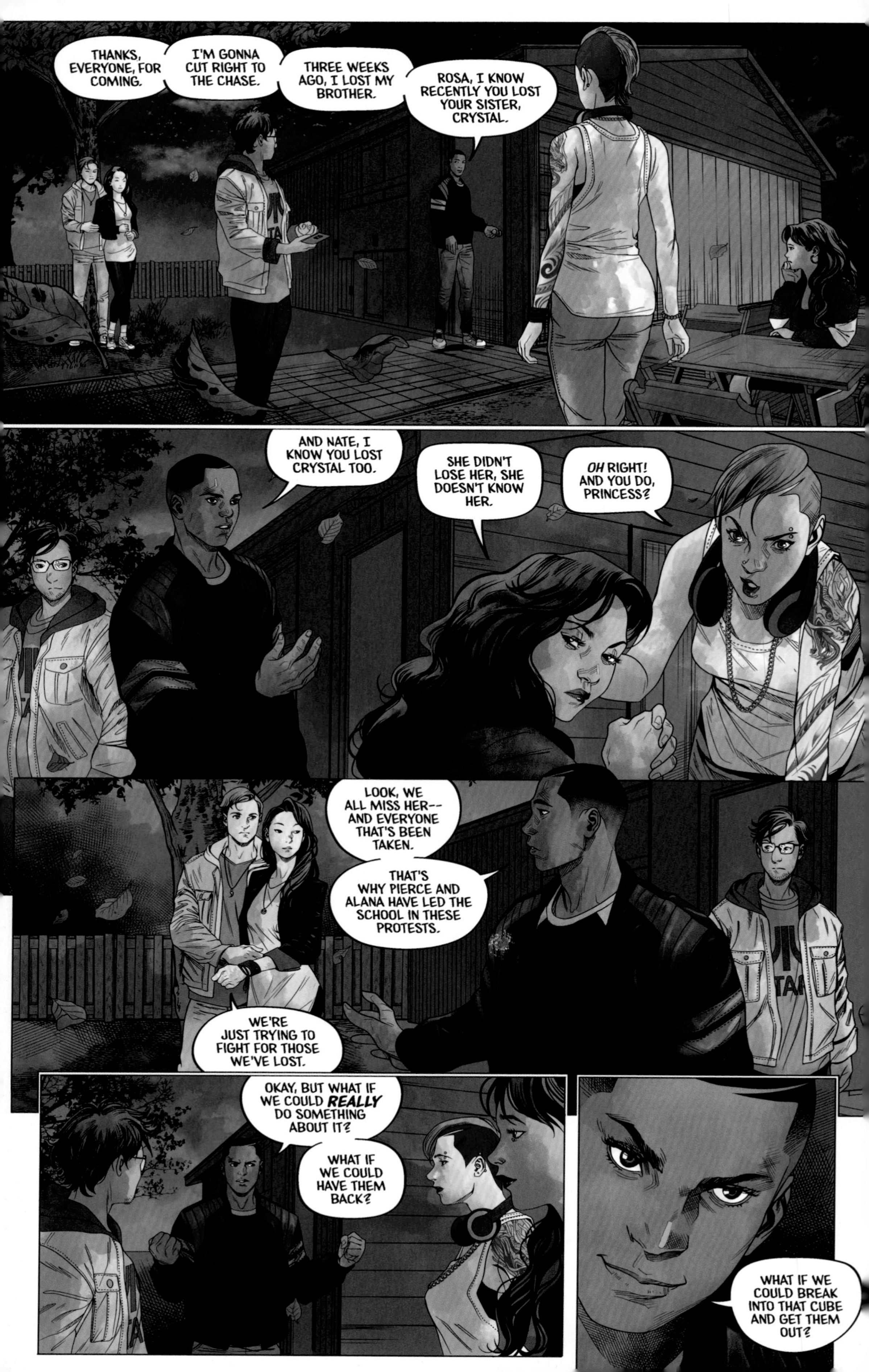
THANKS, EVERYONE, FOR COMING.
I'M GONNA CUT RIGHT TO THE CHASE.
THREE WEEKS AGO, I LOST MY BROTHER.
ROSA, I KNOW RECENTLY YOU LOST YOUR SISTER, CRYSTAL.
AND NATE, I KNOW YOU LOST CRYSTAL TOO.
SHE DIDN'T LOSE HER, SHE DOESN'T KNOW HER.
OH RIGHT! AND YOU DO, PRINCESS?
LOOK, WE ALL MISS HER-- AND EVERYONE THAT'S BEEN TAKEN.
THAT'S WHY PIERCE AND ALANA HAVE LED THE SCHOOL IN THESE PROTESTS.
WE'RE JUST TRYING TO FIGHT FOR THOSE WE'VE LOST.
OKAY, BUT WHAT IF WE COULD REALLY DO SOMETHING ABOUT IT?
WHAT IF WE COULD HAVE THEM BACK?
WHAT IF WE COULD BREAK INTO THAT CUBE AND GET THEM OUT?

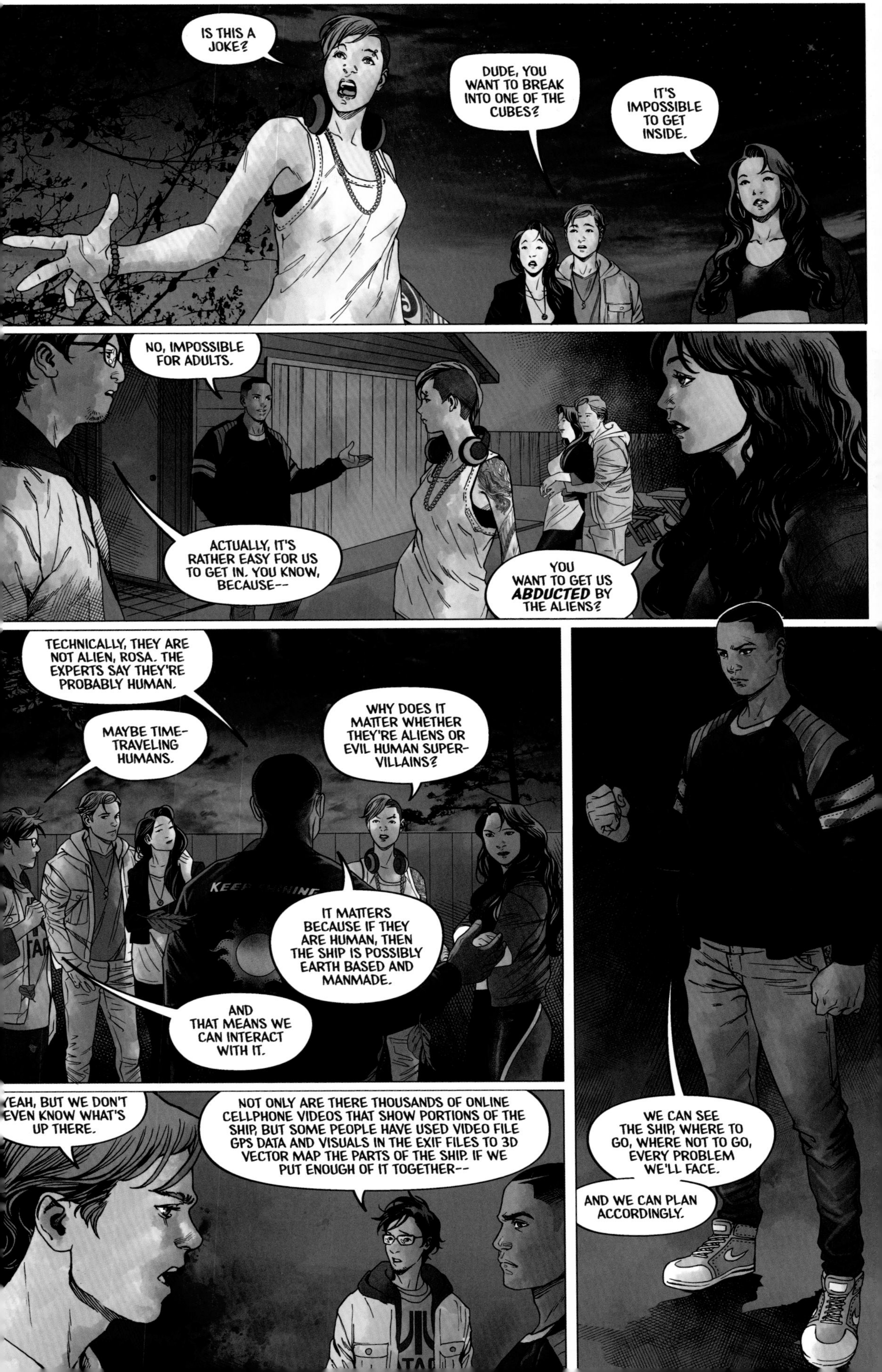
IS THIS A JOKE?
DUDE, YOU WANT TO BREAK INTO ONE OF THE CUBES?
IT'S IMPOSSIBLE TO GET INSIDE.
NO, IMPOSSIBLE FOR ADULTS.
ACTUALLY, IT'S RATHER EASY FOR US TO GET IN. YOU KNOW, BECAUSE--
YOU WANT TO GET US ***ABDUCTED*** BY THE ALIENS?
TECHNICALLY, THEY ARE NOT ALIEN, ROSA. THE EXPERTS SAY THEY'RE PROBABLY HUMAN.
MAYBE TIME-TRAVELING HUMANS.
WHY DOES IT MATTER WHETHER THEY'RE ALIENS OR EVIL HUMAN SUPER-VILLAINS?
IT MATTERS BECAUSE IF THEY ARE HUMAN, THEN THE SHIP IS POSSIBLY EARTH BASED AND MANMADE.
AND THAT MEANS WE CAN INTERACT WITH IT.
YEAH, BUT WE DON'T EVEN KNOW WHAT'S UP THERE.
NOT ONLY ARE THERE THOUSANDS OF ONLINE CELLPHONE VIDEOS THAT SHOW PORTIONS OF THE SHIP, BUT SOME PEOPLE HAVE USED VIDEO FILE GPS DATA AND VISUALS IN THE EXIF FILES TO 3D VECTOR MAP THE PARTS OF THE SHIP. IF WE PUT ENOUGH OF IT TOGETHER--
WE CAN SEE THE SHIP, WHERE TO GO, WHERE NOT TO GO, EVERY PROBLEM WE'LL FACE.
AND WE CAN PLAN ACCORDINGLY.

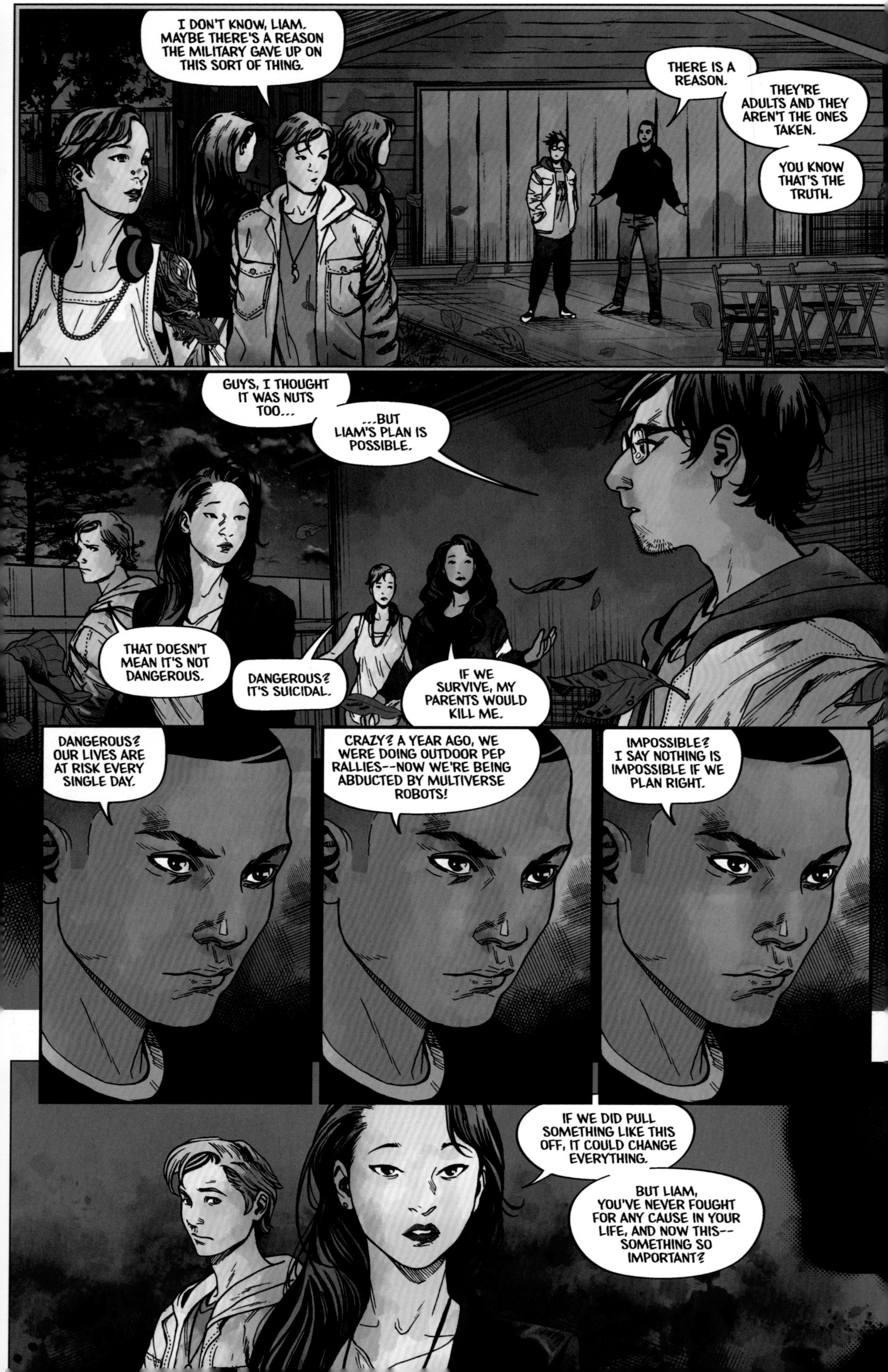
I DON'T KNOW, LIAM. MAYBE THERE'S A REASON THE MILITARY GAVE UP ON THIS SORT OF THING.
THERE IS A REASON.
THEY'RE ADULTS AND THEY AREN'T THE ONES TAKEN.
YOU KNOW THAT'S THE TRUTH.
GUYS, I THOUGHT IT WAS NUTS TOO...
...BUT LIAM'S PLAN IS POSSIBLE.
THAT DOESN'T MEAN IT'S NOT DANGEROUS.
DANGEROUS? IT'S SUICIDAL.
IF WE SURVIVE, MY PARENTS WOULD KILL ME.
DANGEROUS? OUR LIVES ARE AT RISK EVERY SINGLE DAY.
CRAZY? A YEAR AGO, WE WERE DOING OUTDOOR PEP RALLIES--NOW WE'RE BEING ABDUCTED BY MULTIVERSE ROBOTS!
IMPOSSIBLE? I SAY NOTHING IS IMPOSSIBLE IF WE PLAN RIGHT.
IF WE DID PULL SOMETHING LIKE THIS OFF, IT COULD CHANGE EVERYTHING.
BUT LIAM, YOU'VE NEVER FOUGHT FOR ANY CAUSE IN YOUR LIFE, AND NOW THIS--SOMETHING SO IMPORTANT?

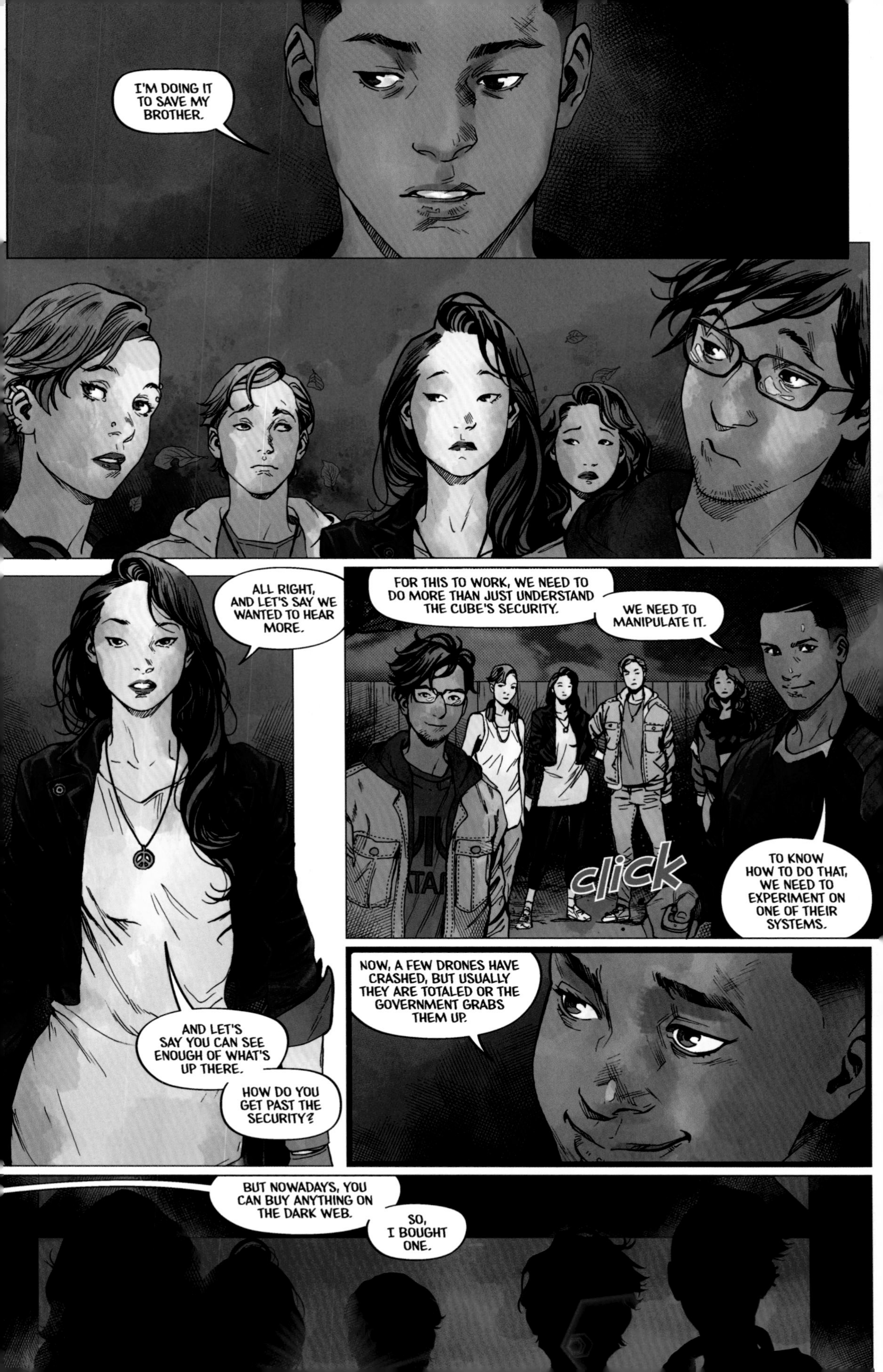
I'M DOING IT TO SAVE MY BROTHER.
ALL RIGHT, AND LET'S SAY WE WANTED TO HEAR MORE.
AND LET'S SAY YOU CAN SEE ENOUGH OF WHAT'S UP THERE.
HOW DO YOU GET PAST THE SECURITY?
FOR THIS TO WORK, WE NEED TO DO MORE THAN JUST UNDERSTAND THE CUBE'S SECURITY.
WE NEED TO MANIPULATE IT.
CLICK
TO KNOW HOW TO DO THAT, WE NEED TO EXPERIMENT ON ONE OF THEIR SYSTEMS.
NOW, A FEW DRONES HAVE CRASHED, BUT USUALLY THEY ARE TOTALED OR THE GOVERNMENT GRABS THEM UP.
BUT NOWADAYS, YOU CAN BUY ANYTHING ON THE DARK WEB.
SO, I BOUGHT ONE.

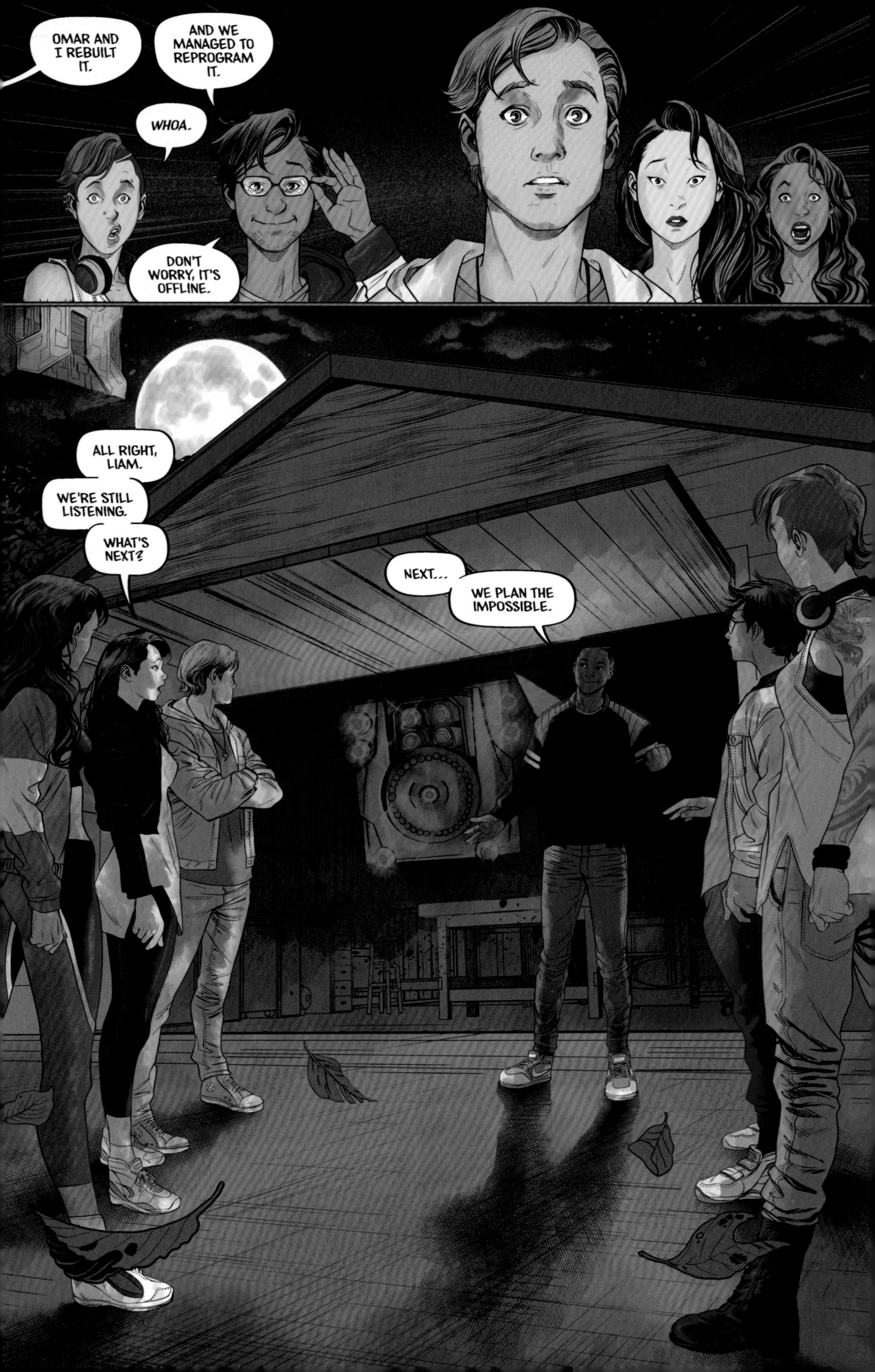
OMAR AND I REBUILT IT.
AND WE MANAGED TO REPROGRAM IT.
WHOA.
DON'T WORRY, IT'S OFFLINE.
ALL RIGHT, LIAM.
WE'RE STILL LISTENING.
WHAT'S NEXT?
NEXT...
WE PLAN THE IMPOSSIBLE.

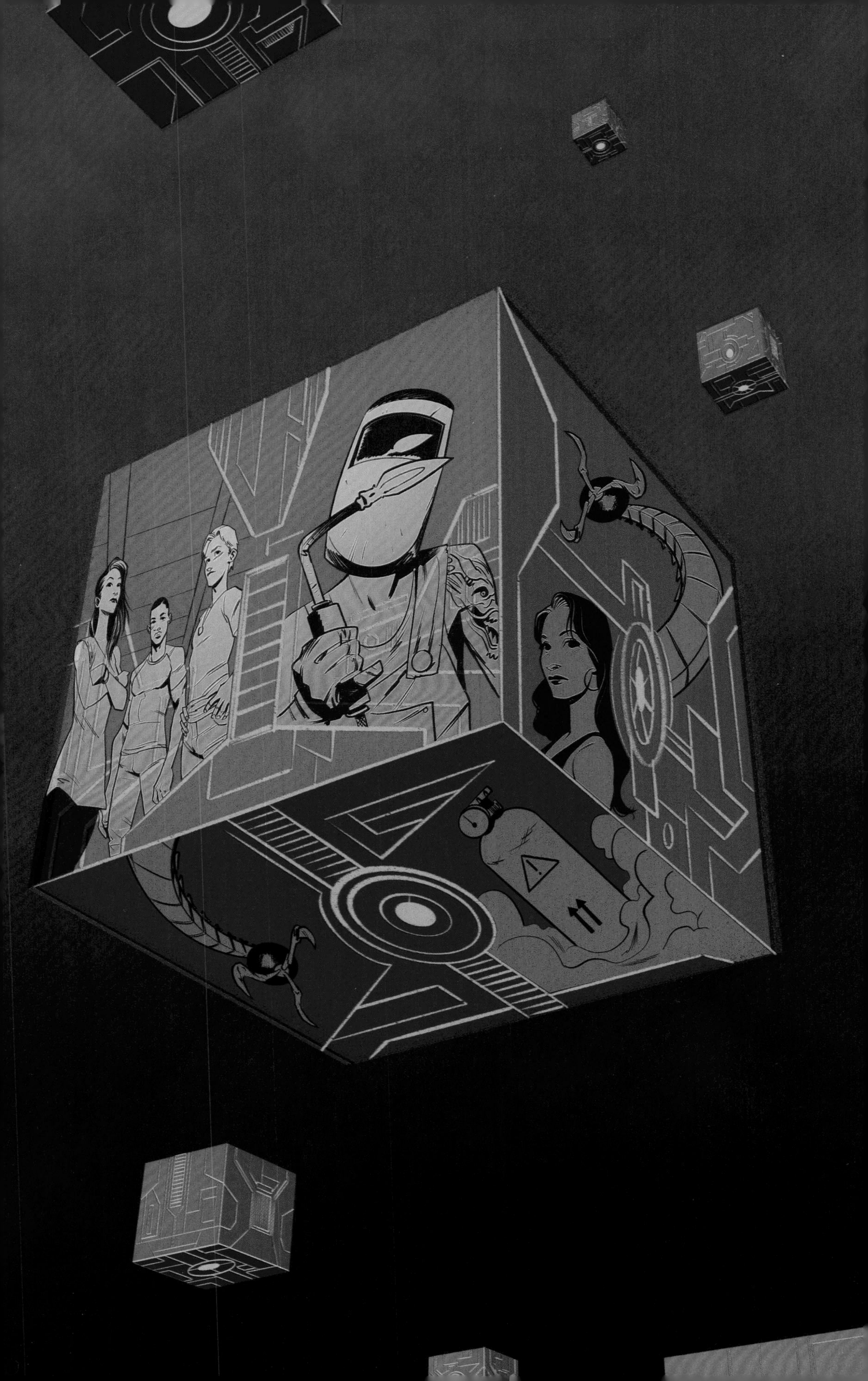

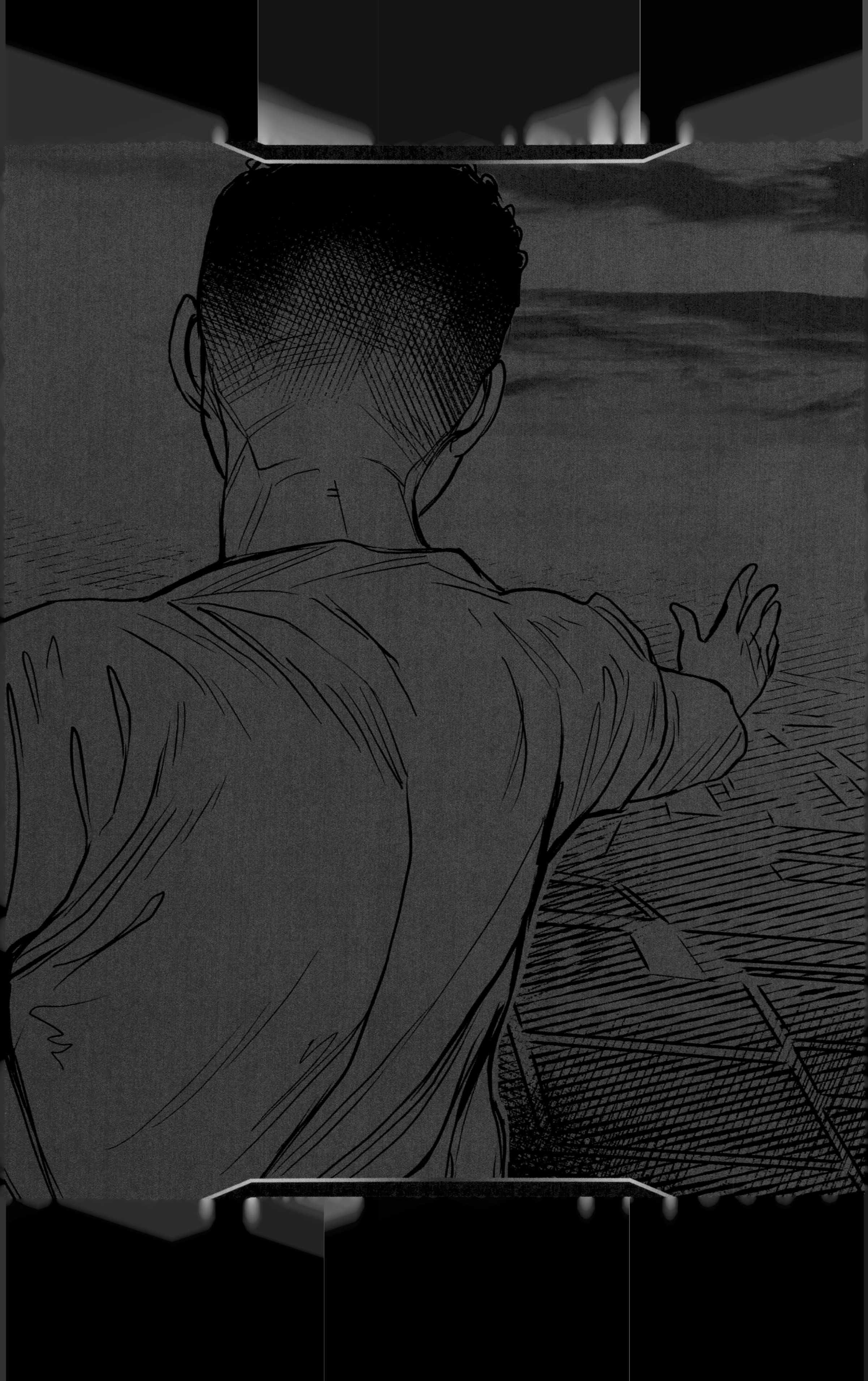

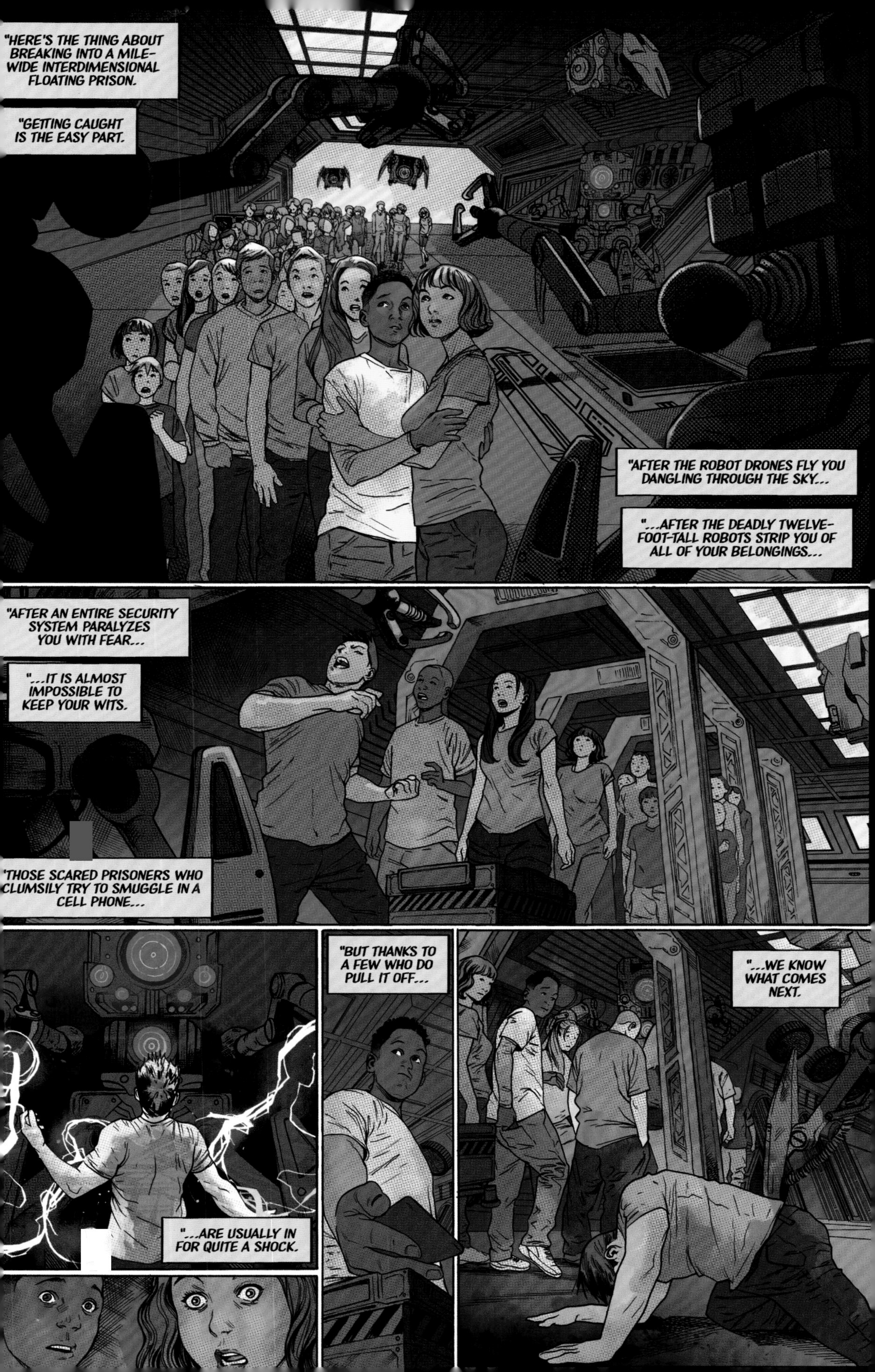
"HERE'S THE THING ABOUT BREAKING INTO A MILE-WIDE INTERDIMENSIONAL FLOATING PRISON.
"GETTING CAUGHT IS THE EASY PART.
"AFTER THE ROBOT DRONES FLY YOU DANGLING THROUGH THE SKY...
"...AFTER THE DEADLY TWELVE-FOOT-TALL ROBOTS STRIP YOU OF ALL OF YOUR BELONGINGS...
"AFTER AN ENTIRE SECURITY SYSTEM PARALYZES YOU WITH FEAR...
"...IT IS ALMOST IMPOSSIBLE TO KEEP YOUR WITS.
"THOSE SCARED PRISONERS WHO CLUMSILY TRY TO SMUGGLE IN A CELL PHONE...
"...ARE USUALLY IN FOR QUITE A SHOCK.
"BUT THANKS TO A FEW WHO DO PULL IT OFF...
"...WE KNOW WHAT COMES NEXT.

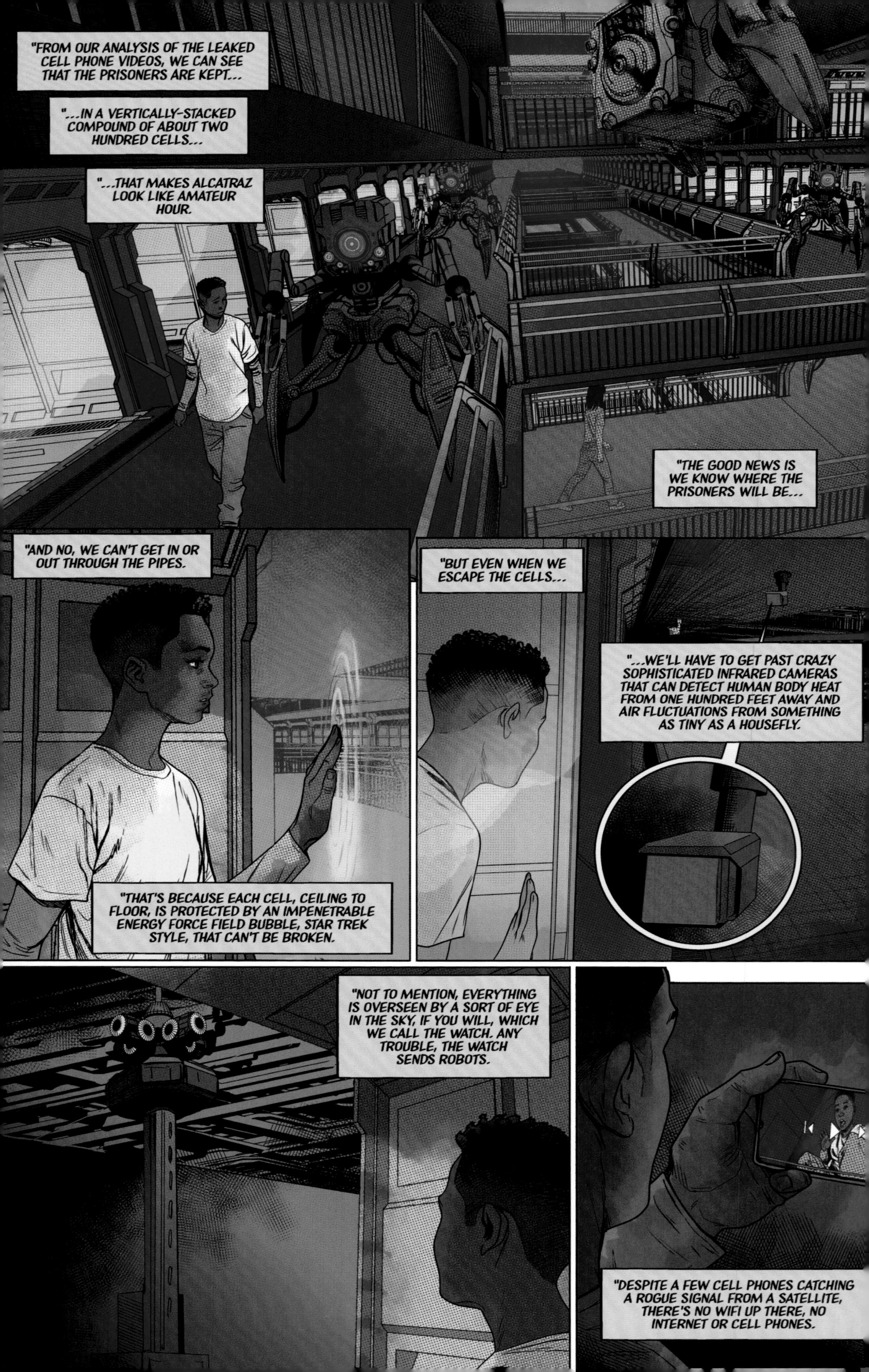
"FROM OUR ANALYSIS OF THE LEAKED CELL PHONE VIDEOS, WE CAN SEE THAT THE PRISONERS ARE KEPT...
"...IN A VERTICALLY-STACKED COMPOUND OF ABOUT TWO HUNDRED CELLS...
"...THAT MAKES ALCATRAZ LOOK LIKE AMATEUR HOUR.
"THE GOOD NEWS IS WE KNOW WHERE THE PRISONERS WILL BE...
"AND NO, WE CAN'T GET IN OR OUT THROUGH THE PIPES.
"THAT'S BECAUSE EACH CELL, CEILING TO FLOOR, IS PROTECTED BY AN IMPENETRABLE ENERGY FORCE FIELD BUBBLE, STAR TREK STYLE, THAT CAN'T BE BROKEN.
"BUT EVEN WHEN WE ESCAPE THE CELLS...
"...WE'LL HAVE TO GET PAST CRAZY SOPHISTICATED INFRARED CAMERAS THAT CAN DETECT HUMAN BODY HEAT FROM ONE HUNDRED FEET AWAY AND AIR FLUCTUATIONS FROM SOMETHING AS TINY AS A HOUSEFLY.
"NOT TO MENTION, EVERYTHING IS OVERSEEN BY A SORT OF EYE IN THE SKY, IF YOU WILL, WHICH WE CALL THE WATCH. ANY TROUBLE, THE WATCH SENDS ROBOTS.
"DESPITE A FEW CELL PHONES CATCHING A ROGUE SIGNAL FROM A SATELLITE, THERE'S NO WIFI UP THERE, NO INTERNET OR CELL PHONES.

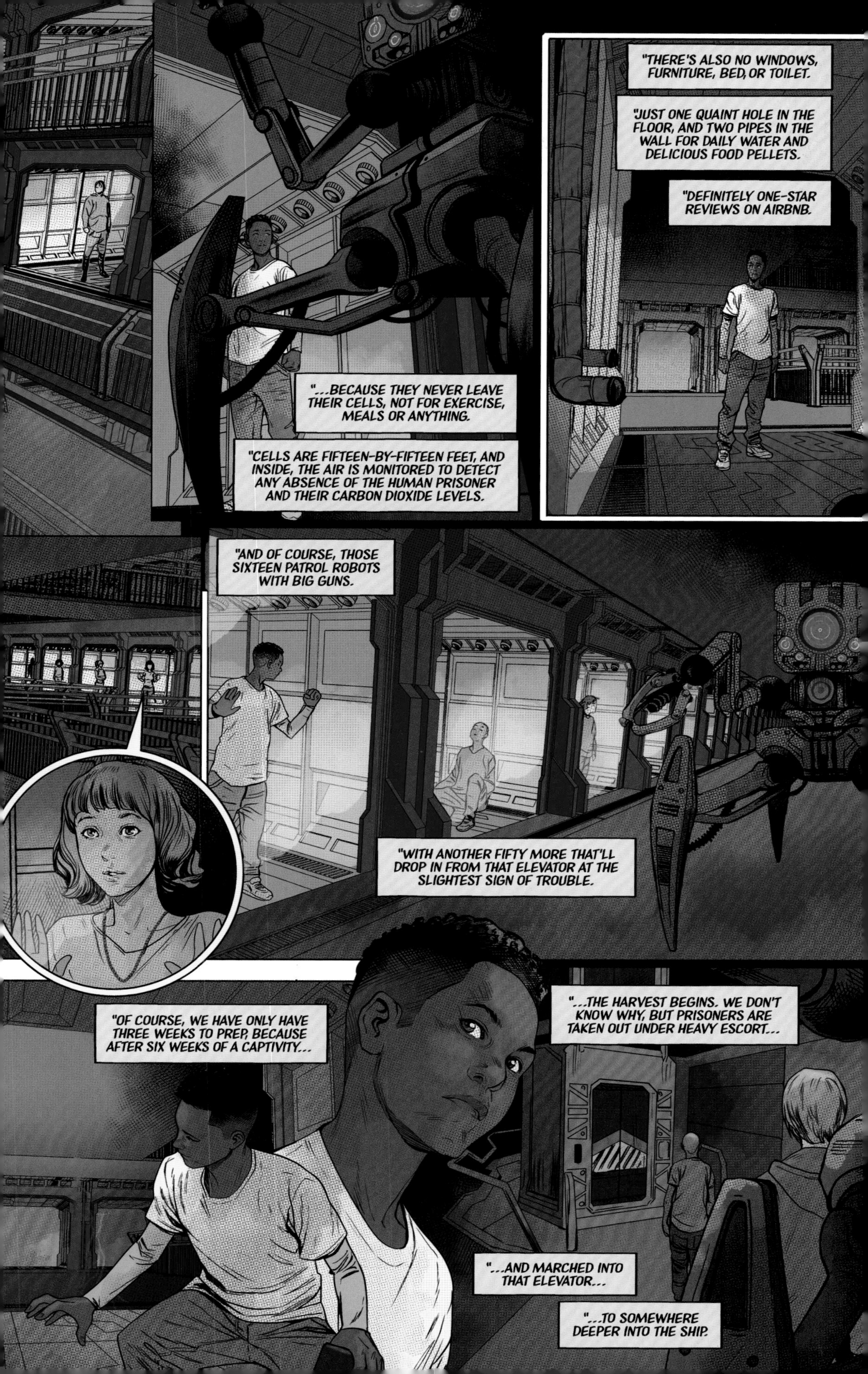
"...BECAUSE THEY NEVER LEAVE THEIR CELLS, NOT FOR EXERCISE, MEALS OR ANYTHING.
"CELLS ARE FIFTEEN-BY-FIFTEEN FEET, AND INSIDE, THE AIR IS MONITORED TO DETECT ANY ABSENCE OF THE HUMAN PRISONER AND THEIR CARBON DIOXIDE LEVELS.
"THERE'S ALSO NO WINDOWS, FURNITURE, BED, OR TOILET.
"JUST ONE QUAINT HOLE IN THE FLOOR, AND TWO PIPES IN THE WALL FOR DAILY WATER AND DELICIOUS FOOD PELLETS.
"DEFINITELY ONE-STAR REVIEWS ON AIRBNB.
"AND OF COURSE, THOSE SIXTEEN PATROL ROBOTS WITH BIG GUNS.
"WITH ANOTHER FIFTY MORE THAT'LL DROP IN FROM THAT ELEVATOR AT THE SLIGHTEST SIGN OF TROUBLE.
"OF COURSE, WE HAVE ONLY HAVE THREE WEEKS TO PREP, BECAUSE AFTER SIX WEEKS OF A CAPTIVITY...
"...THE HARVEST BEGINS. WE DON'T KNOW WHY, BUT PRISONERS ARE TAKEN OUT UNDER HEAVY ESCORT...
"...AND MARCHED INTO THAT ELEVATOR...
"...TO SOMEWHERE DEEPER INTO THE SHIP.

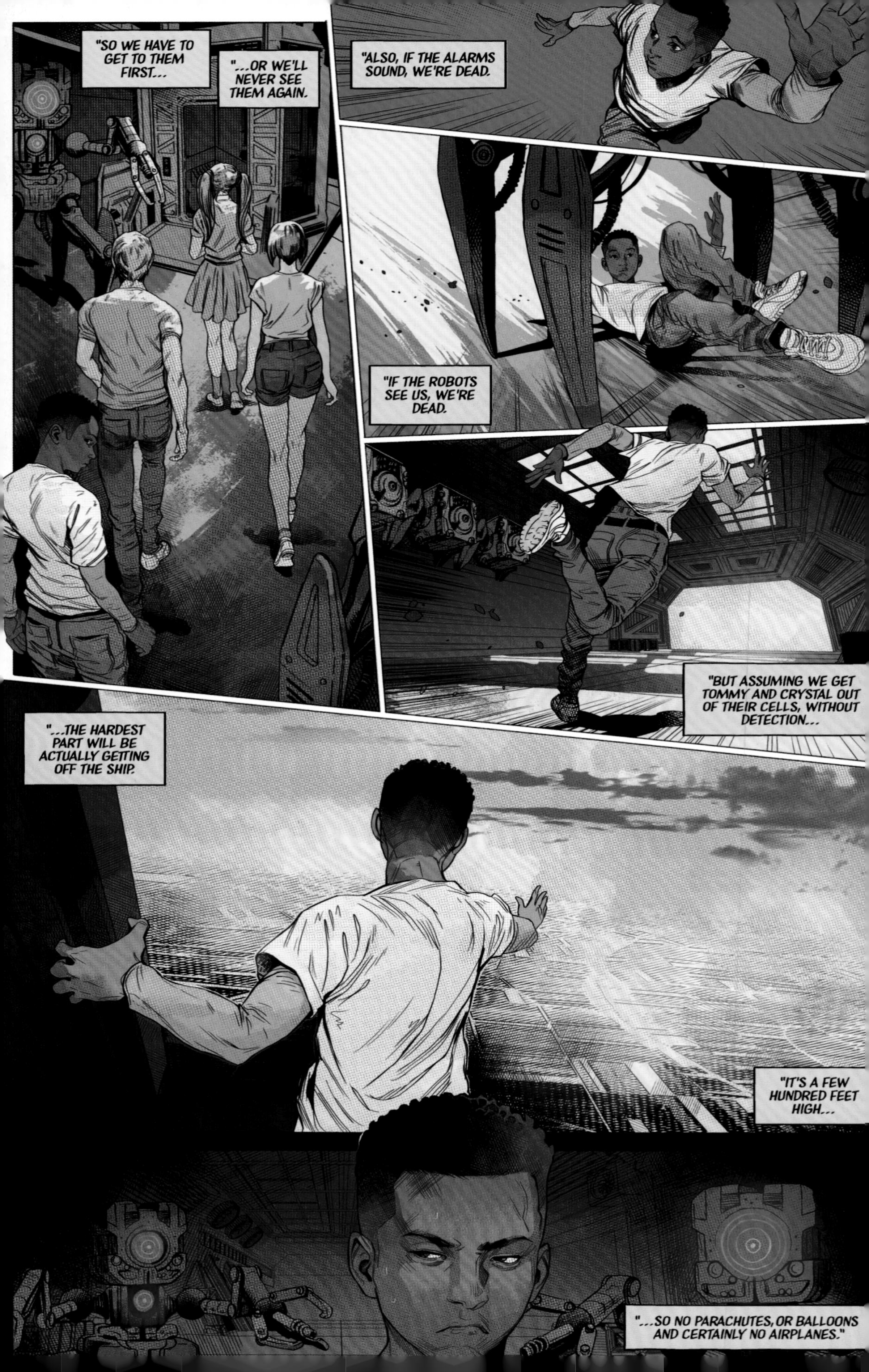
"SO WE HAVE TO GET TO THEM FIRST...
"...OR WE'LL NEVER SEE THEM AGAIN.
"ALSO, IF THE ALARMS SOUND, WE'RE DEAD.
"IF THE ROBOTS SEE US, WE'RE DEAD.
"BUT ASSUMING WE GET TOMMY AND CRYSTAL OUT OF THEIR CELLS, WITHOUT DETECTION...
"...THE HARDEST PART WILL BE ACTUALLY GETTING OFF THE SHIP.
"IT'S A FEW HUNDRED FEET HIGH...
"...SO NO PARACHUTES, OR BALLOONS AND CERTAINLY NO AIRPLANES."

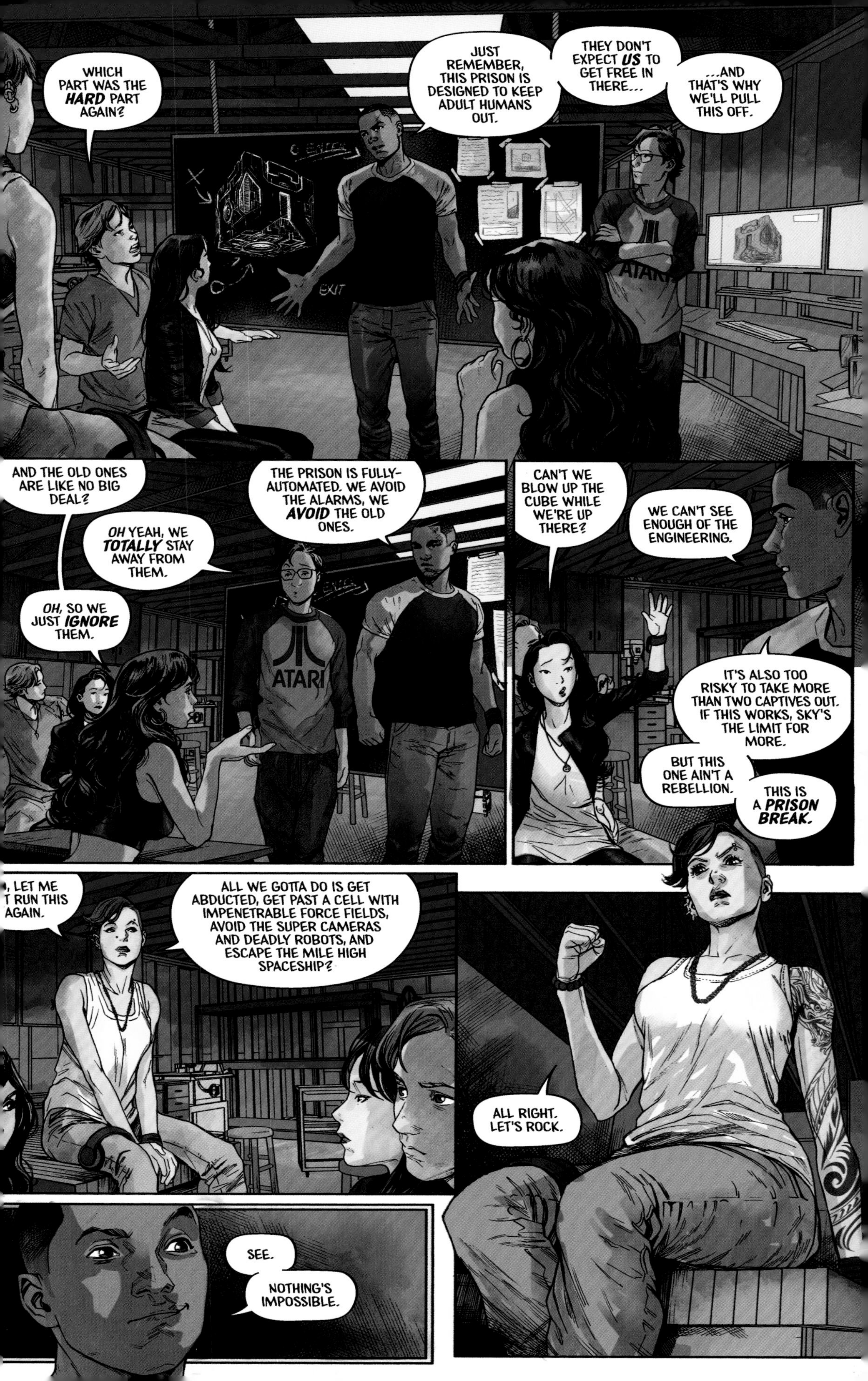
WHICH PART WAS THE HARD PART AGAIN?
JUST REMEMBER, THIS PRISON IS DESIGNED TO KEEP ADULT HUMANS OUT.
THEY DON'T EXPECT US TO GET FREE IN THERE...
...AND THAT'S WHY WE'LL PULL THIS OFF.
EXIT
AND THE OLD ONES ARE LIKE NO BIG DEAL?
THE PRISON IS FULLY-AUTOMATED. WE AVOID THE ALARMS, WE AVOID THE OLD ONES.
OH YEAH, WE TOTALLY STAY AWAY FROM THEM.
OH, SO WE JUST IGNORE THEM.
ATARI
CAN'T WE BLOW UP THE CUBE WHILE WE'RE UP THERE?
WE CAN'T SEE ENOUGH OF THE ENGINEERING.
IT'S ALSO TOO RISKY TO TAKE MORE THAN TWO CAPTIVES OUT. IF THIS WORKS, SKY'S THE LIMIT FOR MORE.
BUT THIS ONE AIN'T A REBELLION.
THIS IS A PRISON BREAK.
, LET ME T RUN THIS AGAIN.
ALL WE GOTTA DO IS GET ABDUCTED, GET PAST A CELL WITH IMPENETRABLE FORCE FIELDS, AVOID THE SUPER CAMERAS AND DEADLY ROBOTS, AND ESCAPE THE MILE HIGH SPACESHIP?
ALL RIGHT. LET'S ROCK.
SEE.
NOTHING'S IMPOSSIBLE.

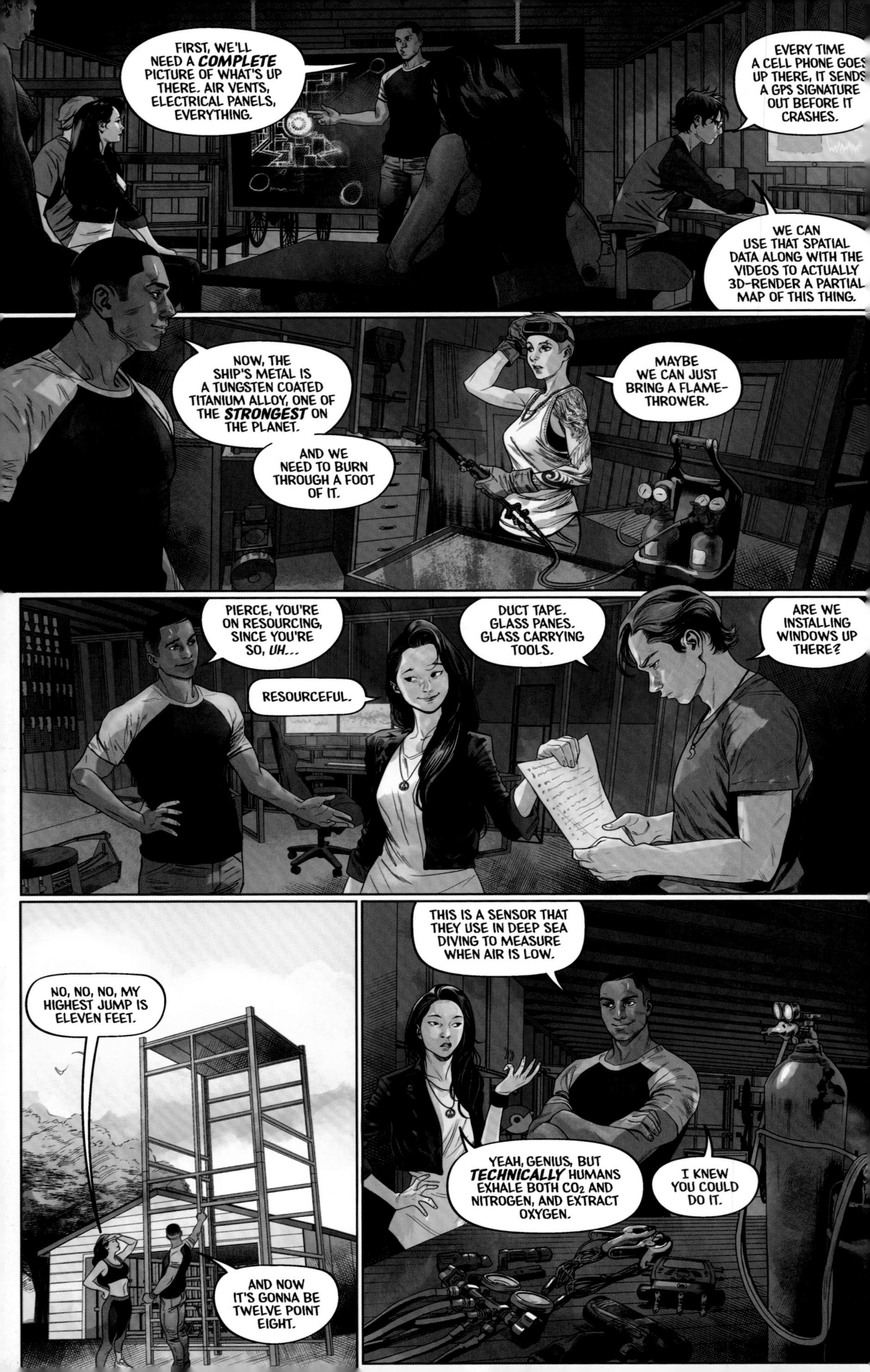
FIRST, WE'LL NEED A COMPLETE PICTURE OF WHAT'S UP THERE. AIR VENTS, ELECTRICAL PANELS, EVERYTHING.
EVERY TIME A CELL PHONE GOES UP THERE, IT SENDS A GPS SIGNATURE OUT BEFORE IT CRASHES.
WE CAN USE THAT SPATIAL DATA ALONG WITH THE VIDEOS TO ACTUALLY 3D-RENDER A PARTIAL MAP OF THIS THING.
NOW, THE SHIP'S METAL IS A TUNGSTEN COATED TITANIUM ALLOY, ONE OF THE STRONGEST ON THE PLANET.
AND WE NEED TO BURN THROUGH A FOOT OF IT.
MAYBE WE CAN JUST BRING A FLAME-THROWER.
PIERCE, YOU'RE ON RESOURCING, SINCE YOU'RE SO, UH...
RESOURCEFUL.
DUCT TAPE. GLASS PANES. GLASS CARRYING TOOLS.
ARE WE INSTALLING WINDOWS UP THERE?
NO, NO, NO, MY HIGHEST JUMP IS ELEVEN FEET.
AND NOW IT'S GONNA BE TWELVE POINT EIGHT.
THIS IS A SENSOR THAT THEY USE IN DEEP SEA DIVING TO MEASURE WHEN AIR IS LOW.
YEAH, GENIUS, BUT TECHNICALLY HUMANS EXHALE BOTH CO_2 AND NITROGEN, AND EXTRACT OXYGEN.
I KNEW YOU COULD DO IT.

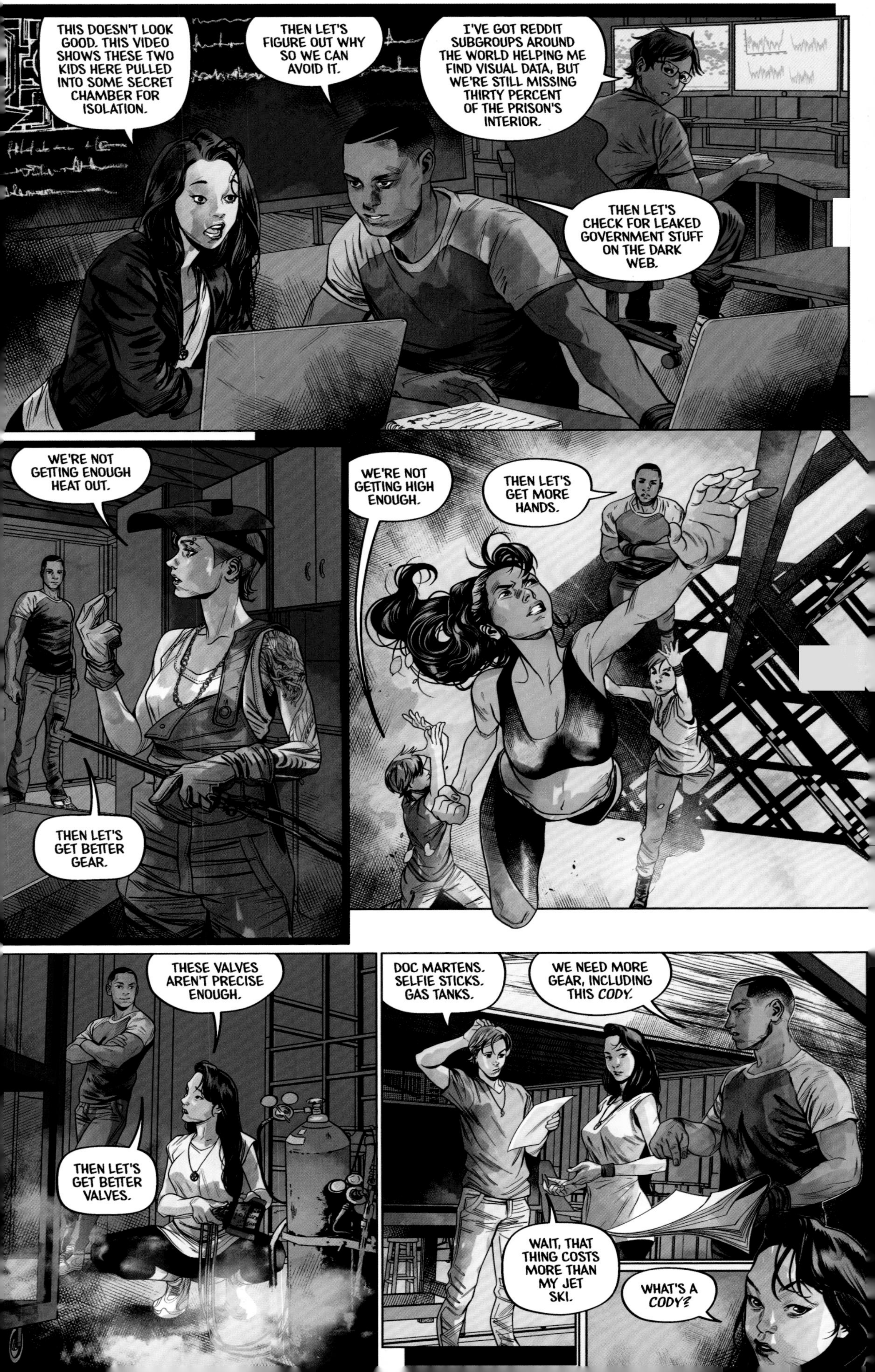

THIS DOESN'T LOOK GOOD. THIS VIDEO SHOWS THESE TWO KIDS HERE PULLED INTO SOME SECRET CHAMBER FOR ISOLATION.
THEN LET'S FIGURE OUT WHY SO WE CAN AVOID IT.
I'VE GOT REDDIT SUBGROUPS AROUND THE WORLD HELPING ME FIND VISUAL DATA, BUT WE'RE STILL MISSING THIRTY PERCENT OF THE PRISON'S INTERIOR.
THEN LET'S CHECK FOR LEAKED GOVERNMENT STUFF ON THE DARK WEB.
WE'RE NOT GETTING ENOUGH HEAT OUT.
THEN LET'S GET BETTER GEAR.
WE'RE NOT GETTING HIGH ENOUGH.
THEN LET'S GET MORE HANDS.
THESE VALVES AREN'T PRECISE ENOUGH.
THEN LET'S GET BETTER VALVES.
DOC MARTENS. SELFIE STICKS. GAS TANKS.
WE NEED MORE GEAR, INCLUDING THIS *CODY*.
WAIT, THAT THING COSTS MORE THAN MY JET SKI.
WHAT'S A *CODY*?

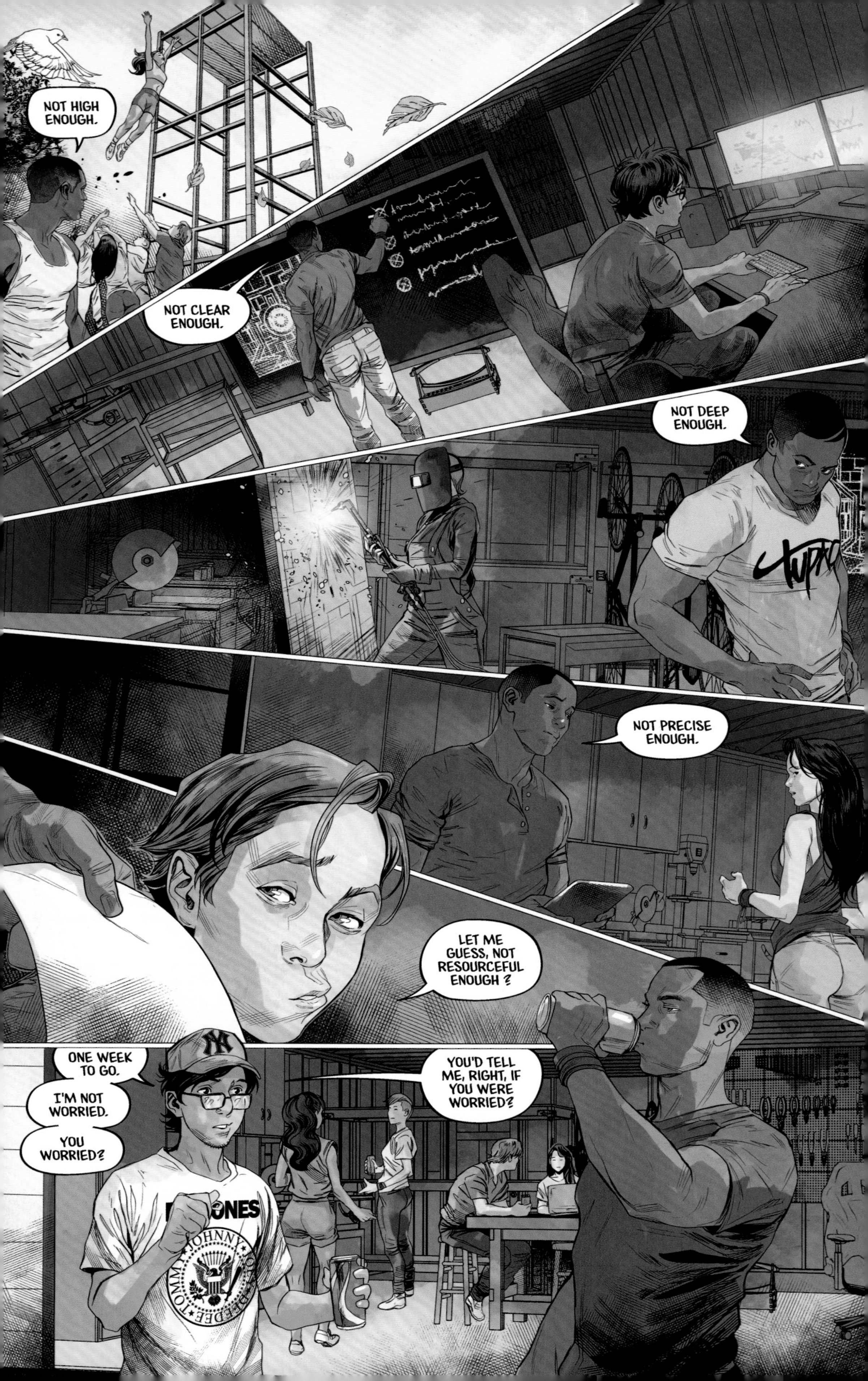
NOT HIGH ENOUGH.
NOT CLEAR ENOUGH.
NOT DEEP ENOUGH.
NOT PRECISE ENOUGH.
LET ME GUESS, NOT RESOURCEFUL ENOUGH?
ONE WEEK TO GO.
I'M NOT WORRIED.
YOU WORRIED?
YOU'D TELL ME, RIGHT, IF YOU WERE WORRIED?

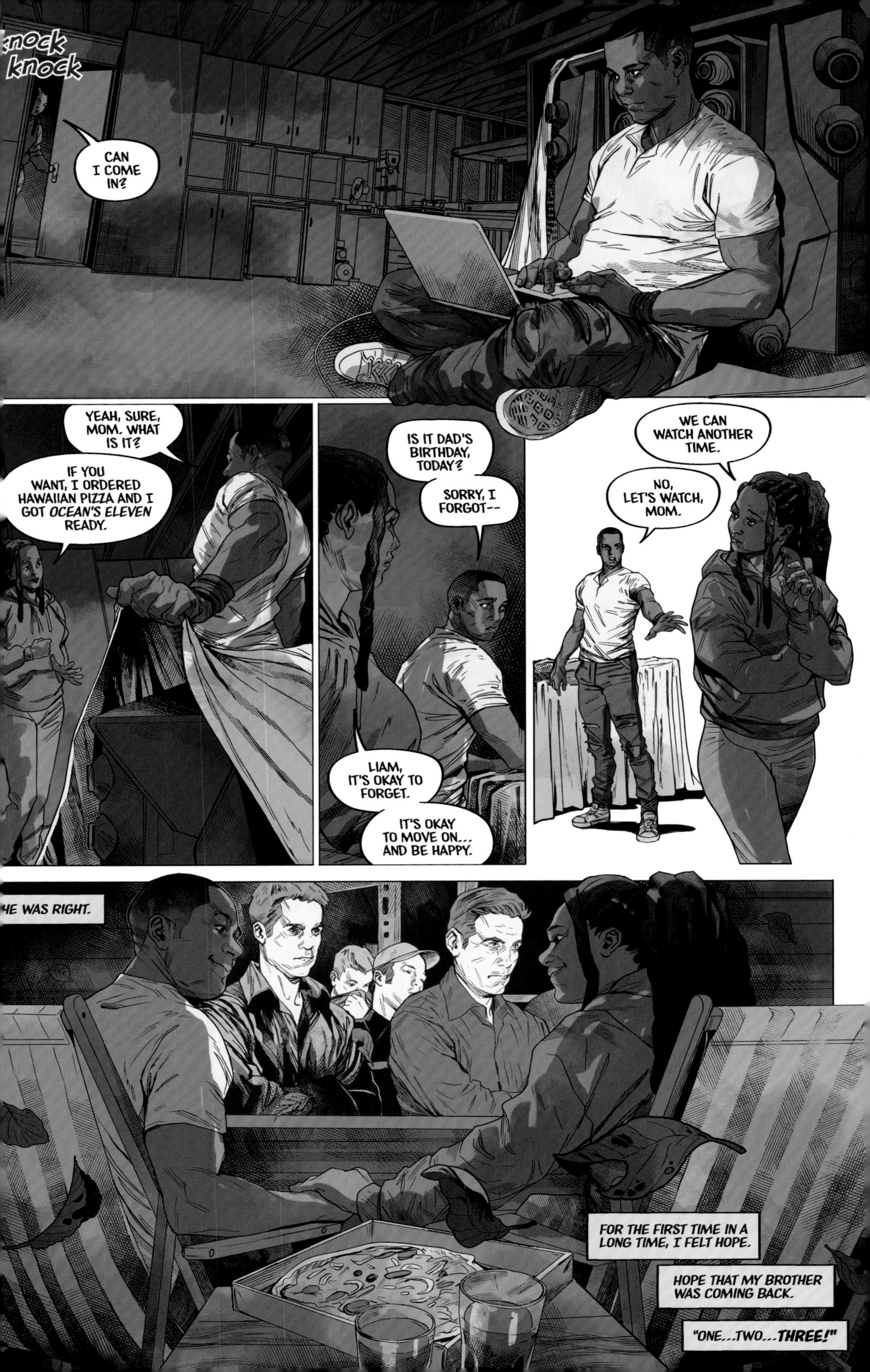
knock knock
CAN I COME IN?
YEAH, SURE, MOM. WHAT IS IT?
IF YOU WANT, I ORDERED HAWAIIAN PIZZA AND I GOT OCEAN'S ELEVEN READY.
IS IT DAD'S BIRTHDAY, TODAY?
SORRY, I FORGOT--
LIAM, IT'S OKAY TO FORGET.
IT'S OKAY TO MOVE ON... AND BE HAPPY.
WE CAN WATCH ANOTHER TIME.
NO, LET'S WATCH, MOM.
HE WAS RIGHT.
FOR THE FIRST TIME IN A LONG TIME, I FELT HOPE.
HOPE THAT MY BROTHER WAS COMING BACK.
"ONE...TWO...THREE!"

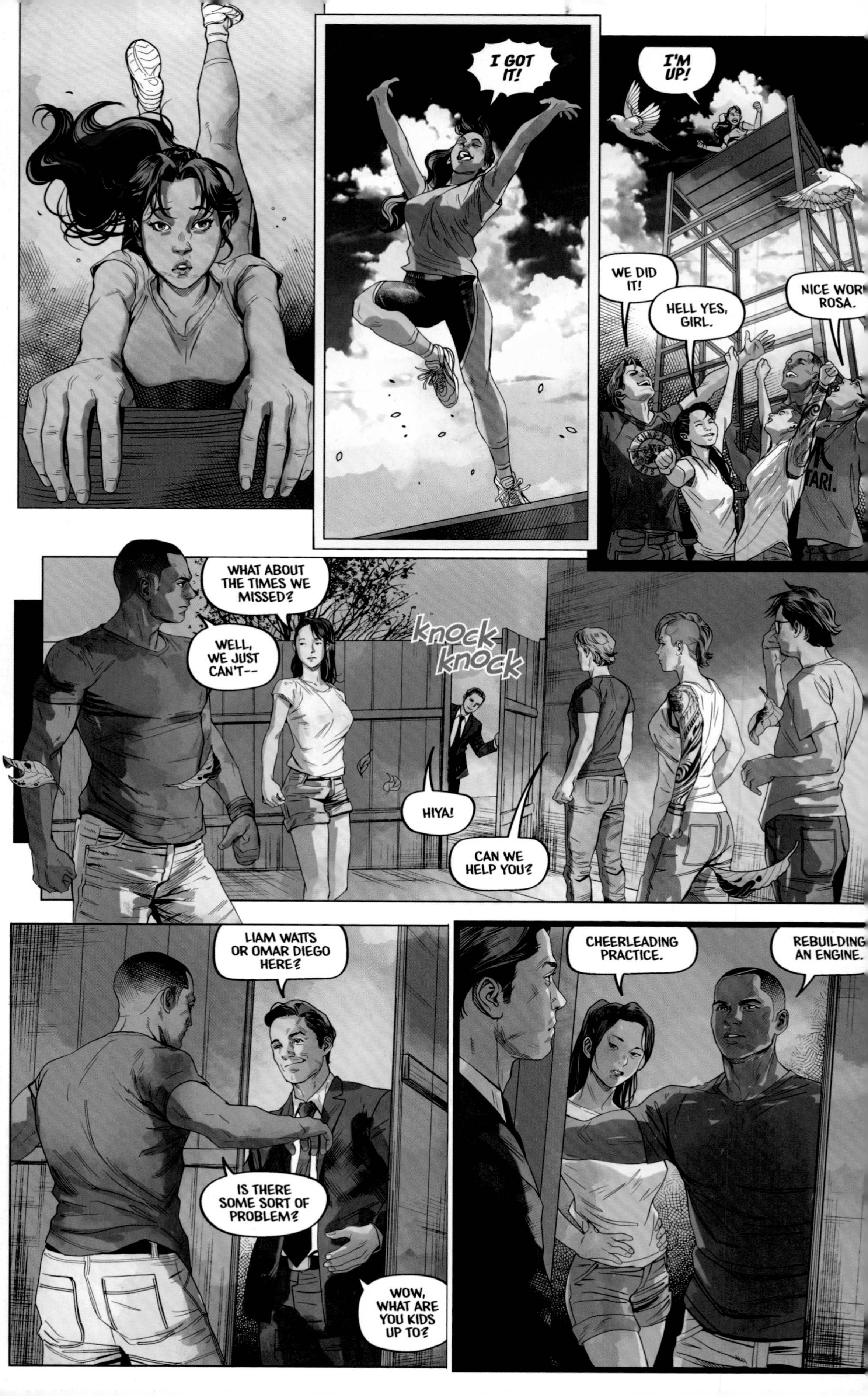
I GOT IT!
I'M UP!
WE DID IT!
HELL YES, GIRL.
NICE WOR
ROSA.
WHAT ABOUT THE TIMES WE MISSED?
WELL, WE JUST CAN'T--
knock knock
HIYA!
CAN WE HELP YOU?
LIAM WATTS OR OMAR DIEGO HERE?
IS THERE SOME SORT OF PROBLEM?
WOW, WHAT ARE YOU KIDS UP TO?
CHEERLEADING PRACTICE.
REBUILDING AN ENGINE.

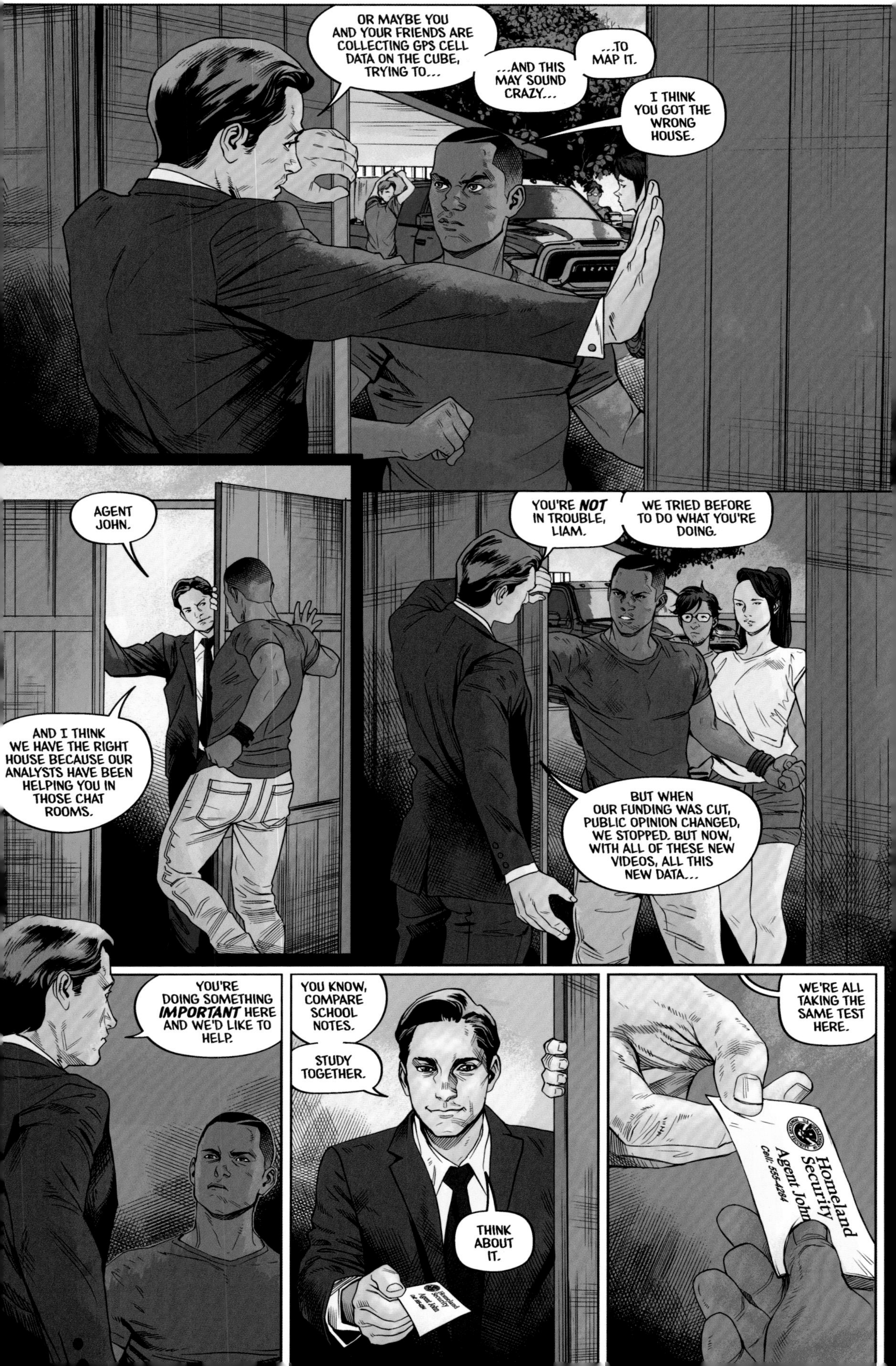
OR MAYBE YOU AND YOUR FRIENDS ARE COLLECTING GPS CELL DATA ON THE CUBE, TRYING TO...
...AND THIS MAY SOUND CRAZY...
...TO MAP IT.
I THINK YOU GOT THE WRONG HOUSE.
AGENT JOHN.
AND I THINK WE HAVE THE RIGHT HOUSE BECAUSE OUR ANALYSTS HAVE BEEN HELPING YOU IN THOSE CHAT ROOMS.
YOU'RE *NOT* IN TROUBLE, LIAM.
WE TRIED BEFORE TO DO WHAT YOU'RE DOING.
BUT WHEN OUR FUNDING WAS CUT, PUBLIC OPINION CHANGED, WE STOPPED. BUT NOW, WITH ALL OF THESE NEW VIDEOS, ALL THIS NEW DATA...
YOU'RE DOING SOMETHING *IMPORTANT* HERE AND WE'D LIKE TO HELP.
YOU KNOW, COMPARE SCHOOL NOTES.
STUDY TOGETHER.
THINK ABOUT IT.
WE'RE ALL TAKING THE SAME TEST HERE.
Homeland Security
Agent John
Cell: 555-4284

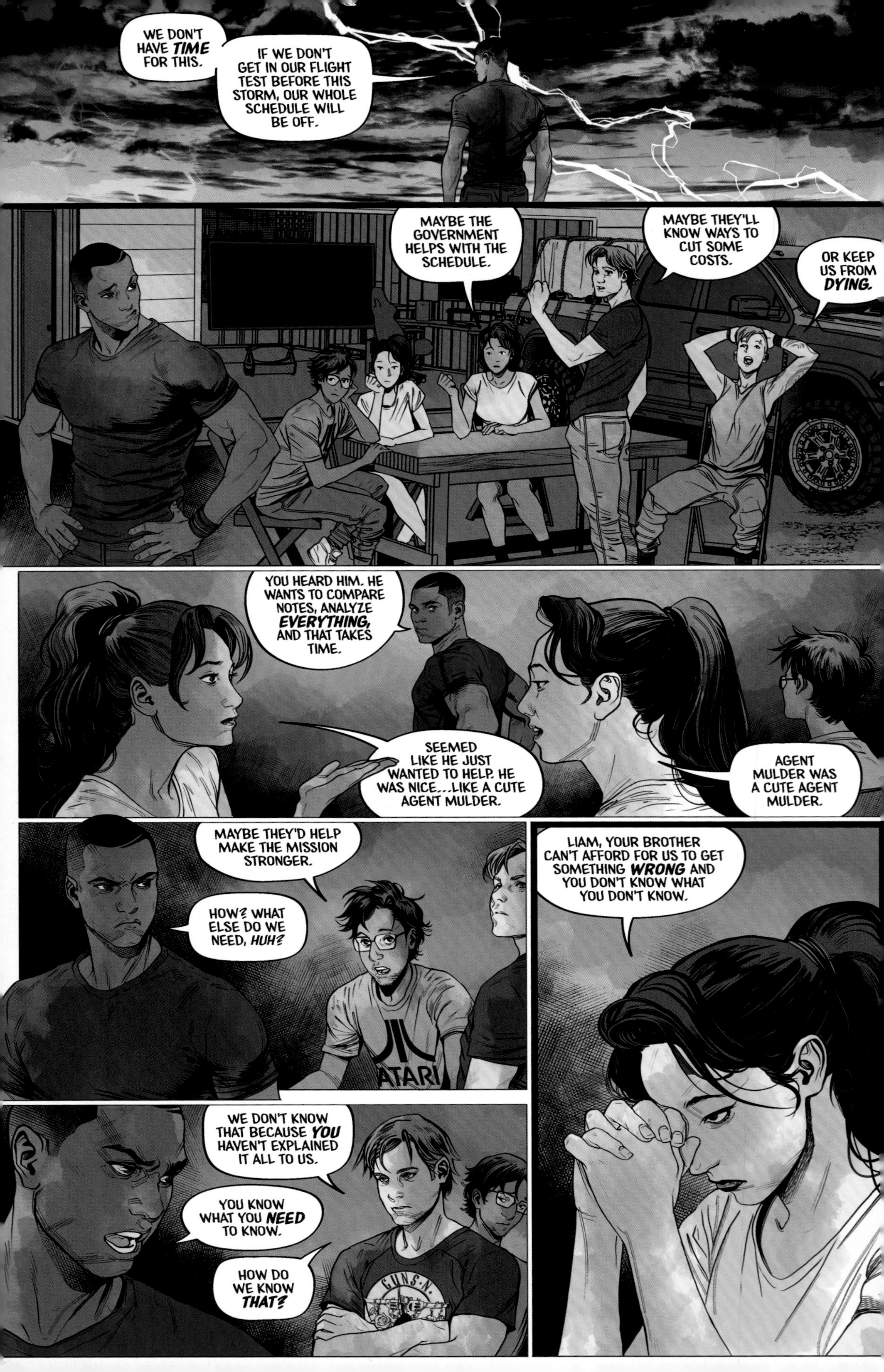
WE DON'T HAVE TIME FOR THIS.
IF WE DON'T GET IN OUR FLIGHT TEST BEFORE THIS STORM, OUR WHOLE SCHEDULE WILL BE OFF.
MAYBE THE GOVERNMENT HELPS WITH THE SCHEDULE.
MAYBE THEY'LL KNOW WAYS TO CUT SOME COSTS.
OR KEEP US FROM DYING.
YOU HEARD HIM. HE WANTS TO COMPARE NOTES, ANALYZE EVERYTHING, AND THAT TAKES TIME.
SEEMED LIKE HE JUST WANTED TO HELP. HE WAS NICE...LIKE A CUTE AGENT MULDER.
AGENT MULDER WAS A CUTE AGENT MULDER.
MAYBE THEY'D HELP MAKE THE MISSION STRONGER.
HOW? WHAT ELSE DO WE NEED, HUH?
ATARI
LIAM, YOUR BROTHER CAN'T AFFORD FOR US TO GET SOMETHING WRONG AND YOU DON'T KNOW WHAT YOU DON'T KNOW.
WE DON'T KNOW THAT BECAUSE YOU HAVEN'T EXPLAINED IT ALL TO US.
YOU KNOW WHAT YOU NEED TO KNOW.
HOW DO WE KNOW THAT?

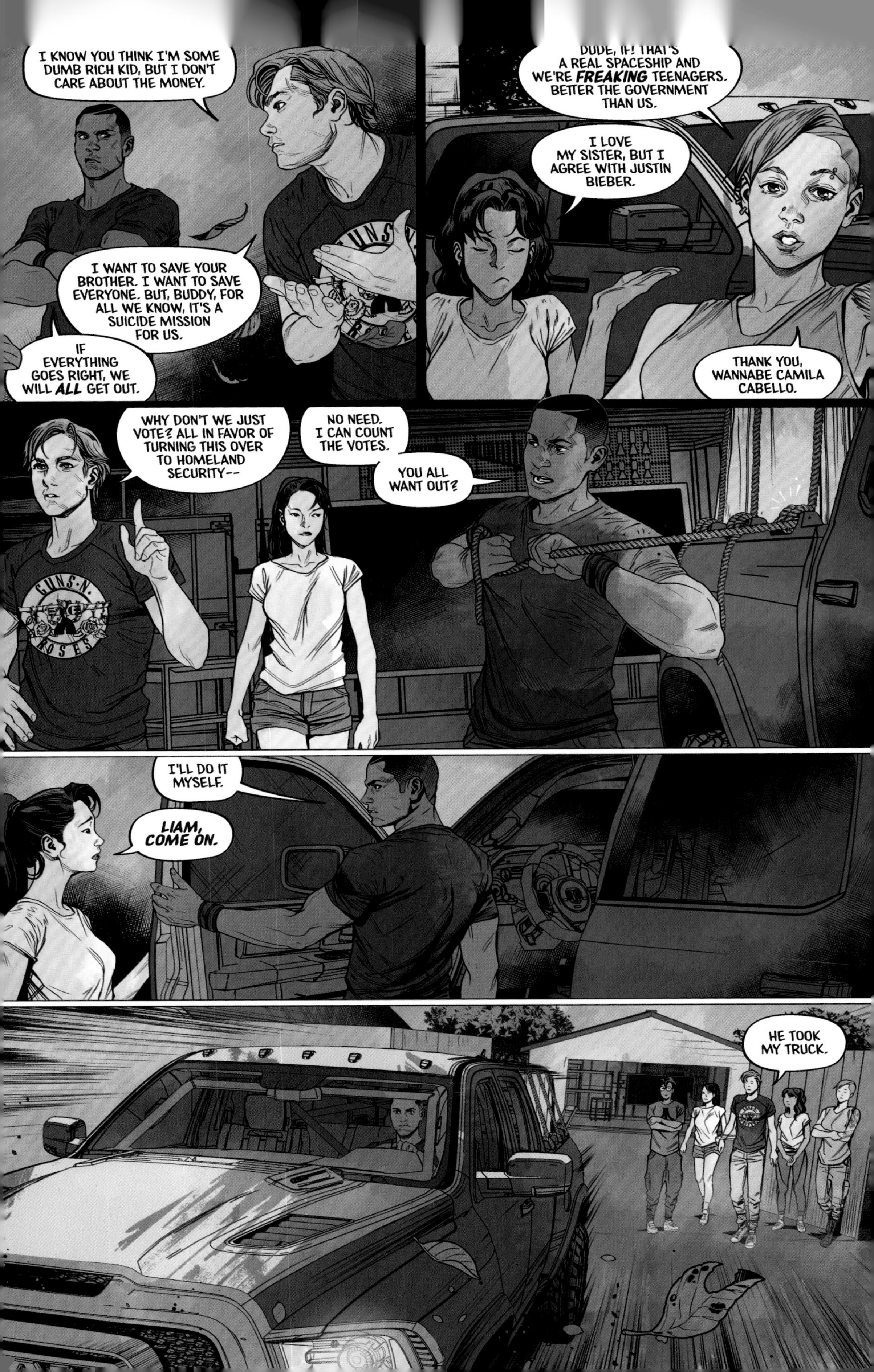
I KNOW YOU THINK I'M SOME DUMB RICH KID, BUT I DON'T CARE ABOUT THE MONEY.
I WANT TO SAVE YOUR BROTHER. I WANT TO SAVE EVERYONE. BUT, BUDDY, FOR ALL WE KNOW, IT'S A SUICIDE MISSION FOR US.
IF EVERYTHING GOES RIGHT, WE WILL ALL GET OUT.
DUDE, IF! THAT'S A REAL SPACESHIP AND WE'RE FREAKING TEENAGERS. BETTER THE GOVERNMENT THAN US.
I LOVE MY SISTER, BUT I AGREE WITH JUSTIN BIEBER.
THANK YOU, WANNABE CAMILA CABELLO.
WHY DON'T WE JUST VOTE? ALL IN FAVOR OF TURNING THIS OVER TO HOMELAND SECURITY--
NO NEED. I CAN COUNT THE VOTES.
YOU ALL WANT OUT?
I'LL DO IT MYSELF.
LIAM, COME ON.
HE TOOK MY TRUCK.

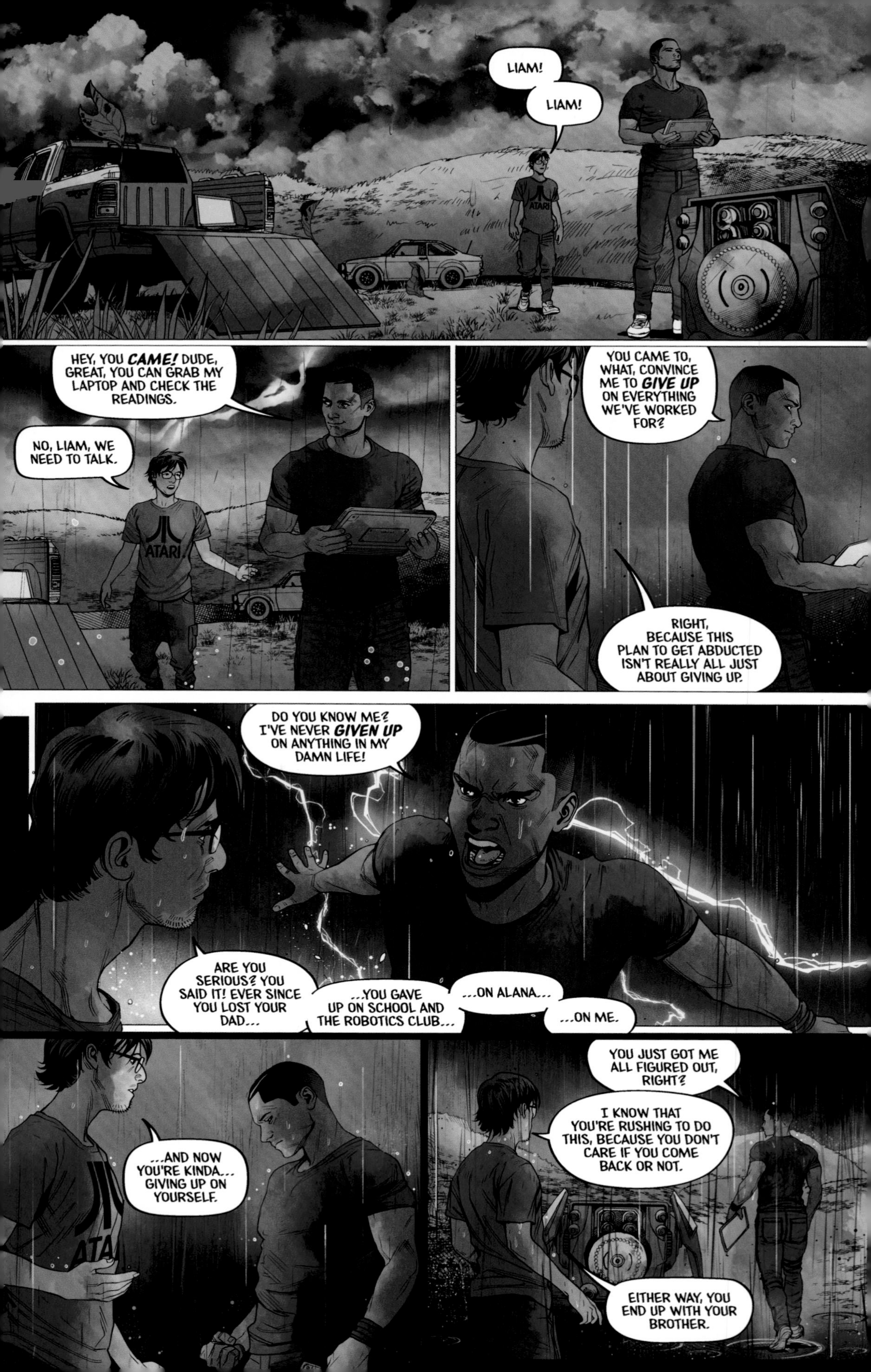
LIAM!
LIAM!
HEY, YOU CAME! DUDE, GREAT, YOU CAN GRAB MY LAPTOP AND CHECK THE READINGS.
NO, LIAM, WE NEED TO TALK.
YOU CAME TO, WHAT, CONVINCE ME TO GIVE UP ON EVERYTHING WE'VE WORKED FOR?
RIGHT, BECAUSE THIS PLAN TO GET ABDUCTED ISN'T REALLY ALL JUST ABOUT GIVING UP.
DO YOU KNOW ME? I'VE NEVER GIVEN UP ON ANYTHING IN MY DAMN LIFE!
ARE YOU SERIOUS? YOU SAID IT! EVER SINCE YOU LOST YOUR DAD...
...YOU GAVE UP ON SCHOOL AND THE ROBOTICS CLUB...
...ON ALANA...
...ON ME.
...AND NOW YOU'RE KINDA... GIVING UP ON YOURSELF.
YOU JUST GOT ME ALL FIGURED OUT, RIGHT?
I KNOW THAT YOU'RE RUSHING TO DO THIS, BECAUSE YOU DON'T CARE IF YOU COME BACK OR NOT.
EITHER WAY, YOU END UP WITH YOUR BROTHER.

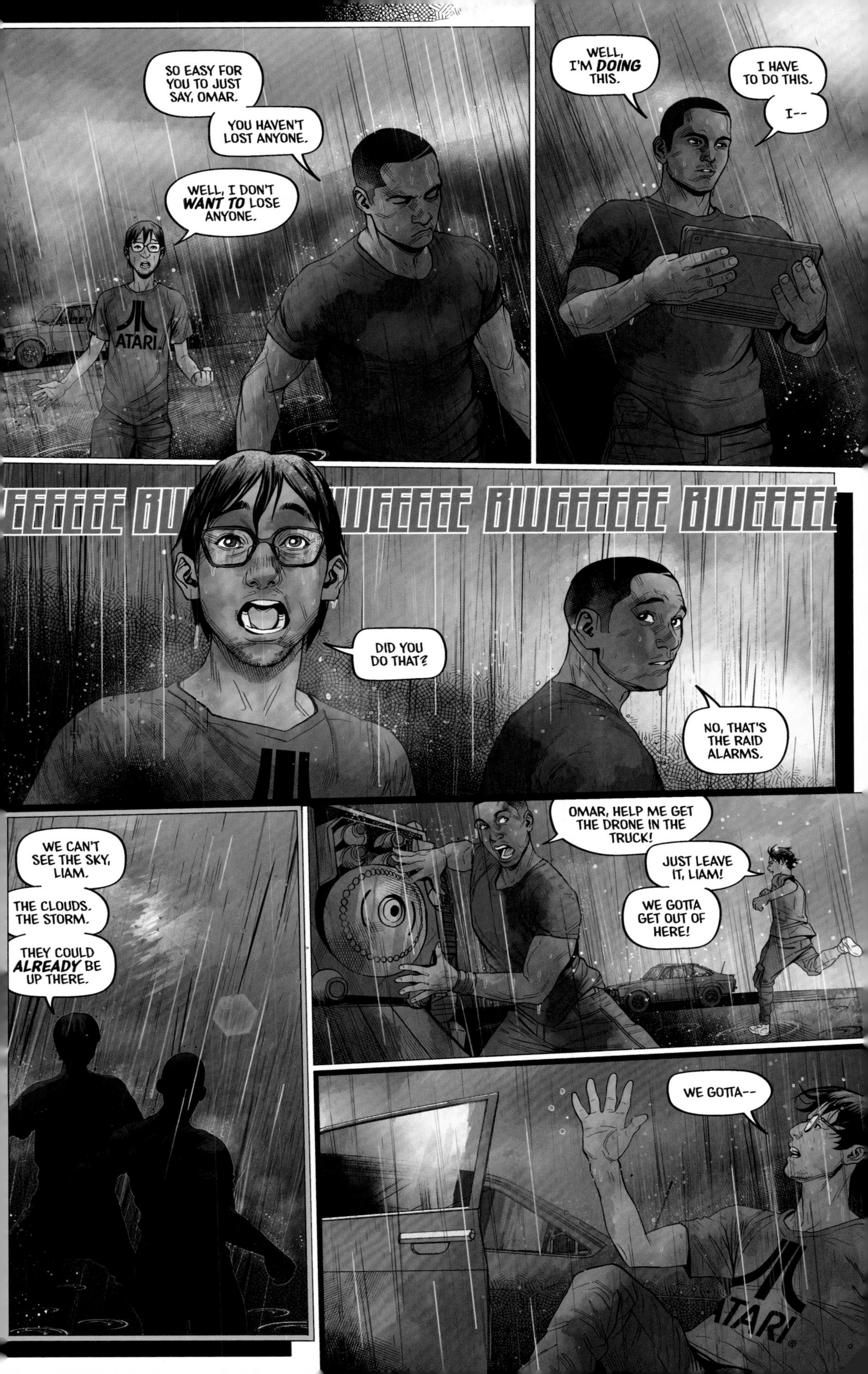
SO EASY FOR YOU TO JUST SAY, OMAR.
YOU HAVEN'T LOST ANYONE.
WELL, I DON'T WANT TO LOSE ANYONE.
WELL, I'M DOING THIS.
I HAVE TO DO THIS.
I--
BWEEEEEE BWEEEEEE BWEEEEEE
DID YOU DO THAT?
NO, THAT'S THE RAID ALARMS.
WE CAN'T SEE THE SKY, LIAM.
THE CLOUDS. THE STORM.
THEY COULD ALREADY BE UP THERE.
OMAR, HELP ME GET THE DRONE IN THE TRUCK!
JUST LEAVE IT, LIAM!
WE GOTTA GET OUT OF HERE!
WE GOTTA--

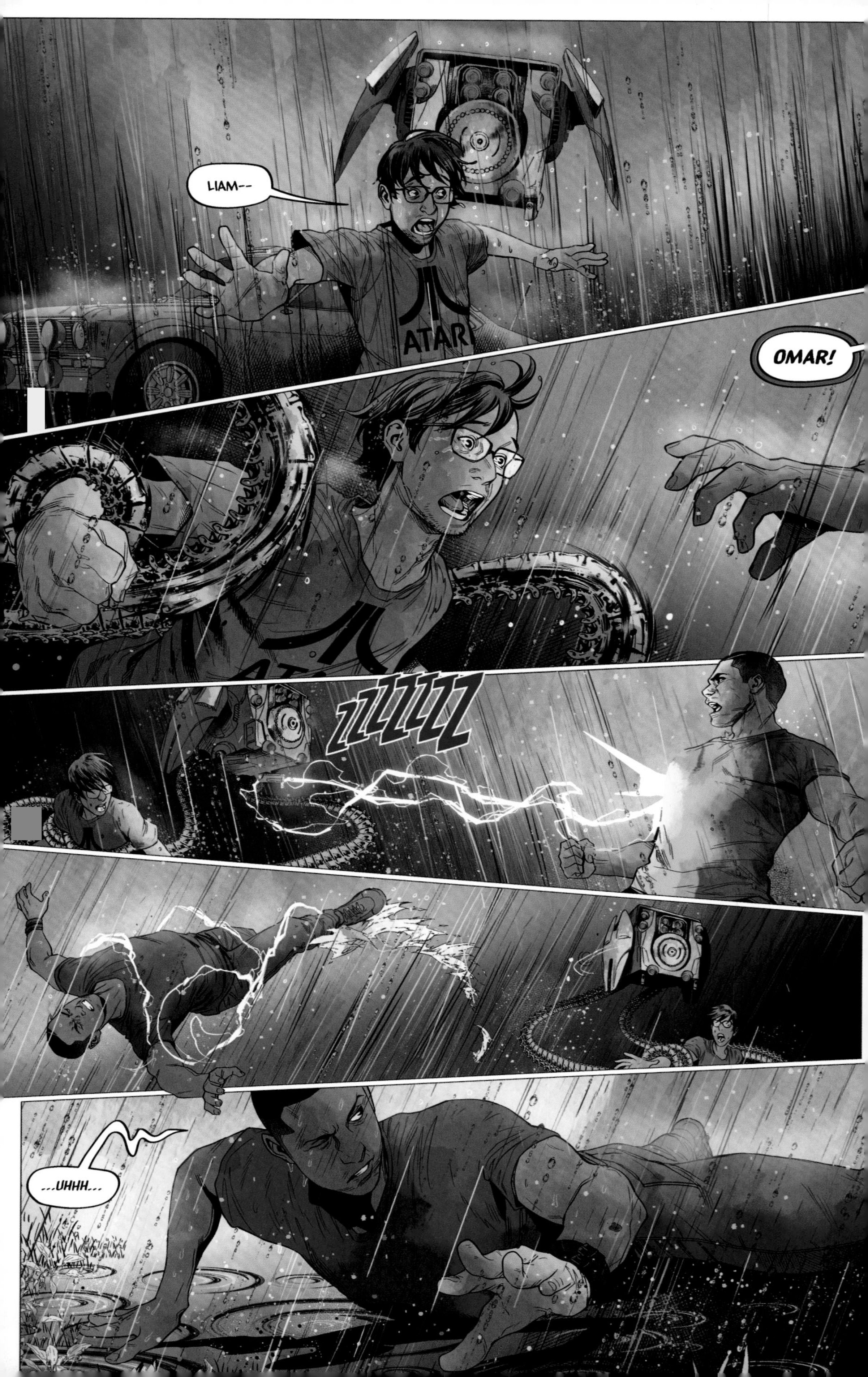
LIAM--
OMAR!
ZZZZZZZ
...UHHH...

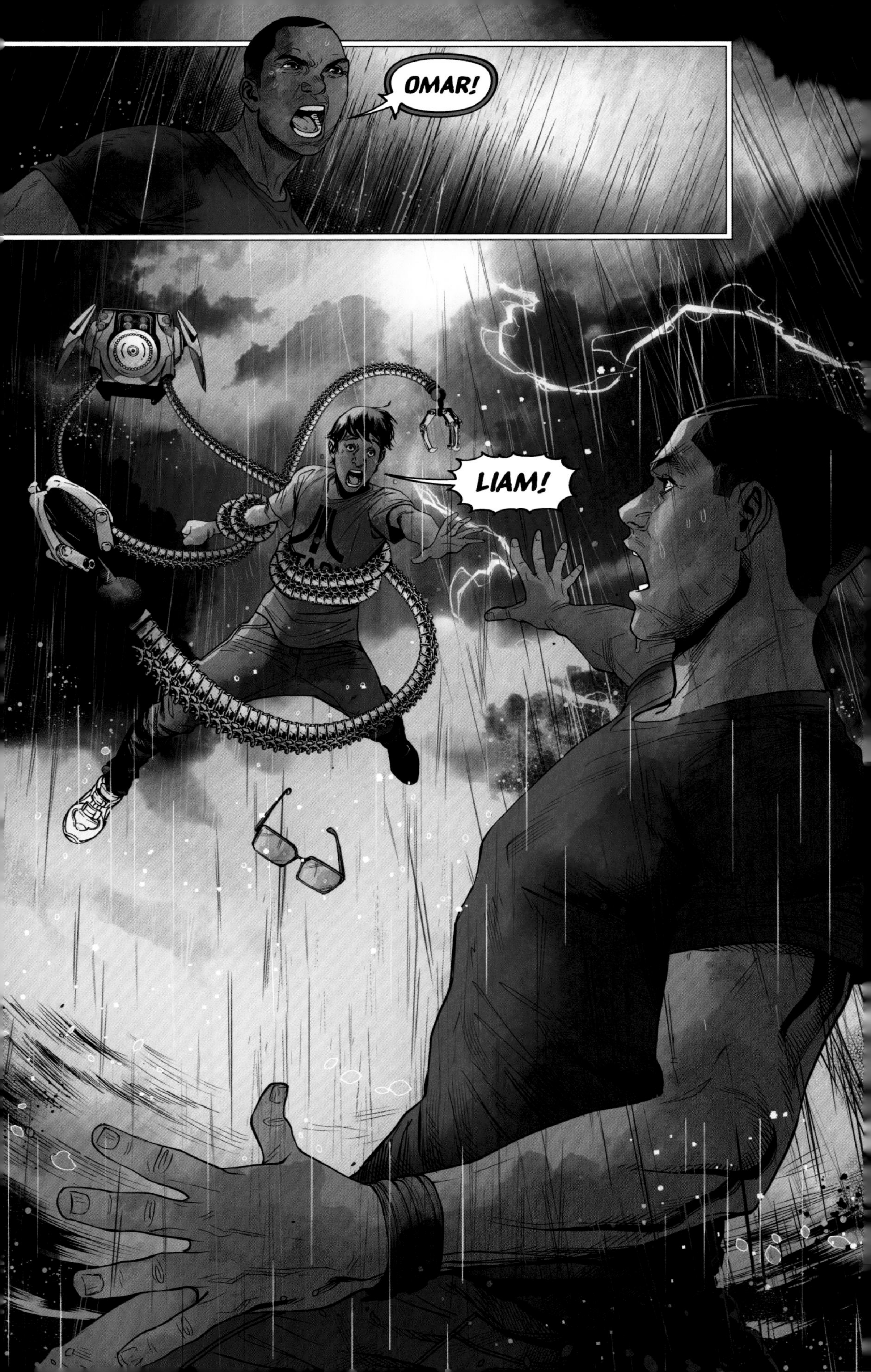
OMAR!
LIAM!

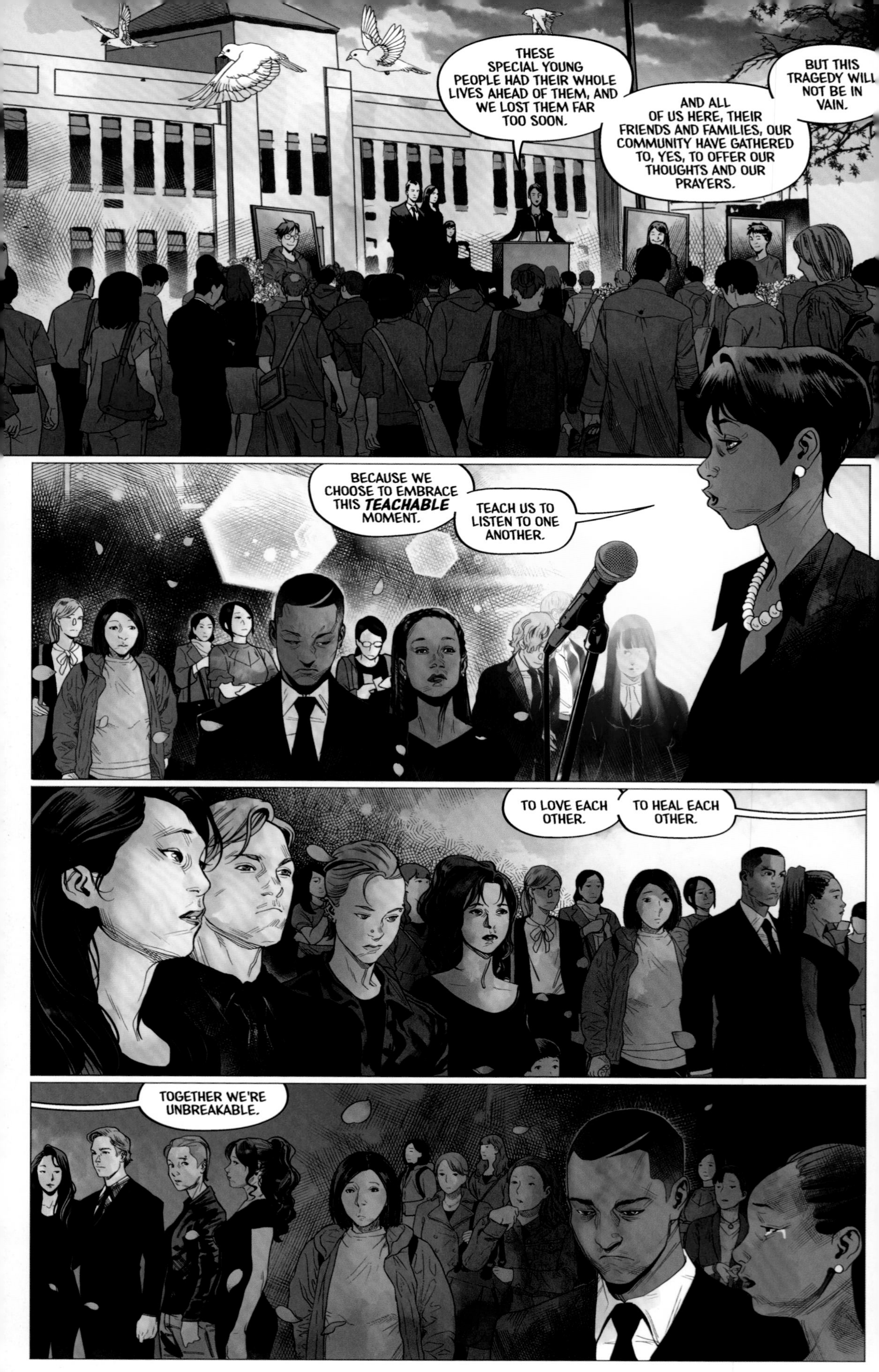
THESE SPECIAL YOUNG PEOPLE HAD THEIR WHOLE LIVES AHEAD OF THEM, AND WE LOST THEM FAR TOO SOON.
AND ALL OF US HERE, THEIR FRIENDS AND FAMILIES, OUR COMMUNITY HAVE GATHERED TO, YES, TO OFFER OUR THOUGHTS AND OUR PRAYERS.
BUT THIS TRAGEDY WILL NOT BE IN VAIN.
BECAUSE WE CHOOSE TO EMBRACE THIS *TEACHABLE* MOMENT.
TEACH US TO LISTEN TO ONE ANOTHER.
TO LOVE EACH OTHER.
TO HEAL EACH OTHER.
TOGETHER WE'RE UNBREAKABLE.

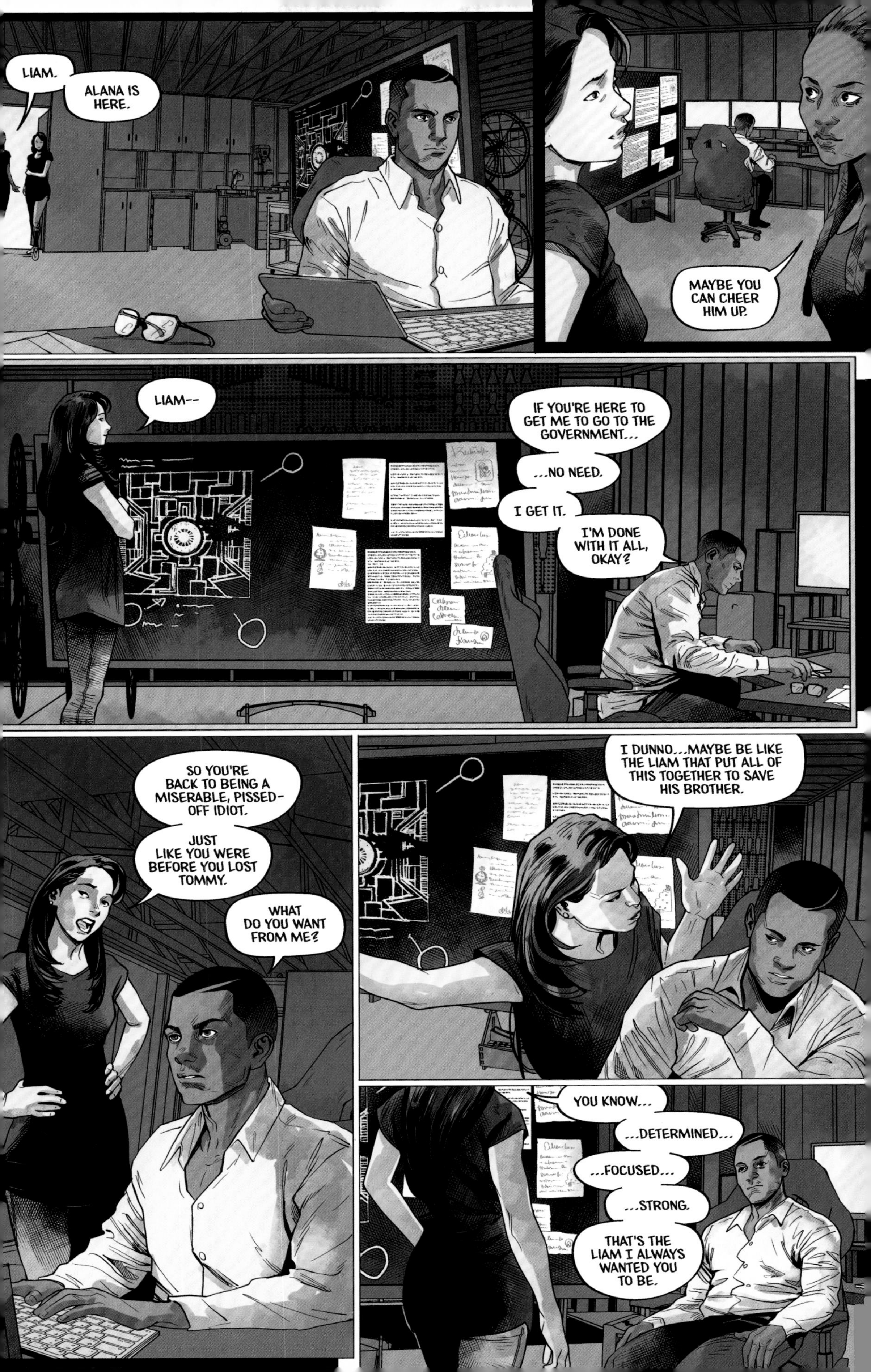

LIAM.
ALANA IS HERE.
MAYBE YOU CAN CHEER HIM UP.
LIAM--
IF YOU'RE HERE TO GET ME TO GO TO THE GOVERNMENT...
...NO NEED.
I GET IT.
I'M DONE WITH IT ALL, OKAY?
SO YOU'RE BACK TO BEING A MISERABLE, PISSED-OFF IDIOT.
JUST LIKE YOU WERE BEFORE YOU LOST TOMMY.
WHAT DO YOU WANT FROM ME?
I DUNNO...MAYBE BE LIKE THE LIAM THAT PUT ALL OF THIS TOGETHER TO SAVE HIS BROTHER.
YOU KNOW...
...DETERMINED...
...FOCUSED...
...STRONG.
THAT'S THE LIAM I ALWAYS WANTED YOU TO BE.

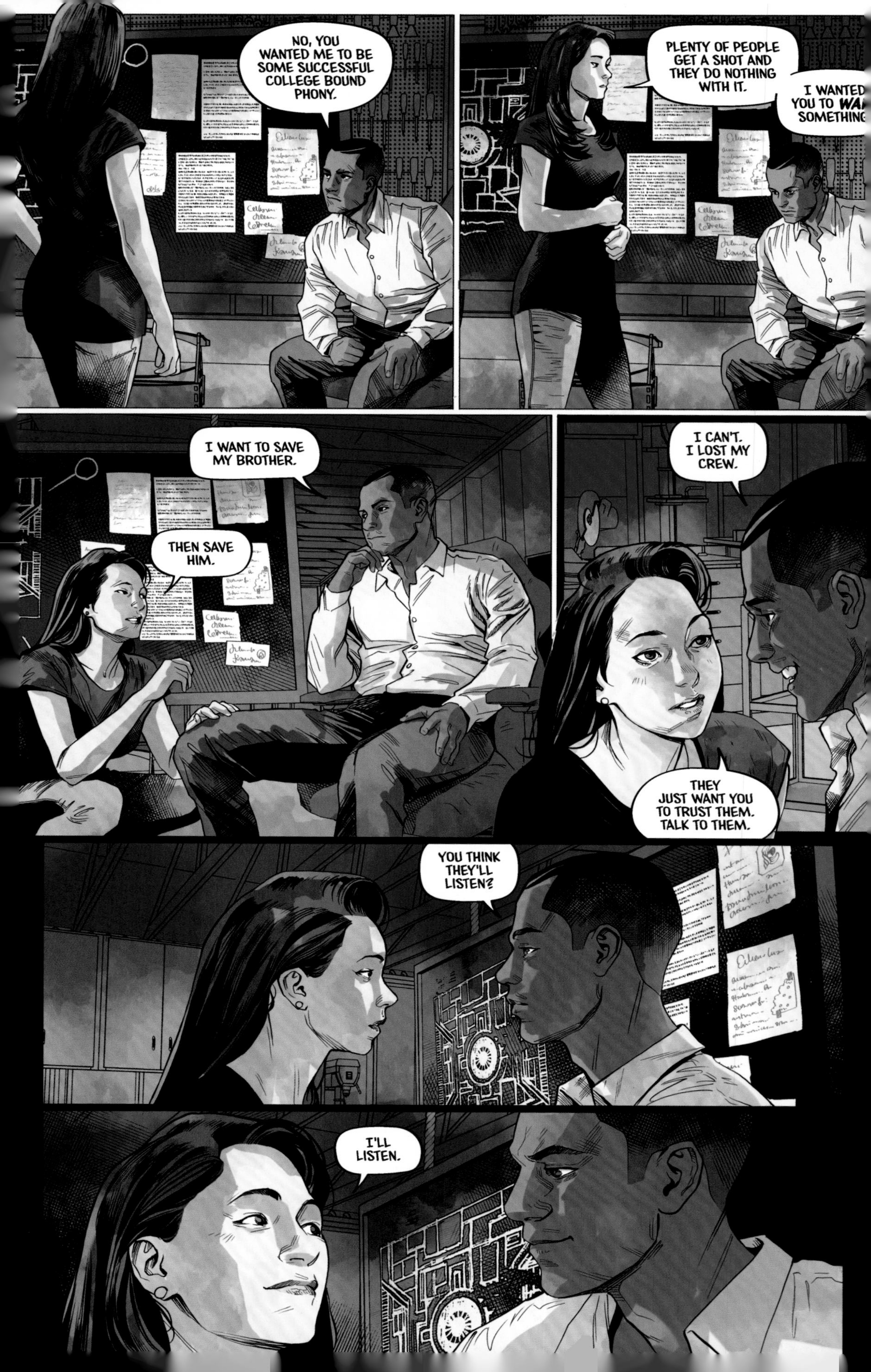

NO, YOU WANTED ME TO BE SOME SUCCESSFUL COLLEGE BOUND PHONY.
PLENTY OF PEOPLE GET A SHOT AND THEY DO NOTHING WITH IT.
I WANTED YOU TO WA
SOMETHING
I WANT TO SAVE MY BROTHER.
THEN SAVE HIM.
I CAN'T. I LOST MY CREW.
THEY JUST WANT YOU TO TRUST THEM. TALK TO THEM.
YOU THINK THEY'LL LISTEN?
I'LL LISTEN.

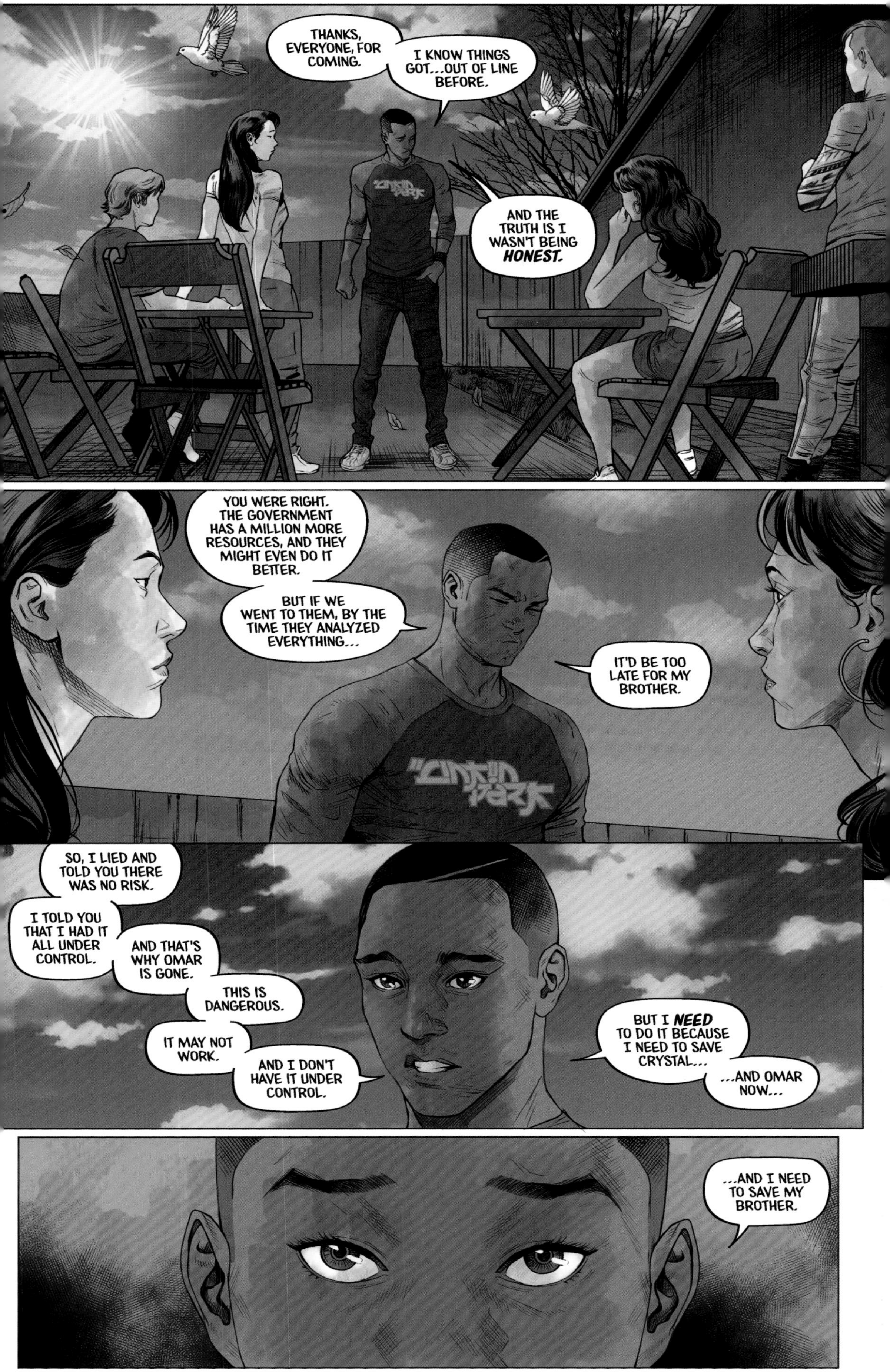
THANKS, EVERYONE, FOR COMING.
I KNOW THINGS GOT...OUT OF LINE BEFORE.
AND THE TRUTH IS I WASN'T BEING *HONEST.*
YOU WERE RIGHT. THE GOVERNMENT HAS A MILLION MORE RESOURCES, AND THEY MIGHT EVEN DO IT BETTER.
BUT IF WE WENT TO THEM, BY THE TIME THEY ANALYZED EVERYTHING...
IT'D BE TOO LATE FOR MY BROTHER.
SO, I LIED AND TOLD YOU THERE WAS NO RISK.
I TOLD YOU THAT I HAD IT ALL UNDER CONTROL.
AND THAT'S WHY OMAR IS GONE.
THIS IS DANGEROUS.
IT MAY NOT WORK.
AND I DON'T HAVE IT UNDER CONTROL.
BUT I *NEED* TO DO IT BECAUSE I NEED TO SAVE CRYSTAL...
...AND OMAR NOW...
...AND I NEED TO SAVE MY BROTHER.

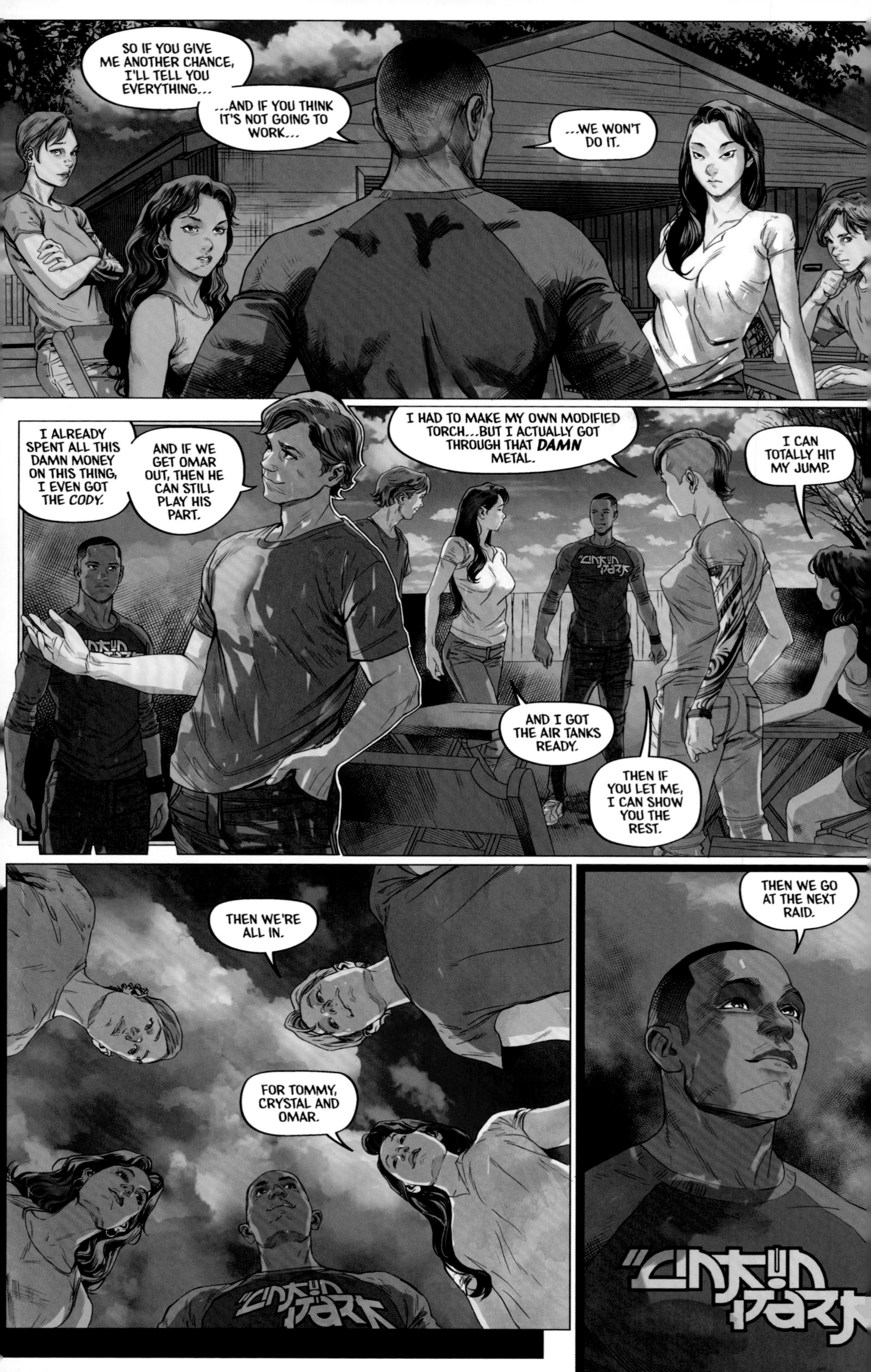
SO IF YOU GIVE ME ANOTHER CHANCE, I'LL TELL YOU EVERYTHING...
...AND IF YOU THINK IT'S NOT GOING TO WORK...
...WE WON'T DO IT.
I ALREADY SPENT ALL THIS DAMN MONEY ON THIS THING, I EVEN GOT THE *CODY.*
AND IF WE GET OMAR OUT, THEN HE CAN STILL PLAY HIS PART.
I HAD TO MAKE MY OWN MODIFIED TORCH...BUT I ACTUALLY GOT THROUGH THAT ***DAMN*** METAL.
I CAN TOTALLY HIT MY JUMP.
AND I GOT THE AIR TANKS READY.
THEN IF YOU LET ME, I CAN SHOW YOU THE REST.
THEN WE'RE ALL IN.
FOR TOMMY, CRYSTAL AND OMAR.
THEN WE GO AT THE NEXT RAID.

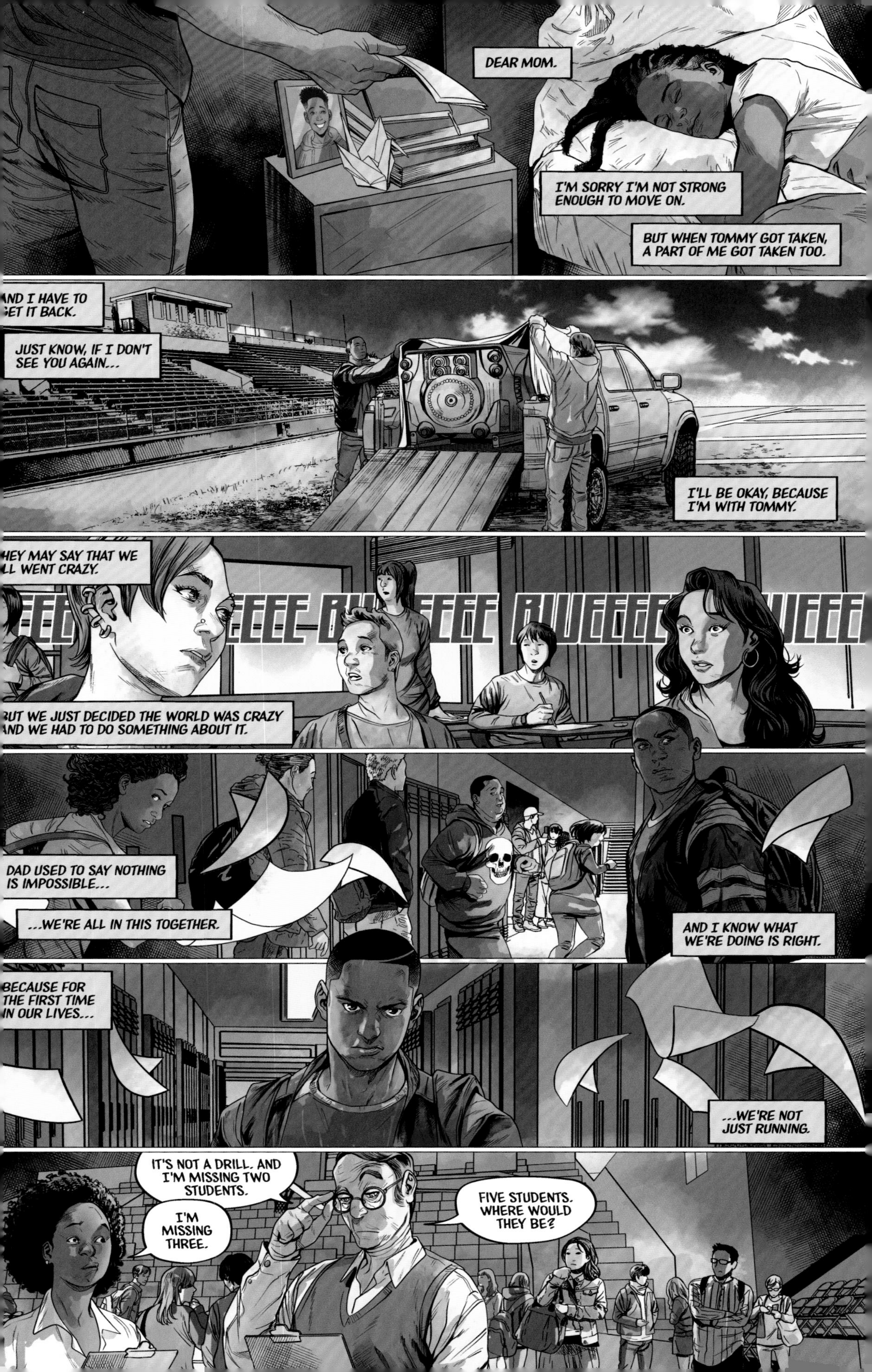
DEAR MOM.
I'M SORRY I'M NOT STRONG ENOUGH TO MOVE ON.
BUT WHEN TOMMY GOT TAKEN, A PART OF ME GOT TAKEN TOO.
AND I HAVE TO GET IT BACK.
JUST KNOW, IF I DON'T SEE YOU AGAIN...
I'LL BE OKAY, BECAUSE I'M WITH TOMMY.
THEY MAY SAY THAT WE ALL WENT CRAZY.
BUT WE JUST DECIDED THE WORLD WAS CRAZY AND WE HAD TO DO SOMETHING ABOUT IT.
DAD USED TO SAY NOTHING IS IMPOSSIBLE...
...WE'RE ALL IN THIS TOGETHER.
AND I KNOW WHAT WE'RE DOING IS RIGHT.
BECAUSE FOR THE FIRST TIME IN OUR LIVES...
...WE'RE NOT JUST RUNNING.
IT'S NOT A DRILL. AND I'M MISSING TWO STUDENTS.
I'M MISSING THREE.
FIVE STUDENTS. WHERE WOULD THEY BE?

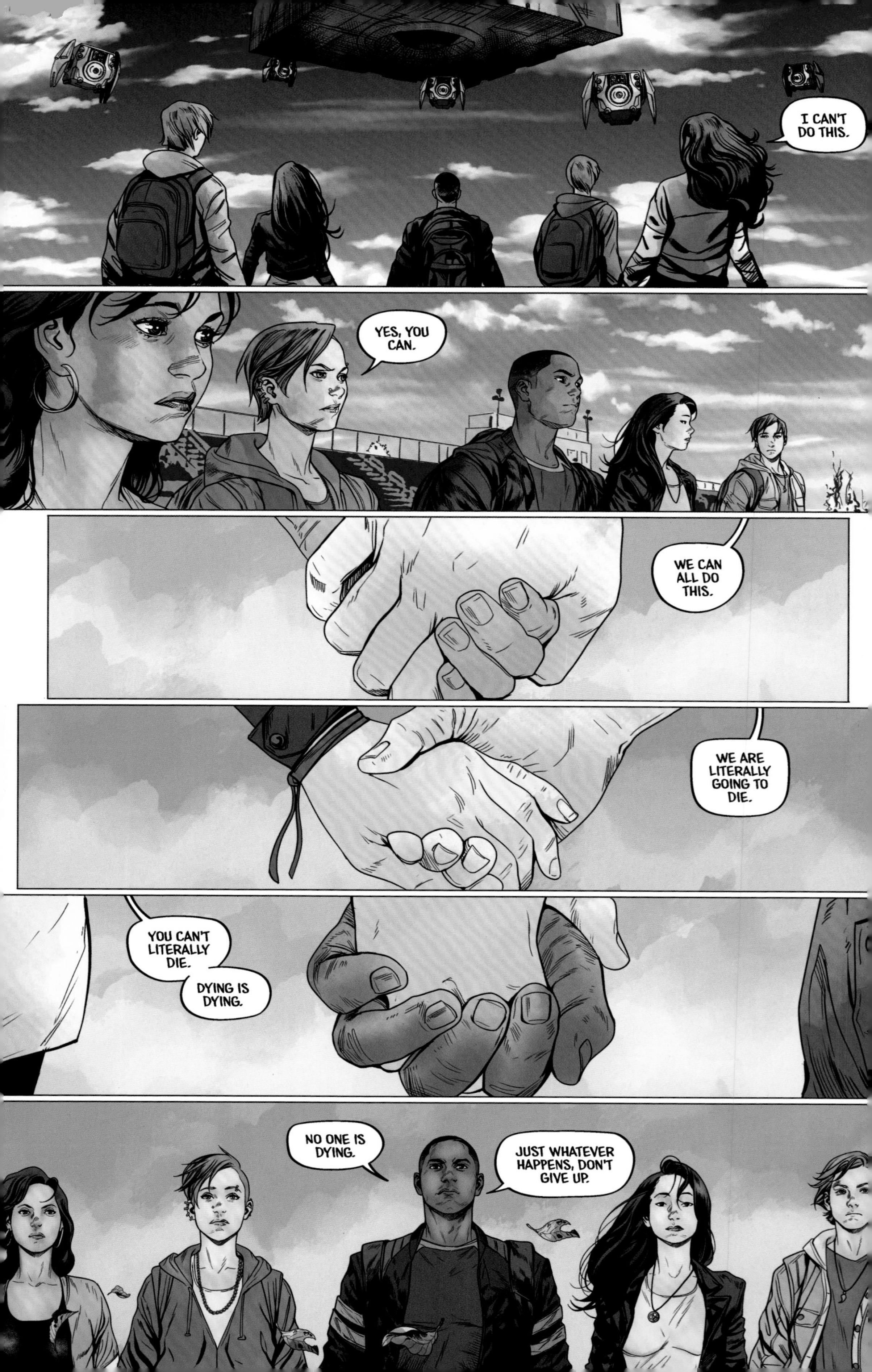

I CAN'T DO THIS.
YES, YOU CAN.
WE CAN ALL DO THIS.
WE ARE LITERALLY GOING TO DIE.
YOU CAN'T LITERALLY DIE.
DYING IS DYING.
NO ONE IS DYING.
JUST WHATEVER HAPPENS, DON'T GIVE UP.

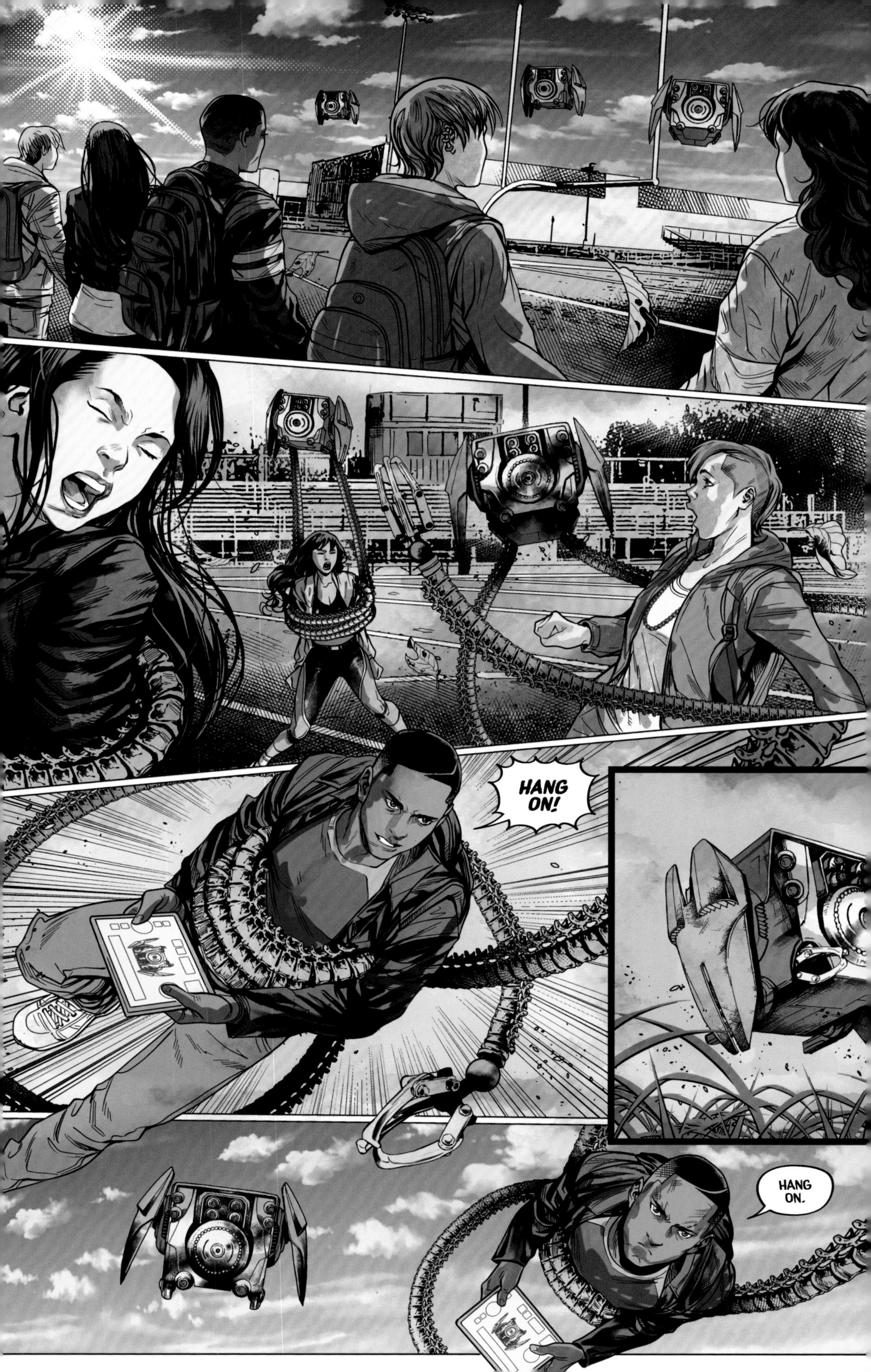
HANG ON!
HANG ON.

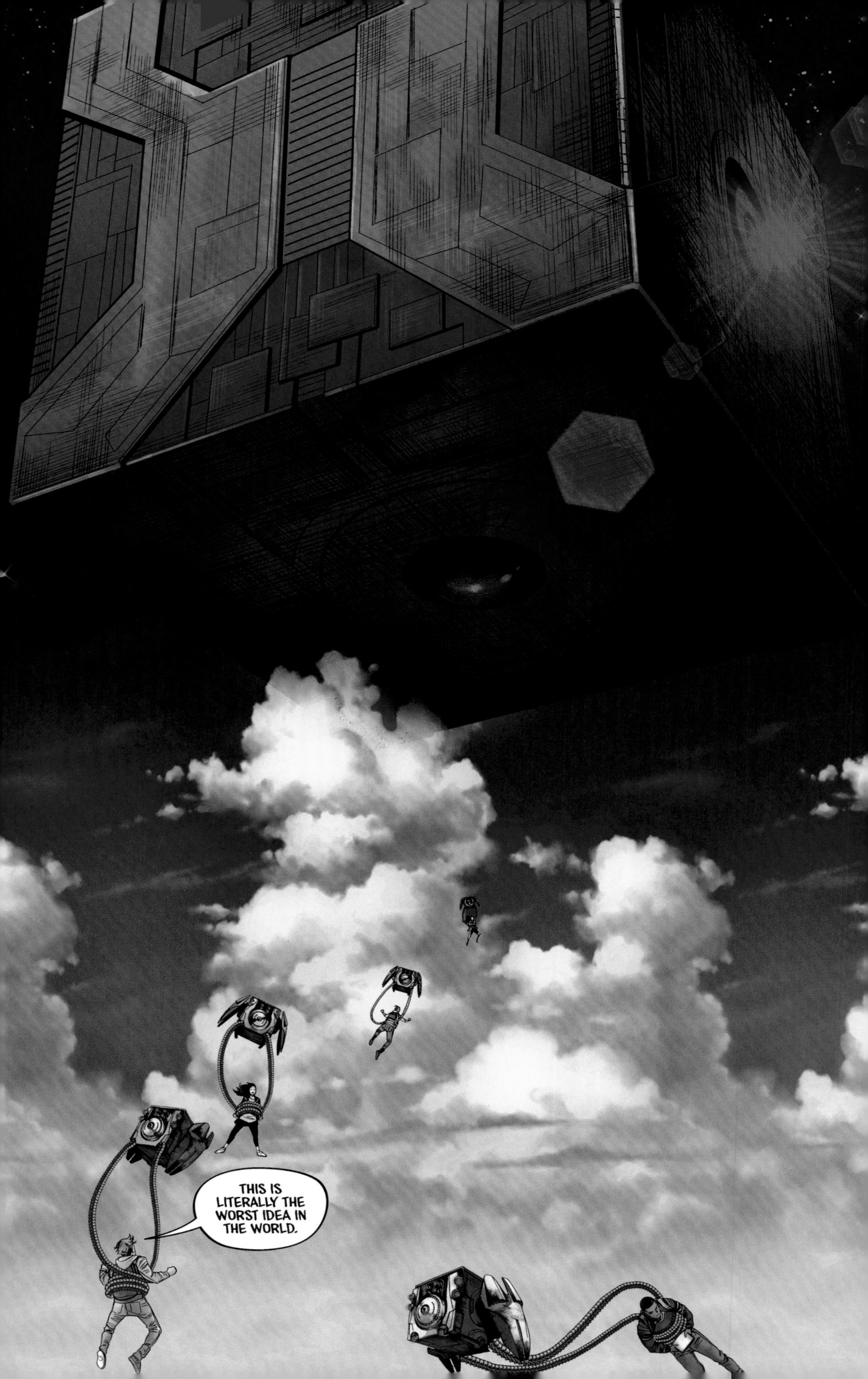
THIS IS LITERALLY THE WORST IDEA IN THE WORLD.

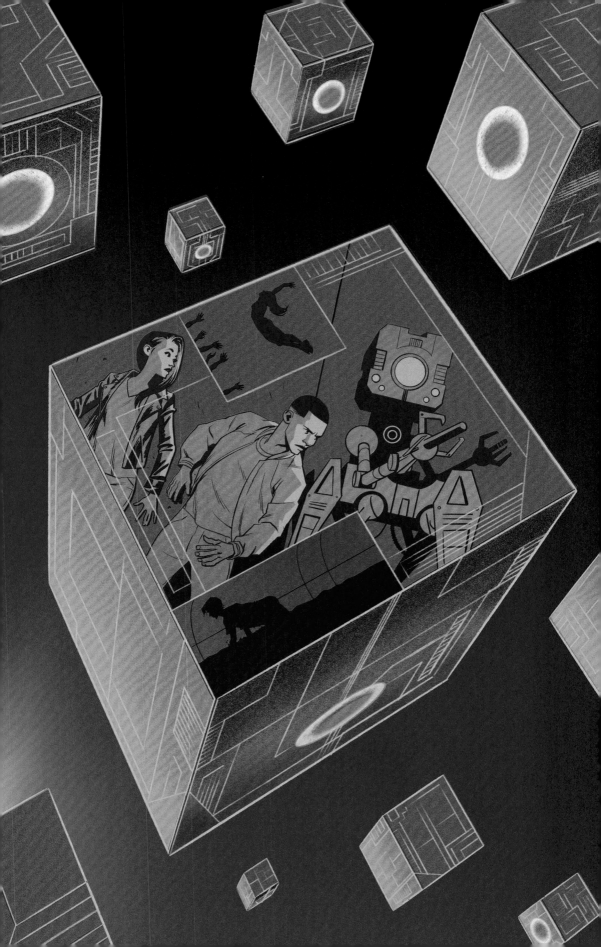

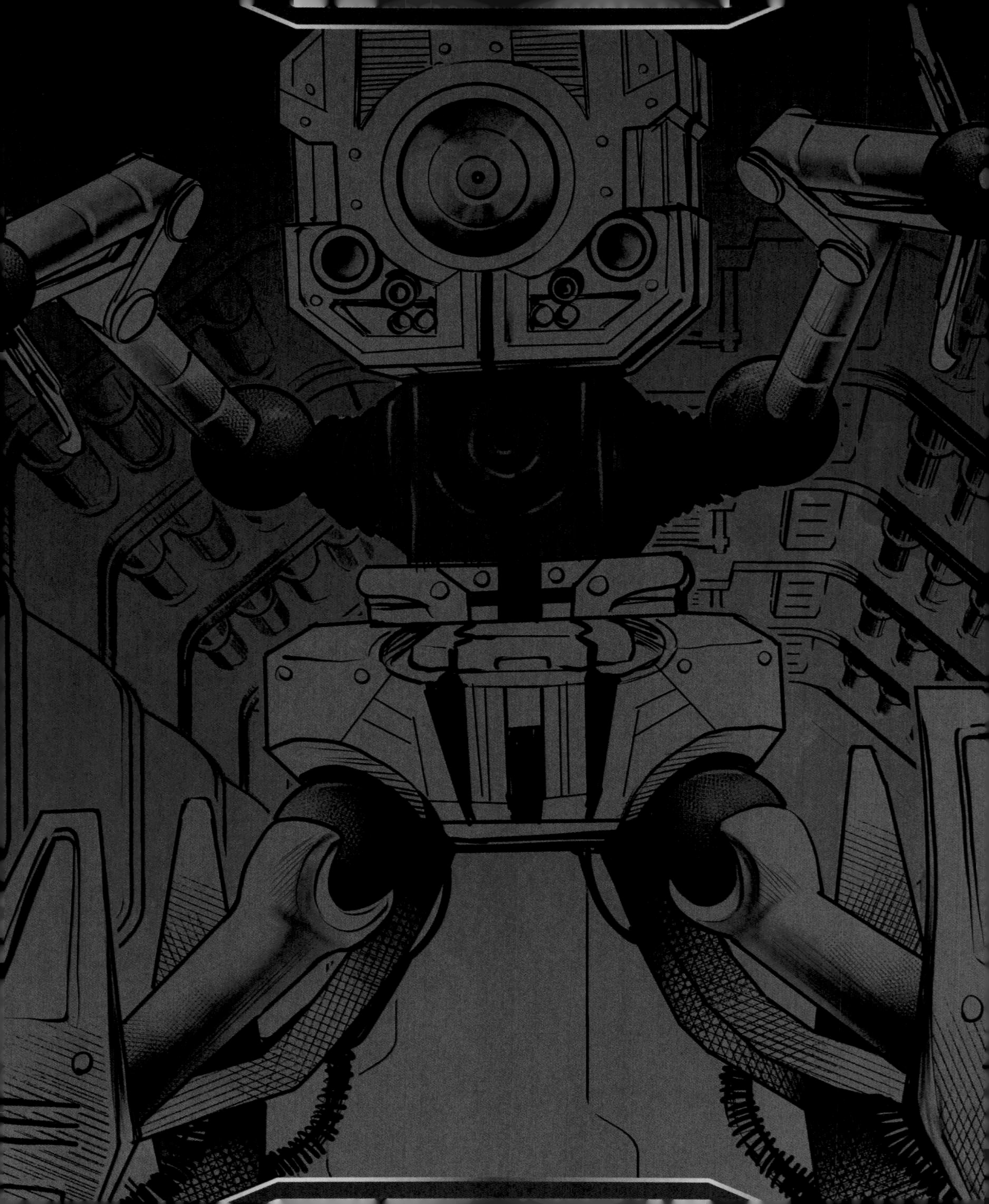

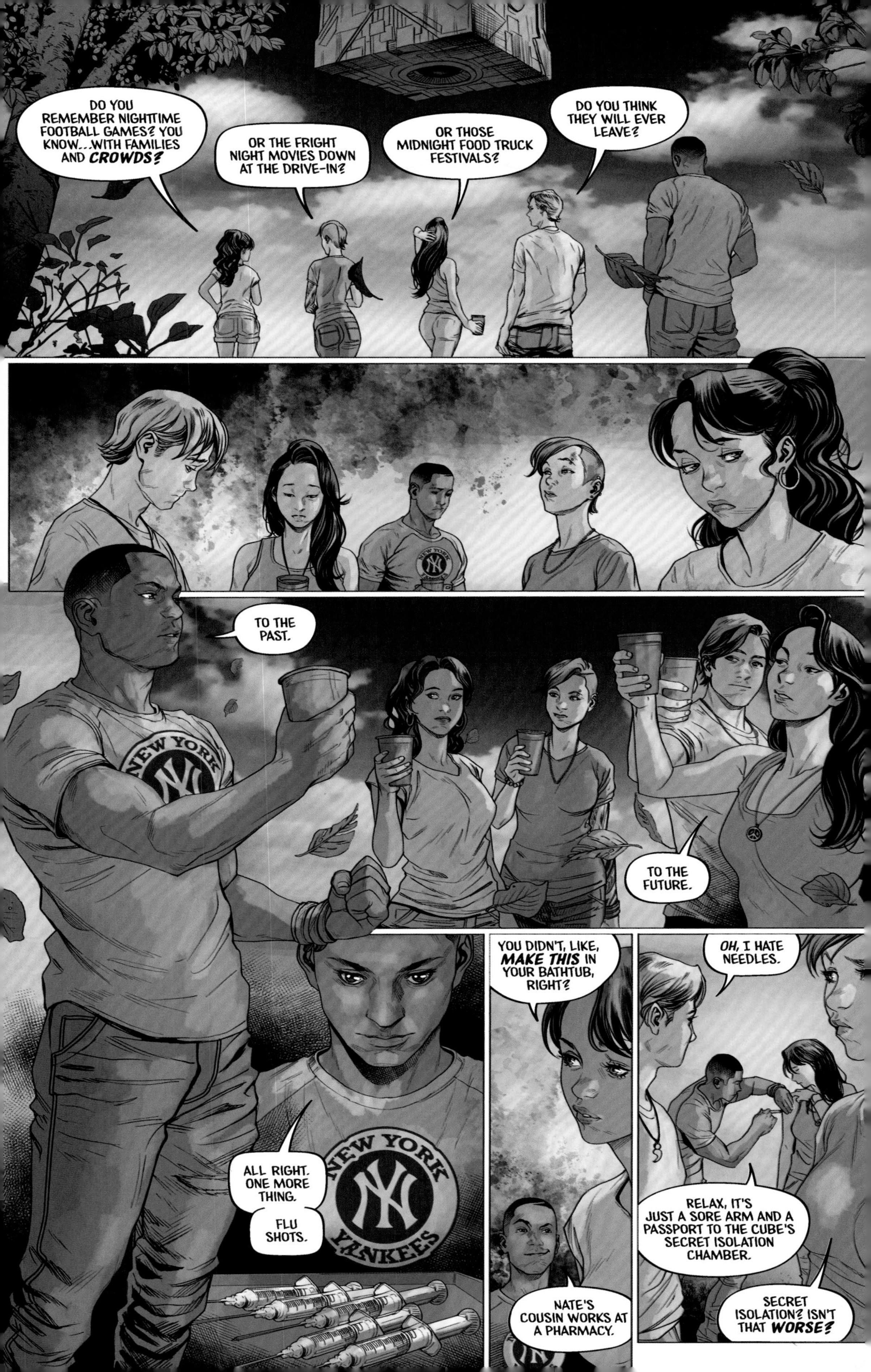
DO YOU REMEMBER NIGHTTIME FOOTBALL GAMES? YOU KNOW...WITH FAMILIES AND CROWDS?
OR THE FRIGHT NIGHT MOVIES DOWN AT THE DRIVE-IN?
OR THOSE MIDNIGHT FOOD TRUCK FESTIVALS?
DO YOU THINK THEY WILL EVER LEAVE?
TO THE PAST.
TO THE FUTURE.
ALL RIGHT. ONE MORE THING.
FLU SHOTS.
YOU DIDN'T, LIKE, MAKE THIS IN YOUR BATHTUB, RIGHT?
NATE'S COUSIN WORKS AT A PHARMACY.
OH, I HATE NEEDLES.
RELAX, IT'S JUST A SORE ARM AND A PASSPORT TO THE CUBE'S SECRET ISOLATION CHAMBER.
SECRET ISOLATION? ISN'T THAT WORSE?

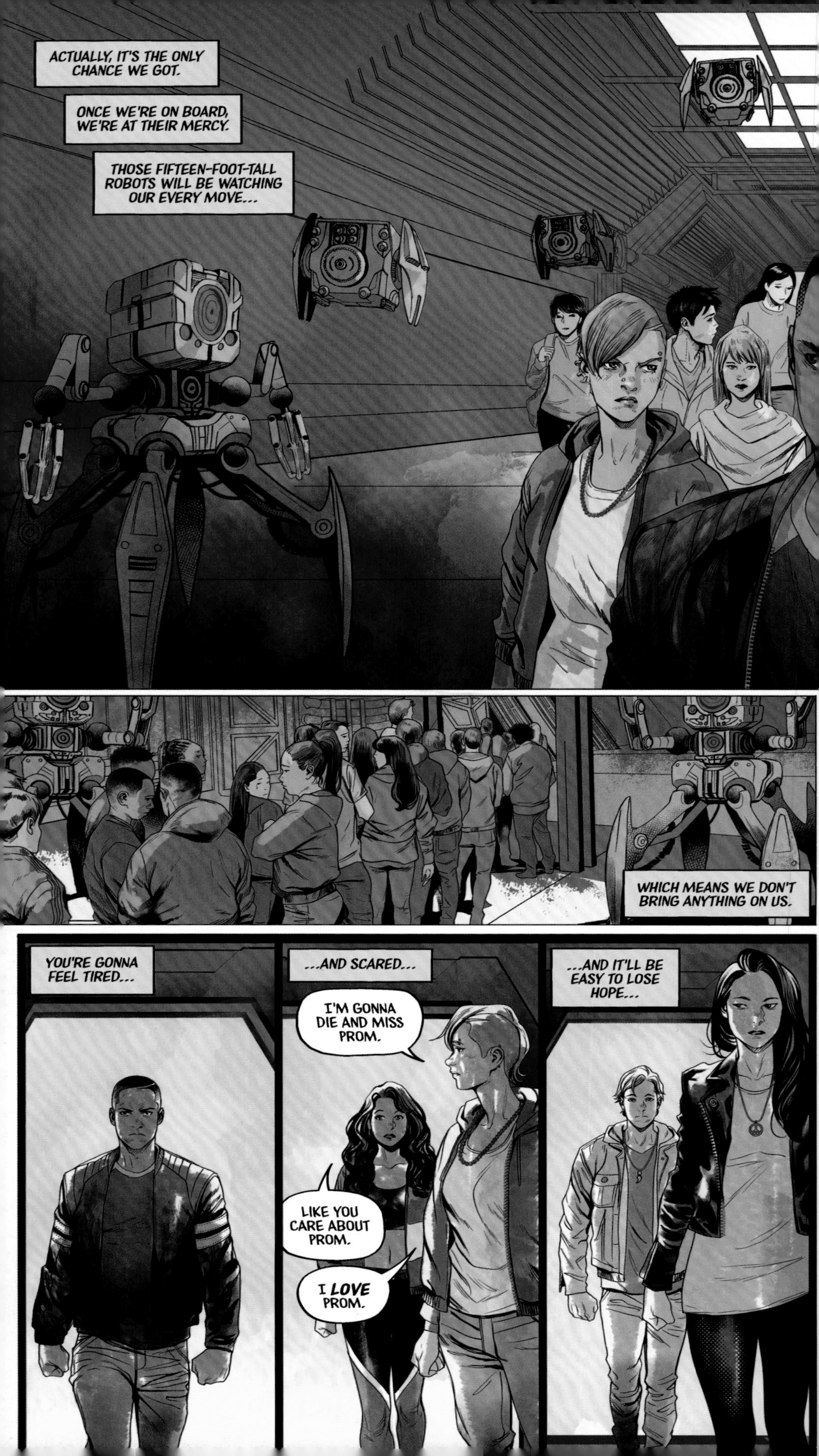
ACTUALLY, IT'S THE ONLY CHANCE WE GOT.
ONCE WE'RE ON BOARD, WE'RE AT THEIR MERCY.
THOSE FIFTEEN-FOOT-TALL ROBOTS WILL BE WATCHING OUR EVERY MOVE...
WHICH MEANS WE DON'T BRING ANYTHING ON US.
YOU'RE GONNA FEEL TIRED...
...AND SCARED...
I'M GONNA DIE AND MISS PROM.
LIKE YOU CARE ABOUT PROM.
I **LOVE** PROM.
...AND IT'LL BE EASY TO LOSE HOPE...

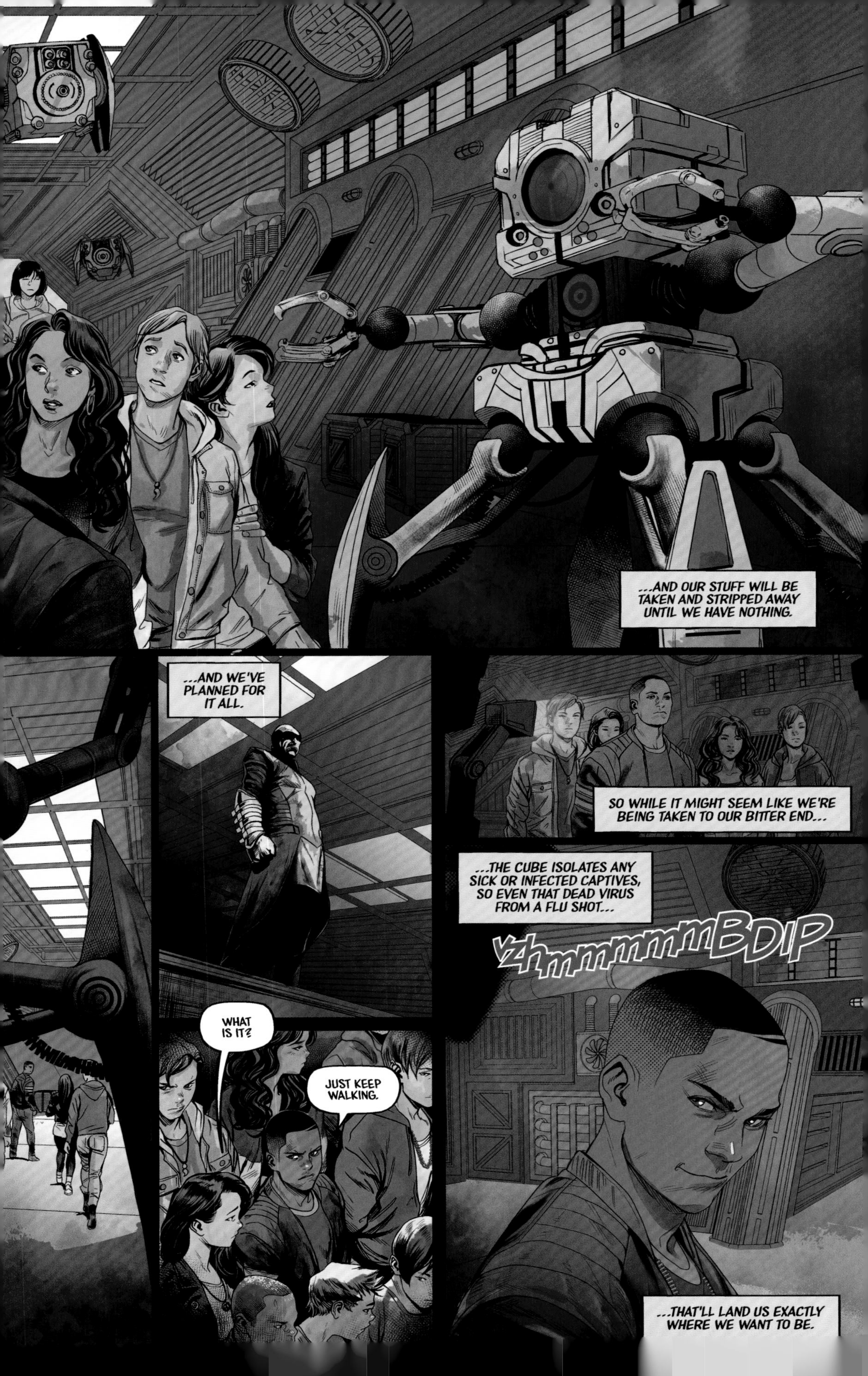
...AND OUR STUFF WILL BE TAKEN AND STRIPPED AWAY UNTIL WE HAVE NOTHING.
...AND WE'VE PLANNED FOR IT ALL.
SO WHILE IT MIGHT SEEM LIKE WE'RE BEING TAKEN TO OUR BITTER END...
...THE CUBE ISOLATES ANY SICK OR INFECTED CAPTIVES, SO EVEN THAT DEAD VIRUS FROM A FLU SHOT...
VZHMMMMMMBDIP
WHAT IS IT?
JUST KEEP WALKING.
...THAT'LL LAND US EXACTLY WHERE WE WANT TO BE.

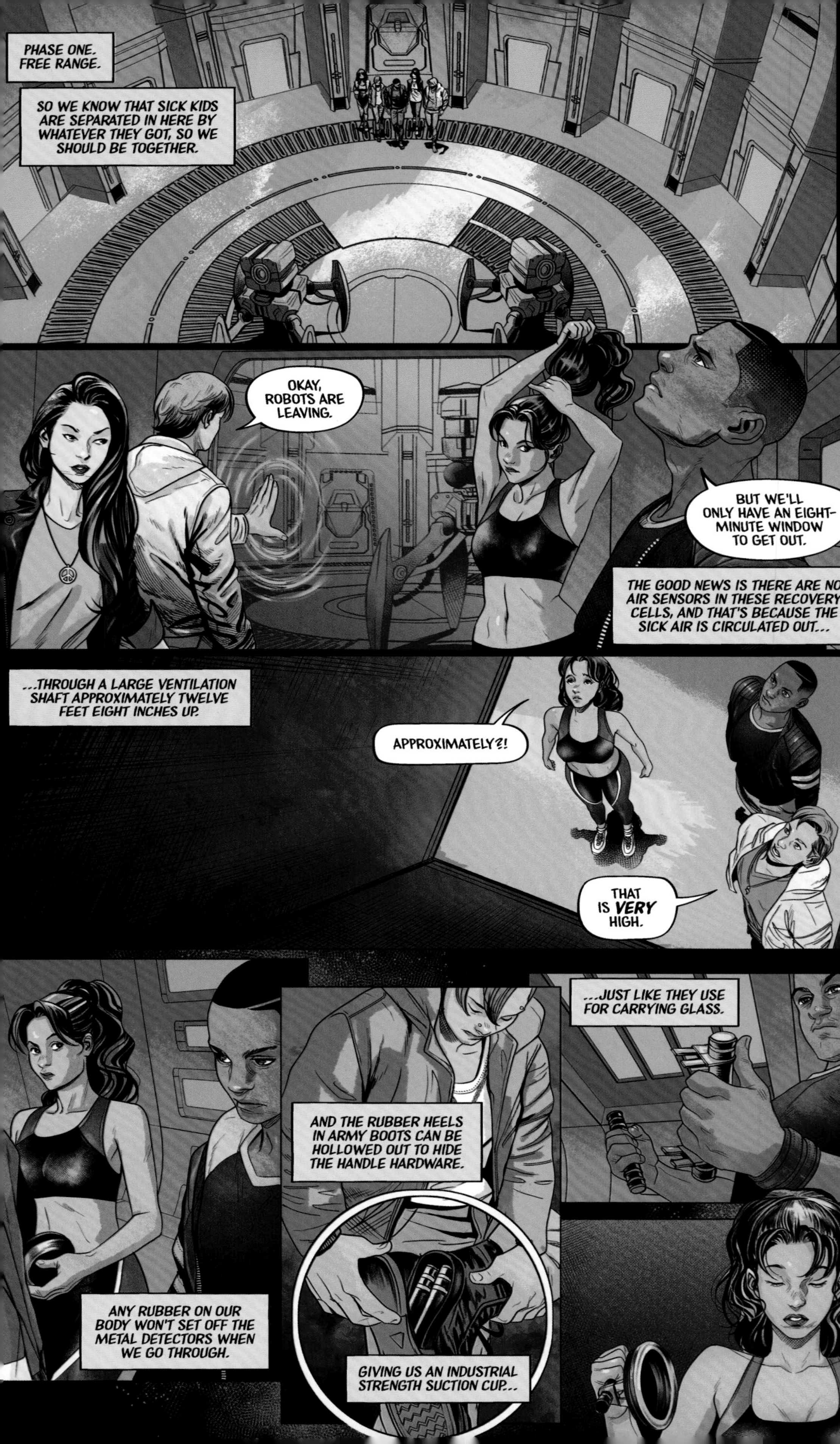

PHASE ONE. FREE RANGE.
SO WE KNOW THAT SICK KIDS ARE SEPARATED IN HERE BY WHATEVER THEY GOT, SO WE SHOULD BE TOGETHER.
OKAY, ROBOTS ARE LEAVING.
BUT WE'LL ONLY HAVE AN EIGHT-MINUTE WINDOW TO GET OUT.
THE GOOD NEWS IS THERE ARE NO AIR SENSORS IN THESE RECOVERY CELLS, AND THAT'S BECAUSE THE SICK AIR IS CIRCULATED OUT...
...THROUGH A LARGE VENTILATION SHAFT APPROXIMATELY TWELVE FEET EIGHT INCHES UP.
APPROXIMATELY?!
THAT IS VERY HIGH.
AND THE RUBBER HEELS IN ARMY BOOTS CAN BE HOLLOWED OUT TO HIDE THE HANDLE HARDWARE.
ANY RUBBER ON OUR BODY WON'T SET OFF THE METAL DETECTORS WHEN WE GO THROUGH.
GIVING US AN INDUSTRIAL STRENGTH SUCTION CUP...
...JUST LIKE THEY USE FOR CARRYING GLASS.

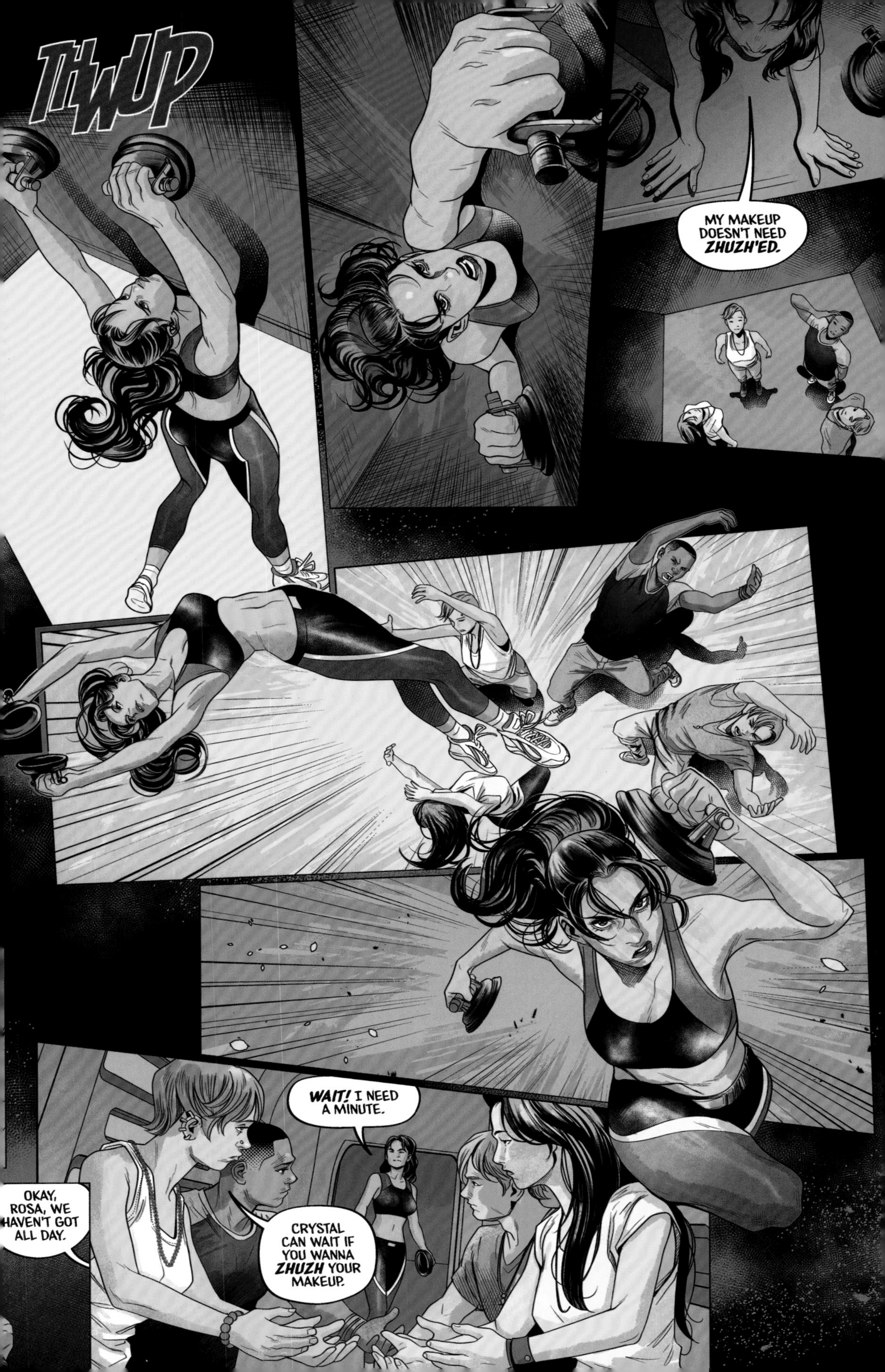
THWUP
MY MAKEUP DOESN'T NEED ZHUZH'ED.
WAIT! I NEED A MINUTE.
OKAY, ROSA, WE HAVEN'T GOT ALL DAY.
CRYSTAL CAN WAIT IF YOU WANNA ZHUZH YOUR MAKEUP.

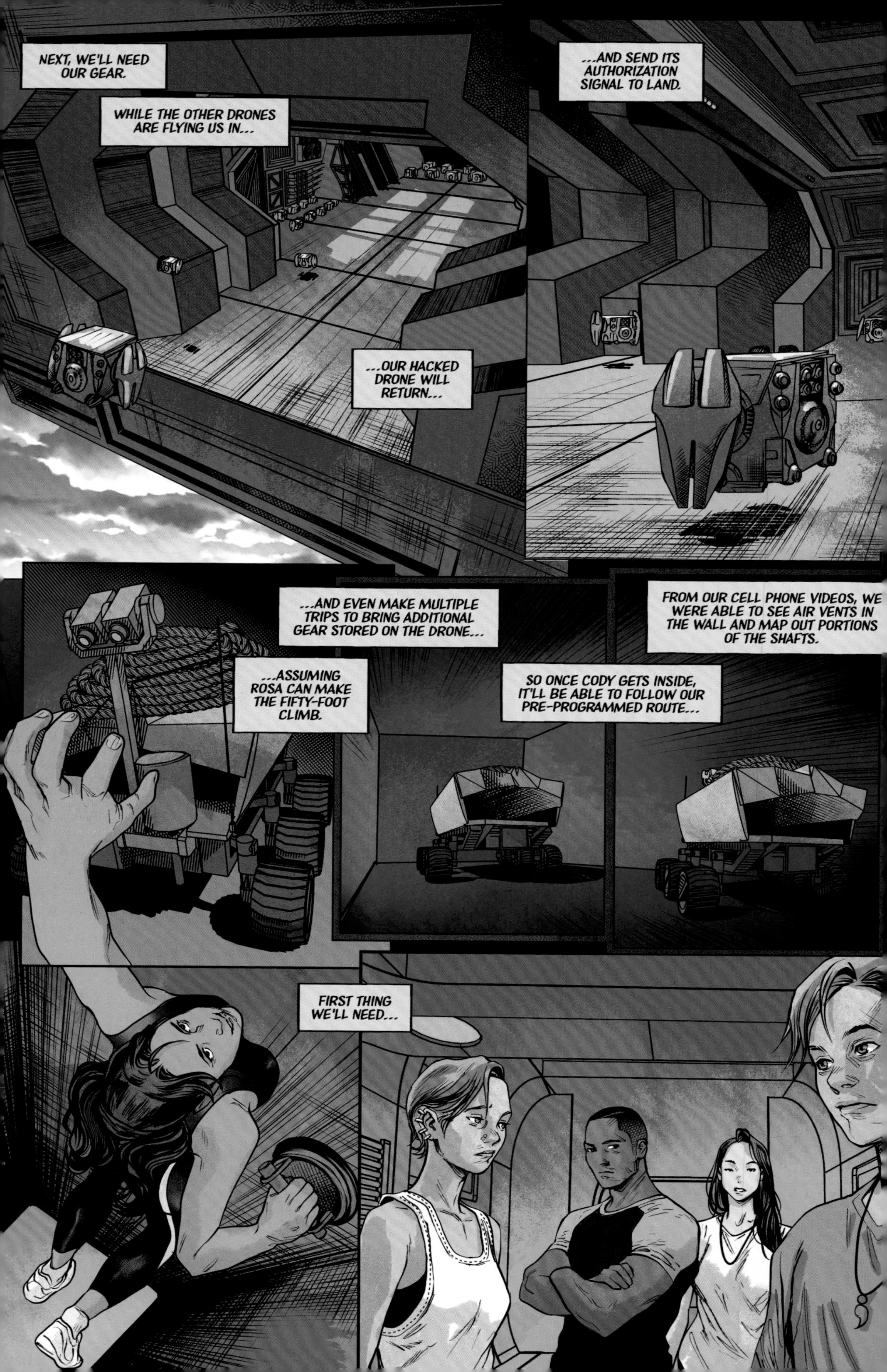
NEXT, WE'LL NEED OUR GEAR.
WHILE THE OTHER DRONES ARE FLYING US IN...
...OUR HACKED DRONE WILL RETURN...
...AND SEND ITS AUTHORIZATION SIGNAL TO LAND.
...AND EVEN MAKE MULTIPLE TRIPS TO BRING ADDITIONAL GEAR STORED ON THE DRONE...
...ASSUMING ROSA CAN MAKE THE FIFTY-FOOT CLIMB.
FROM OUR CELL PHONE VIDEOS, WE WERE ABLE TO SEE AIR VENTS IN THE WALL AND MAP OUT PORTIONS OF THE SHAFTS.
SO ONCE CODY GETS INSIDE, IT'LL BE ABLE TO FOLLOW OUR PRE-PROGRAMMED ROUTE...
FIRST THING WE'LL NEED...

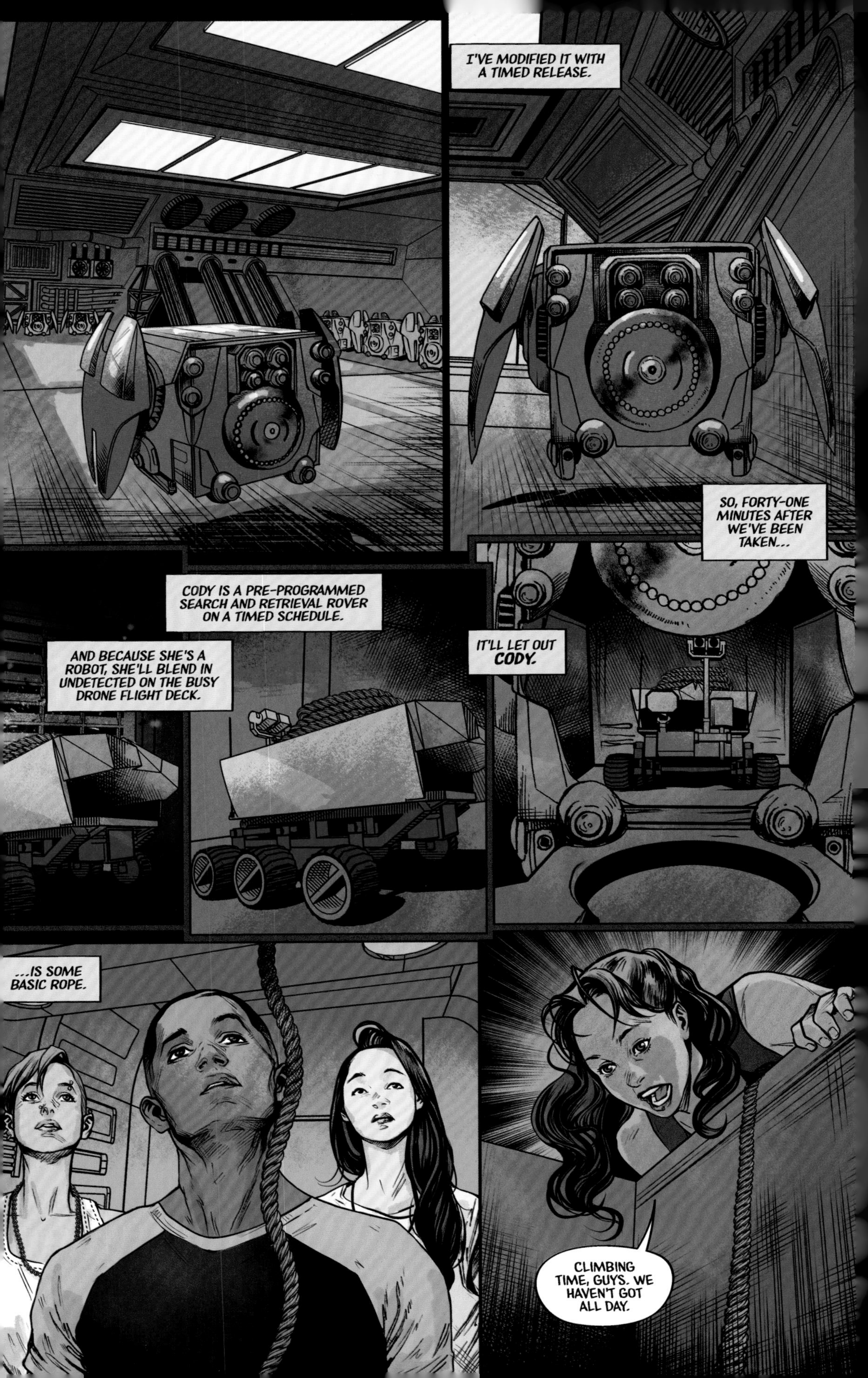
I'VE MODIFIED IT WITH A TIMED RELEASE.
SO, FORTY-ONE MINUTES AFTER WE'VE BEEN TAKEN...
IT'LL LET OUT CODY.
CODY IS A PRE-PROGRAMMED SEARCH AND RETRIEVAL ROVER ON A TIMED SCHEDULE.
AND BECAUSE SHE'S A ROBOT, SHE'LL BLEND IN UNDETECTED ON THE BUSY DRONE FLIGHT DECK.
...IS SOME BASIC ROPE.
CLIMBING TIME, GUYS. WE HAVEN'T GOT ALL DAY.

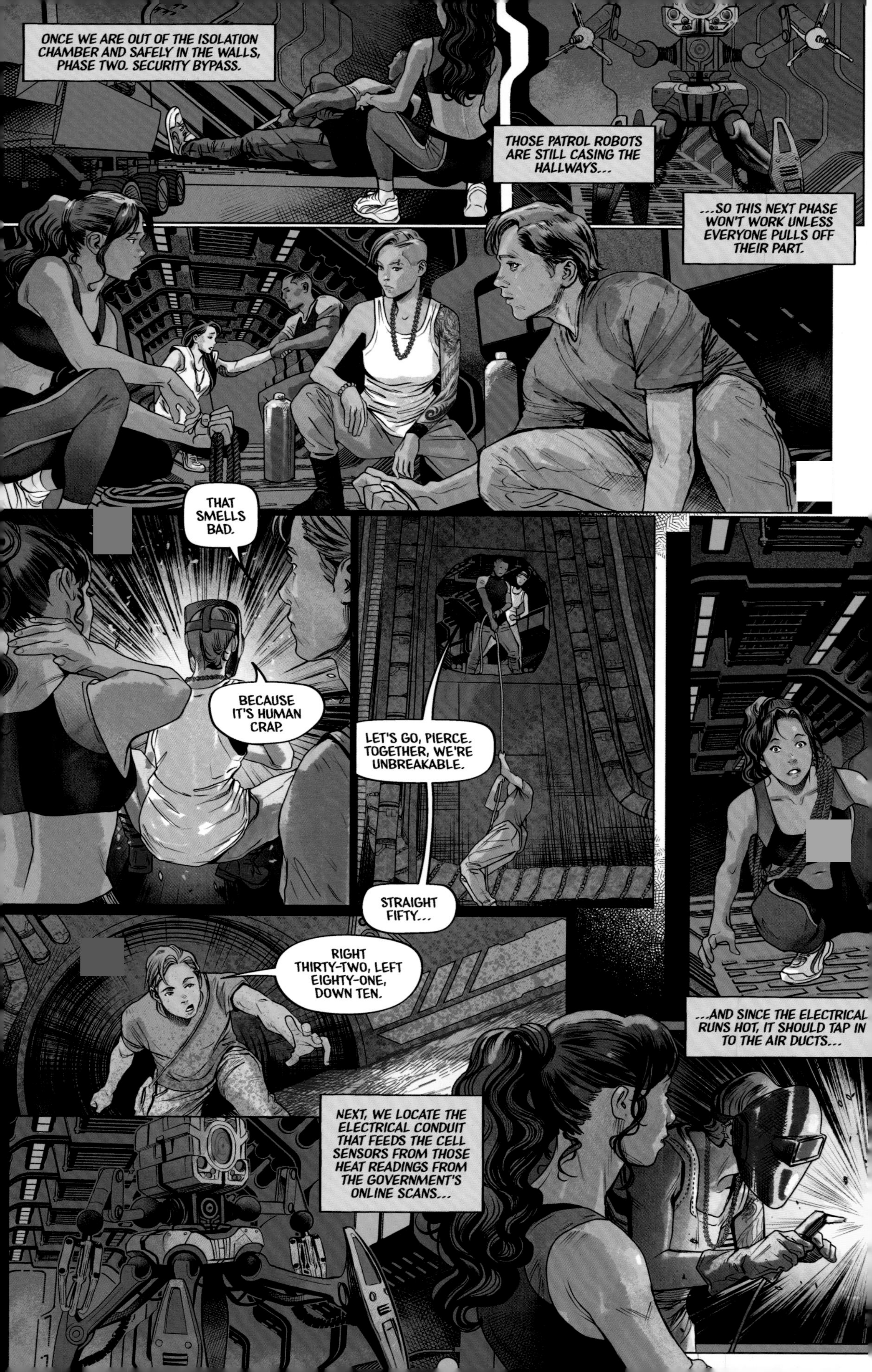
ONCE WE ARE OUT OF THE ISOLATION CHAMBER AND SAFELY IN THE WALLS, PHASE TWO. SECURITY BYPASS.
THOSE PATROL ROBOTS ARE STILL CASING THE HALLWAYS...
...SO THIS NEXT PHASE WON'T WORK UNLESS EVERYONE PULLS OFF THEIR PART.
THAT SMELLS BAD.
BECAUSE IT'S HUMAN CRAP.
LET'S GO, PIERCE. TOGETHER, WE'RE UNBREAKABLE.
STRAIGHT FIFTY...
RIGHT THIRTY-TWO, LEFT EIGHTY-ONE, DOWN TEN.
...AND SINCE THE ELECTRICAL RUNS HOT, IT SHOULD TAP IN TO THE AIR DUCTS...
NEXT, WE LOCATE THE ELECTRICAL CONDUIT THAT FEEDS THE CELL SENSORS FROM THOSE HEAT READINGS FROM THE GOVERNMENT'S ONLINE SCANS...

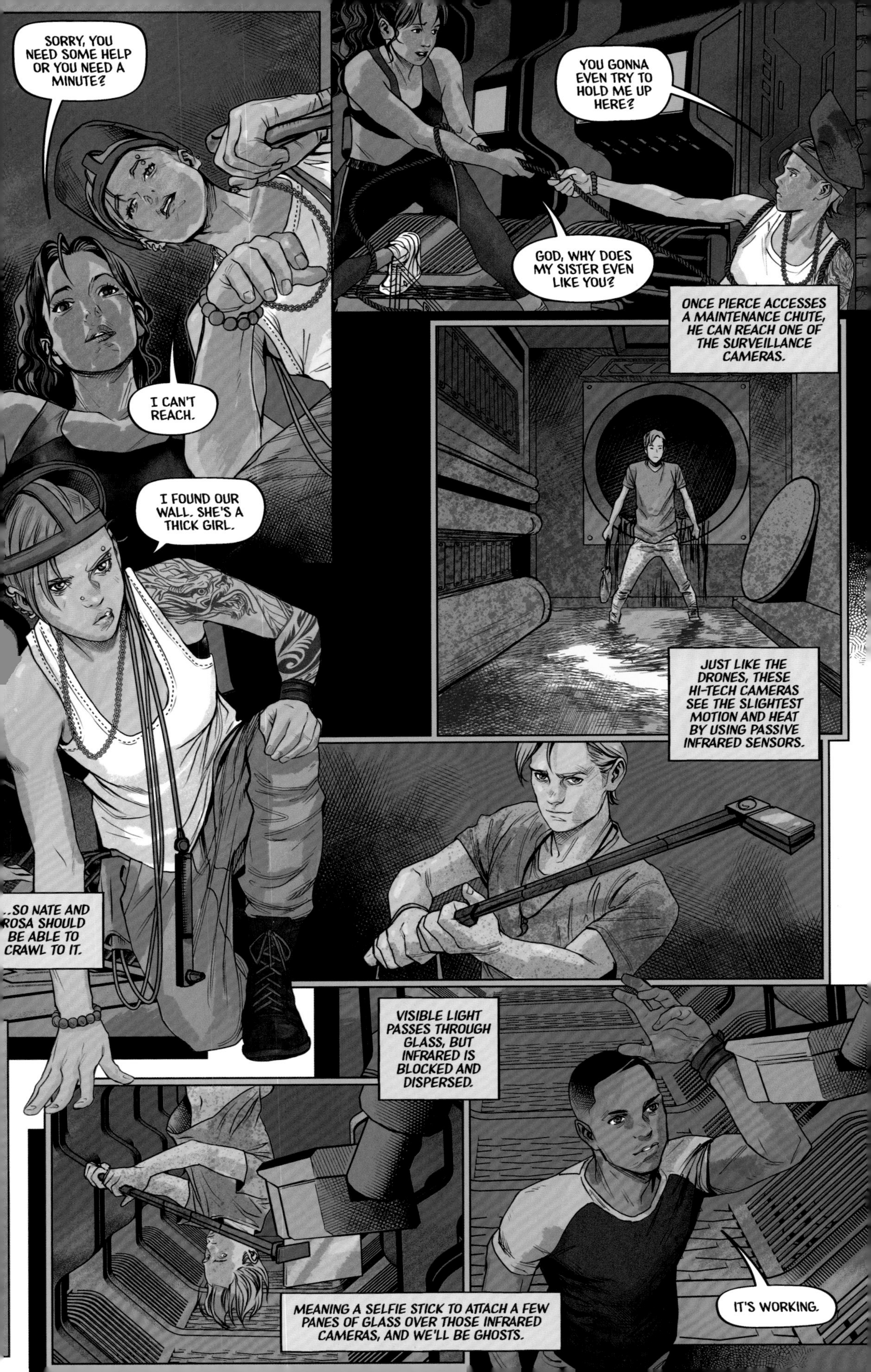
SORRY, YOU NEED SOME HELP OR YOU NEED A MINUTE?
I CAN'T REACH.
YOU GONNA EVEN TRY TO HOLD ME UP HERE?
GOD, WHY DOES MY SISTER EVEN LIKE YOU?
I FOUND OUR WALL. SHE'S A THICK GIRL.
...SO NATE AND ROSA SHOULD BE ABLE TO CRAWL TO IT.
ONCE PIERCE ACCESSES A MAINTENANCE CHUTE, HE CAN REACH ONE OF THE SURVEILLANCE CAMERAS.
JUST LIKE THE DRONES, THESE HI-TECH CAMERAS SEE THE SLIGHTEST MOTION AND HEAT BY USING PASSIVE INFRARED SENSORS.
VISIBLE LIGHT PASSES THROUGH GLASS, BUT INFRARED IS BLOCKED AND DISPERSED.
MEANING A SELFIE STICK TO ATTACH A FEW PANES OF GLASS OVER THOSE INFRARED CAMERAS, AND WE'LL BE GHOSTS.
IT'S WORKING.

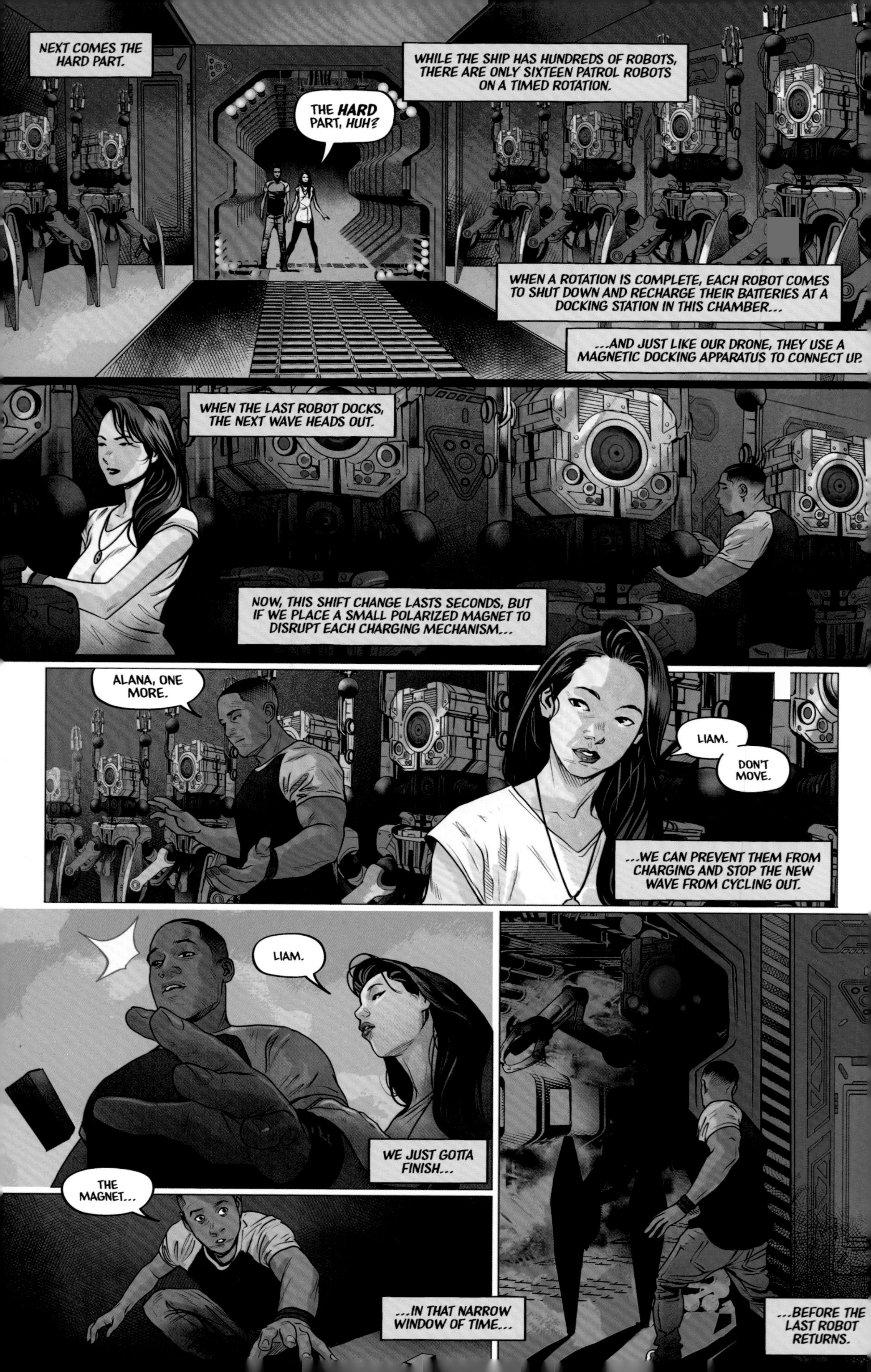
NEXT COMES THE HARD PART.
THE HARD PART, HUH?
WHILE THE SHIP HAS HUNDREDS OF ROBOTS, THERE ARE ONLY SIXTEEN PATROL ROBOTS ON A TIMED ROTATION.
WHEN A ROTATION IS COMPLETE, EACH ROBOT COMES TO SHUT DOWN AND RECHARGE THEIR BATTERIES AT A DOCKING STATION IN THIS CHAMBER...
...AND JUST LIKE OUR DRONE, THEY USE A MAGNETIC DOCKING APPARATUS TO CONNECT UP.
WHEN THE LAST ROBOT DOCKS, THE NEXT WAVE HEADS OUT.
NOW, THIS SHIFT CHANGE LASTS SECONDS, BUT IF WE PLACE A SMALL POLARIZED MAGNET TO DISRUPT EACH CHARGING MECHANISM...
ALANA, ONE MORE.
LIAM.
DON'T MOVE.
...WE CAN PREVENT THEM FROM CHARGING AND STOP THE NEW WAVE FROM CYCLING OUT.
LIAM.
WE JUST GOTTA FINISH...
THE MAGNET...
...IN THAT NARROW WINDOW OF TIME...
...BEFORE THE LAST ROBOT RETURNS.

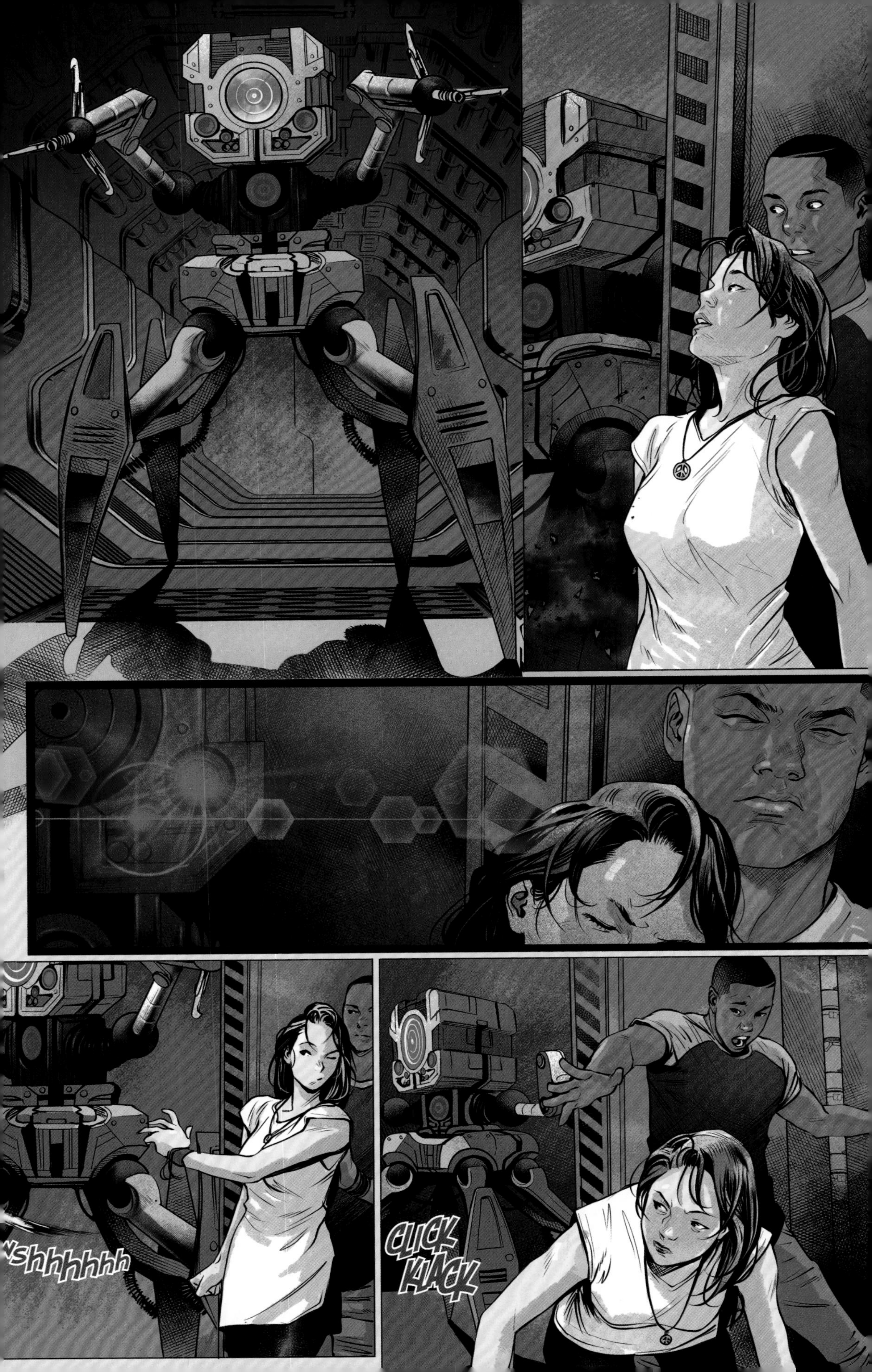

VSHHHHHH
CLICK
KLACK

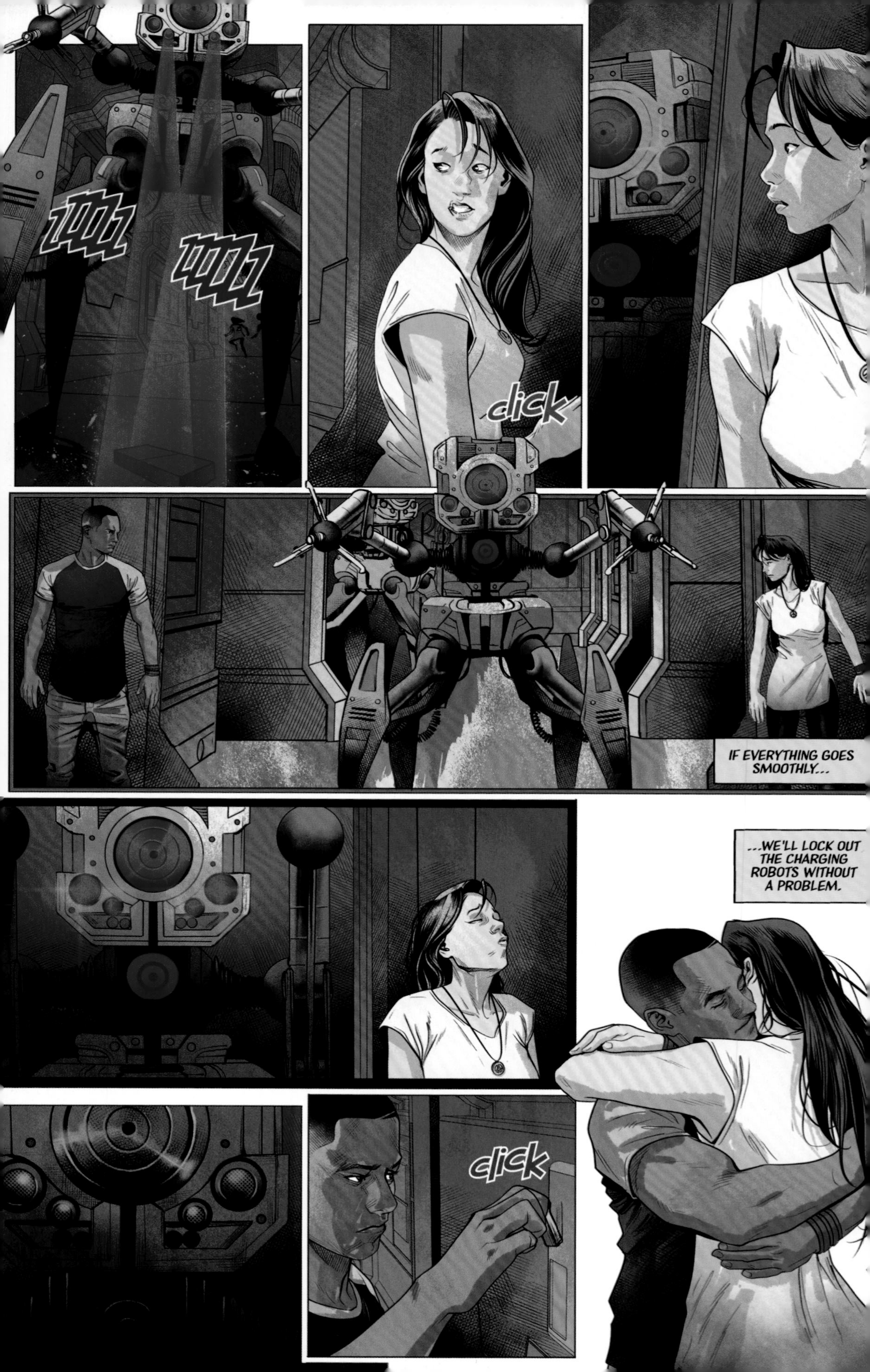
zzzz
zzzz
click
IF EVERYTHING GOES SMOOTHLY...
...WE'LL LOCK OUT THE CHARGING ROBOTS WITHOUT A PROBLEM.
click

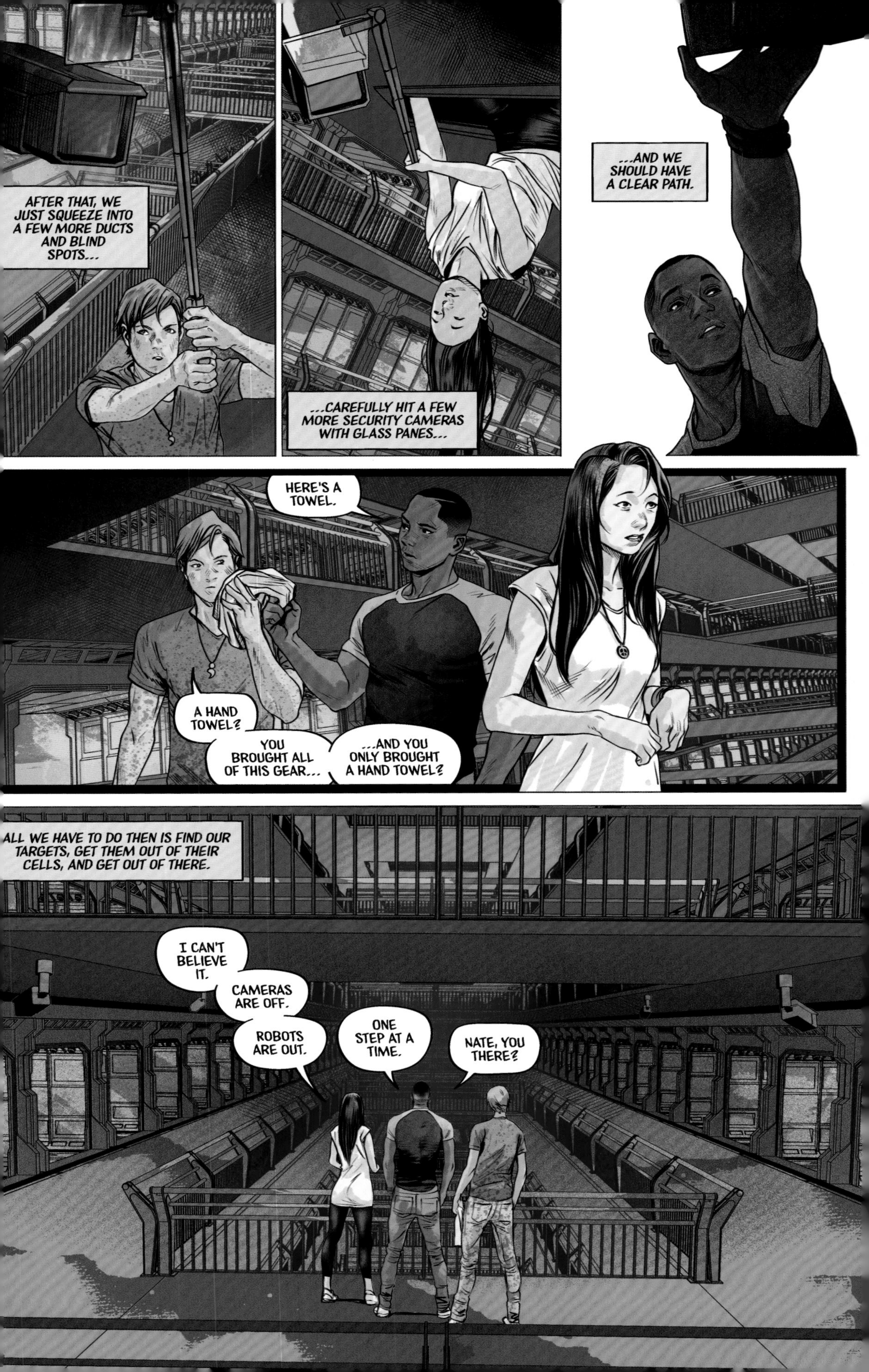
AFTER THAT, WE JUST SQUEEZE INTO A FEW MORE DUCTS AND BLIND SPOTS...
...CAREFULLY HIT A FEW MORE SECURITY CAMERAS WITH GLASS PANES...
...AND WE SHOULD HAVE A CLEAR PATH.
HERE'S A TOWEL.
A HAND TOWEL?
YOU BROUGHT ALL OF THIS GEAR...
...AND YOU ONLY BROUGHT A HAND TOWEL?
ALL WE HAVE TO DO THEN IS FIND OUR TARGETS, GET THEM OUT OF THEIR CELLS, AND GET OUT OF THERE.
I CAN'T BELIEVE IT.
CAMERAS ARE OFF.
ROBOTS ARE OUT.
ONE STEP AT A TIME.
NATE, YOU THERE?

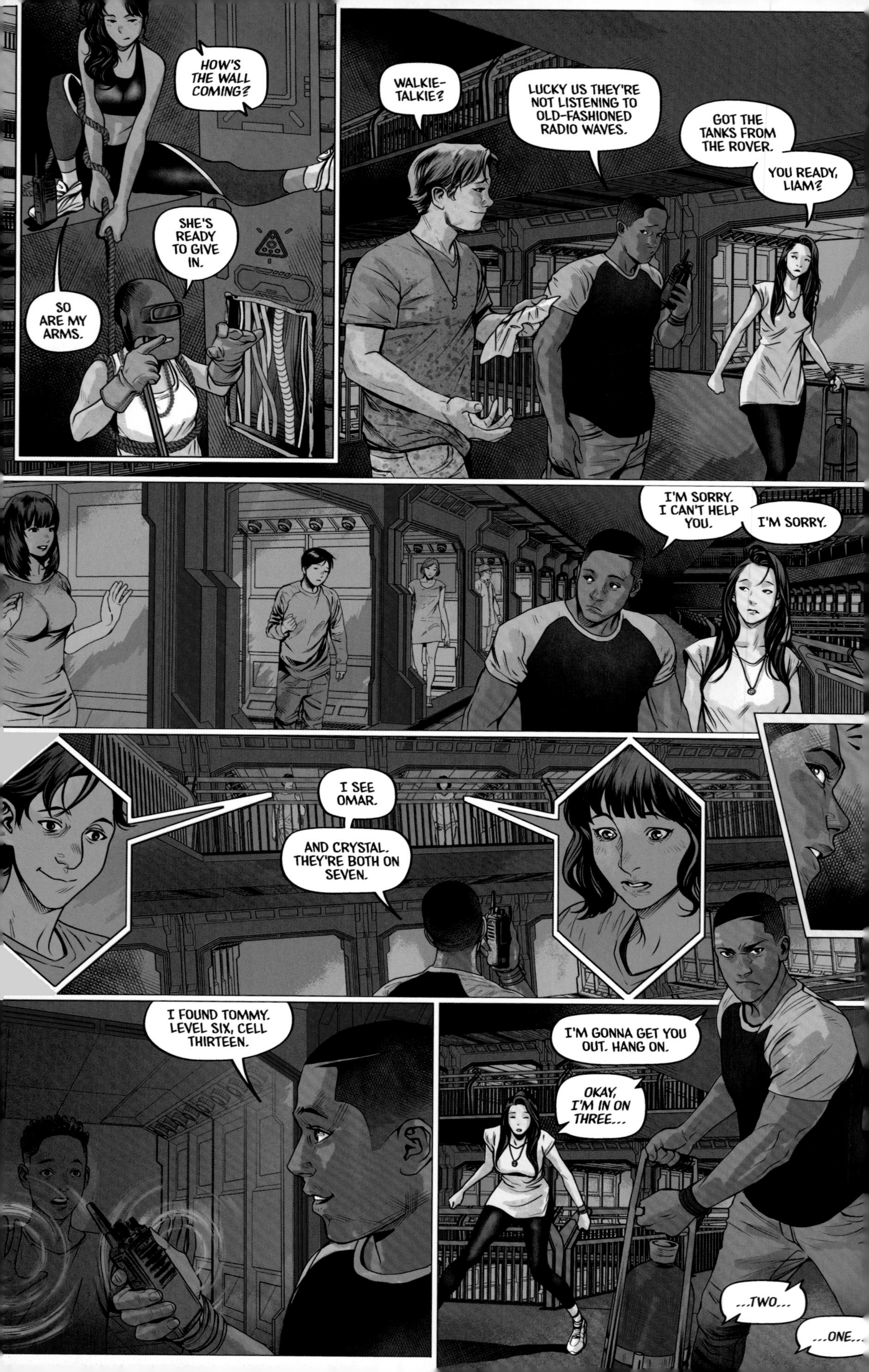
HOW'S THE WALL COMING?
SHE'S READY TO GIVE IN.
SO ARE MY ARMS.
WALKIE-TALKIE?
LUCKY US THEY'RE NOT LISTENING TO OLD-FASHIONED RADIO WAVES.
GOT THE TANKS FROM THE ROVER.
YOU READY, LIAM?
I'M SORRY. I CAN'T HELP YOU.
I'M SORRY.
I SEE OMAR.
AND CRYSTAL. THEY'RE BOTH ON SEVEN.
I FOUND TOMMY. LEVEL SIX, CELL THIRTEEN.
I'M GONNA GET YOU OUT. HANG ON.
OKAY, I'M IN ON THREE...
...TWO...
...ONE...

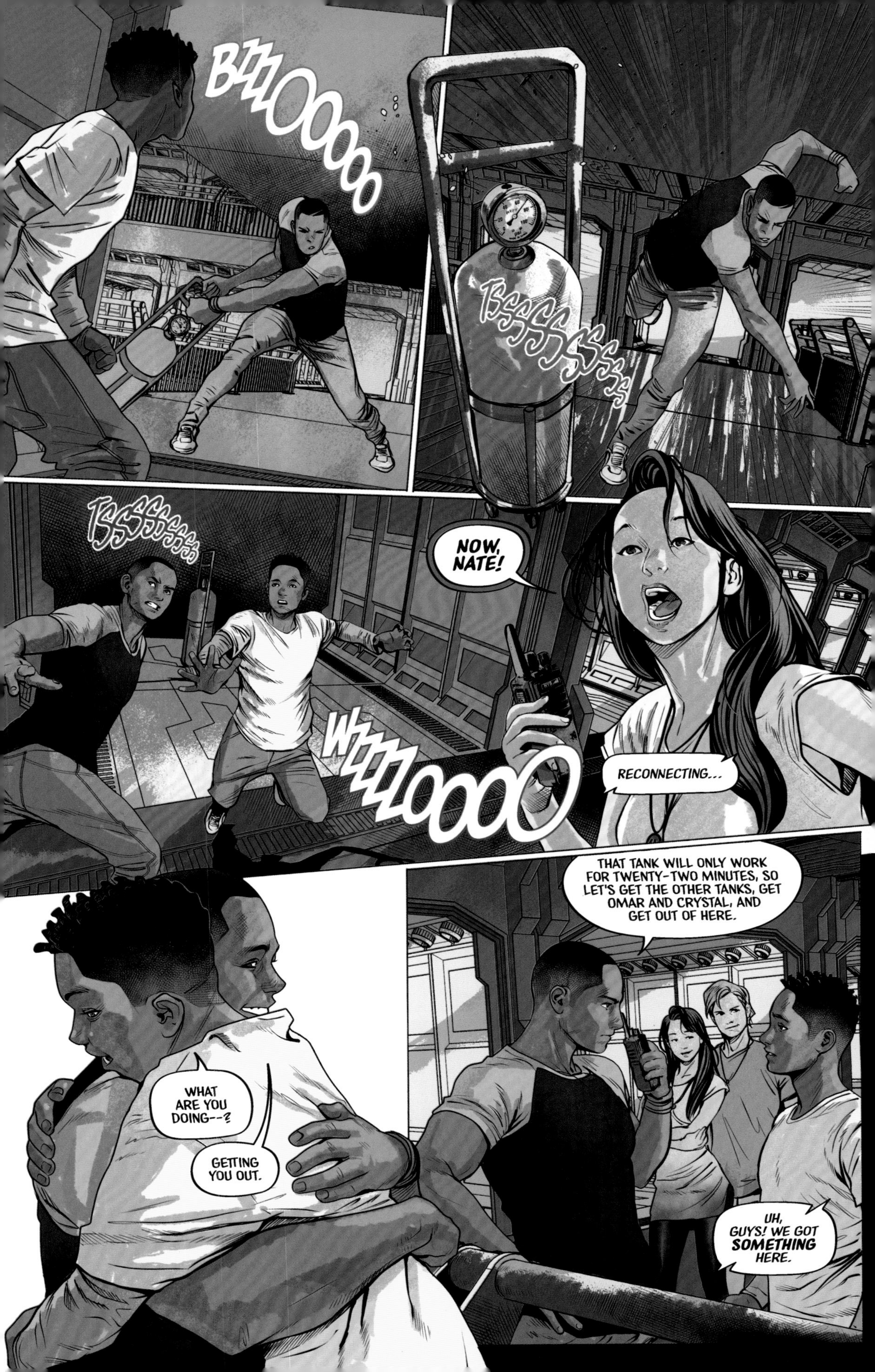
BZZZOOOOO
TSSSSSSSSS
TSSSSSSSS
NOW, NATE!
WZZZOOOOO
RECONNECTING...
THAT TANK WILL ONLY WORK FOR TWENTY-TWO MINUTES, SO LET'S GET THE OTHER TANKS, GET OMAR AND CRYSTAL, AND GET OUT OF HERE.
WHAT ARE YOU DOING--?
GETTING YOU OUT.
UH, GUYS! WE GOT **SOMETHING** HERE.

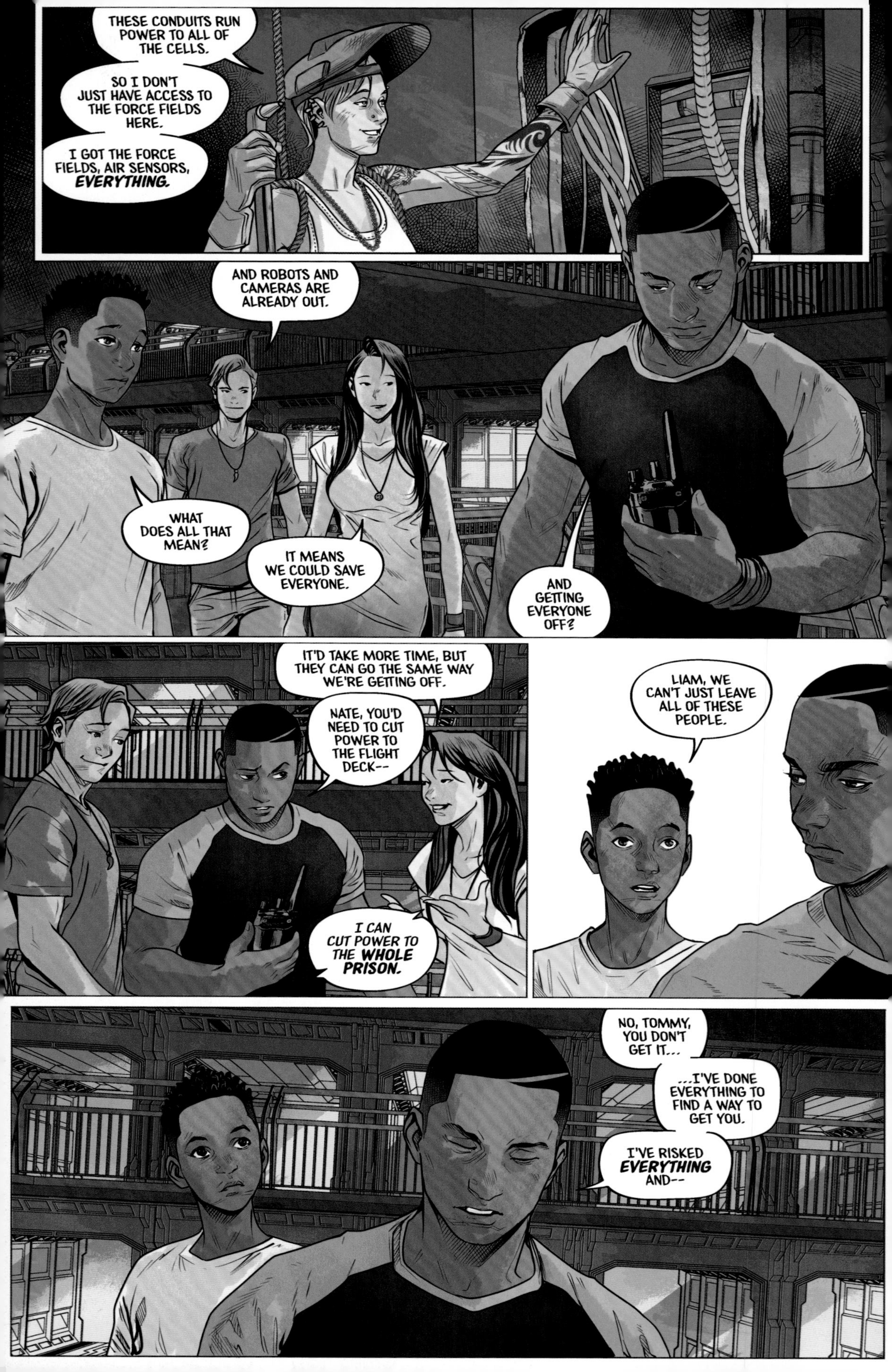
THESE CONDUITS RUN POWER TO ALL OF THE CELLS.
SO I DON'T JUST HAVE ACCESS TO THE FORCE FIELDS HERE.
I GOT THE FORCE FIELDS, AIR SENSORS, ***EVERYTHING.***
AND ROBOTS AND CAMERAS ARE ALREADY OUT.
WHAT DOES ALL THAT MEAN?
IT MEANS WE COULD SAVE EVERYONE.
AND GETTING EVERYONE OFF?
IT'D TAKE MORE TIME, BUT THEY CAN GO THE SAME WAY WE'RE GETTING OFF.
NATE, YOU'D NEED TO CUT POWER TO THE FLIGHT DECK--
I CAN CUT POWER TO THE **WHOLE PRISON.**
LIAM, WE CAN'T JUST LEAVE ALL OF THESE PEOPLE.
NO, TOMMY, YOU DON'T GET IT...
...I'VE DONE EVERYTHING TO FIND A WAY TO GET YOU.
I'VE RISKED ***EVERYTHING*** AND--

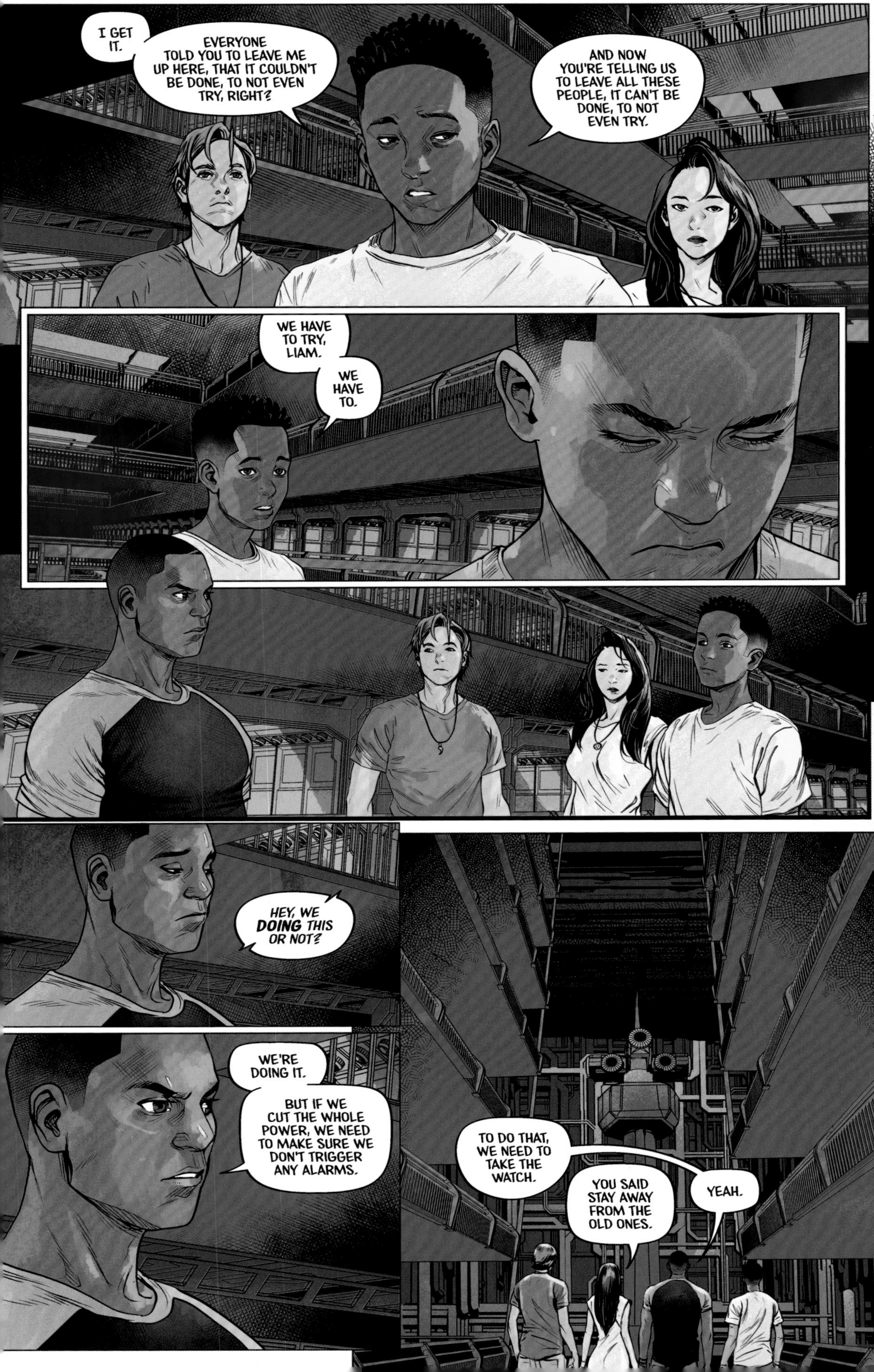
I GET IT.
EVERYONE TOLD YOU TO LEAVE ME UP HERE, THAT IT COULDN'T BE DONE, TO NOT EVEN TRY, RIGHT?
AND NOW YOU'RE TELLING US TO LEAVE ALL THESE PEOPLE, IT CAN'T BE DONE, TO NOT EVEN TRY.
WE HAVE TO TRY, LIAM.
WE HAVE TO.
HEY, WE DOING THIS OR NOT?
WE'RE DOING IT.
BUT IF WE CUT THE WHOLE POWER, WE NEED TO MAKE SURE WE DON'T TRIGGER ANY ALARMS.
TO DO THAT, WE NEED TO TAKE THE WATCH.
YOU SAID STAY AWAY FROM THE OLD ONES.
YEAH.

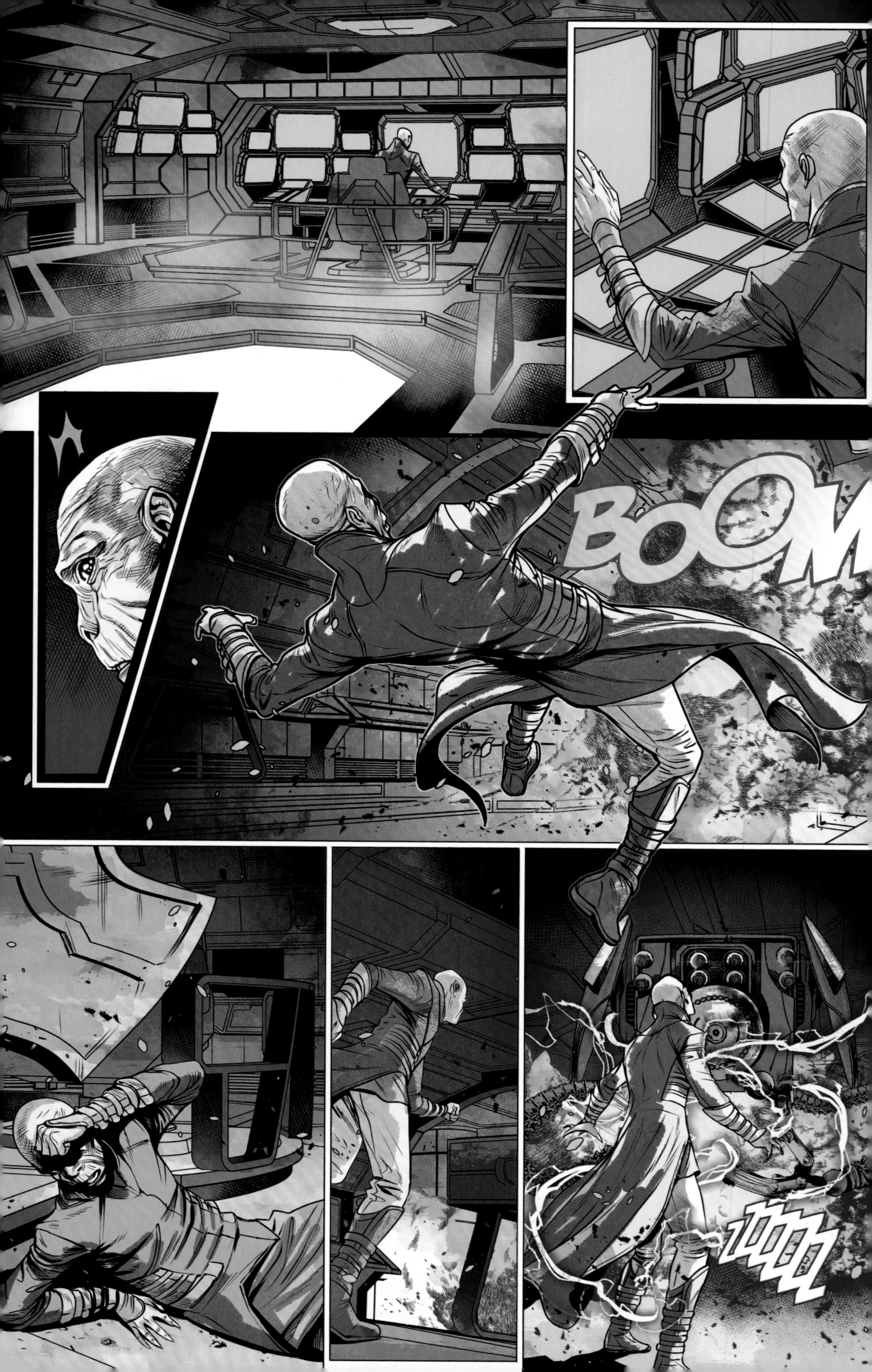
BOOM

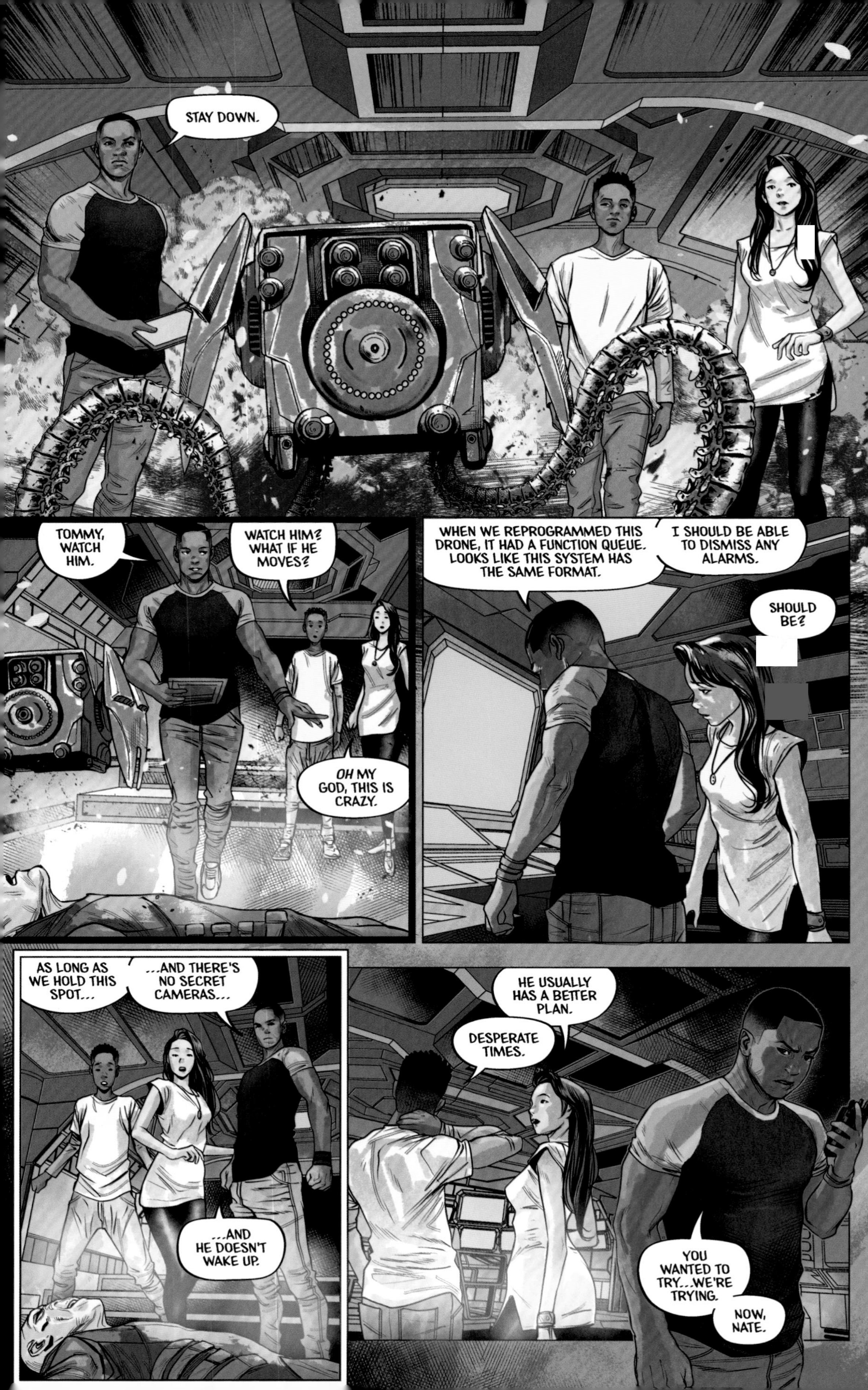
STAY DOWN.
TOMMY, WATCH HIM.
WATCH HIM? WHAT IF HE MOVES?
OH MY GOD, THIS IS CRAZY.
WHEN WE REPROGRAMMED THIS DRONE, IT HAD A FUNCTION QUEUE. LOOKS LIKE THIS SYSTEM HAS THE SAME FORMAT.
I SHOULD BE ABLE TO DISMISS ANY ALARMS.
SHOULD BE?
AS LONG AS WE HOLD THIS SPOT...
...AND THERE'S NO SECRET CAMERAS...
...AND HE DOESN'T WAKE UP.
HE USUALLY HAS A BETTER PLAN.
DESPERATE TIMES.
YOU WANTED TO TRY...WE'RE TRYING.
NOW, NATE.

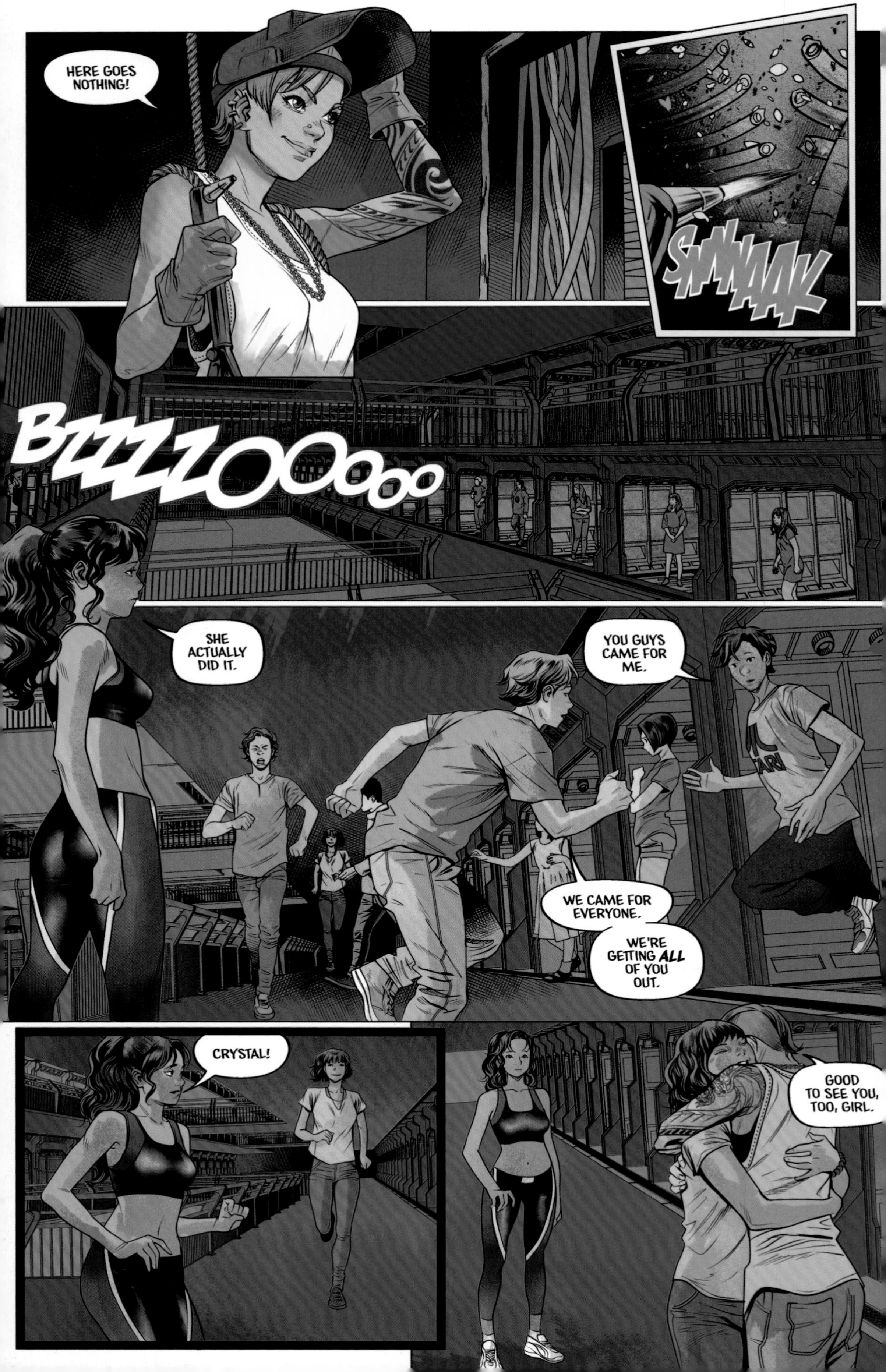

HERE GOES NOTHING!
SHWAAAK
BZZZOOooo
SHE ACTUALLY DID IT.
YOU GUYS CAME FOR ME.
WE CAME FOR EVERYONE.
WE'RE GETTING ALL OF YOU OUT.
CRYSTAL!
GOOD TO SEE YOU, TOO, GIRL.

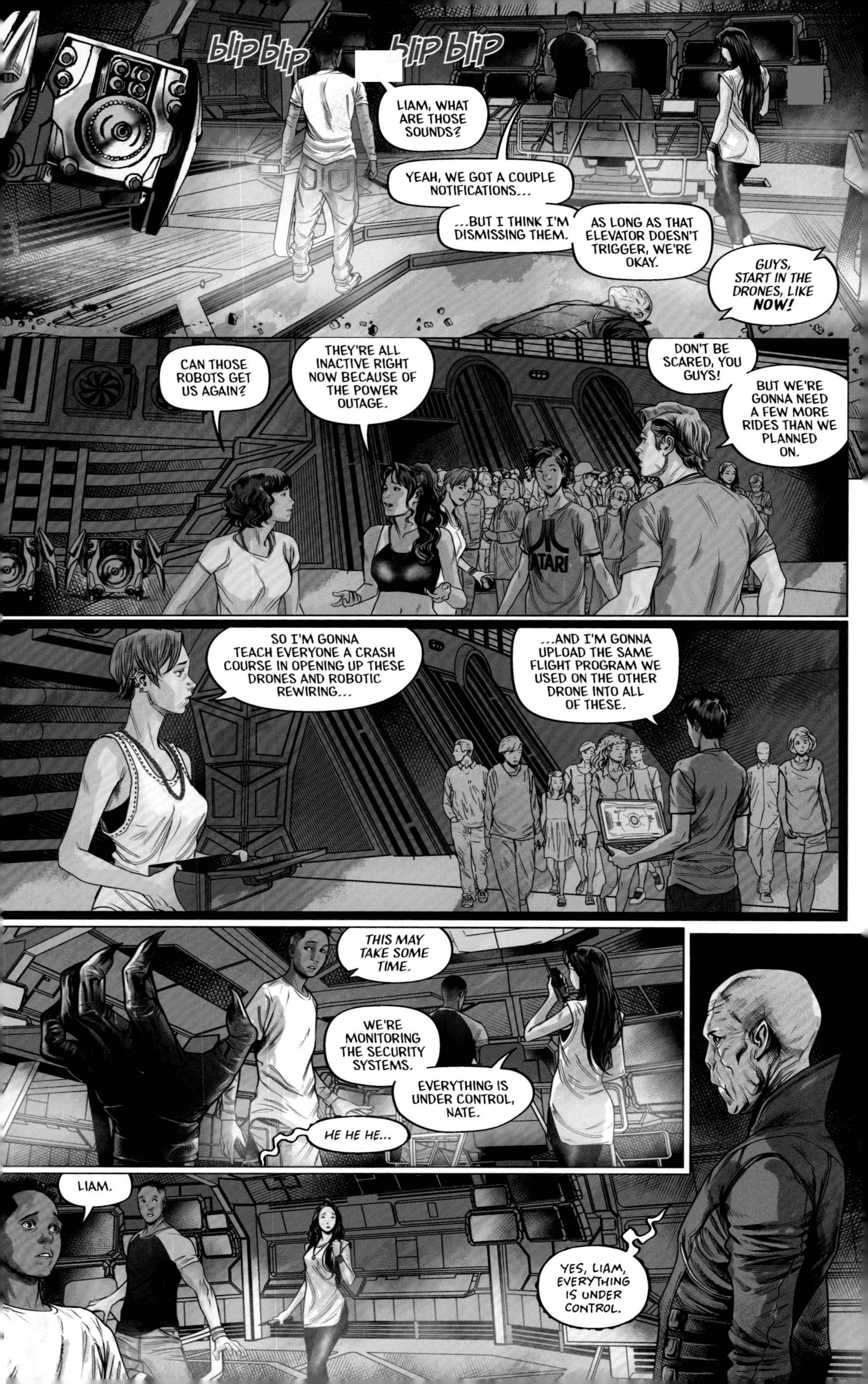
blip blip
blip blip
LIAM, WHAT ARE THOSE SOUNDS?
YEAH, WE GOT A COUPLE NOTIFICATIONS...
...BUT I THINK I'M DISMISSING THEM.
AS LONG AS THAT ELEVATOR DOESN'T TRIGGER, WE'RE OKAY.
GUYS, START IN THE DRONES, LIKE NOW!
CAN THOSE ROBOTS GET US AGAIN?
THEY'RE ALL INACTIVE RIGHT NOW BECAUSE OF THE POWER OUTAGE.
DON'T BE SCARED, YOU GUYS!
BUT WE'RE GONNA NEED A FEW MORE RIDES THAN WE PLANNED ON.
ATARI
SO I'M GONNA TEACH EVERYONE A CRASH COURSE IN OPENING UP THESE DRONES AND ROBOTIC REWIRING...
...AND I'M GONNA UPLOAD THE SAME FLIGHT PROGRAM WE USED ON THE OTHER DRONE INTO ALL OF THESE.
THIS MAY TAKE SOME TIME.
WE'RE MONITORING THE SECURITY SYSTEMS.
EVERYTHING IS UNDER CONTROL, NATE.
HE HE HE...
LIAM.
YES, LIAM, EVERYTHING IS UNDER CONTROL.

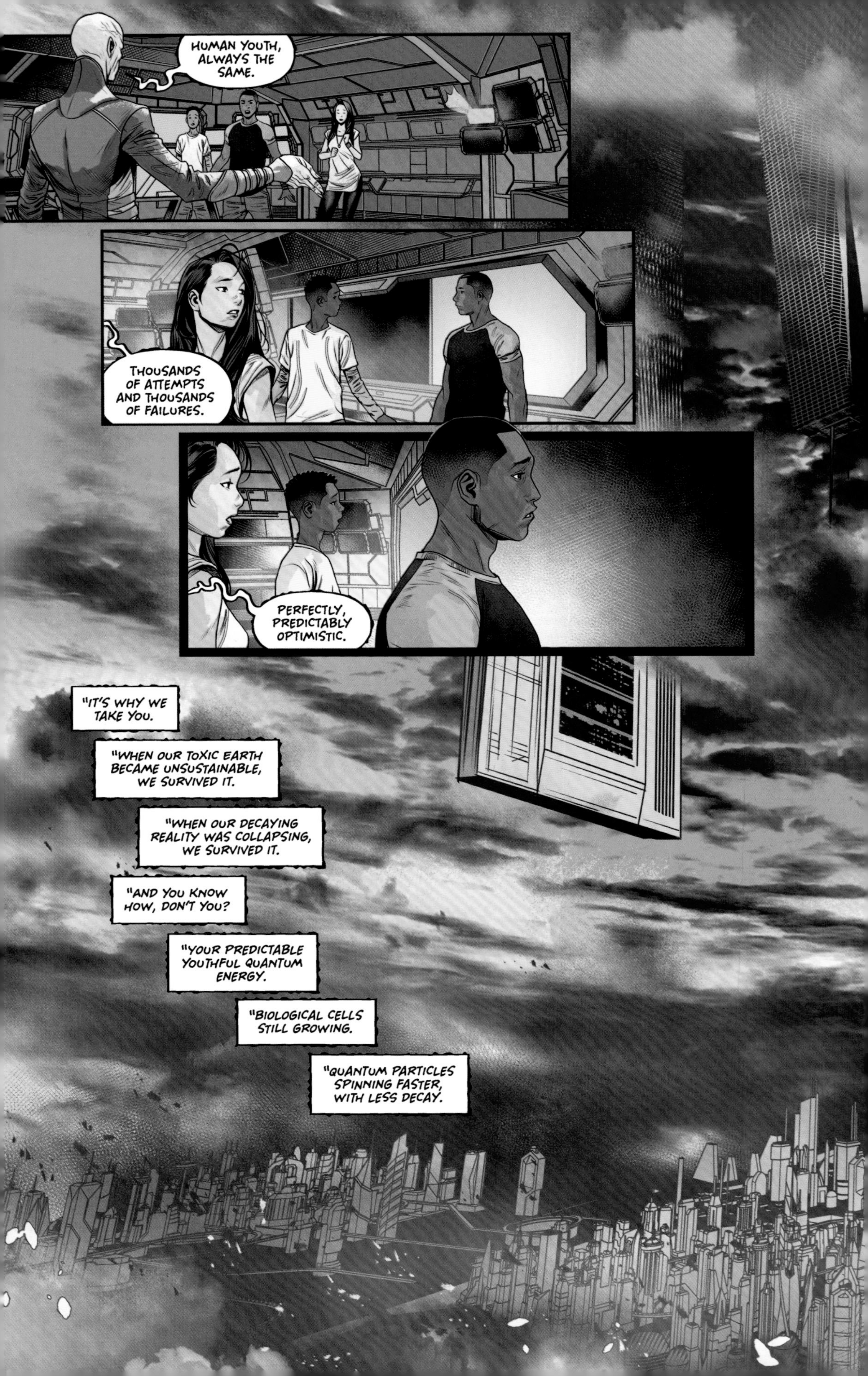
HUMAN YOUTH, ALWAYS THE SAME.
THOUSANDS OF ATTEMPTS AND THOUSANDS OF FAILURES.
PERFECTLY, PREDICTABLY OPTIMISTIC.
"IT'S WHY WE TAKE YOU.
"WHEN OUR TOXIC EARTH BECAME UNSUSTAINABLE, WE SURVIVED IT.
"WHEN OUR DECAYING REALITY WAS COLLAPSING, WE SURVIVED IT.
"AND YOU KNOW HOW, DON'T YOU?
"YOUR PREDICTABLE YOUTHFUL QUANTUM ENERGY.
"BIOLOGICAL CELLS STILL GROWING.
"QUANTUM PARTICLES SPINNING FASTER, WITH LESS DECAY.

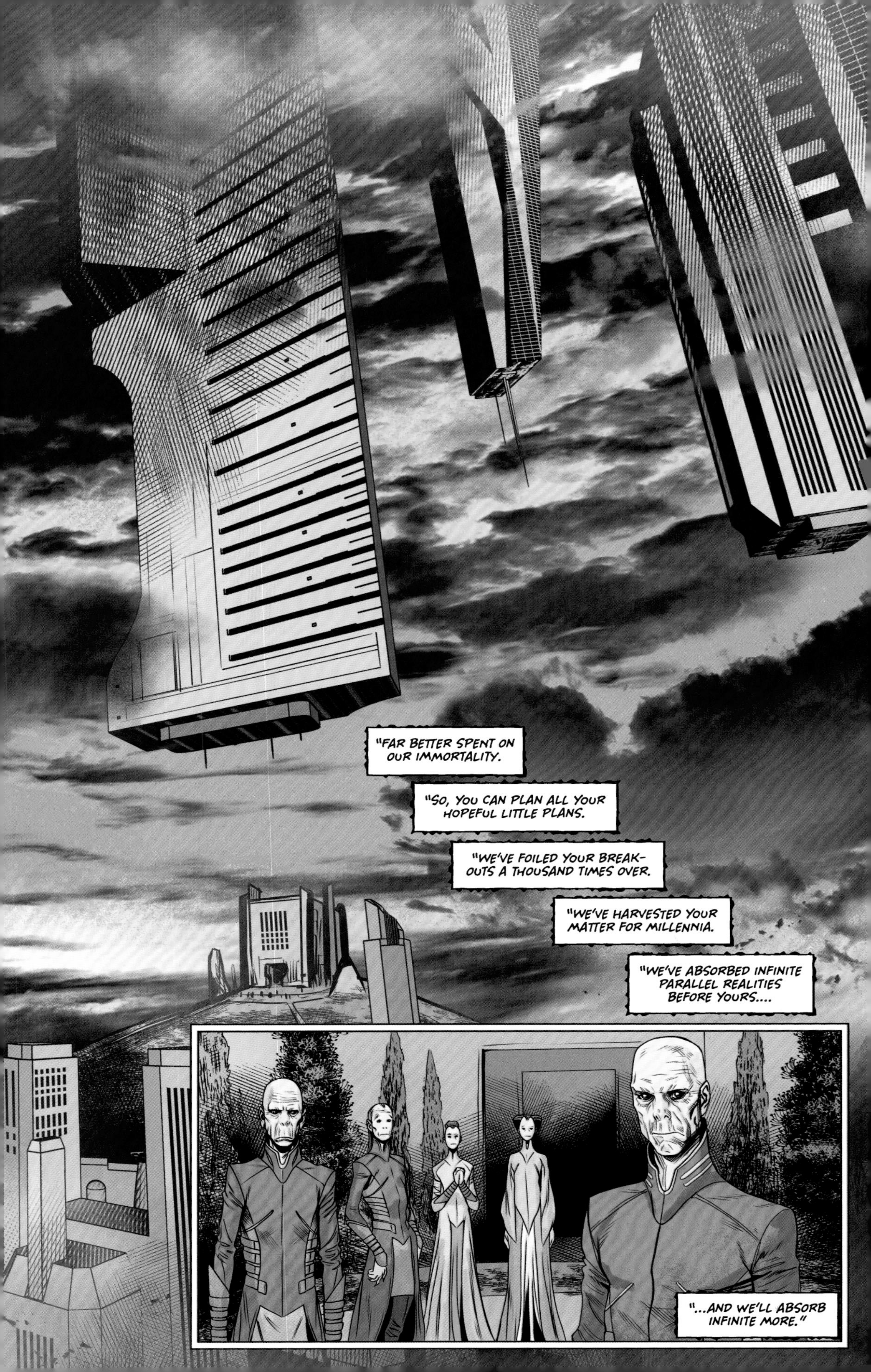
"FAR BETTER SPENT ON OUR IMMORTALITY.
"SO, YOU CAN PLAN ALL YOUR HOPEFUL LITTLE PLANS.
"WE'VE FOILED YOUR BREAK-OUTS A THOUSAND TIMES OVER.
"WE'VE HARVESTED YOUR MATTER FOR MILLENNIA.
"WE'VE ABSORBED INFINITE PARALLEL REALITIES BEFORE YOURS....
"...AND WE'LL ABSORB INFINITE MORE."

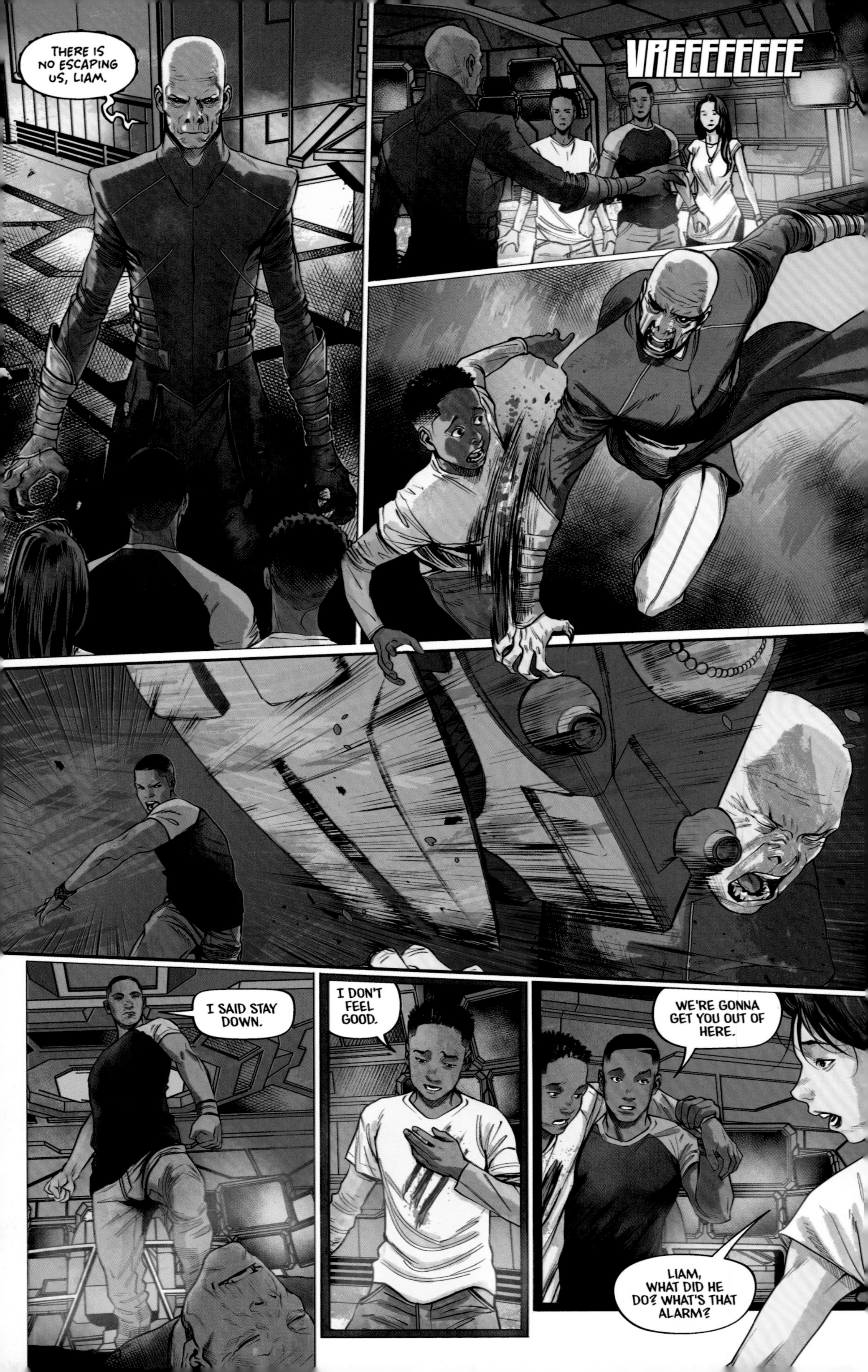
THERE IS NO ESCAPING US, LIAM.
VREEEEEEEE
I SAID STAY DOWN.
I DON'T FEEL GOOD.
WE'RE GONNA GET YOU OUT OF HERE.
LIAM, WHAT DID HE DO? WHAT'S THAT ALARM?

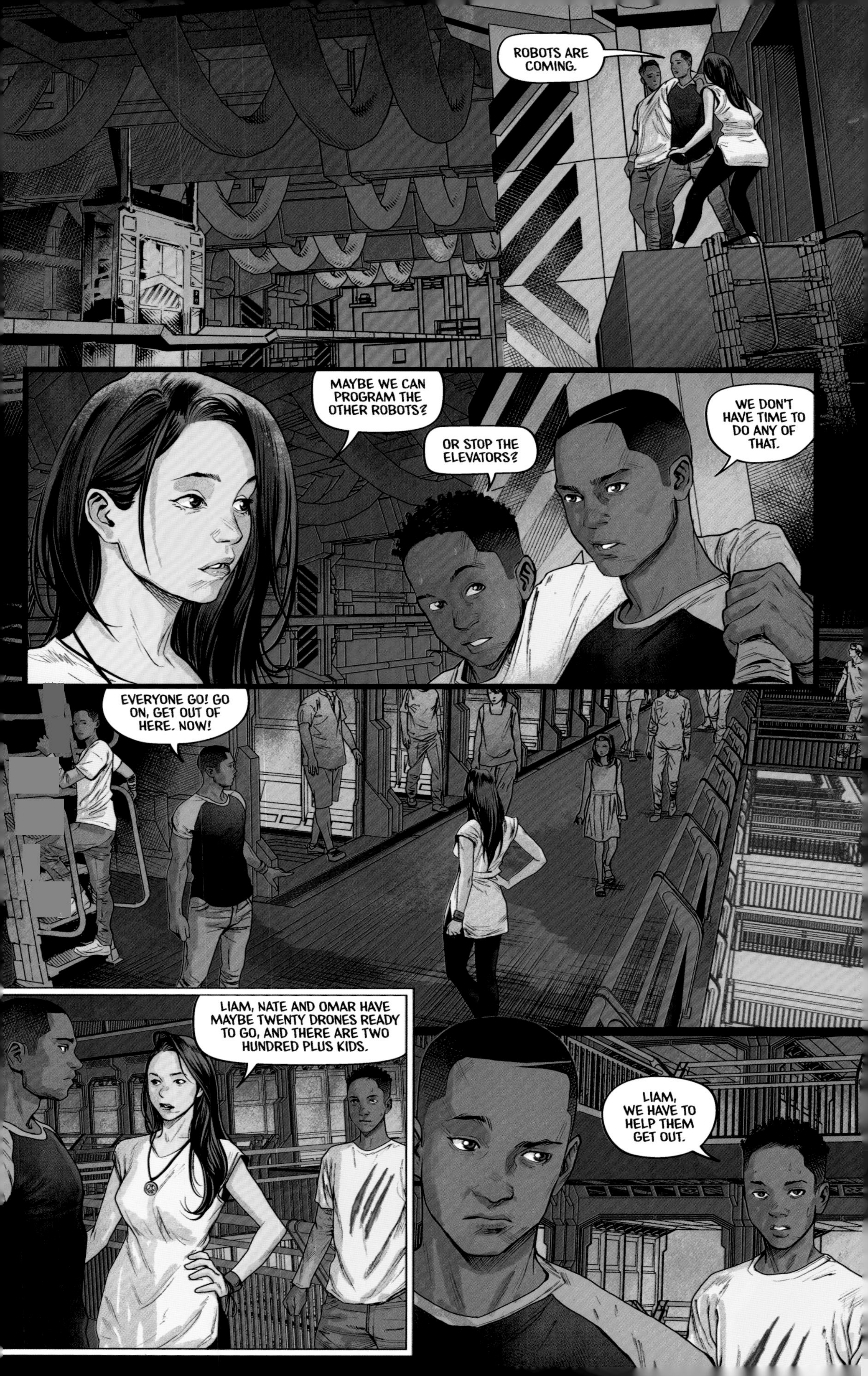
ROBOTS ARE COMING.
MAYBE WE CAN PROGRAM THE OTHER ROBOTS?
OR STOP THE ELEVATORS?
WE DON'T HAVE TIME TO DO ANY OF THAT.
EVERYONE GO! GO ON, GET OUT OF HERE. NOW!
LIAM, NATE AND OMAR HAVE MAYBE TWENTY DRONES READY TO GO, AND THERE ARE TWO HUNDRED PLUS KIDS.
LIAM, WE HAVE TO HELP THEM GET OUT.

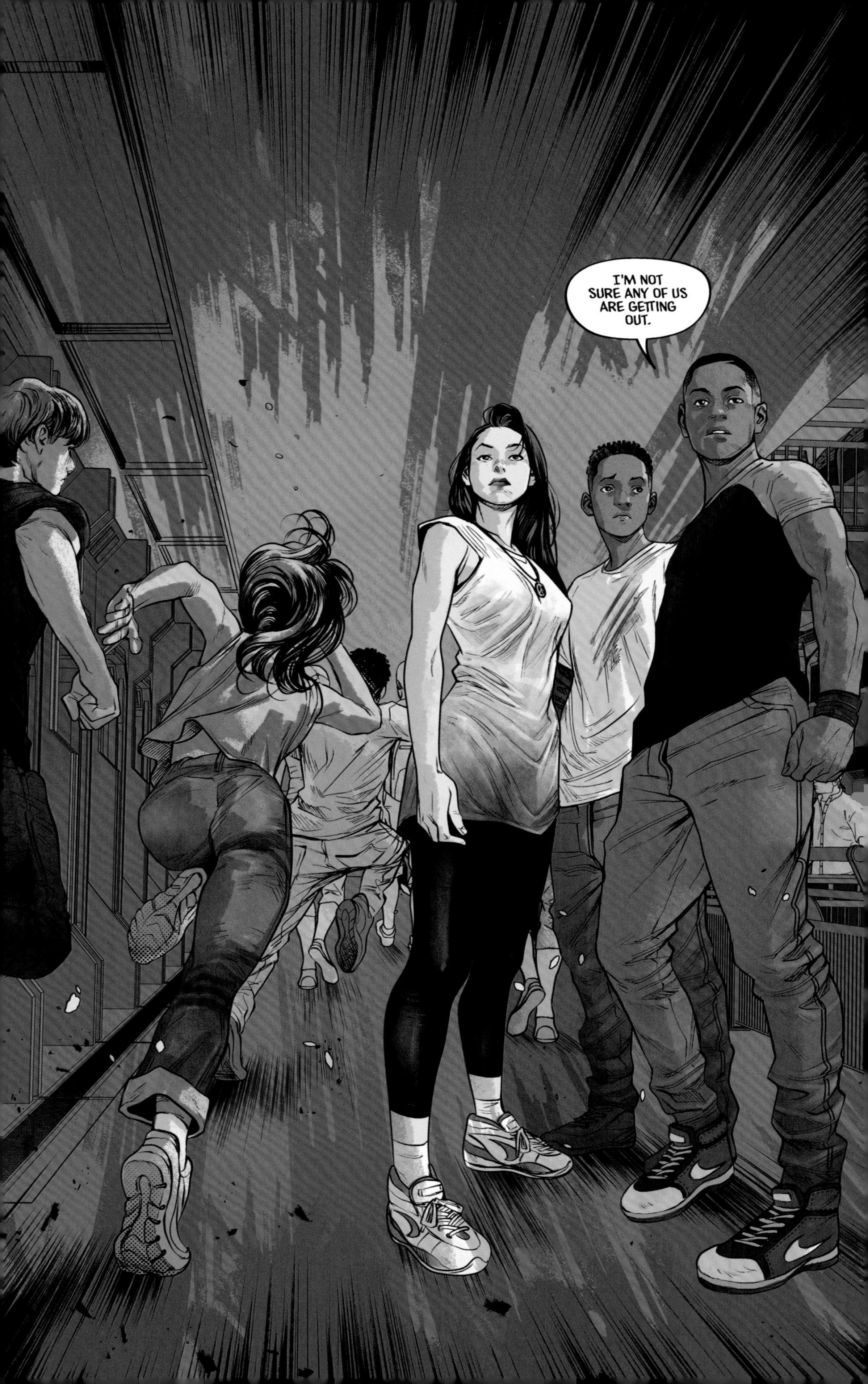
I'M NOT SURE ANY OF US ARE GETTING OUT.

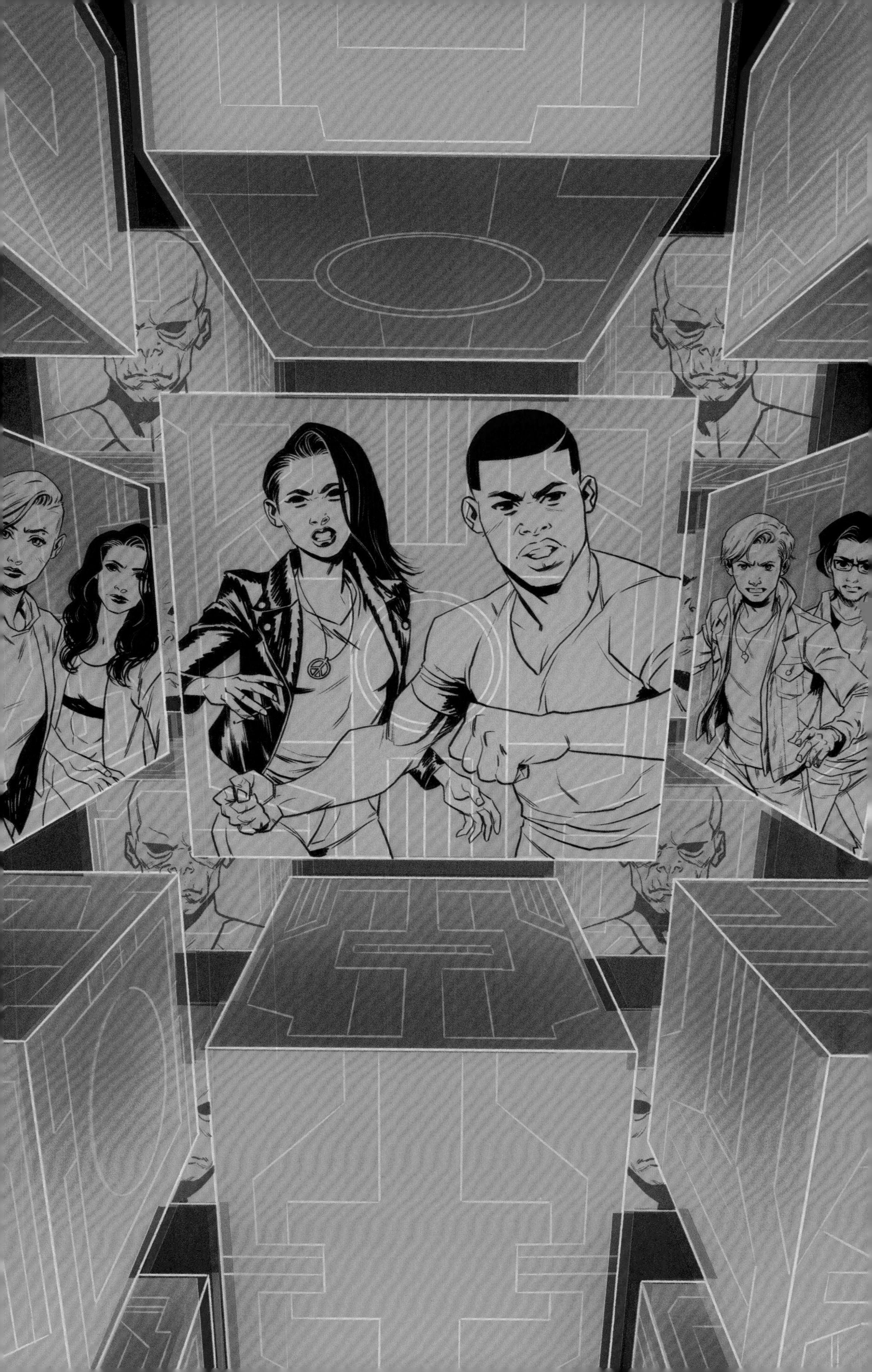

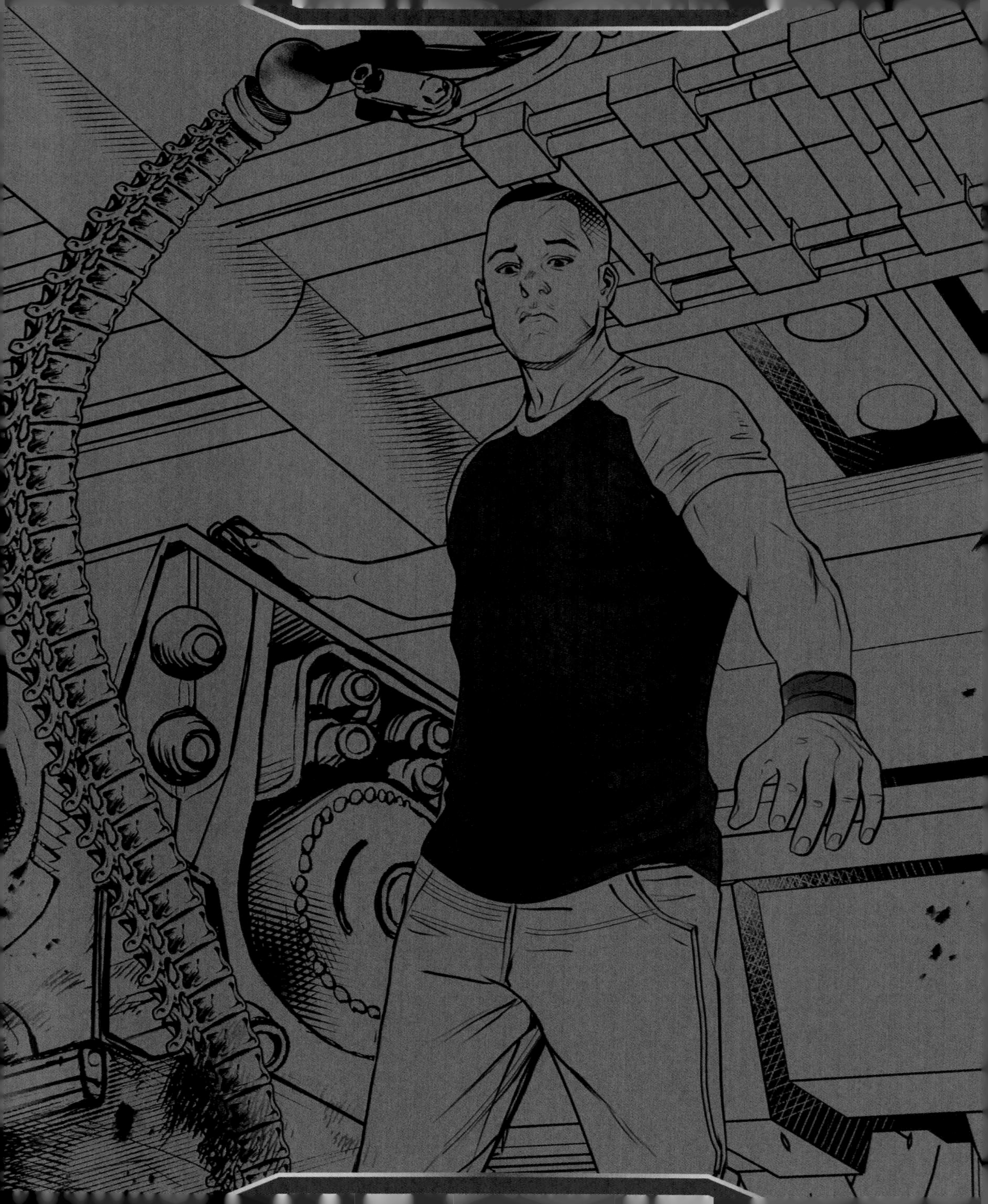

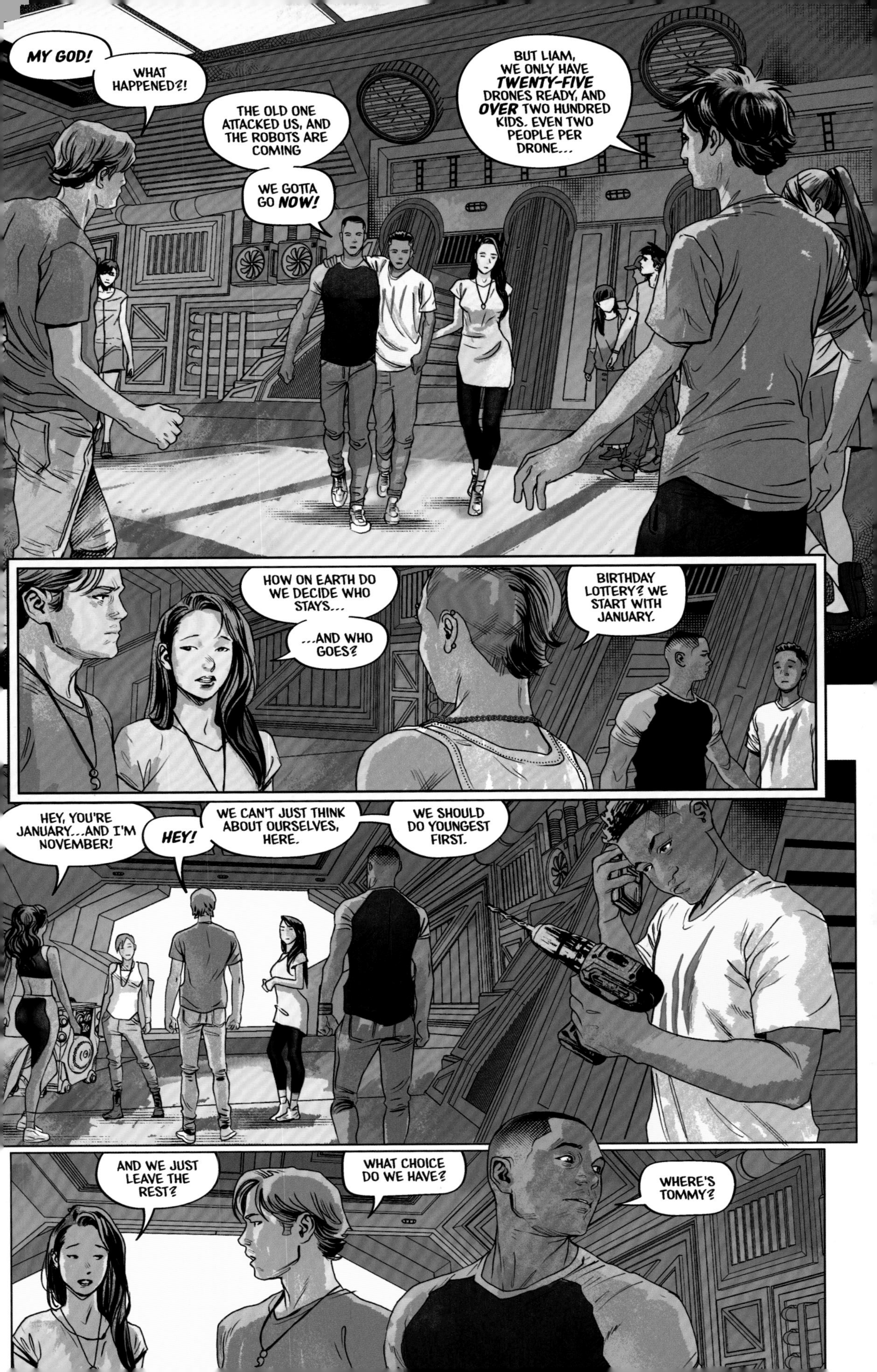

MY GOD!
WHAT HAPPENED?!
THE OLD ONE ATTACKED US, AND THE ROBOTS ARE COMING
WE GOTTA GO NOW!
BUT LIAM, WE ONLY HAVE TWENTY-FIVE DRONES READY, AND OVER TWO HUNDRED KIDS. EVEN TWO PEOPLE PER DRONE...
HOW ON EARTH DO WE DECIDE WHO STAYS...
...AND WHO GOES?
BIRTHDAY LOTTERY? WE START WITH JANUARY.
HEY, YOU'RE JANUARY...AND I'M NOVEMBER!
HEY!
WE CAN'T JUST THINK ABOUT OURSELVES, HERE.
WE SHOULD DO YOUNGEST FIRST.
AND WE JUST LEAVE THE REST?
WHAT CHOICE DO WE HAVE?
WHERE'S TOMMY?

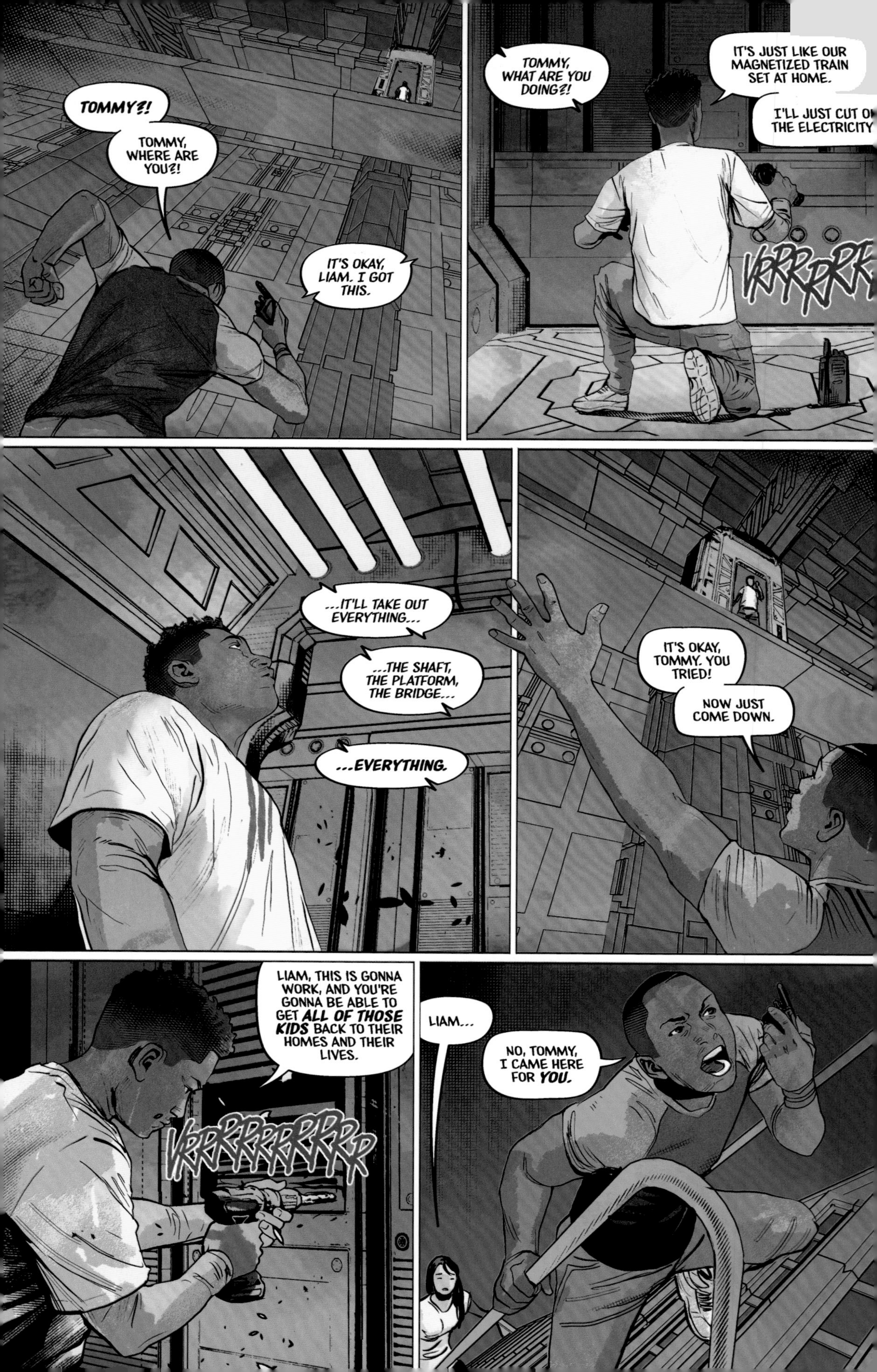

TOMMY?!
TOMMY, WHERE ARE YOU?!
IT'S OKAY, LIAM. I GOT THIS.
TOMMY, WHAT ARE YOU DOING?!
IT'S JUST LIKE OUR MAGNETIZED TRAIN SET AT HOME.
I'LL JUST CUT O
THE ELECTRICITY
VRRRRRR
...IT'LL TAKE OUT EVERYTHING...
...THE SHAFT, THE PLATFORM, THE BRIDGE...
...EVERYTHING.
IT'S OKAY, TOMMY. YOU TRIED!
NOW JUST COME DOWN.
LIAM, THIS IS GONNA WORK, AND YOU'RE GONNA BE ABLE TO GET ALL OF THOSE KIDS BACK TO THEIR HOMES AND THEIR LIVES.
VRRRRRRRRRRR
LIAM...
NO, TOMMY, I CAME HERE FOR YOU.

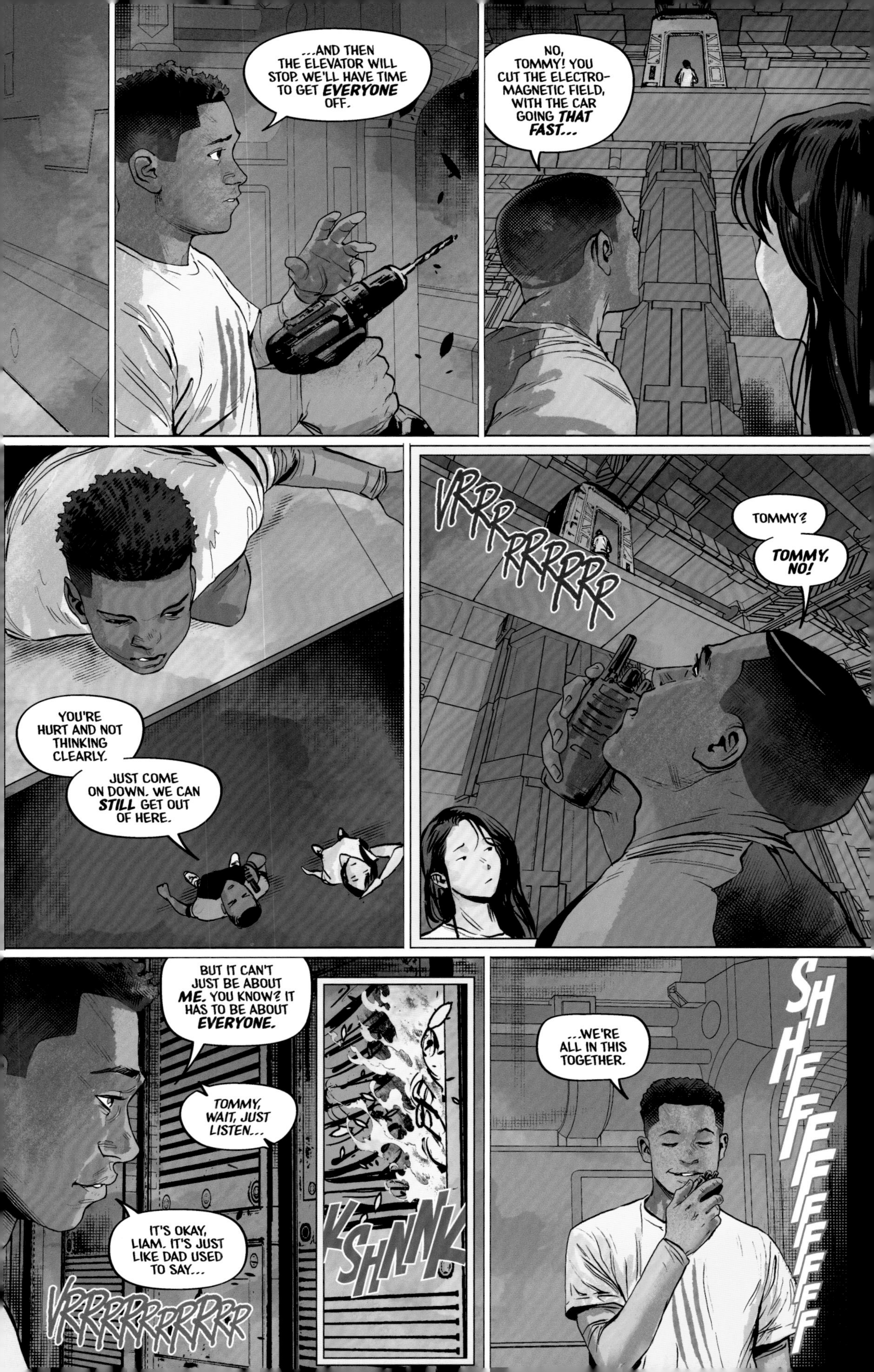
...AND THEN THE ELEVATOR WILL STOP. WE'LL HAVE TIME TO GET EVERYONE OFF.
NO, TOMMY! YOU CUT THE ELECTRO-MAGNETIC FIELD, WITH THE CAR GOING THAT FAST...
YOU'RE HURT AND NOT THINKING CLEARLY.
JUST COME ON DOWN. WE CAN STILL GET OUT OF HERE.
VRRRRRRRRR
TOMMY?
TOMMY, NO!
BUT IT CAN'T JUST BE ABOUT ME. YOU KNOW? IT HAS TO BE ABOUT EVERYONE.
TOMMY, WAIT, JUST LISTEN...
IT'S OKAY, LIAM. IT'S JUST LIKE DAD USED TO SAY...
VRRRRRRRRRRR
KSHNNK
...WE'RE ALL IN THIS TOGETHER.
SHHFFFFFFFFF

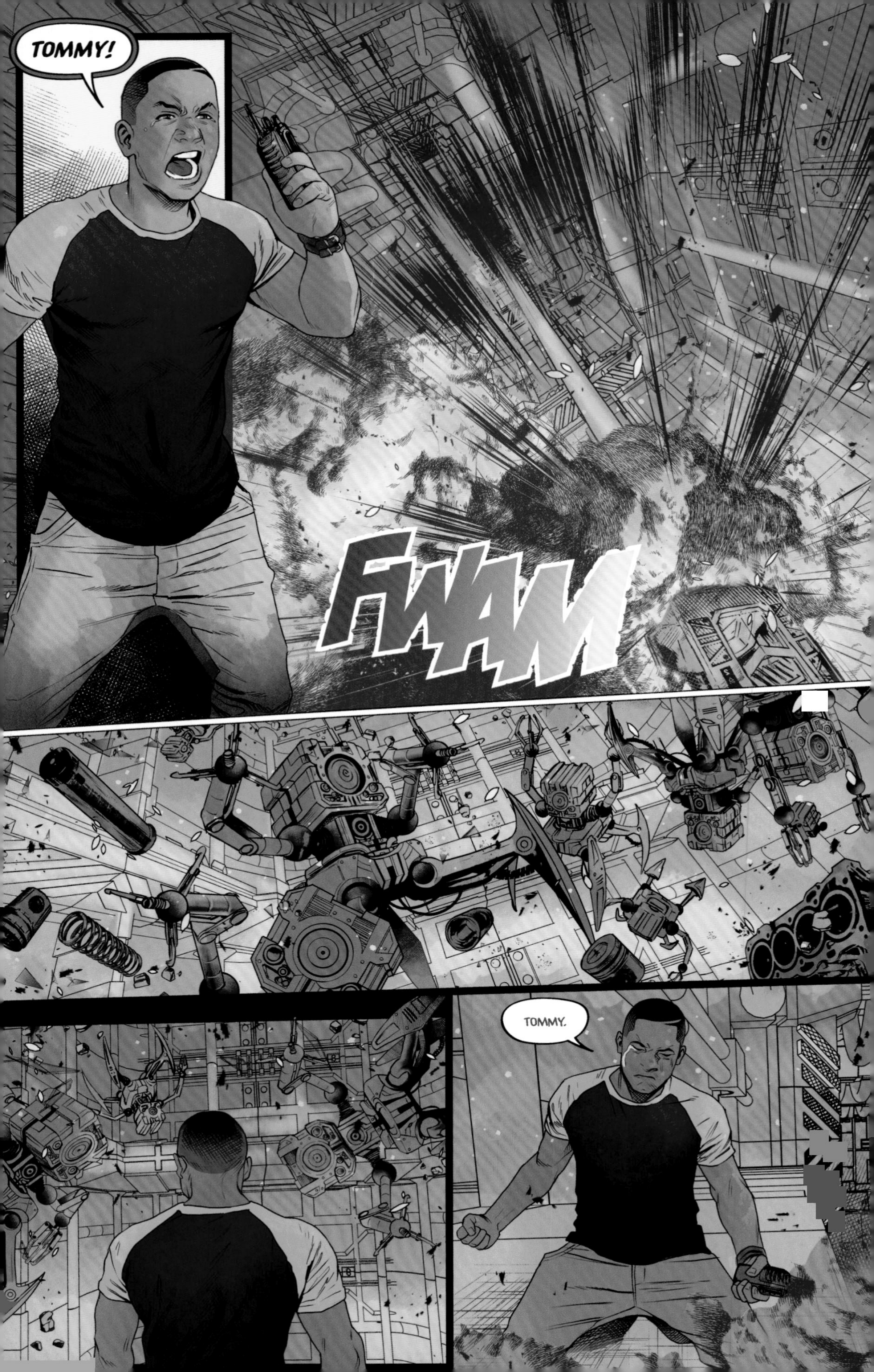

TOMMY!
FWAM
TOMMY.

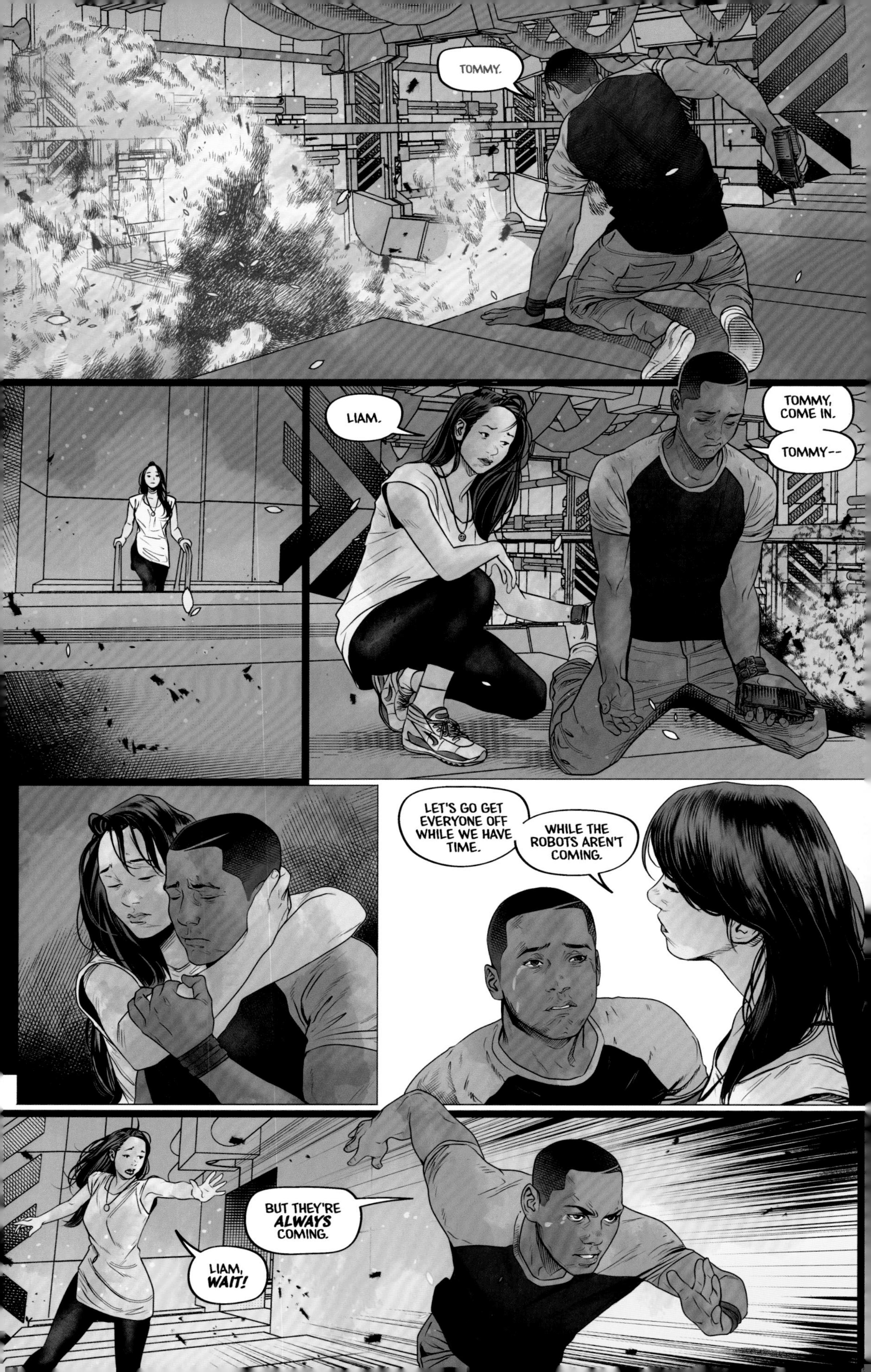
TOMMY.
LIAM.
TOMMY, COME IN.
TOMMY--
LET'S GO GET EVERYONE OFF WHILE WE HAVE TIME.
WHILE THE ROBOTS AREN'T COMING.
BUT THEY'RE *ALWAYS* COMING.
LIAM, *WAIT!*

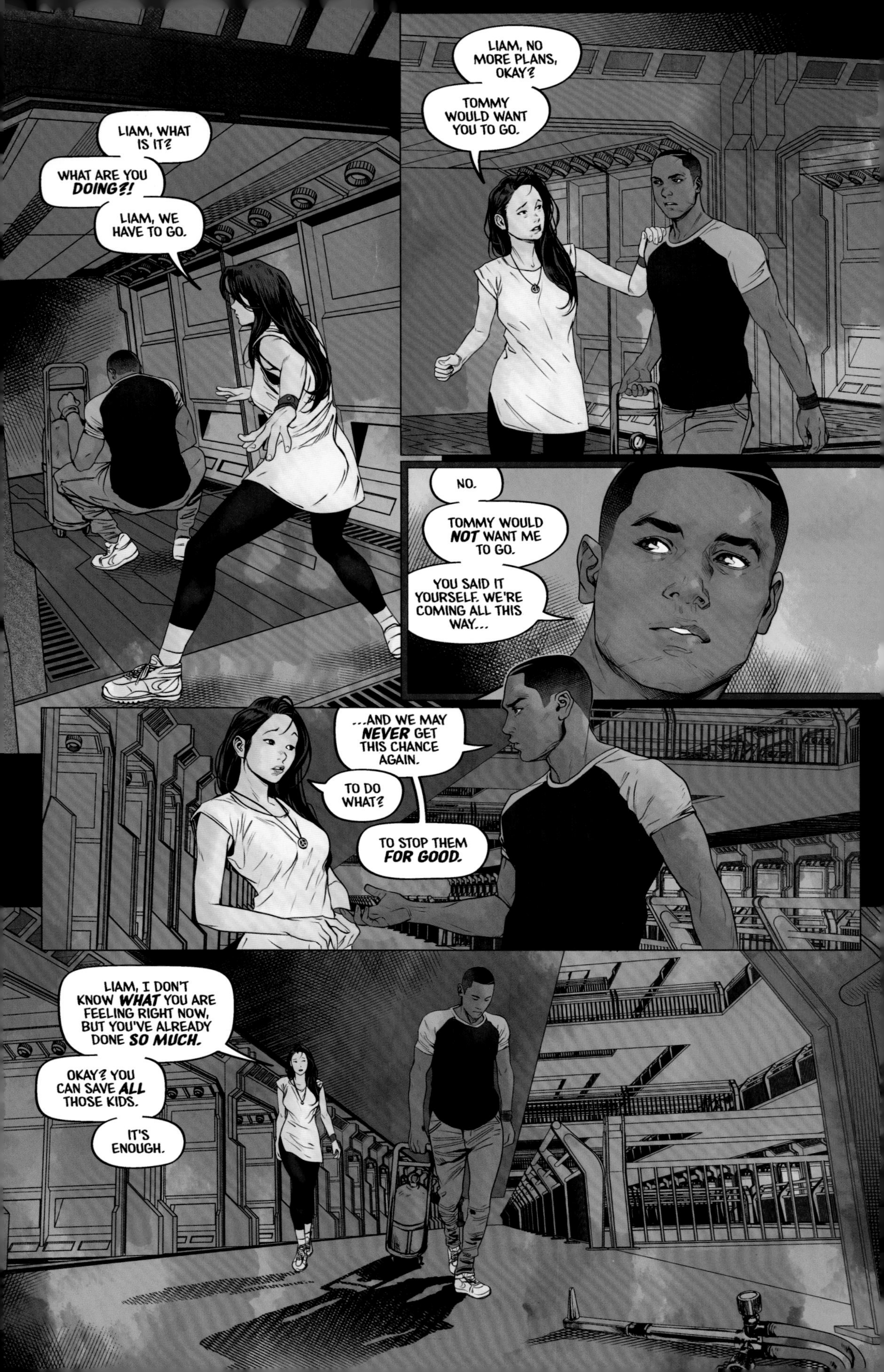
LIAM, WHAT IS IT?
WHAT ARE YOU DOING?!
LIAM, WE HAVE TO GO.
LIAM, NO MORE PLANS, OKAY?
TOMMY WOULD WANT YOU TO GO.
NO.
TOMMY WOULD NOT WANT ME TO GO.
YOU SAID IT YOURSELF. WE'RE COMING ALL THIS WAY...
...AND WE MAY NEVER GET THIS CHANCE AGAIN.
TO DO WHAT?
TO STOP THEM FOR GOOD.
LIAM, I DON'T KNOW WHAT YOU ARE FEELING RIGHT NOW, BUT YOU'VE ALREADY DONE SO MUCH.
OKAY? YOU CAN SAVE ALL THOSE KIDS.
IT'S ENOUGH.

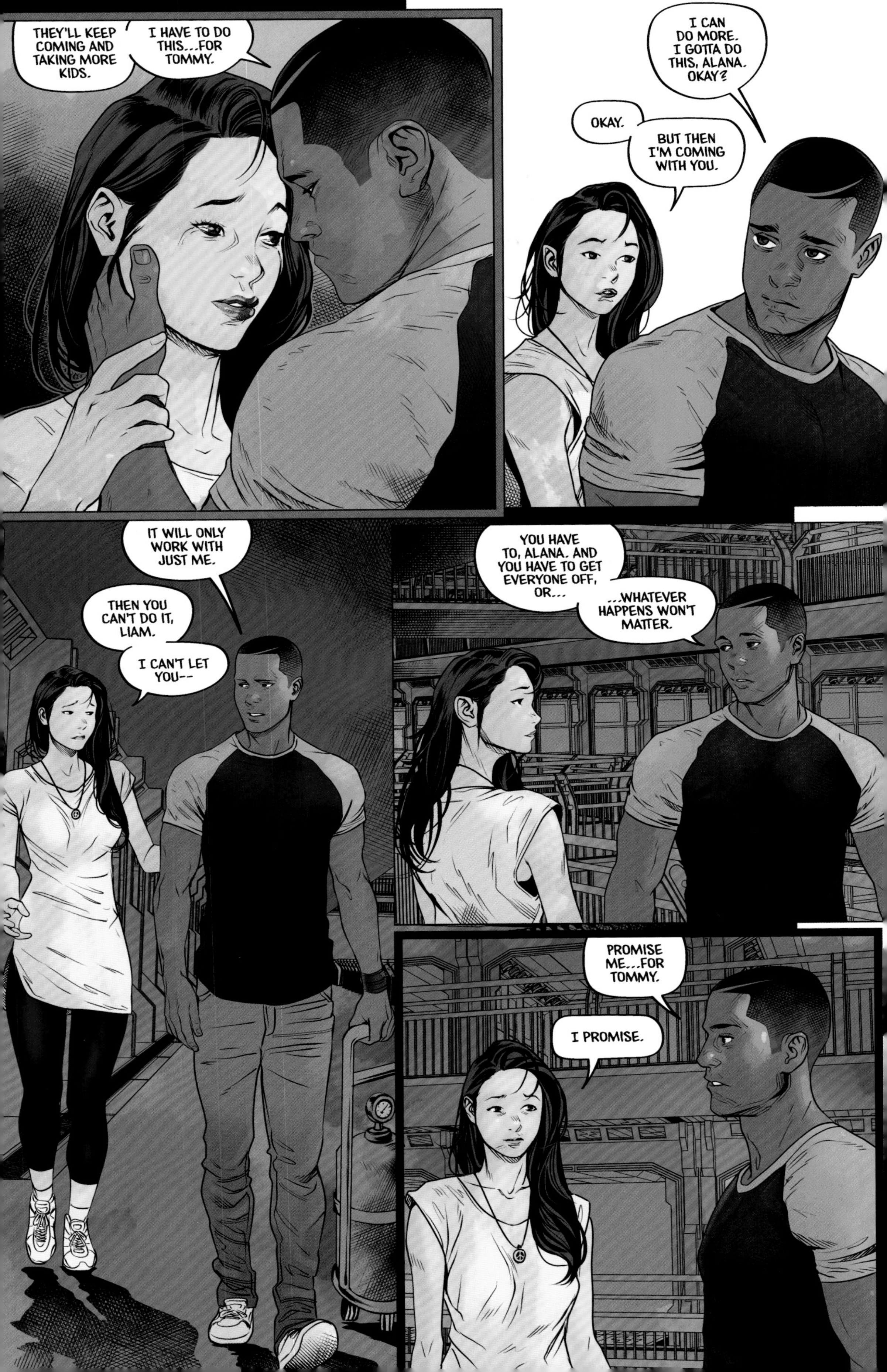
THEY'LL KEEP COMING AND TAKING MORE KIDS.
I HAVE TO DO THIS...FOR TOMMY.
I CAN DO MORE. I GOTTA DO THIS, ALANA. OKAY?
OKAY.
BUT THEN I'M COMING WITH YOU.
IT WILL ONLY WORK WITH JUST ME.
THEN YOU CAN'T DO IT, LIAM.
I CAN'T LET YOU--
YOU HAVE TO, ALANA. AND YOU HAVE TO GET EVERYONE OFF, OR...
...WHATEVER HAPPENS WON'T MATTER.
PROMISE ME...FOR TOMMY.
I PROMISE.

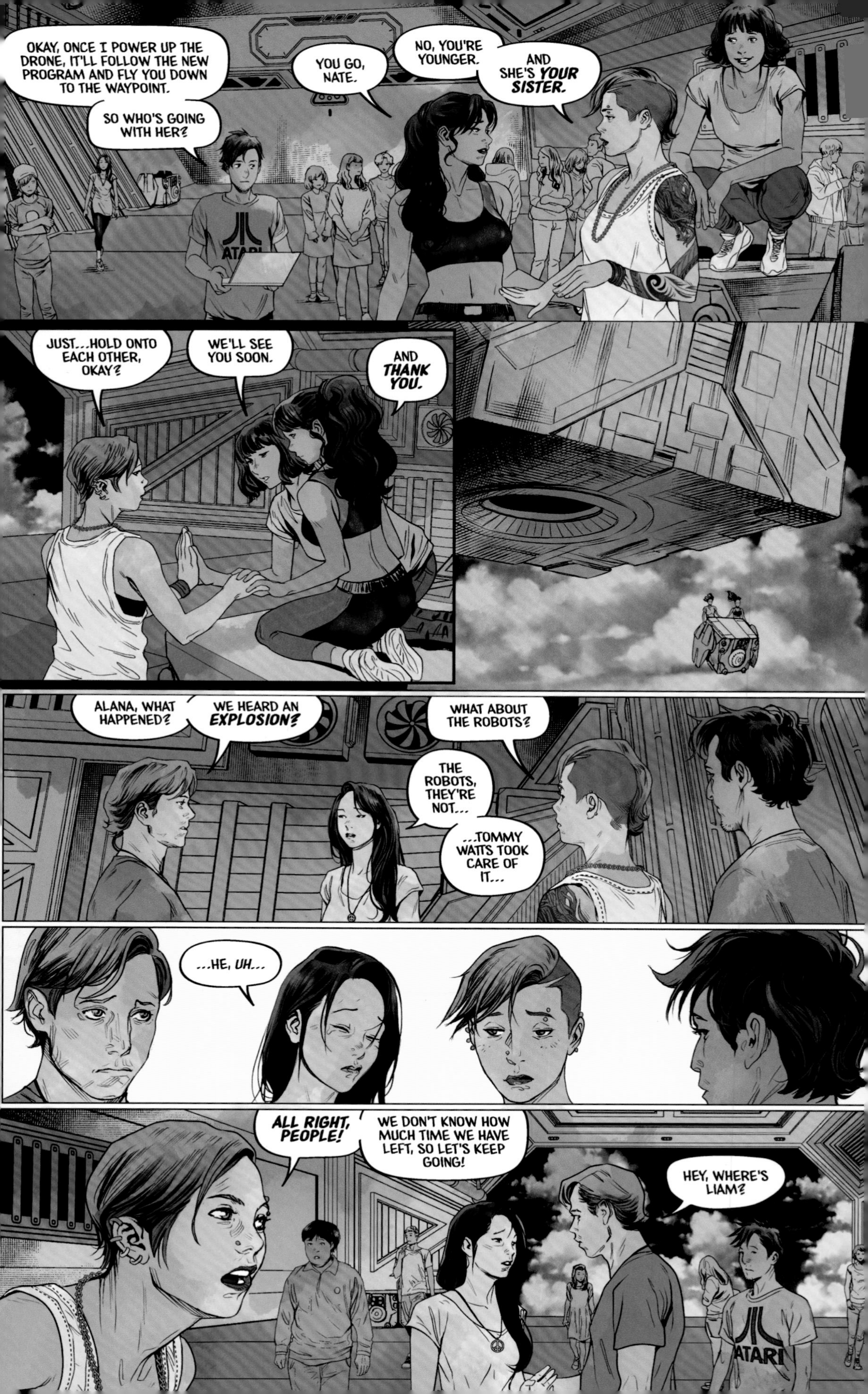
OKAY, ONCE I POWER UP THE DRONE, IT'LL FOLLOW THE NEW PROGRAM AND FLY YOU DOWN TO THE WAYPOINT.
SO WHO'S GOING WITH HER?
YOU GO, NATE.
NO, YOU'RE YOUNGER.
AND SHE'S YOUR SISTER.
JUST...HOLD ONTO EACH OTHER, OKAY?
WE'LL SEE YOU SOON.
AND THANK YOU.
ALANA, WHAT HAPPENED?
WE HEARD AN EXPLOSION?
WHAT ABOUT THE ROBOTS?
THE ROBOTS, THEY'RE NOT...
...TOMMY WATTS TOOK CARE OF IT...
...HE, UH...
ALL RIGHT, PEOPLE!
WE DON'T KNOW HOW MUCH TIME WE HAVE LEFT, SO LET'S KEEP GOING!
HEY, WHERE'S LIAM?

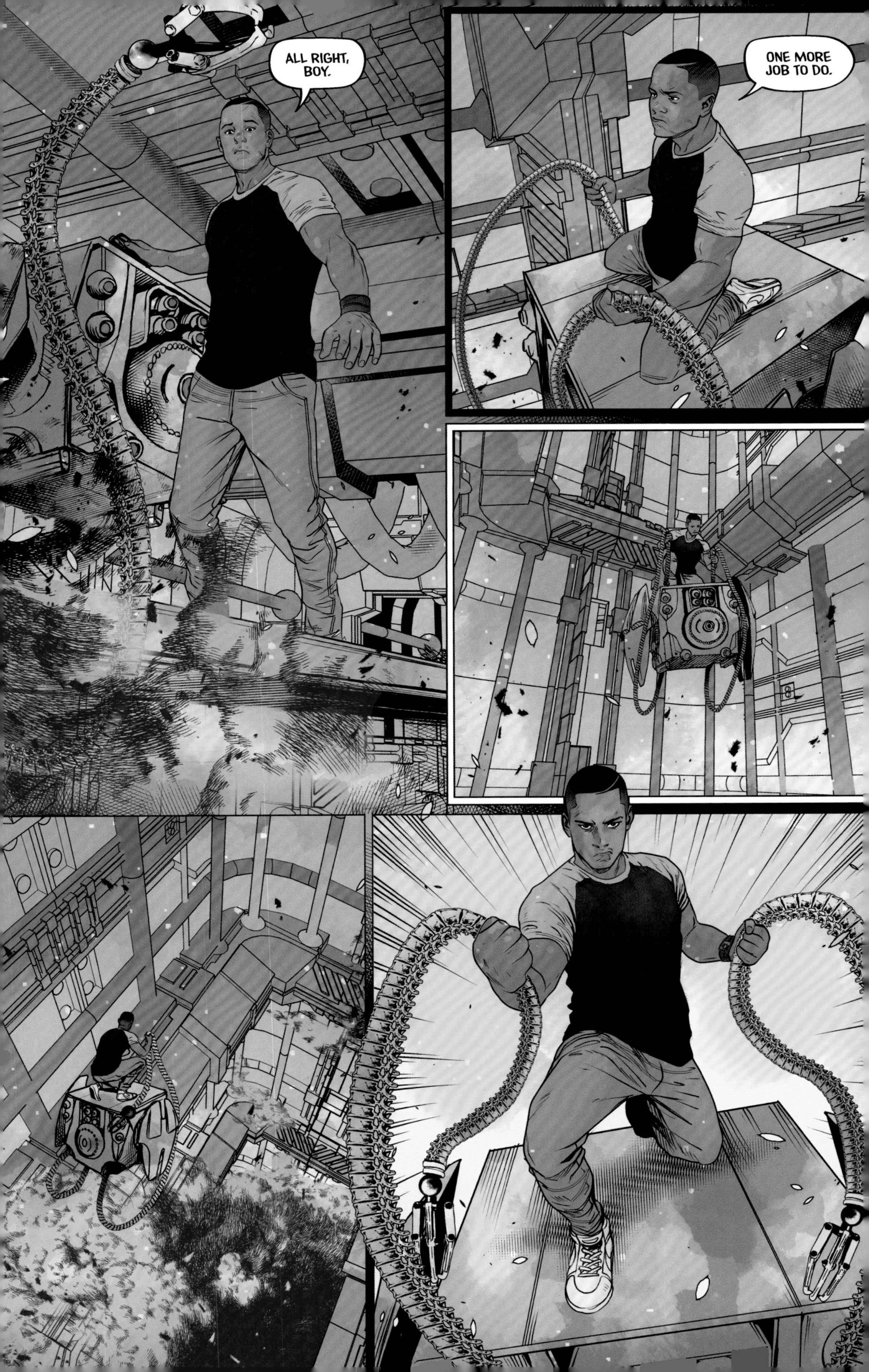
ALL RIGHT, BOY.
ONE MORE JOB TO DO.

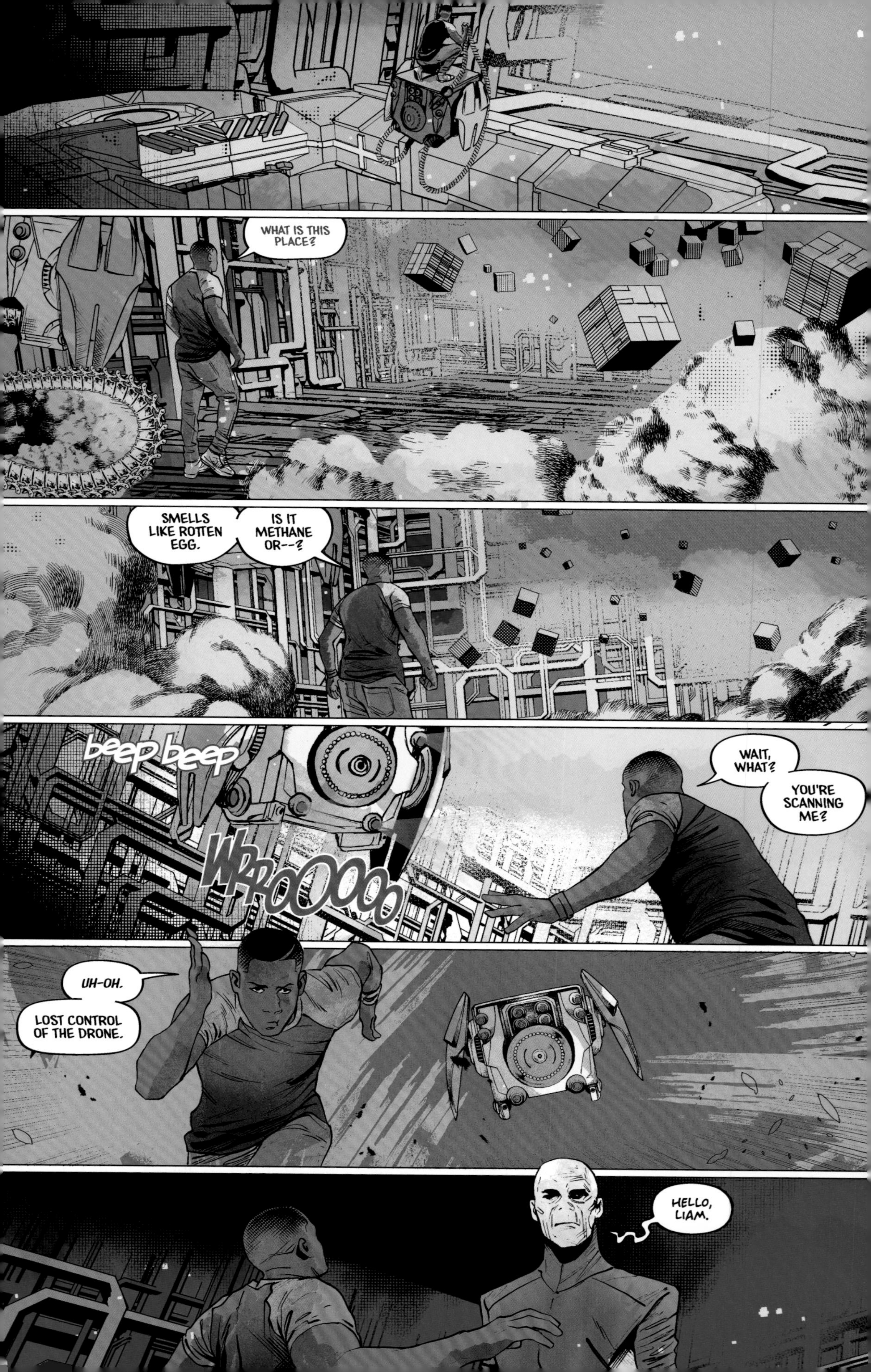
WHAT IS THIS PLACE?
SMELLS LIKE ROTTEN EGG.
IS IT METHANE OR--?
beep beep
WRROOOOOO
WAIT, WHAT?
YOU'RE SCANNING ME?
UH-OH.
LOST CONTROL OF THE DRONE.
HELLO, LIAM.

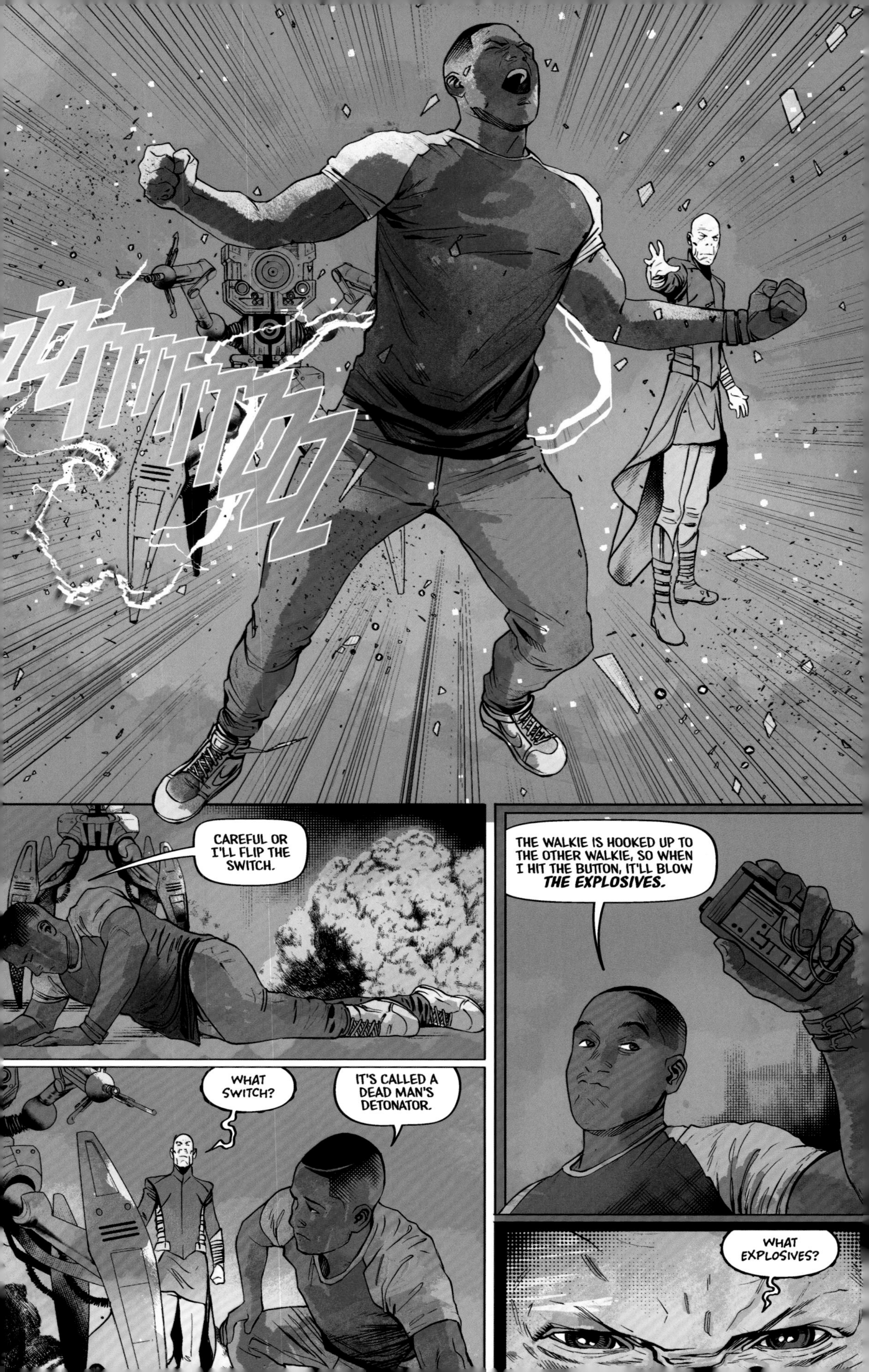
ZZTTTTTTZZZ
CAREFUL OR I'LL FLIP THE SWITCH.
THE WALKIE IS HOOKED UP TO THE OTHER WALKIE, SO WHEN I HIT THE BUTTON, IT'LL BLOW THE EXPLOSIVES.
WHAT SWITCH?
IT'S CALLED A DEAD MAN'S DETONATOR.
WHAT EXPLOSIVES?

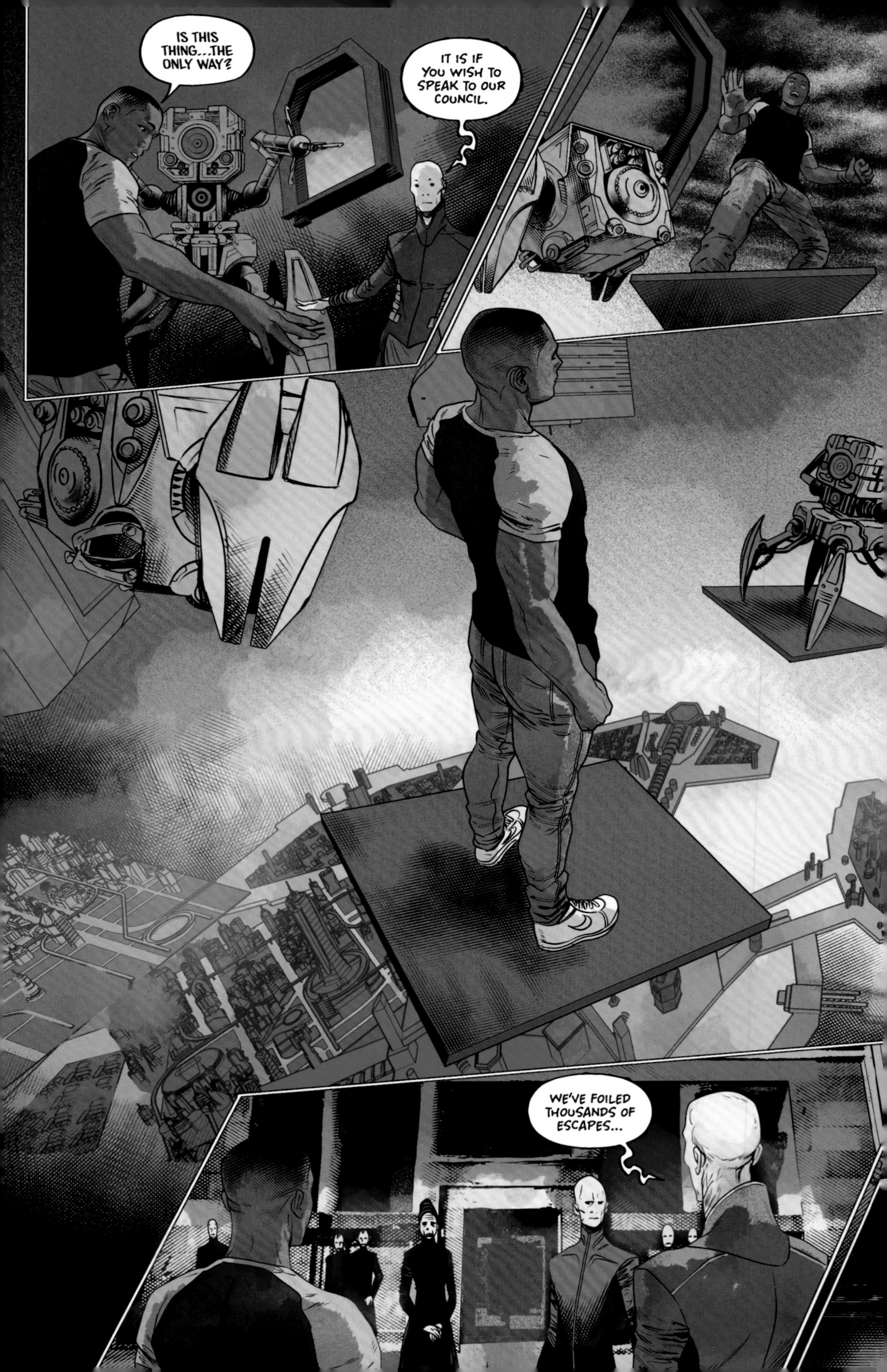
IS THIS THING...THE ONLY WAY?
IT IS IF YOU WISH TO SPEAK TO OUR COUNCIL.
WE'VE FOILED THOUSANDS OF ESCAPES...

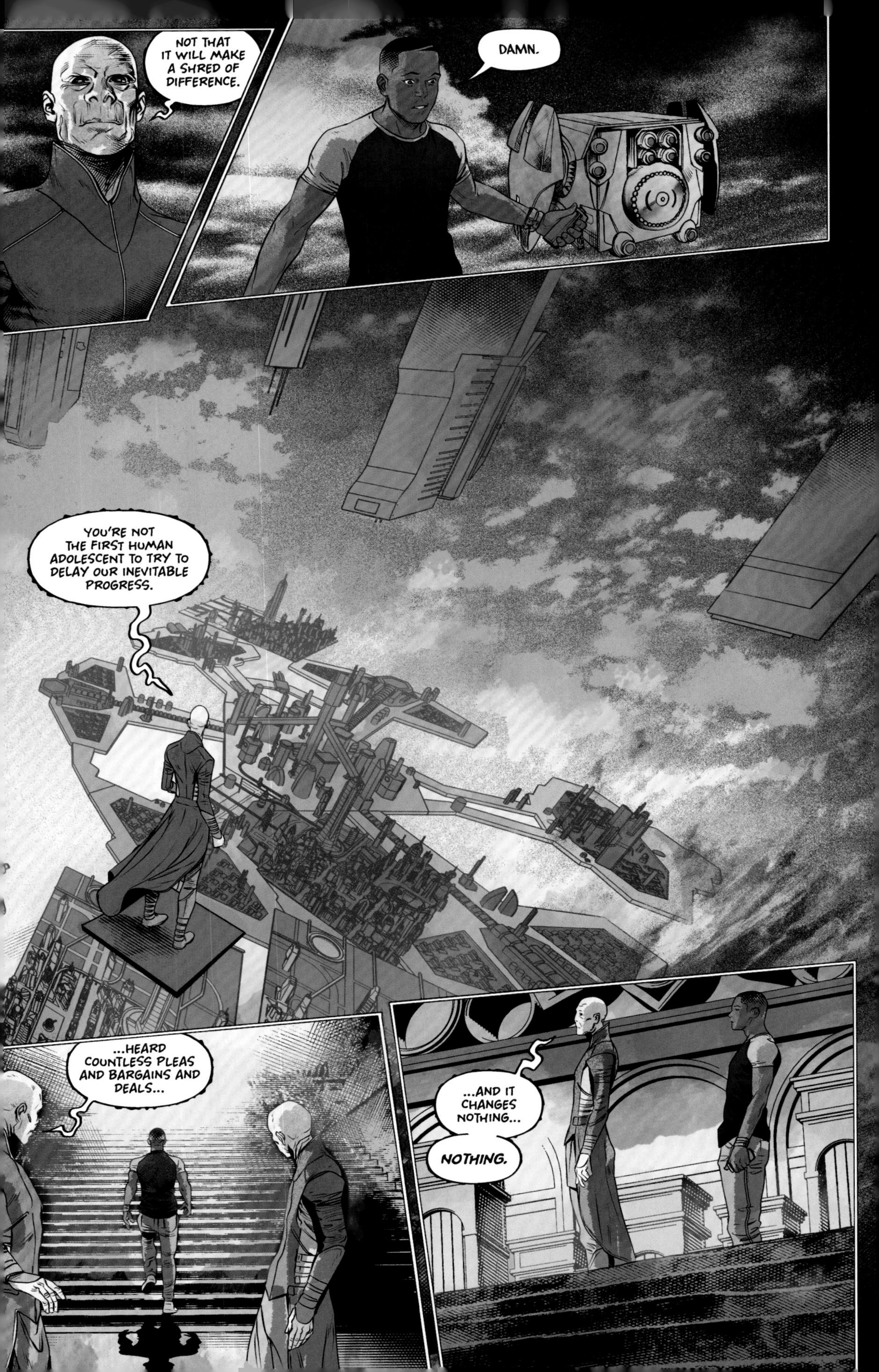
NOT THAT IT WILL MAKE A SHRED OF DIFFERENCE.
DAMN.
YOU'RE NOT THE FIRST HUMAN ADOLESCENT TO TRY TO DELAY OUR INEVITABLE PROGRESS.
...HEARD COUNTLESS PLEAS AND BARGAINS AND DEALS...
...AND IT CHANGES NOTHING...
NOTHING.

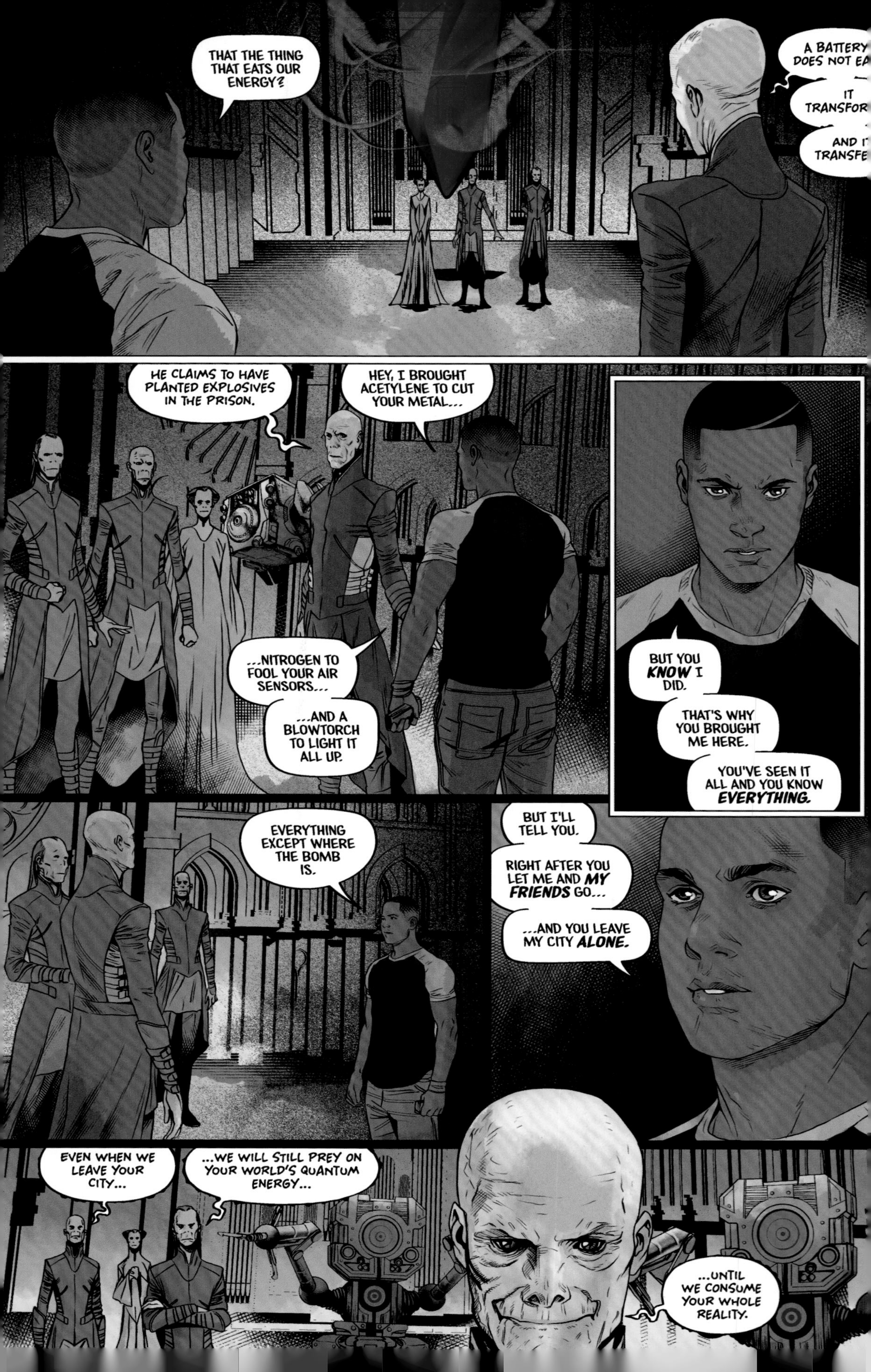
THAT THE THING THAT EATS OUR ENERGY?
A BATTERY DOES NOT EA
IT TRANSFOR
AND I TRANSFE
HE CLAIMS TO HAVE PLANTED EXPLOSIVES IN THE PRISON.
HEY, I BROUGHT ACETYLENE TO CUT YOUR METAL...
...NITROGEN TO FOOL YOUR AIR SENSORS...
...AND A BLOWTORCH TO LIGHT IT ALL UP.
BUT YOU KNOW I DID.
THAT'S WHY YOU BROUGHT ME HERE.
YOU'VE SEEN IT ALL AND YOU KNOW EVERYTHING.
EVERYTHING EXCEPT WHERE THE BOMB IS.
BUT I'LL TELL YOU.
RIGHT AFTER YOU LET ME AND MY FRIENDS GO...
...AND YOU LEAVE MY CITY ALONE.
EVEN WHEN WE LEAVE YOUR CITY...
...WE WILL STILL PREY ON YOUR WORLD'S QUANTUM ENERGY...
...UNTIL WE CONSUME YOUR WHOLE REALITY.

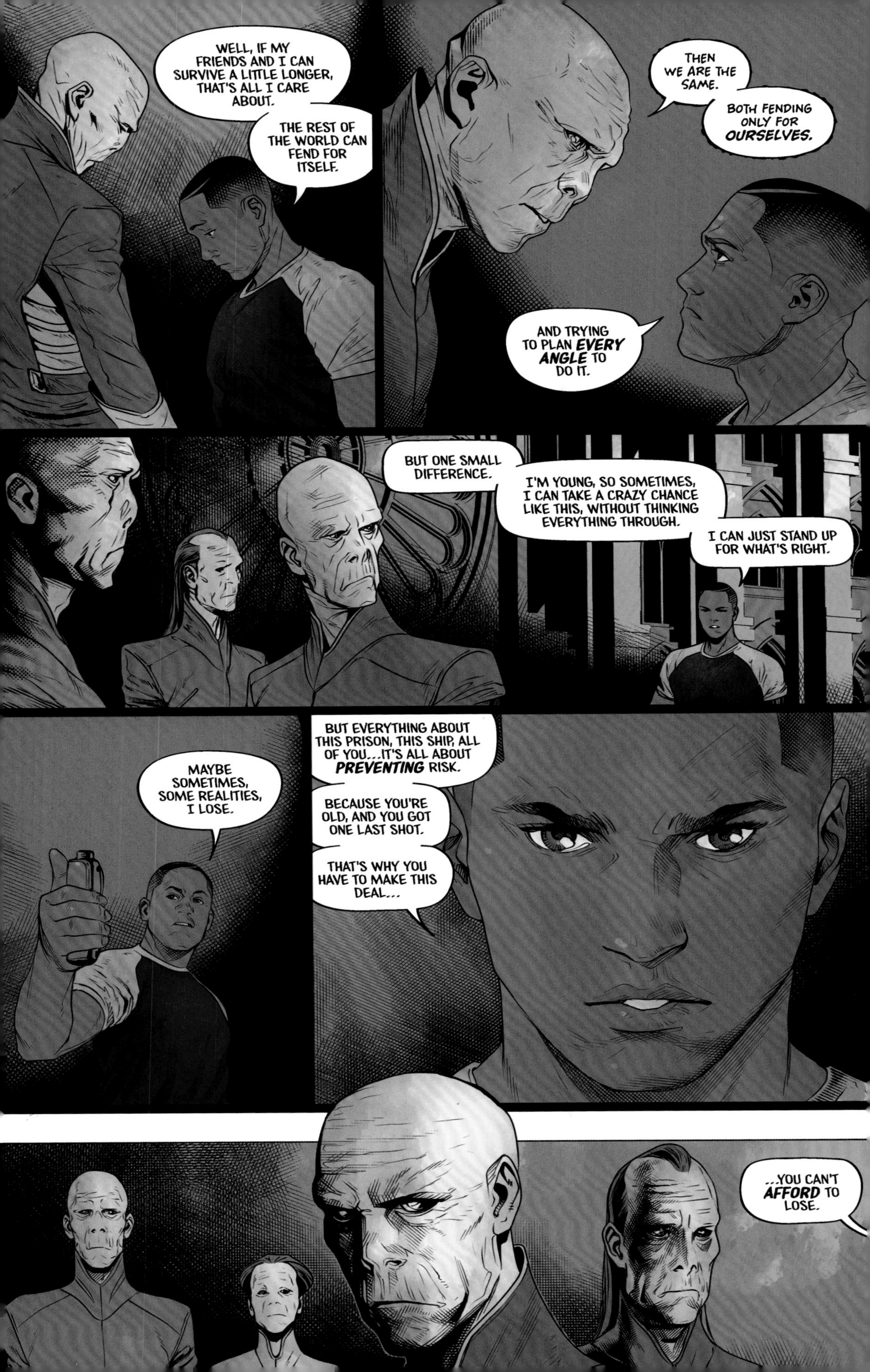
WELL, IF MY FRIENDS AND I CAN SURVIVE A LITTLE LONGER, THAT'S ALL I CARE ABOUT.
THE REST OF THE WORLD CAN FEND FOR ITSELF.
THEN WE ARE THE SAME.
BOTH FENDING ONLY FOR OURSELVES.
AND TRYING TO PLAN EVERY ANGLE TO DO IT.
BUT ONE SMALL DIFFERENCE.
I'M YOUNG, SO SOMETIMES, I CAN TAKE A CRAZY CHANCE LIKE THIS, WITHOUT THINKING EVERYTHING THROUGH.
I CAN JUST STAND UP FOR WHAT'S RIGHT.
MAYBE SOMETIMES, SOME REALITIES, I LOSE.
BUT EVERYTHING ABOUT THIS PRISON, THIS SHIP, ALL OF YOU...IT'S ALL ABOUT PREVENTING RISK.
BECAUSE YOU'RE OLD, AND YOU GOT ONE LAST SHOT.
THAT'S WHY YOU HAVE TO MAKE THIS DEAL...
...YOU CAN'T AFFORD TO LOSE.

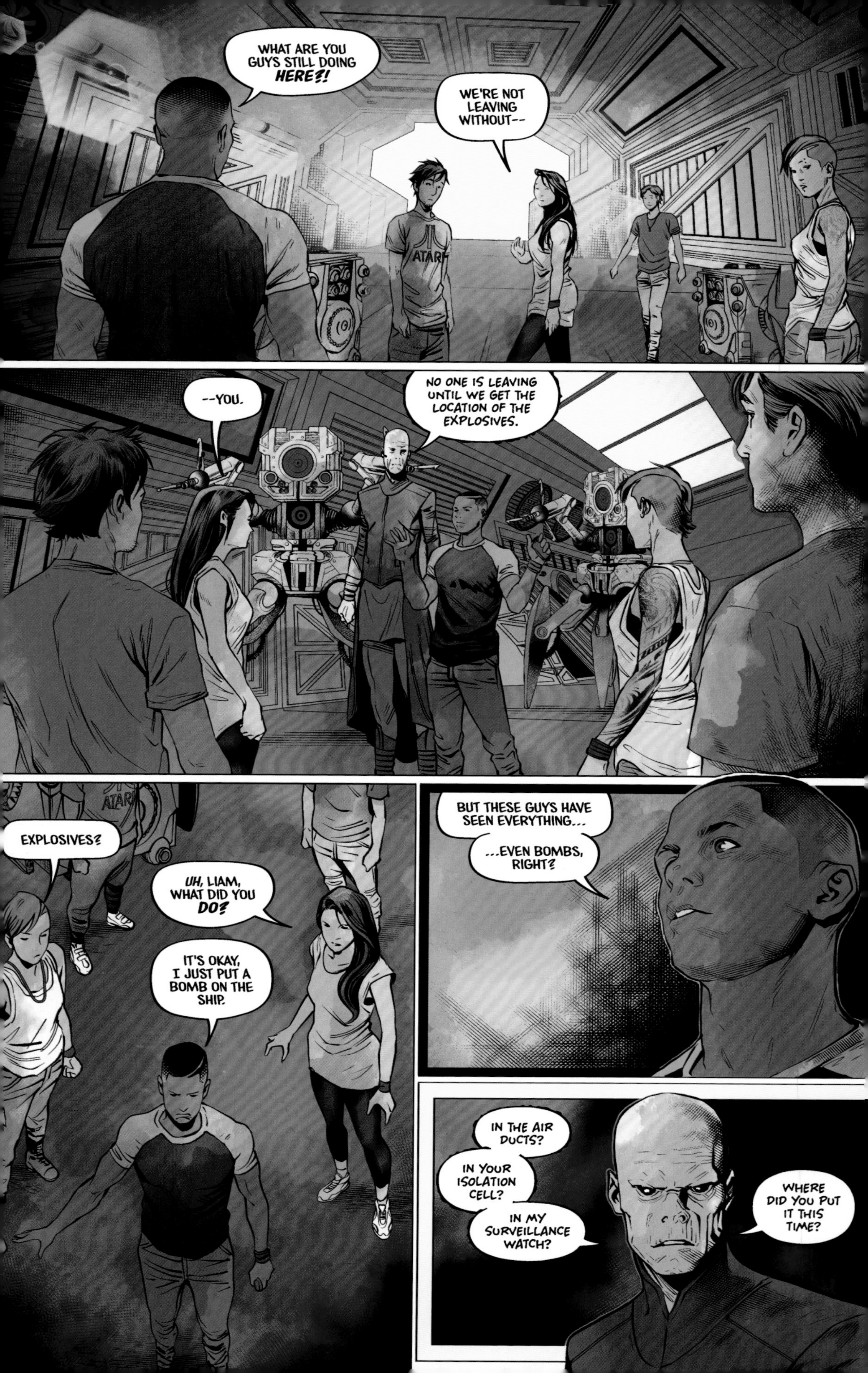
WHAT ARE YOU GUYS STILL DOING HERE?!
WE'RE NOT LEAVING WITHOUT--
ATARI
--YOU.
NO ONE IS LEAVING UNTIL WE GET THE LOCATION OF THE EXPLOSIVES.
EXPLOSIVES?
UH, LIAM, WHAT DID YOU DO?
IT'S OKAY, I JUST PUT A BOMB ON THE SHIP.
BUT THESE GUYS HAVE SEEN EVERYTHING...
...EVEN BOMBS, RIGHT?
IN THE AIR DUCTS?
IN YOUR ISOLATION CELL?
IN MY SURVEILLANCE WATCH?
WHERE DID YOU PUT IT THIS TIME?

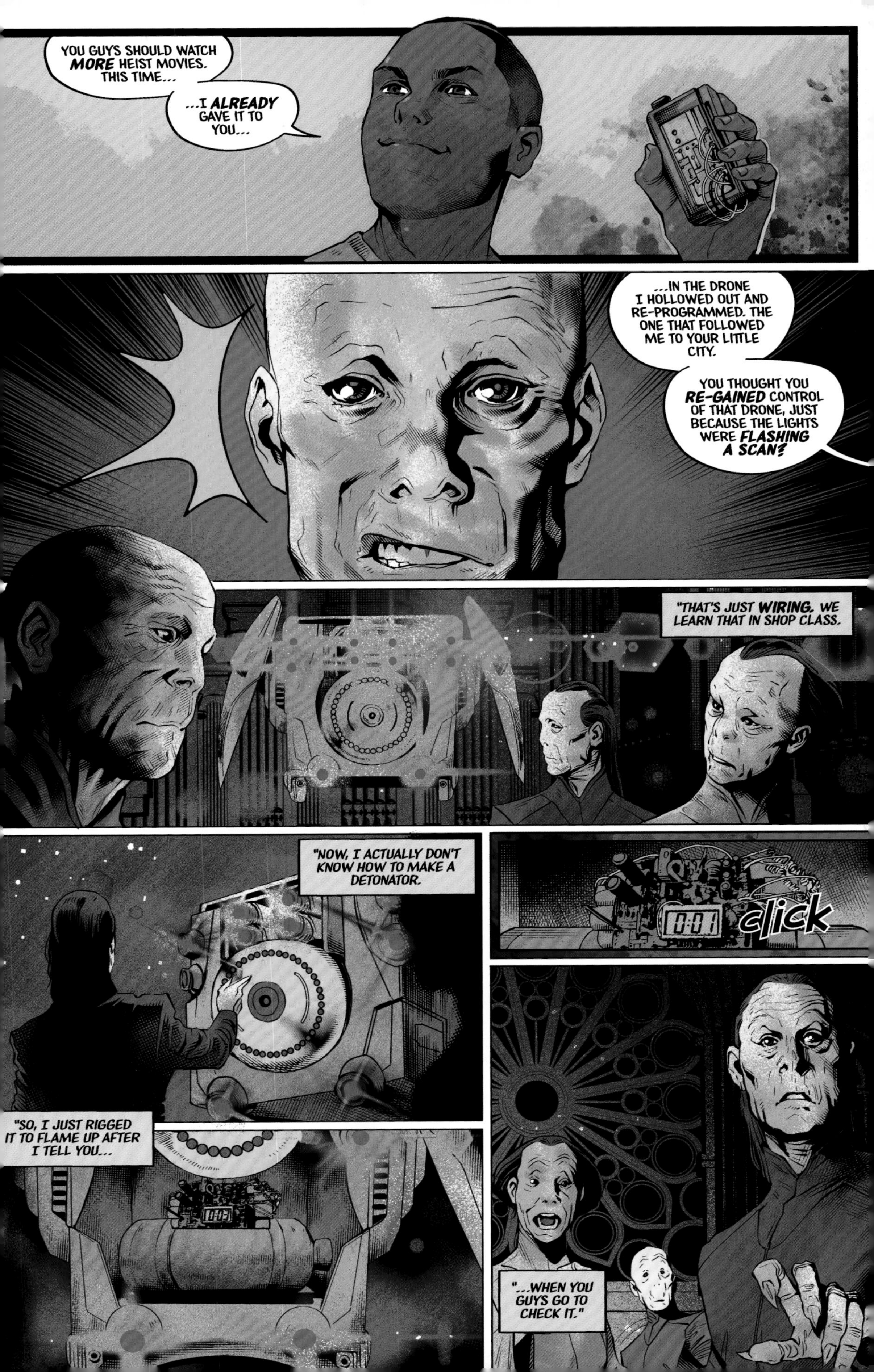

YOU GUYS SHOULD WATCH MORE HEIST MOVIES. THIS TIME...
...I ALREADY GAVE IT TO YOU...
...IN THE DRONE I HOLLOWED OUT AND RE-PROGRAMMED. THE ONE THAT FOLLOWED ME TO YOUR LITTLE CITY.
YOU THOUGHT YOU RE-GAINED CONTROL OF THAT DRONE, JUST BECAUSE THE LIGHTS WERE FLASHING A SCAN?
"THAT'S JUST WIRING. WE LEARN THAT IN SHOP CLASS.
"NOW, I ACTUALLY DON'T KNOW HOW TO MAKE A DETONATOR.
0:01
click
"SO, I JUST RIGGED IT TO FLAME UP AFTER I TELL YOU...
"...WHEN YOU GUYS GO TO CHECK IT."

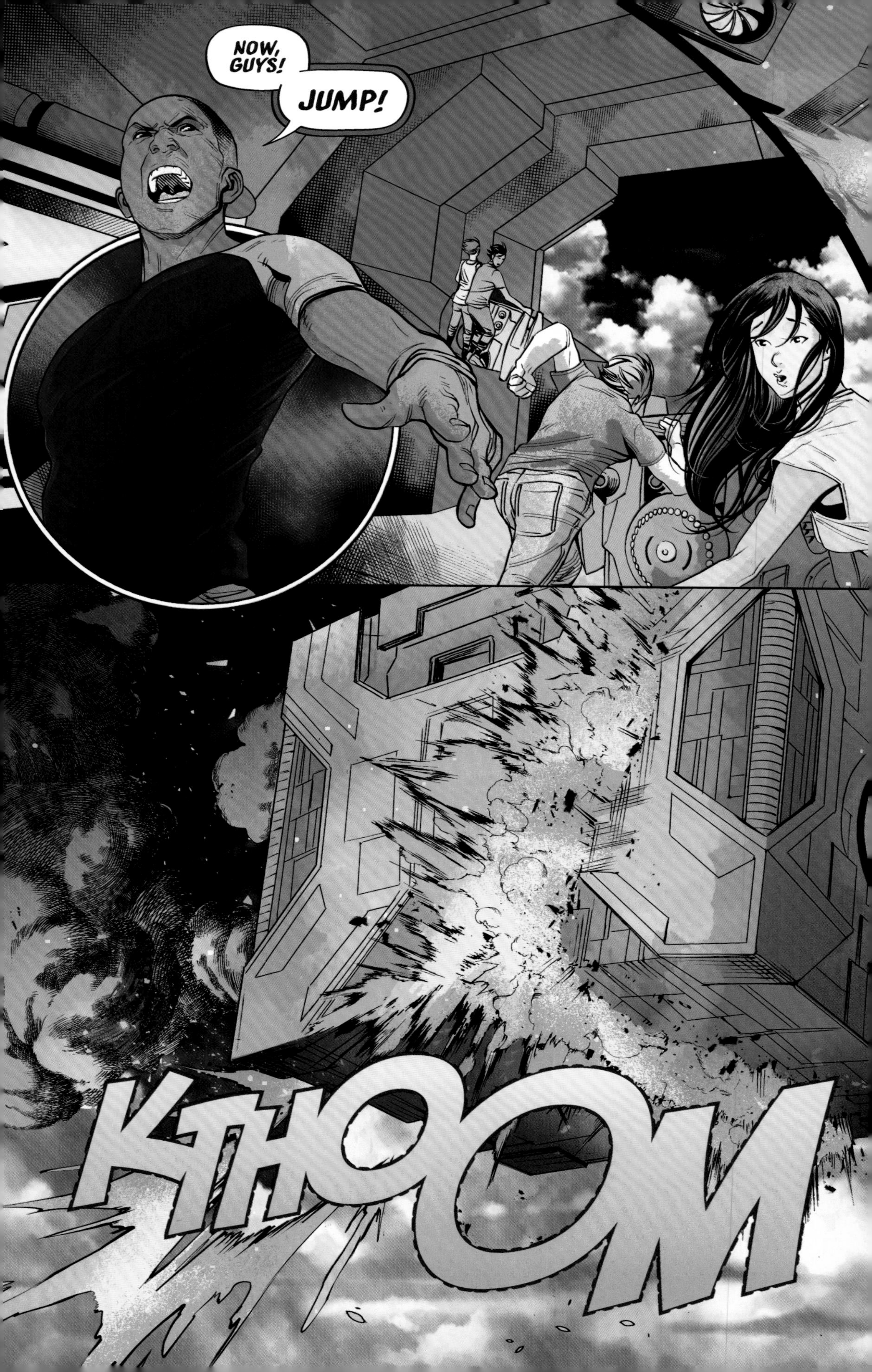
NOW, GUYS!
JUMP!
KHOOM

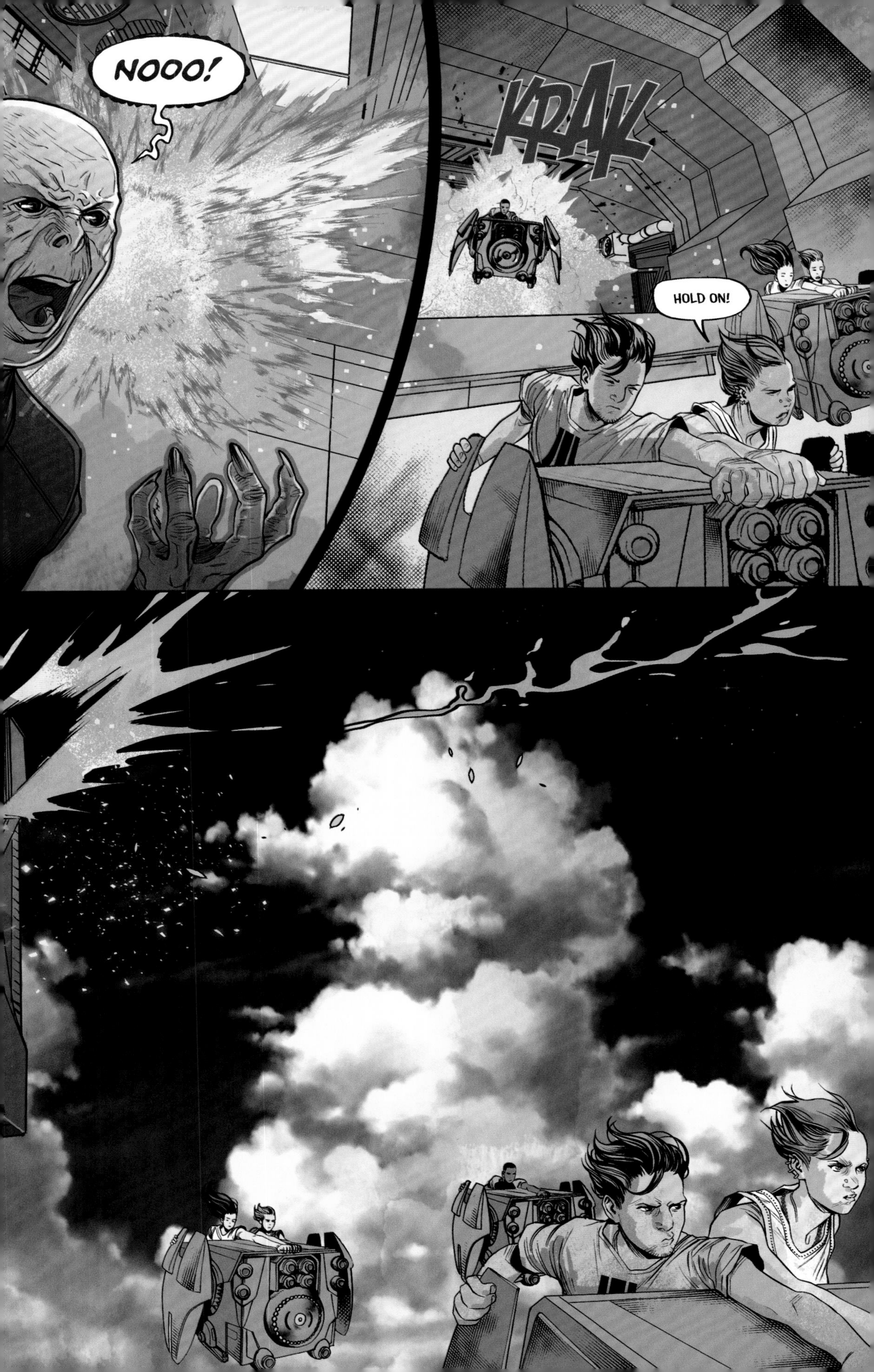
NOOO!
KRAK
HOLD ON!

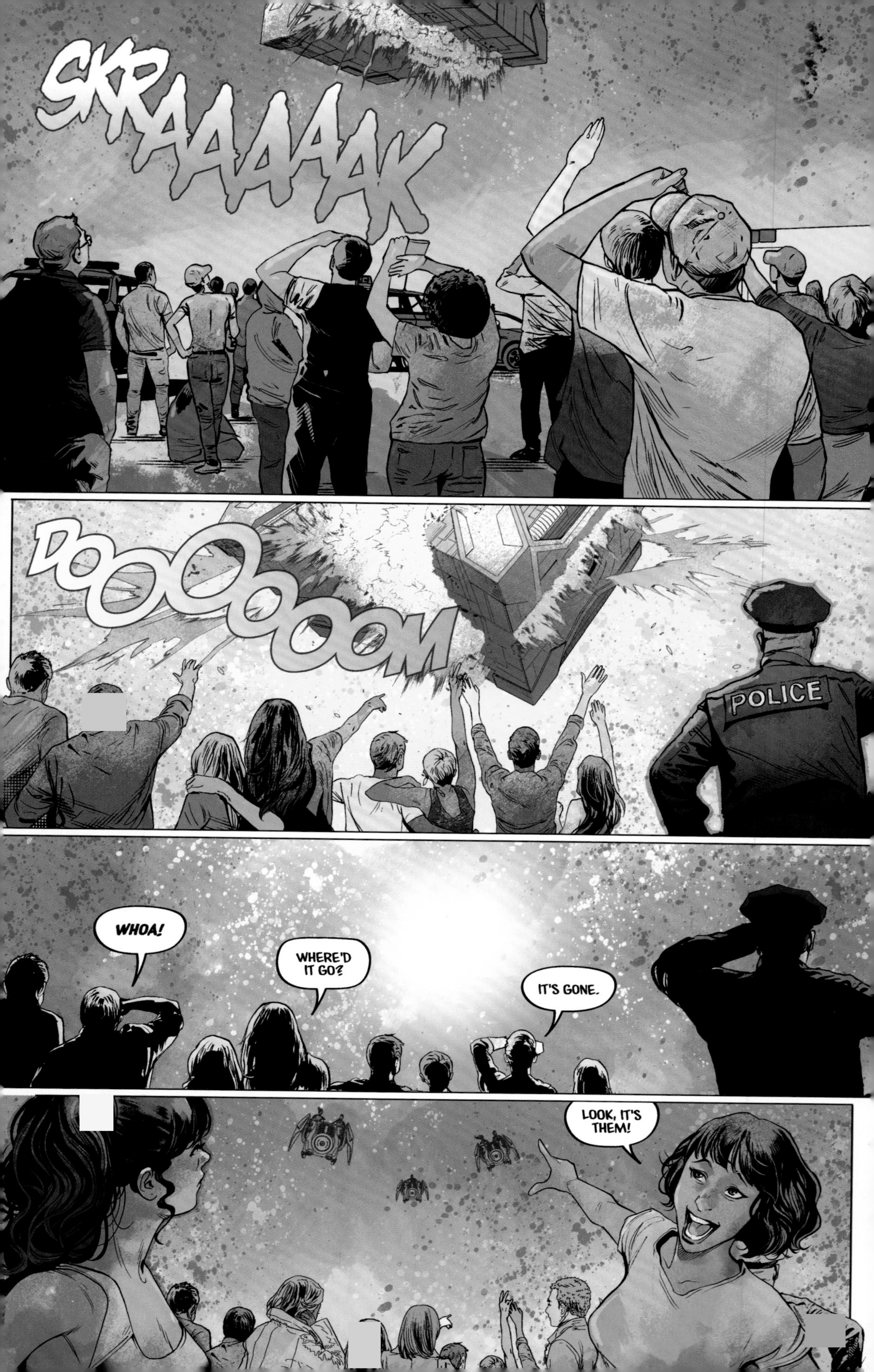
SKRAAAAAK
DOOOOOOOM
POLICE
WHOA!
WHERE'D IT GO?
IT'S GONE.
LOOK, IT'S THEM!

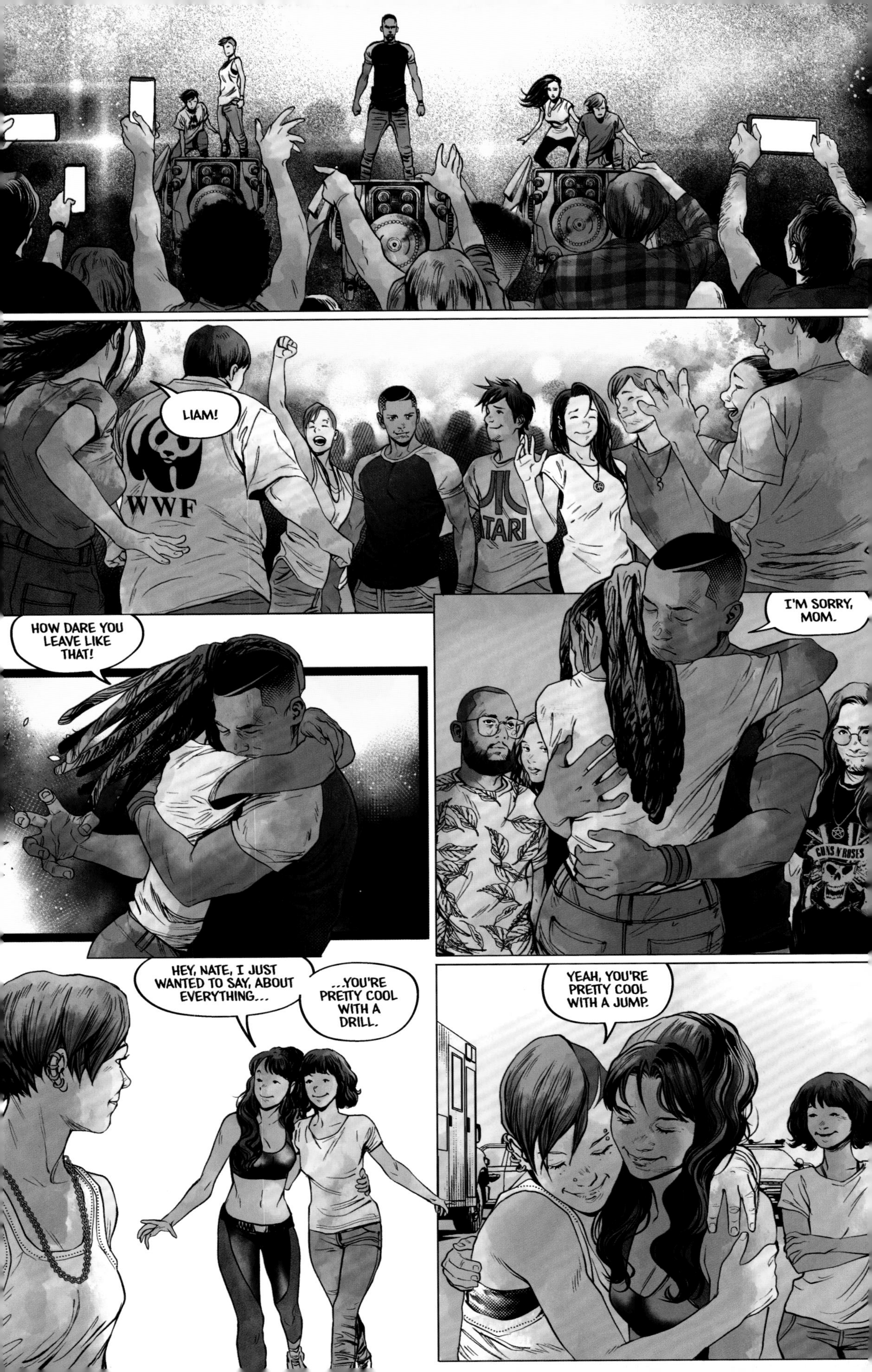

LIAM!
HOW DARE YOU LEAVE LIKE THAT!
I'M SORRY, MOM.
HEY, NATE, I JUST WANTED TO SAY, ABOUT EVERYTHING...
...YOU'RE PRETTY COOL WITH A DRILL.
YEAH, YOU'RE PRETTY COOL WITH A JUMP.

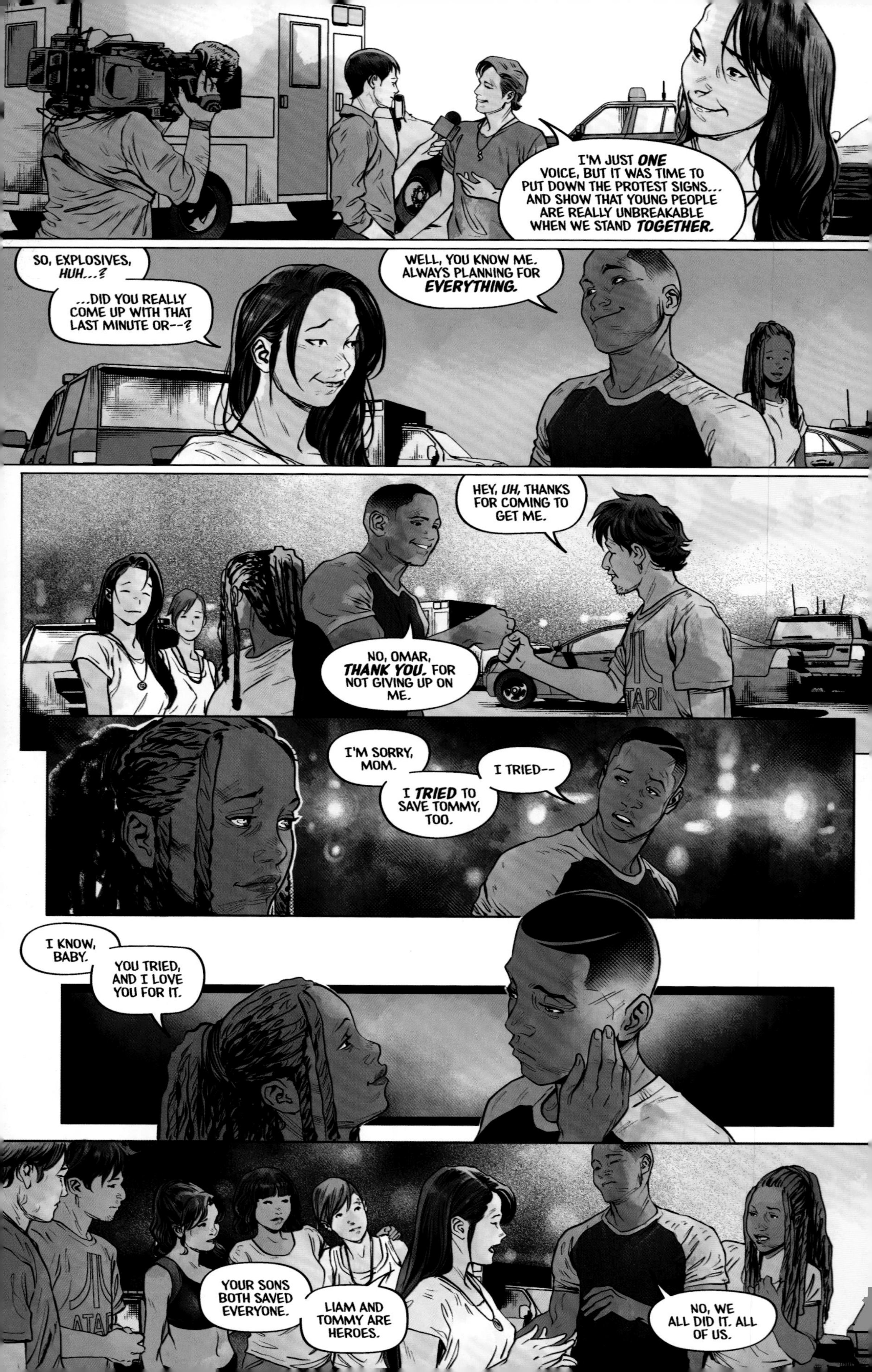
I'M JUST ONE VOICE, BUT IT WAS TIME TO PUT DOWN THE PROTEST SIGNS... AND SHOW THAT YOUNG PEOPLE ARE REALLY UNBREAKABLE WHEN WE STAND TOGETHER.
SO, EXPLOSIVES, HUH...?
...DID YOU REALLY COME UP WITH THAT LAST MINUTE OR--?
WELL, YOU KNOW ME. ALWAYS PLANNING FOR EVERYTHING.
HEY, UH, THANKS FOR COMING TO GET ME.
NO, OMAR, THANK YOU. FOR NOT GIVING UP ON ME.
I'M SORRY, MOM.
I TRIED--
I TRIED TO SAVE TOMMY, TOO.
I KNOW, BABY.
YOU TRIED, AND I LOVE YOU FOR IT.
YOUR SONS BOTH SAVED EVERYONE.
LIAM AND TOMMY ARE HEROES.
NO, WE ALL DID IT. ALL OF US.

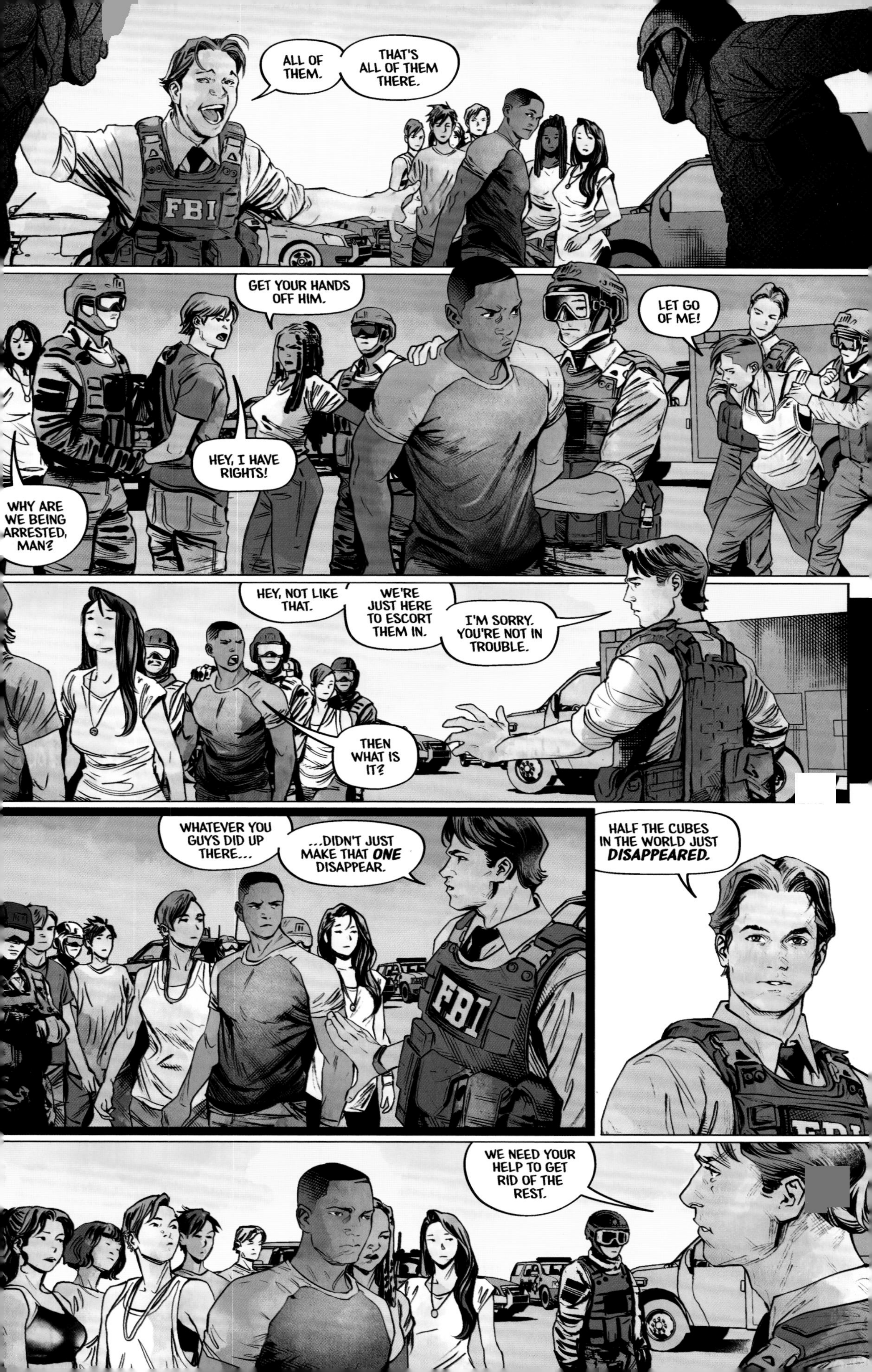
ALL OF THEM.
THAT'S ALL OF THEM THERE.
GET YOUR HANDS OFF HIM.
LET GO OF ME!
HEY, I HAVE RIGHTS!
WHY ARE WE BEING ARRESTED, MAN?
HEY, NOT LIKE THAT.
WE'RE JUST HERE TO ESCORT THEM IN.
I'M SORRY. YOU'RE NOT IN TROUBLE.
THEN WHAT IS IT?
WHATEVER YOU GUYS DID UP THERE...
...DIDN'T JUST MAKE THAT ONE DISAPPEAR.
HALF THE CUBES IN THE WORLD JUST DISAPPEARED.
WE NEED YOUR HELP TO GET RID OF THE REST.

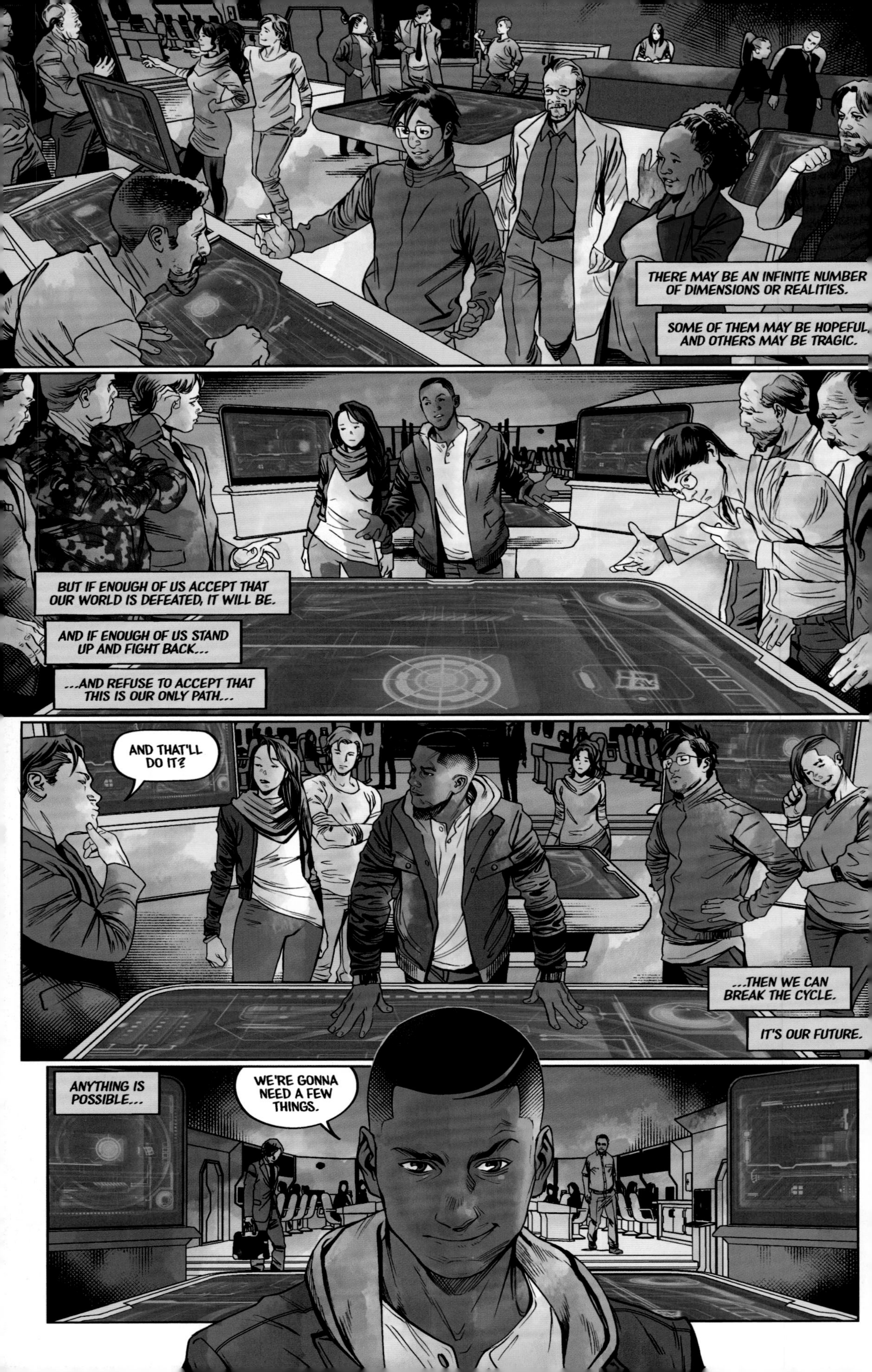
THERE MAY BE AN INFINITE NUMBER OF DIMENSIONS OR REALITIES.
SOME OF THEM MAY BE HOPEFUL, AND OTHERS MAY BE TRAGIC.
BUT IF ENOUGH OF US ACCEPT THAT OUR WORLD IS DEFEATED, IT WILL BE.
AND IF ENOUGH OF US STAND UP AND FIGHT BACK...
...AND REFUSE TO ACCEPT THAT THIS IS OUR ONLY PATH...
AND THAT'LL DO IT?
...THEN WE CAN BREAK THE CYCLE.
IT'S OUR FUTURE.
ANYTHING IS POSSIBLE...
WE'RE GONNA NEED A FEW THINGS.

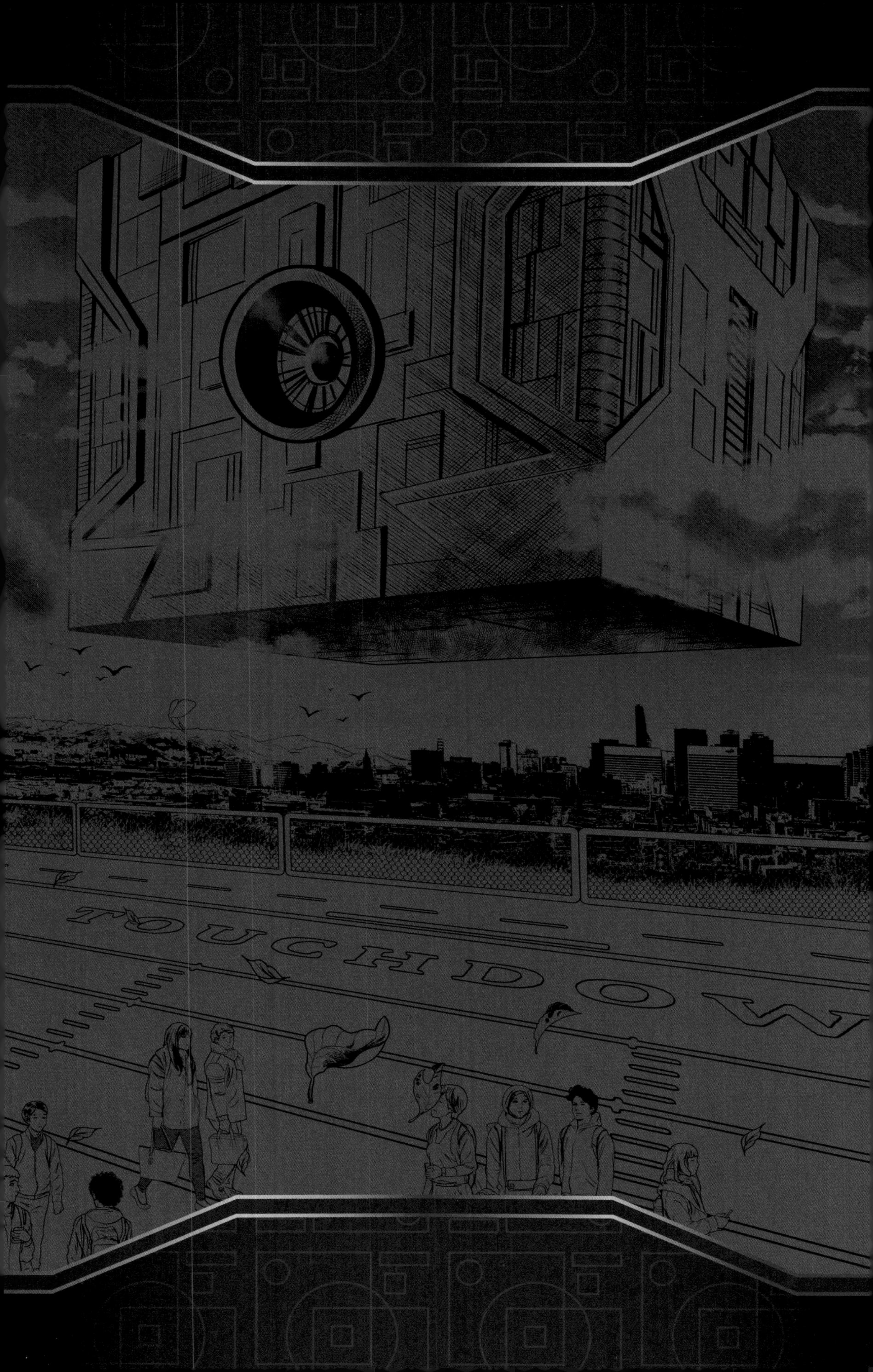
TOUCHDOW

I NEVER HAD TO HIDE UNDER MY DESK FOR AN ACTIVE-SHOOTER DRILL. I DIDN'T GROW UP WORRYING ABOUT OUR AIR BECOMING TOO TOXIC WITH ASH TO BREATHE. AS A CHILD, I HARDLY EVER WONDERED ABOUT THE SAFETY OF MY DRINKING WATER, LET ALONE THE FUTURE OF OUR PLANET OR OUR COUNTRY.

What the hell have we done?

Our young people are inheriting a world wrought with existential challenges and out-of-control crises. And older generations—and by *older*, I mean my generation, too—have all allowed ourselves to be overwhelmed by these conflicts while we settle with compromise, pragmatism, or heartless apathy. Our youth have never felt more abandoned, and these dilemmas are hanging over them like weights in the sky. And as a parent to young children, I'm ashamed.

BREAK OUT is a story of mysterious Cube spaceships that appear out of thin air all around the world. We don't know where they came from, but we know why they are here: to take young people. Only young people, between the ages of ten and twenty. Imprisoned in their strange floating detention centers. The Cubes don't respond to our calls. Our military can't stop them. And so our planet accepts the loss of young people simply as the new normal. Just go about your day, kids. Nothing to worry about.

The story centers on Liam Watts, a clever high-school senior whose younger brother, Tommy, is taken. So Liam does something unexpected. He studies the spaceships. He assembles a crew. And he plans a breakout.

While the plot of our series is a classic prison-break structure, underneath the cool sci-fi skin is a heartfelt story about losing those we love and how we transform that pain into action, change, and heroism. With such important subject matter, Dark Horse and the entire *BREAK OUT* creative team wanted to create a series that elevated an ordinary YA teenage adventure into a substantial, thought-provoking narrative. Wilton Santos, Jason Wordie, Jim Campbell, and I all tirelessly evaluated every creative choice to ensure the characters' ordinary world of entrapment and chaos would come across.

On the one hand, it's your standard YA teenage heist adventure, right? We definitely played with conventions from classic heist tales like *The Italian Job* and *Ocean's Eleven*, and we worked diligently to create the most impossible of escapes with an advanced interdimensional prison.

But this isn't *The Breakfast Club*.

Our series had to capture what it feels like to be a young person right now facing all this chaos. They face a normalization of fear and doubt. And we tell them to let it go.

But our youth are fighters. They may be the strongest generation yet. And they've had enough. This is a series about how young people fight back. How they save us.

How they BREAK OUT.

ZACK KAPLAN

ART BY FRANCESCO FRANCAVILLA

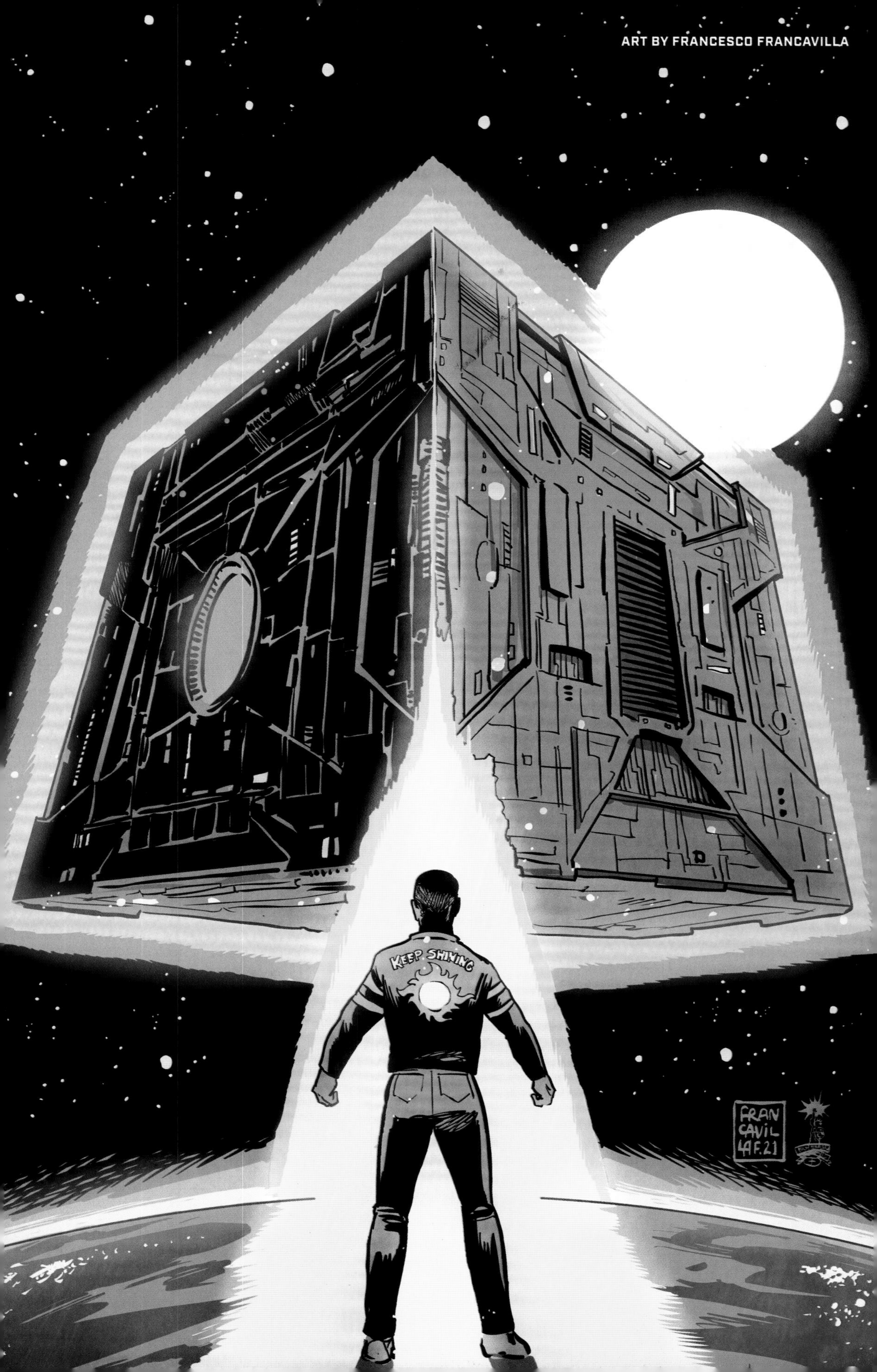
KEEP SHINING
FRAN
CAVIL
LA F.21

ART BY JACOB PHILLIPS

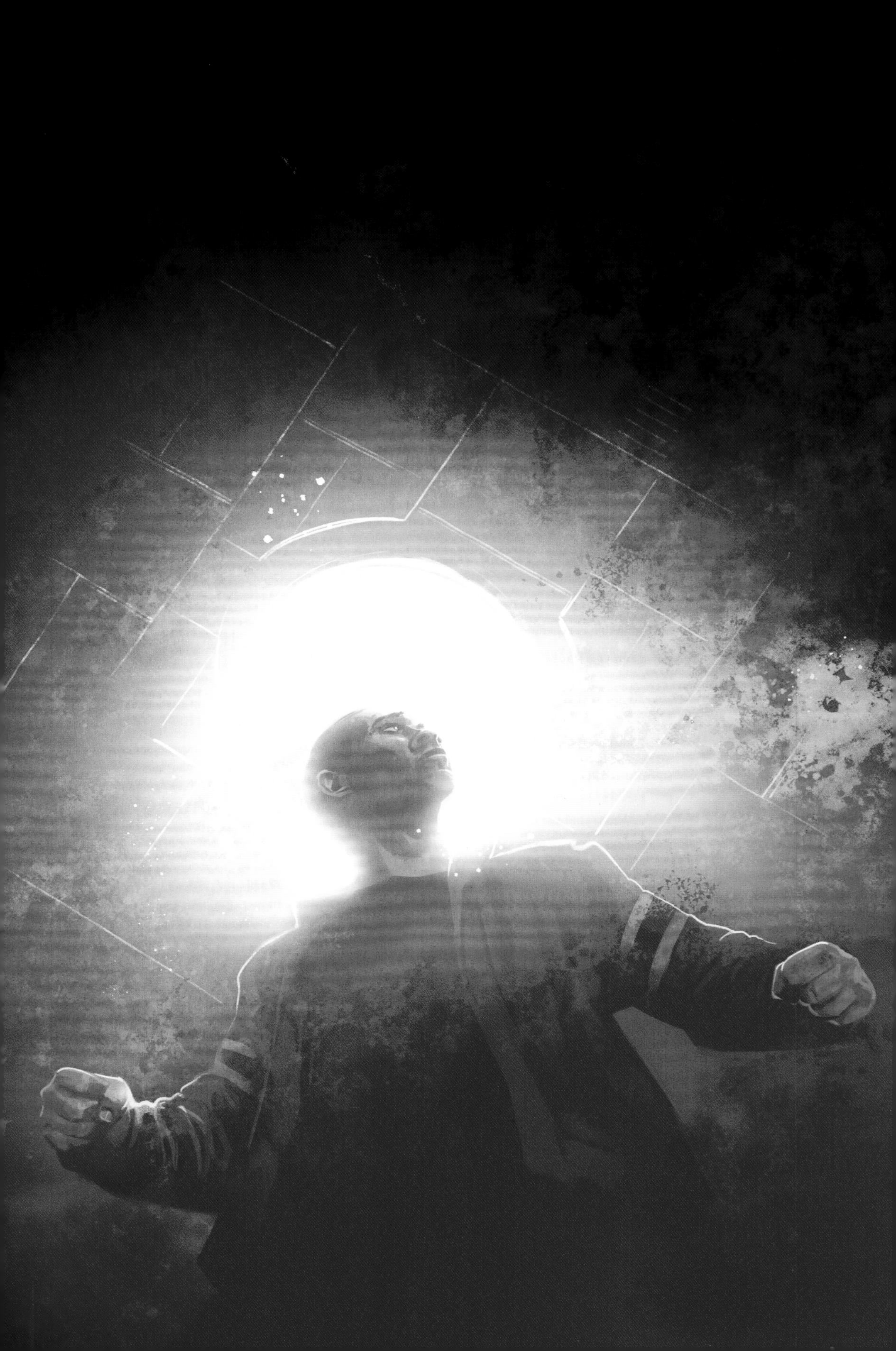

ART BY JORGE FORNÉS

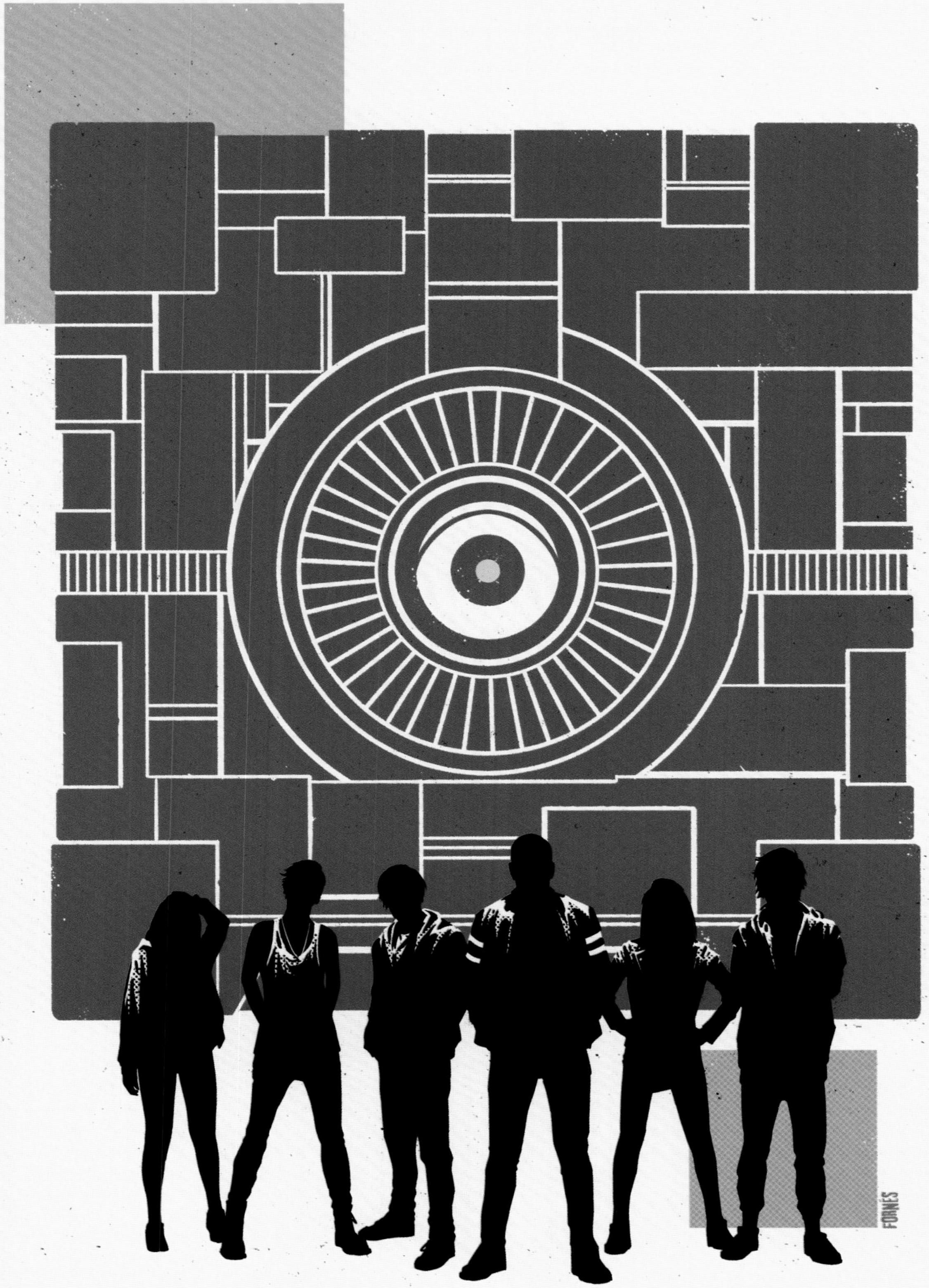
FORNÉS

ART BY JAHNOY LINDSAY

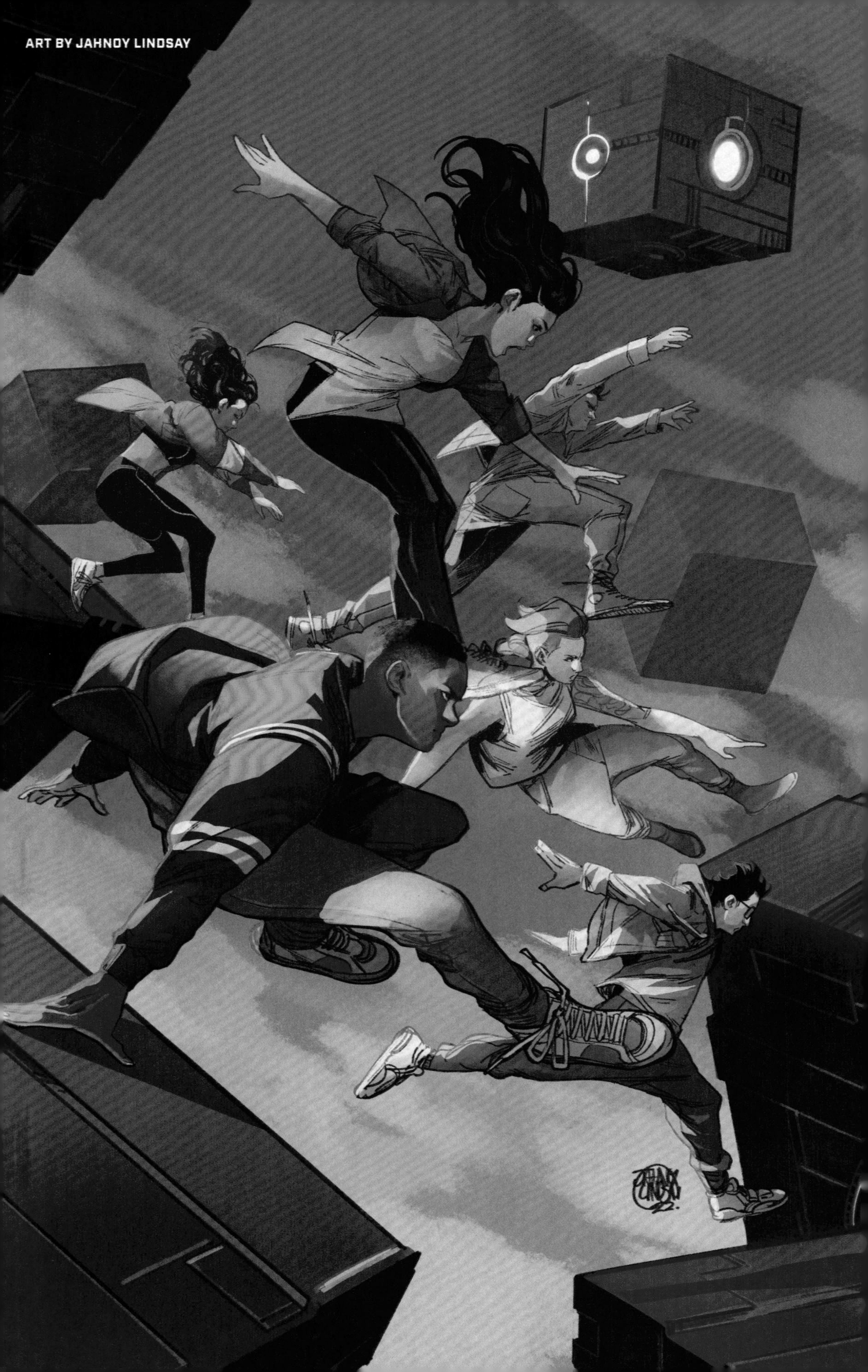

ART BY WILTON SANTOS

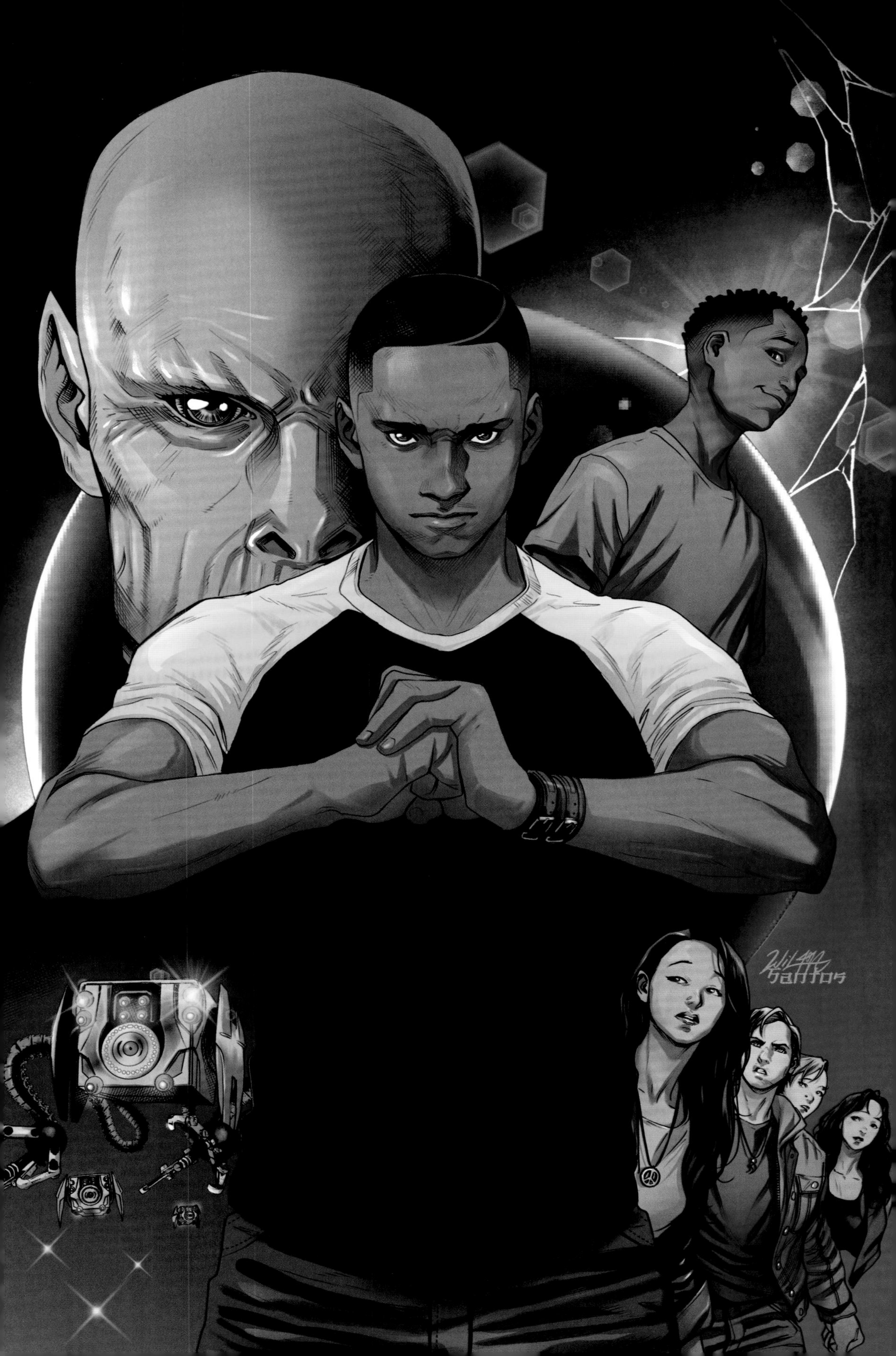

Wilton Santos

ART BY WILTON SANTOS

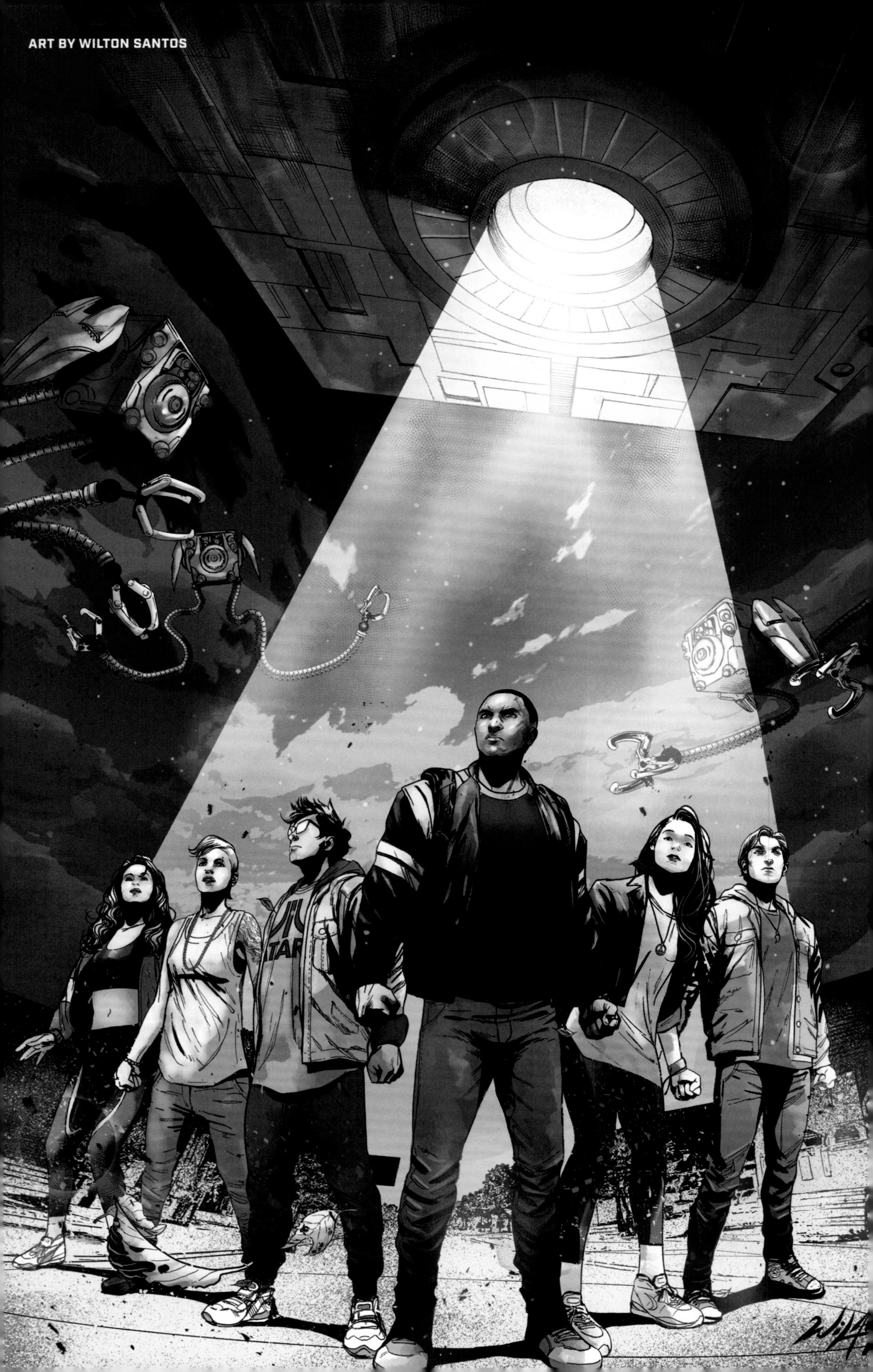

CHARACTER DESIGNS

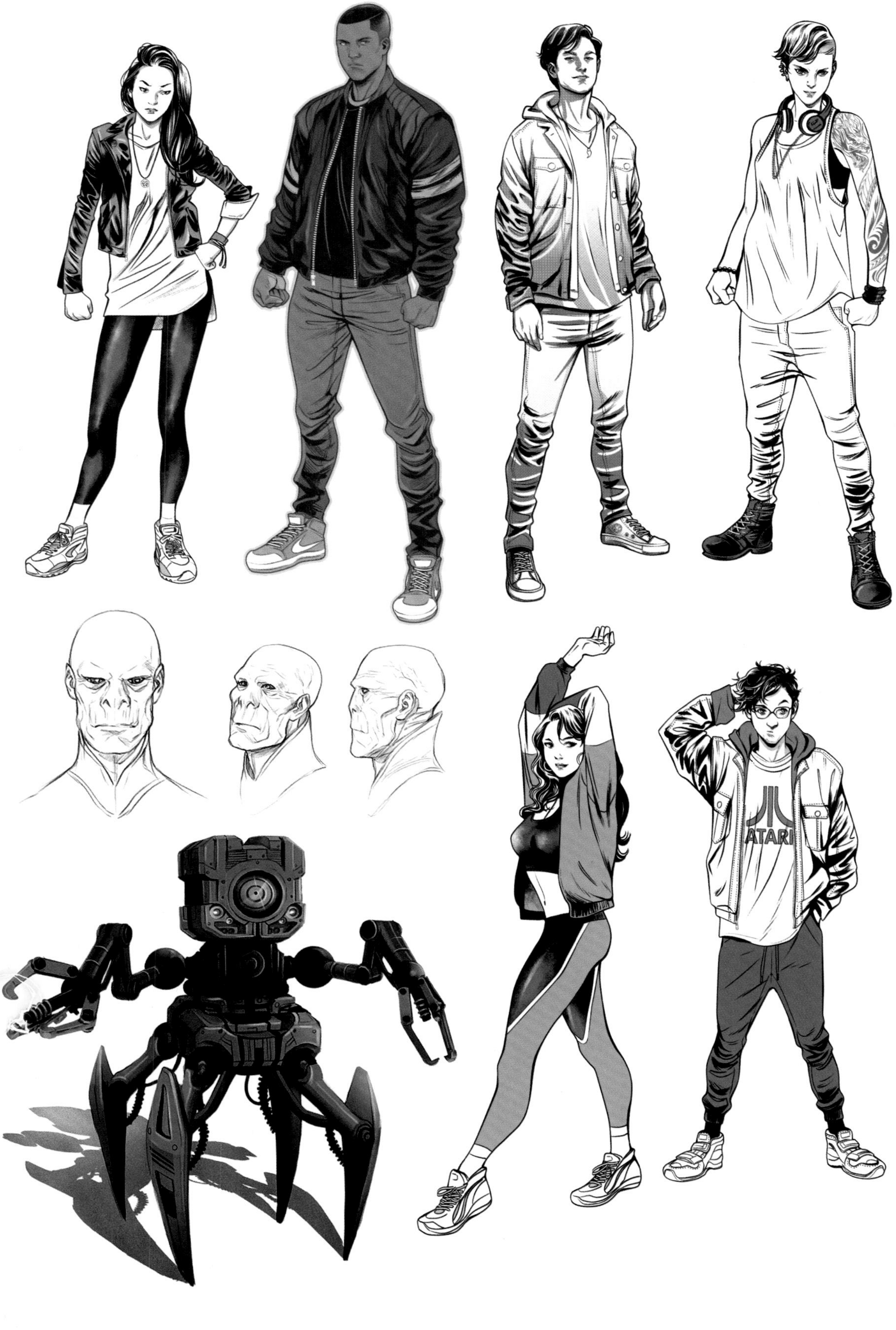
ATARI

"If you think there's no room left in your life for another superhero comic, *Black Hammer* might just prove you wrong."—IGN

BLACK HAMMER™

ONCE THEY WERE HEROES, but the age of heroes has long since passed. Banished from existence by a multiversal crisis, the old champions of Spiral City—Abraham Slam, Golden Gail, Colonel Weird, Madame Dragonfly, and Barbalien—now lead simple lives in an idyllic, timeless farming village from which there is no escape! And yet, the universe isn't done with them—it's time for one last grand adventure.

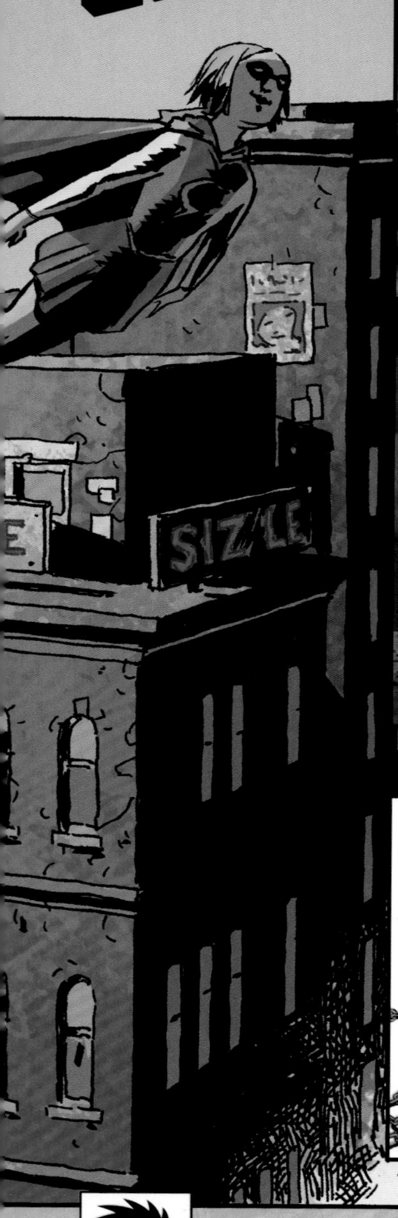

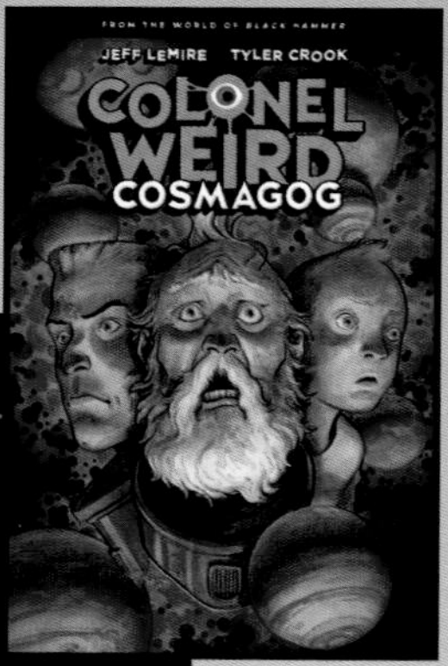

FROM THE WORLD OF BLACK HAMMER
JEFF LEMIRE TYLER CROOK
COLONEL WEIRD
COSMAGOG

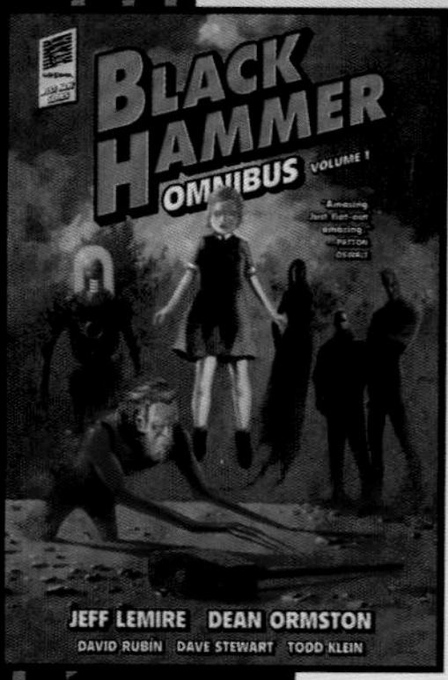

BLACK HAMMER
OMNIBUS VOLUME 1
JEFF LEMIRE DEAN ORMSTON
DAVID RUBIN DAVE STEWART TODD KLEIN

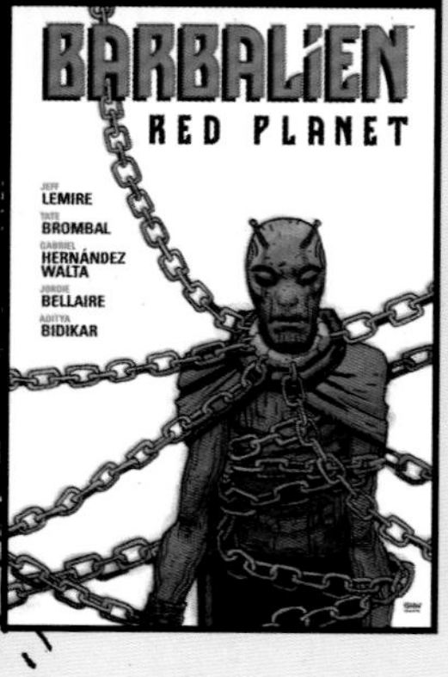

FROM THE WORLD OF BLACK HAMMER
BARBALIEN
RED PLANET
JEFF LEMIRE
TATE BROMBAL
GABRIEL HERNÁNDEZ WALTA
JORDIE BELLAIRE
ADITYA BIDIKAR

BLACK HAMMER
Written by Jeff Lemire • Art by Dean Ormston

LIBRARY EDITION VOLUME 1
978-1-50671-073-0 • $49.99

LIBRARY EDITION VOLUME 2
978-1-50671-185-0 • $49.99

OMNIBUS VOLUME 1
978-1-50673-146-9 • $29.99

VOLUME 1: SECRET ORIGINS
978-1-61655-786-7 • $14.99

VOLUME 2: THE EVENT
978-1-50670-198-1 • $19.99

VOLUME 3: AGE OF DOOM PART ONE
978-1-50670-389-3 • $19.99

VOLUME 4: AGE OF DOOM PART TWO
978-1-50670-816-4 • $19.99

VOLUME 5: BLACK HAMMER REBORN PART ONE
Art by Caitlin Yarsky
978-1-50671-426-4 • $19.99

VOLUME 6: BLACK HAMMER REBORN PART TWO
Written by Jeff Lemire, Art by Malachi Ward and Matthew Sheean
978-1-50671-515-5 • $19.99

VOLUME 7: BLACK HAMMER REBORN PART THREE
978-1-50672-015-9 • $19.99

THE WORLD OF BLACK HAMMER

LIBRARY EDITION VOLUME 1
978-1-50671-995-5 • $49.99

LIBRARY EDITION VOLUME 2
978-1-50671-996-2 • $49.99

LIBRARY EDITION VOLUME 3
978-1-50671-997-9 • $49.99

LIBRARY EDITION VOLUME 4
978-1-50672-601-4 • $49.99

SHERLOCK FRANKENSTEIN & THE LEGION OF EVIL
Written by Jeff Lemire
Art by David Rubín
978-1-50670-526-2 • $17.99

DOCTOR ANDROMEDA & THE KINGDOM OF LOST TOMORROWS
Written by Jeff Lemire
Art by Max Fiumara
978-1-50672-329-7 • $19.99

THE UNBELIEVABLE UNTEENS: FROM THE WORLD OF BLACK HAMMER VOLUME 1
Written by Jeff Lemire
Art by Tyler Crook, Tonci Zonjic, Ray Fawkes, and others
978-1-50672-436-2 • $19.99

THE QUANTUM AGE: FROM THE WORLD OF BLACK HAMMER VOLUME 1
Written by Jeff Lemire
Art by Wilfredo Torres
978-1-50670-841-6 • $19.99

BLACK HAMMER '45: FROM THE WORLD OF BLACK HAMMER
Written by Jeff Lemire and Ray Fawkes
Art by Matt Kindt and Sharlene Kindt
978-1-50670-850-8 • $17.99

COLONEL WEIRD—COSMAGOG: FROM THE WORLD OF BLACK HAMMER
Written by Jeff Lemire
Art by Tyler Crook
978-1-50671-516-2 • $19.99

BLACK HAMMER: STREETS OF SPIRAL
Written by Jeff Lemire, Tate Brombal, and Ray Fawkes
Art by Dean Ormston, Matt Kindt, Tyler Crook, and others
978-1-50670-941-3 • $19.99

BLACK HAMMER/JUSTICE LEAGUE: HAMMER OF JUSTICE!
Written by Jeff Lemire
Art by Michael Walsh
978-1-50671-099-0 • $29.99

BARBALIEN: RED PLANET
Written by Jeff Lemire and Tate Brombal
Art by Gabriel Hernández Walta and Jordie Bellaire
978-1-50671-580-3 • $19.99

SKULLDIGGER AND SKELETON BOY
Written by Jeff Lemire
Art by Tonci Zonjic
978-1-50671-033-4 • $19.99

BLACK HAMMER VISIONS VOLUME 1
Written by Patton Oswalt, Geoff Johns, Chip Zdarsky, and Mariko Tamaki
Art by Johnnie Christmas, Scott Kollins, and Diego Olortegui
978-1-50672-326-6 • $24.99

VOLUME 2
Written by Kelly Thompson, Scott Snyder, Cecil Castelluci, and Cullen Bunn
Art by David Rubín, Matthew Sheean, Melissa Duffy, and others
978-1-50672-551-2 • $24.99

THE LAST DAYS OF BLACK HAMMER: FROM THE WORLD OF BLACK HAMMER
Written by Jeff Lemire
Art by Stefano Simeone
978-1-50673-112-4 • $19.99

DARK HORSE BOOKS

AVAILABLE AT YOUR LOCAL COMICS SHOP OR BOOKSTORE

TO FIND A COMICS SHOP IN YOUR AREA, VISIT COMICSHOPLOCATOR.COM.
For more information or to order direct, visit darkhorse.com.

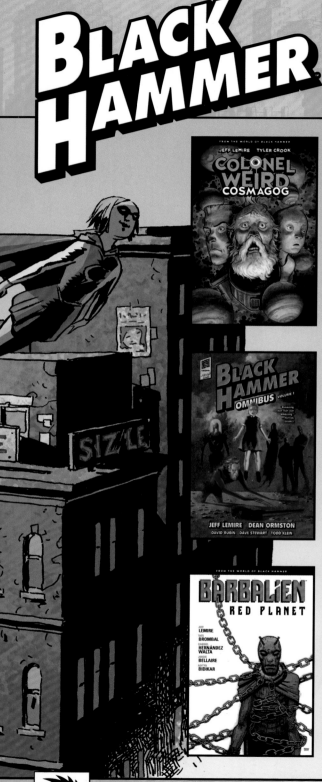